GHOST

GIFTS

ALSO BY LAURA SPINELLA

Beautiful Disaster

Perfect Timing

Writing as L. J. Wilson

Ruby Ink

The Mission

GHOST
GIFTS

LAURA SPINELLA

Montlake
Romance

Text copyright © 2016 Laura Spinella
All rights reserved.

Published by Montlake Romance, Seattle

www.apub.com

Amazon, the Amazon logo, and Montlake Romance are trademarks of Amazon.com, Inc., or its affiliates.

ISBN-13: 9781503950771
ISBN-10: 1503950778

Cover design by Marc J. Cohen

Printed in the United States of America

For Jamie, because it's her turn.
And for Peter Daley, who didn't get enough turns.

CHAPTER
ONE

Holyoke, Massachusetts
Twenty Years Ago

The sky cartwheeled overhead. A Ferris wheel continued on, carrying Aubrey Ellis past amber-tinged treetops and stringy power lines that looked like black spaghetti. She counted church steeples. This town had three to the north. Heaven disappeared, carrying Aubrey closer to earth. On the approach, Aubrey felt like any normal thirteen-year-old girl, in particular the kind who didn't speak to the dead. The scenery leveled and the view changed. Carnival crowds thinned as she circled past Carmine, who manned the controls. "One more time, please!"

"Once more, Miss Ellis, then it's back to work! Your grandmother will take us to task for slacking on the job." But his mustache stretched wide over a grin. Aubrey relaxed, her long arms resting lazily across the seat back. Her chin tipped upward and she indulged in nothingness, a soft breeze touching her face like a kiss. A cornflower September sky domed high while a white moon awaited its cue. Cool nutty air rode with her, and Aubrey breathed deep with each turn of the Ferris wheel. It was the Heinz-Bodette carnival's largest, most spectacular ride. But soon cycles would come full circle and leaves would decay, signaling another season's end. The troupe and equipment would break down into smaller units and retreat to various winter haunts. Some went to storage and some went to Albuquerque.

Aubrey inhaled halfway and the autumn air transformed. A chemical odor, like gasoline but stronger, seeped into her lungs. She inched forward, looking right and left, trying to match the smell to an earthly event below. There were only signs that a carnival had come to town: Sugared-up children begging for one more ride and another game of chance. The parents who'd spent their money on made-in-China memories, their children's bellies filled with cotton candy and funnel cake. Aubrey saw nothing that explained the pungent air. The growing stench made her gag, and she pressed her hand to her mouth.

As she passed by Carmine, he asked, "Miss Ellis . . . Aubrey, are you all right?" But it was too late to stop the spinning machinery and Aubrey circled on. Their catch and release gaze broke, her gondola rising above the idyllic New England scene. Unable to hold her breath any longer, Aubrey gasped for air. Her lungs filled. She prayed for a simple gas-main leak and looked toward the pointy steeples. Religion offered few clues. At the Ferris wheel's peak, Aubrey stood and the gondola wobbled from its winch. There was nothing to note. She shuffled onto her knees and peered over the back of the seat. Ferris wheels were stingy about a downward view, and the only thing Aubrey could see was the top of a man's hat in the gondola below. He wore a fedora, like the ones she'd seen in old movies.

On putrid air a name filtered up: *"Georgie . . ."*

Aubrey faced forward and sat, her insides cramping with the grip of a python. She braced for what came next. There hadn't been an incident since June, and she'd lulled herself into thinking the dead might never come again. On her tongue came the taste of candy, a Mary Jane, peanut buttery and sweet. It layered with the acrid chemical smell. Fear and flavor were a potent combination, too potent, and Aubrey thrust her head over the side, retching onto the grass below. A late lunch hit with a splat, thankfully missing Carmine. As her gondola approached, he grabbed the metal frame and wrestled it to a halt.

"You should have yelled down. I would have gotten you off faster!"

Aubrey waved one gangly arm, wiping tears from her eyes with her other hand. "There wasn't time. It happened too fast." Carmine helped her out of the gondola, but it did little to resolve the sensation of being trapped. The name *Georgie* drilled into Aubrey's ears. The chemical smell burned. The taste of the Mary Jane was opposing and strong. Carmine's hand rested on her shoulder as everyday embarrassment nudged its way in. "I'll . . . I'll clean it up," she said, glancing at the mess. Towns had strict ordinances about waste disposal, and Aubrey supposed vomit on their pretty fairgrounds violated the rules.

"Joe will take care of it." Carmine pressed the walkie-talkie in his hand. "Charlotte, are you nearby? Aubrey could use you."

"What's the problem, Carmine? I'm waist-deep in receipts." Husky laughter echoed through the device. "And we know that's a substantial waist!"

He traded another look with Aubrey who nodded. "We, um . . . she's had an encounter of sorts. She looks a little peaked . . . I think she could—"

A crackle cut in. "I'll be right there."

Carmine smiled thinly. "Your grandmother will be right here."

Aubrey tried to focus on the physical bits and pieces of Carmine. Sometimes it had a settling effect. His dark winged-tipped hair went with his wing-tipped shoes, his mustache and Roman nose perfecting his master-of-ceremonies façade. Aubrey was relieved it was Carmine; he understood that this was neither motion sickness nor malady, not even the result of a teenage candy binge. There was the possibility of insanity, which Aubrey had yet to rule out. Complementing the idea of insanity were the images of marbles currently rolling around Aubrey's head. She saw black aggies and oxbloods, the word *keepsies* hammering over and over. She had no idea how she knew the names for the marbles or why they were there.

Aubrey's hand balled into the layers of fabric, her sweatshirt and tie-dyed Heinz-Bodette apron twisting as she gripped the fabric. It dizzied her to glance down. The swimming colors had made Aubrey uneasy from the moment troupe seamstress, Yvette, handed Aubrey her apron last spring. She closed her eyes and tried to breathe plain air. Vomiting was bad enough, but the potential humiliation of losing bladder and bowel could never be discounted. A voice thrummed in her ears, an adamant plea that she speak to *Georgie*. She heard arguing over marbles and Mary Janes. More distantly, she sensed fear and sorrow. On ordinary sound waves a rider yelled from above, "Hey, you ever lettin' us off this thing?"

Aubrey's trembling hand remained in Carmine's steadier one. He glanced at the control switch. "Hang on. I had to reboot the motor. It'll just be a minute." He winked at Aubrey. "Let them wait, honey."

Aubrey coughed, swiping her hand across her watery mouth. A caftan-covered Charley approached like a giant seabird, her grandmother swooping in to protect her charge. Thick fingers, a ring on nearly every one, cupped her granddaughter's chin. Aubrey peered into murky blue-gray eyes that looked like her own.

As Carmine quietly recounted the details to Charley, the marionette creases on her face pushed into a smile. It was equally wooden. "Would you look at that, Carmine? The child's pale as a ghost."

"Not funny," Aubrey said. The creases did what wood couldn't, bending into a frown.

Charley pulled her granddaughter tight to her. "I know, sweetie . . . I know."

"If you want to take her back to the motor coach, I'll get these folks down."

Charley glanced at the motionless wheel. "Yes, get them down before somebody threatens to sue," she said. "Why don't we do that, Aubrey? We'll hide out inside the Winnie, watch an old black and white—Cary Grant, maybe Montgomery Clift—until we get the heck out of Dodge."

Aubrey moved a few steps from the Ferris wheel, wanting to do just that. But in the last year, hiding hadn't proved useful. "I'd rather get it over with. It won't give up."

Charley sighed. "The same way they looked for your father." Thick silver hair shimmied along her shoulders. She surveyed the crowd as if she might see whoever sought out her granddaughter. "Why don't we give it a try? Who says we can't outsmart—"

Aubrey broke from their conversation as the man in the fedora hat exited his gondola. She'd noticed him three or four rides ago. It didn't seem like he was in the mood for a carnival ride. Aubrey knew his name. He slipped into the crowd and she chased after him, her long legs and Keds spiraling. "George!" There was no response. Aubrey jammed her feet to a stop. *"Georgie!"* The man turned. The look on his face did a free fall.

"What did you say?"

"Georgie."

Charley was close behind. "Aubrey, slow down. He won't understand. You're going too fast."

She glanced over her shoulder. "I want it done. I want him to go away and leave me alone. I hate this!"

"Hey, I didn't do nothin' to the kid here!"

"No, not you." Aubrey's voice was sure, but her body said otherwise, her knees buckling and a trickle of urine soaking her underpants. "You're Georgie."

Aubrey watched his eyes shift between her own sweaty face and Charley. "I'm George Everett. I haven't been Georgie for decades. Not since . . . since I was a kid."

"Not since Roy."

He stepped back.

Aubrey forced her line of vision onto a solid earthly element, the grass beneath her feet. Touch was better, but the man's tone said he wasn't open to holding Aubrey's hand.

"He calls you Georgie. The two of you came here every summer when the carnival was in town."

"How . . . how do you know . . . ? That was years ago."

"Roy told me." Aubrey dragged her hand through her dark hair. At the crown, a fistful knotted in her grip. Squeezing seemed like a way to get the information out and her gaze rose to a bewildered George. "The Ferris wheel. It was your favorite ride . . . both of you. You'd come here every year when our carnival was in Holyoke just to ride it."

"That was decades before you were even born." George's mouth gaped. "I don't understand . . . "

"Neither do I!" Aubrey spat back. "But Roy is here. He wants you to know it's not your fault, that you should stop feeling bad about him."

"What's not my fault?"

"His death." Aubrey plucked at the colorful apron. It had grown increasingly uncomfortable, like the chemicals had soaked through to her skin. Needing more answers than she had to give, Aubrey glared at George. She stepped closer and sniffed. "What's that stink? Did he die in a plane crash? Was it an accident?"

No response came from George. On her shoulder, she felt Charley's hand. But in an abstract line of vision, one no other human could see, a young man appeared. He wavered in between aged oaks and the popcorn machine. His skin was shredded; he was dirty and sweat covered, wearing fatigues and blood . . . dog tags. His face was both pleading and dead. Aubrey realized her misstep. Roy hadn't died in any factory accident.

"Napalm," George said. "Roy died in Vietnam. It was an overload of chemical weapons. It wasn't even the enemy. Human error. But if I had been . . ." As George's explanation hit Aubrey's ears, the image of Roy grew more vivid. "Roy and I . . . we were going to enlist together, be war buddies. We were eighteen. But I don't see how—"

"You didn't do that, did you? You didn't enlist," Aubrey said.

"I . . . My father talked me into college. Roy, he went anyway . . . to war. He didn't have money for college. I was supposed to be there, with him. I . . . I didn't go. But how do you . . . Wait. Wait just a doggone minute." George's wide-eyed look collapsed. He turned toward Charley. "You case your subjects good, don't you, lady? I give you credit. You almost had me. She's good."

Charley's hand squeezed Aubrey's shoulder. "Aubrey, go. Go back to the Winnebago and stay inside. I'll be right there."

"You picked the wrong mark today. George Everett won't be your next carnie scam!"

"My grandmother doesn't scam people!" Aubrey said, anger pushing hard against the aberrant encounter. "She doesn't have anything to do with this."

"Yeah, right. And Roy's been waitin' thirty years for a chance to chat. Think I was born yesterday? Sure, I been coming here since Roy died and before. I ride that Ferris wheel in his memory. But it probably didn't take much for professionals to do their homework, come up with a few specifics. You people travel this circuit every summer."

"That's not what's happening here," Charley said.

"No, of course not."

"If you would just lis—"

"Sure. And for what, a cool fifty, maybe a hundred, I get to hear the whole story? The gawky, sad-eyed kid here provides me with Roy's personal message? No thanks. I know how this stuff works. You make the trip out to the cemetery, come up with some leads—then you look up the poor dead sucker's history. How hard could it be? Hell, they named the damn municipal building after him! The Roy E. Fletcher Complex. I'm sure you had to stop there for your permits."

"I realize how it might sound, Mr. Everett. But no one here is scamming you. My granddaughter has a very unusual, very intense gift. She didn't seek you out. Your friend sought her out. And I will not allow—"

"Save the indignant speech, Mata Hari. You and your underling targeted the wrong mark. You're lucky I don't call the cops!" He turned and started to walk away.

Aubrey pulled away from Charley's hold. "Roy said that the Mary Janes were his, fair and square—so were the aggies and oxbloods. It was *keepsies* . . . whatever that means."

He spun back around, coming so fast that Charley didn't have time to intervene. Aubrey quaked at his stink-eye but held her ground. "Keepsies, kid, is what we played every afternoon, grammar school through junior high. But that's part of your training, right? You mention some obscure fact and play dumb to the rest." His ugly glare turned on Charley, and Aubrey stepped toward her grandmother. "You ought to be ashamed of yourselves. Slick touch though—not sure how you pulled that off." He stalked toward the exit, the words "Lousy carnies!" echoing.

George Everett never looked back. Aubrey supposed it wouldn't have mattered if he had, whether to argue over con artists or even to let her show him the ghost gifts that were now hers. Black aggies and oxbloods, she guessed, rolling around her apron pocket.

◆ ◆ ◆

Two weeks later the Heinz-Bodette Troupe neared the season's end with stops in Chatham and now Surrey, Massachusetts—whirlwind setups and breakdowns. Peak season was behind them. Carnival days competed now with fall renaissance fairs and apple picking. Soon Aubrey and her grandmother would depart to the desert Southwest where they wintered. In that hot, dry place, carnival equipment and teenage psyches could be repaired. Aubrey didn't mind carnival life, although she had little to compare it to. She recalled only bits and pieces of any other existence, and doubted that what she did remember qualified as normal.

Eight years ago, a limo ride between her parents' wake and gravesites marked the transition from that curious life into this one.

Conversation had been sparse during the bleak ride, and the name game had distracted grandmother and granddaughter. *Charley*, they'd both agreed, was a good fit. While the multi-married carnival mistress could be described as many things, *Grandma* was not one of them. Charlotte Antonia Pickford Ellis Heinz Bodette embraced a traveling life, having inherited both halves of the carnival from her former and late husbands, Truman Heinz and Oscar Bodette.

For herself, Aubrey had adapted to this version of domesticity, calling *Winnie* home and the people around her family. Charley was the carnival's matriarch, warm in her boisterous bawdy ways, and everyone, even Aubrey, earned their keep. When she was small, so were the tasks, like feeding the baby goats and sorting tiny plastic prizes. The jobs grew with Aubrey, who now tended to an assortment of carnival duties—everything from running rides to assisting Yvette with costumes. But after the Ferris wheel scene in Holyoke, even everyday chores were ignored. Aubrey remained inside the Winnebago.

Charley had been absent most of this morning, overseeing the setup for their Surrey stop. The town was an idyllic place that all but glowed with traditional family life—something Aubrey usually found fascinating to observe. Today not even Surrey's quaint town common could tempt her. Aubrey stayed sequestered, uninterested in the general public. It wasn't that she feared people. But avoiding them seemed like the best way to elude a gift that did not make her feel safe.

During her self-imposed solitude, Carmine had come by for lessons and yesterday to administer an algebra test. (Before joining the carnival, he'd run one of the toughest, most gang-filled schools in Detroit.) In between schoolwork, Aubrey passed the time by watching black-and-white classics on VHS and reading. Aubrey had fifty-three library cards in her possession, a representative number of the carnival's annual sixty-eight circuit stops. Of course you were supposed to be a resident of whatever town, but Charley had managed to secure one for Aubrey whenever she asked. Maybe, sometimes, carnie sleight of hand facilitated their lives.

Aubrey looked up from her book and peeked past the curtain in the Winnebago. She huffed at the daytime buzz. Joe had the motor cover off the Whip—the carnival's most vomit-inducing ride—while Yvette took a skimpy costume from Maxine, the tattooed lady. At last count, Maxine was her own skin flick, showing off one hundred and twelve separate and unique designs.

Aubrey dropped the curtain and returned to her book—*Watership Down*. The novel was an escape, a comfort title that Yvette had brought from the Surrey Public Library. While Aubrey loved to read, what she wanted to do was write. Not novels or poetry, but real life adventures. Perhaps, she thought, hugging the book, it was the longing to tell a story more incredible than her own. Aubrey was in the midst of wondering if such a thing was even possible when Charley lumbered back inside the Winnebago. From the serious look on her grandmother's face, Aubrey knew her book refuge and solitude were about to end.

"Is it your plan to spend the rest of your life in the confines of a motor home? Granted, it's cozy," Charley said, one rotund arm on the kitchen counter, her other easily reaching to the compact dining table. "But I have to insist on more. Obstacles are going to come your way, Aubrey, and I'd imagine the insult of George Everett won't be the worst of it."

Aubrey closed the book. "I've been thinking about it. You recognized him . . . George Everett. You'd seen him before, didn't you?"

"I'd like to tell you I spotted George Everett at the municipal office—a mark, just as he accused." Charley's jowls shook and her labored breath pulled in. "Luring you into a Dodger-Fagin scam would be an easier life."

"You dreamed about him."

"In Londonderry, New Hampshire. Two nights before his friend, Roy, showed up."

Aubrey nodded. It was the genetics of her gift. On occasion, things worked in tandem. Charley dreamed of a connected earthbound being before Aubrey encountered the spiritual half. "Why didn't you tell me?"

"Oh, Aubrey, you know the answer to that. Dreams aren't a road map. I also dreamed that Oscar's first wife, Vera, came by the carnival to chat. I haven't seen the woman in thirty years. You haven't heard from Oscar, have you?"

"No, I never see anyone I know." Frustrated, Aubrey tossed the book aside. She thought a visit from her mother or father might be reasonable compensation for enduring her *gift*. Nothing like that ever happened. Aubrey's attention was drawn back to Charley as she reached to her lower back. "It's bothering you again, isn't it? I knew Joe putting a board under your mattress wasn't going to fix anything. You need a doctor."

"So he can tell me what I know. That my sciatica is worse, and my lifestyle is a catalyst. Then what? We sell? I don't know about that, Aubrey. I don't know at all . . ." She gave her granddaughter serious consideration. "Oliver Twist's Fagin might not think twice, but I'd miss you when the new owners insist I sweeten the deal by tossing you in." Aubrey bit down on the humor that bubbled. Her grandmother was even parts wit, understanding, and durability. Both carnival life and living with Aubrey demanded as much. Charley tapped her crimson nails on the counter, her stare examining, and Aubrey knew tough love was on today's agenda.

A short time later, the assumption came to fruition. Aubrey stood with Yvette, the two of them manning the duck shooting game. They looked like twin kaleidoscopes, each wearing a neon tie-dyed apron. Aubrey touched the bands of color as she recalled last summer's carnival smocks. It had been Yvette's earthy phase, and the aprons had looked more like brown paper sacks. This year Charley requested vibrant colors, and Yvette, who adhered to the literal translation of everything, had delivered.

Aubrey and Yvette made a good pair. Yvette talked so much about life—the one that she lived and the one that she'd left—that a person hardly had time to reply, much less conjure up the dead. Chances were they'd be too busy to talk anyway. It was a Friday afternoon and

Surrey ordinances didn't allow carnival rides to open until five. Games of chance were the only attractions available.

Rogue boys on bicycles perused the area, darting like bandits from game to game. A man and his granddaughter stopped by. It made Aubrey smile to hand the small girl a pink pony after her grandfather skillfully took down the midsize row of ducks. His recently deceased wife nudged at Aubrey, but she forced silent the woman's faint plea. Among the things she had learned was that the newly dead were far easier to dismiss. Aubrey touched the apron again. Last summer, apparitions were fewer in number, weaker in tone. Aubrey thought about the bright hues of the apron's fabric and the newly dead woman's ability to be heard at all. There was a connection between the two things. Color, she realized, mattered.

The spaces in front of the stalls began to fill. She and Yvette went about their work, resetting the game and doling out prizes. Other shooters came and went, a pair of older boys who challenged one another with duel-like antics, neither winning a thing. Close on their heels came a tall man with dark crew-cut hair. His presence commanded Aubrey's attention. He looked in her direction, though he spoke mostly to Yvette—perhaps because she was an adult and Aubrey was a girl. There was nothing surreal in his demeanor.

Aubrey did note that his hands weren't clean, as if he'd just gotten off work—a laborer, like the men who worked for Charley. Caked under his nails and on them were bits of dried cement. She couldn't peg his age, maybe thirty. He wasn't overly good-looking, but not bad either. Aubrey thought he was average, until he smiled. She heard the man say that he'd learned good aim in the army—a sharpshooter. None of it really mattered, as no entities seemed inbound, trying to attach themselves to the man via Aubrey. It was mercifully silent. Yet her stare remained fixed and her heart fluttered when the man's cement-covered fingers grazed against hers as she took his money, almost the buzz of touching a live electrical wire. Aubrey felt it a second time as she handed him a giant stuffed walrus, their grand prize. He claimed his reward, flashing a smile. "I'm going to give it to my girlfriend. She didn't want to come to the carnival. It'll make up for our spat."

Aubrey wanted to say something back, but her attention was averted. A blond-haired girl—no, a woman—stepped into Aubrey's line of vision, taking the man's place. She was pretty, almost too pretty. There was eye contact, though Aubrey tried to look past her. The man was gone, having vanished into the thick of kiosks, rides, and people. She gave up and turned her attention to the young woman. Instead of asking if she wanted to play, Aubrey was compelled to say, "Can I help you?" The young woman didn't reply, just gave a vague stare as she nodded. "It'll just be a minute," Aubrey said.

In his effort to win, the crew-cut man and his dazzling smile had used sharpshooter aim and a violent approach. Aubrey watched while Yvette finished resetting the ducks. It was a tedious task as he'd succeeded in taking out all but one.

"Okay, we're all set," Yvette said, facing Aubrey. "Hopefully, the next one misses most of them."

Aubrey blinked. Her mind wouldn't let go of the man. An uneasy feeling rumbled. It felt like a volcanic warning that Aubrey needed to escape. She huddled close to her seamstress partner. "Yvette, I . . ." she said quietly, "I have to go to the bathroom. Can you help her?"

The blue of Yvette's irises scanned the perimeter of the duck-shooting booth. "Help who?"

"The girl—" Aubrey turned. The blond woman was gone. Clutching the front of the rainbow-colored apron, Aubrey leaned into the booth's raw wooden edge. She peered right and left. "Huh. She . . . she must have left. She was odd . . . like she was mute or something."

"Are you all right, sweetie? You seem . . . not quite here."

Aubrey rubbed her hands over the dizzying pattern of rainbow tie-dye. "I'm fine," she lied. "I . . . I just need to go. Can you work the booth without me?"

"Charlotte was clear. She wanted . . ." The lines on Yvette's face collapsed into layers as she smiled. "Sure, baby, I can do that." Yvette glanced down. "Hey, where'd these come from? They're awfully pretty . . . purple, for sure." From the counter, she scooped up a handful of delicate, violet-colored flowers. "I don't know what it is about this town, but these flowers grow like crazy around here. With so many stops, it's how I always know we're in Surrey." The fine petals rustled in the late September breeze. A thin grosgrain ribbon bound the stems, the only thing that kept the wind from carrying the flowers away. Aubrey didn't respond. Purple flowers, flowers of any color, were not on her mind.

Instead, Aubrey's head swam with indiscernible babble. Future promises and the crack of a gun, an argument about money—a lot of money. She stifled a gasp. But Yvette diverted her attention, tugging at the elastic edge of Aubrey's apron pocket. She dropped in the flowers.

"Go on now. But if you're going to hide out, put those in a bud-vase next to your grandmother's bed. Flowers are a sure way to keep on Charley's good side."

On her way back to the Winnebago, Aubrey purposely took a path that differed from the one the man with the dazzling smile had taken. Bad feelings receded as she walked. The urge to get to the bathroom wasn't as strong. The only sound that sank in was the crank of carnival music. Nearing the motor home, Aubrey stopped and breathed. She relaxed. Her hand slipped inside the apron pocket as she stretched her neck and shoulders. But the movement ceased when Aubrey withdrew the purple blossoms. In her palm, the flowers had wilted, decayed, and rotted—the heavy burden of death sinking back into Aubrey.

CHAPTER TWO

Surrey, Massachusetts
Present Day

In a conference room where she normally felt at ease, Aubrey tried to focus on the work in front of her. That or maybe just breathing. As the writer and editor of the *Surrey City Press* home portrait feature, her presence was not a requirement, only newsroom courtesy. But the noise was disconcerting, infiltrating. The topic, the newly discovered remains of a girl gone twenty years, made her wish she'd called in sick. She didn't want to be anywhere near the dead, not in this room. Not with that story. Aubrey huddled tighter to the table as her colleagues continued to all speak at once.

Editor in chief, Malcolm Reed, fed a coffee high while reining in his troops. At least it wasn't cigarettes. The excitement was unusual and Aubrey did wonder if there was a defibrillator on site. Who knew how much his tired heart could take? She worried about him like that. Malcolm was three parts seasoned newsman and one part sweet old guy—the kind who wore a velvet glove and a twinkle in his eye.

Aubrey gave up on mental traction and pushed aside photos of a regal Georgian colonial and an unassuming split-level on Harper Street. One of the properties would end up being Sunday's home portrait piece. It would also prove to be the home Aubrey was destined to visit that day.

At the moment, it didn't matter. Common house story or ghostly dwelling—neither thing could compete with current events.

Malcolm had asked that their Monday meeting convene a half hour earlier than scheduled. Aubrey supposed this was in deference to the story at hand. With the exception of herself and sports editor, Dan Coulter, it would consume the *Surrey City Press* staff. Bebe Wang and Ned Allegro aggressively vied for the position of lead reporter. Aubrey couldn't be part of the conference room fervor, but she appreciated the argument. Being named lead reporter in the breaking Missy Flannigan story would be a coup. Particularly in Surrey where news like this came around, well, about once every twenty years.

Malcolm moderated the debate, although his enthusiasm was weak. Aubrey sensed that he'd already made a decision, surely having spent his weekend assessing the options. He gave a noncommittal nod as Ned pointed out his tenure, followed by a subtle hum when Bebe emphasized her investigative skills. Last year she'd exposed the Surrey councilwoman who'd covered up the dope-selling ring operating out of the local car wash. Apparently, her son had run the hot-wax cycle. Aubrey was drawn back to the sound of polite mentoring when Malcolm allowed Kim Jones an opportunity to make a bid. The newbie reporter didn't stand a chance, but that didn't stop her from chiming in with words about her shiny new journalism degree. Not this day, but someday, Kim Jones would have her shot. There was a twinge of envy and Aubrey wrestled it silent. The *Surrey City Press* home portrait section was her calling, not mainstream news, and she breathed easier knowing that was her place.

Aubrey shuffled her real estate listing sheets into a neater pile. In doing so, the fine edge of the paper sliced into her index finger. She pinched closed the split in her skin with her teeth and the faint tang of blood transformed into the taste of Thanksgiving dinner. It seized Aubrey's focus. She abandoned the conference room table talk and stared at the listing sheets. Her gaze alternated between the magnificent colonial located on Surrey's antique row and the characterless split-level on Harper Street—surely both had been host to numerous Thanksgivings. Intuitively, Aubrey rested her hand on top of the listing sheet detailing the lesser property. Before, the paper had been room temperature. Now it emanated heat. It was a clear sign: that was the property she needed to visit.

Satisfied, Aubrey placed the paperwork for the regal Georgian colonial in the discard pile and turned back to the conversation. From her spectator's point of view she listened. The mood had morphed into something more akin to cutthroat reality television: who would Malcolm choose? The *Surrey City Press* staff was capable, but this story was unlikely and vast. Ordinarily, anyone might describe the midsize Massachusetts town as uneventful—a place like a time capsule. Last Friday it felt as if they'd cracked one open when skeletal remains had spilled out from behind Dustin Byrd's basement wall.

Aubrey happened to be in Malcolm's office when the story broke, hearing details of the ghoulish tale via neighbor Stan Entwhistle, who had been minding the Byrds' cats. Dustin Byrd had taken his mother to Foxwoods. Violet liked to play the penny slots and her only son had splurged, the two of them celebrating her seventy-fifth birthday. Entwhistle couldn't locate the felines and decided to look in the basement. What he found was half a foot of rising water. It immediately prompted a phone call to master plumber, Reggie Swanson. But Reggie had trouble locating the leak, and eventually drilled a hole into a sloping section of brick wall. Fishing a camera through, the plumber spied a broken pipe, a backpack, and most disturbing, something that looked like floating bones. It didn't take long for the police to arrive, busting through a wall from which secrets gushed. Behind the brick, which police theorized was a later addition, were Missy Flannigan's backpack and skeletal remains, still dressed in a rat-tattered Surrey State T-shirt and shorts. It was the outfit Missy had been wearing the day she vanished.

A team effort, led by Malcolm, handled immediate coverage of the story. These reportable facts read like a giant billboard, impossible to miss. But now Malcolm had to choose, putting one reporter in charge of investigating and finessing the multifaceted story. Adding to the situation was the onslaught of national media. Twenty years prior, when disappearing girls were more of an anomaly than a sad statistic, national media had descended on Surrey. Over the weekend they'd returned, not only prompted by the grisly discovery of a murdered girl's remains, but also by the fresh news swirling around army veteran Frank Delacort.

He was the man who'd pleaded innocent to Missy's murder but ultimately was convicted of the crime sans body. A Surrey jury of his peers had sentenced him to life in prison. With the discovery of Missy's remains—in the house of a man who now appeared stunningly suspect—Frank's conviction did seem disputable. Aubrey tipped her head, leaning toward Malcolm's edition of the *Surrey City Press*. The headline read: *Did Surrey Rush to Justice?* Maybe they had, maybe they hadn't. Either way, the choice of lead reporter would be critical to how the newspaper covered the story.

From his end of the table, Malcolm urged the conversation to a close. The others had backed off, conceding that the choice was between Ned and Bebe. "Ned . . . Bebe, suffice it to say I'm thoroughly familiar with your work." Malcolm folded his hands as the room awaited the call. He didn't make one, his face nearly as ashen as the day he'd had his heart attack. "You're all fine reporters," he said, pointing around the table. "I have no doubt any one of you would give this story your best. But it appears . . ." His suspenders, shirt, and bony shoulders shifted in one defeated motion. "It seems the decision is out of my hands." The buzz fizzled and Bebe snatched the lead.

"What does that mean, 'out of your hands'?" Her tiny eyes narrowed at Malcolm.

"It means corporate is going to be in on this one. MediaMatters has *suggested* that someone with . . . It seems they've decided to lighten the load for us. At least that's how it was put to me. Due to the compelling nature of this story, they're providing assistance from one of the larger papers." Aubrey sighed. Forty years in newspapers and Malcolm was being undermined by corporate executives. Cumulatively, they couldn't have half his experience. "Listen up," he said, reeling in his disgruntled team. "I don't need to tell you that newspapers are an endangered species. This story is a big-ticket item for MediaMatters. We'll be influencing national media sources. We'll be in the spotlight. They want you all involved. But they also want a reporter of their choosing steering things."

"You're kidding," said Ned. "I've worked a solid fifteen years at this paper. If I haven't earned the right to cover this story . . ." He stopped. His annoyance mirrored his co-workers. "Damn it, Malcolm. You're just going to let corporate take over your newspaper?"

"I'm doing what's necessary to safeguard our existence—which is not a given. In the past two years MediaMatters has shut down a half dozen presses. Cooperation is critical, even if that means letting corporate in on our story." Grumbling faded to conciliatory murmurs. "It's why I called this meeting early. I wanted to give you all the courtesy of a heads-up before the latest addition to our team arrives." He glanced at the wall clock, then at his watch, as if timing his speech. "Rumor has it that punctuality is your new colleague's hallmark." He motioned toward the closed door. Curious looks passed from one person to the next as Malcolm's reporters collectively turned toward the entrance. "I also know you'll do your best to work together. Remember, the story is what's important here."

As the wall clock ticked to precisely eight, the door burst open and Levi St John ploughed through, a large coffee cup balanced on a sizeable stack of folders.

"How did we not see this coming?" Ned slumped, his pen thudding against his notepad. Bebe's thin frame pulled pole-straight, her face a mix of pleasure and surprise. Gwen Trumble, who ran special features, traded glances with Dan Coulter. Aubrey grabbed up her Harper Street listing sheet and hid behind it. Heated pages crinkled in her hands. She felt renewed gratitude for her singular position of home portrait writer and editor. Other than bumping into Levi in the break room, her job guaranteed zero interaction. The last time he'd descended onto *Surrey City Press* territory she hadn't been as fortunate.

Malcolm's health had necessitated a three-month leave of absence a year ago August. Having been the product of a cigarette-smoking generation of reporters, he'd suffered a heart attack right in the middle of the newsroom floor. It was followed by an emergency triple bypass. In his absence, Levi had been MediaMatters' interim choice for editor in chief. Compared to Malcolm, anyone would have been a shock. As it was, corporate saw fit to send a locomotive through their placid newsroom.

Levi worked at MediaMatters' most enduring publication, the *Hartford Standard Speaker*, where he was the city desk editor. Being as the *Surrey City Press* was currently without theirs—Erin Barkley having gone out on maternity leave only last week—it surely added a layer of appeal to his resume. On paper, it was the perfect storm of corporate logic: Levi was a tough reporter with imposing skills. He also had experience with the inner workings of the *Surrey City Press*. What Media-Matters had overlooked was disposition.

Levi folded his tall frame into a chair at the opposite end of the conference room table. The choice would be perceived in one of two ways: It was the seat closest to the door. It was a presumptuous place of authority. Aubrey sensed that her co-workers had settled on the latter. Levi appeared oblivious. He was busy separating his early edition of the *New York Times* from the folders, which he arranged like a flow chart in front of him.

"Good morning, Levi. Glad to see traffic wasn't an issue. Carl Toppan personally called to let me know you'd be available to the *Surrey City Press*. It certainly speaks volumes when the MediaMatters CEO rings up an editor in chief to relay news."

"Thanks . . . right. Malcolm, good to see you." Levi pushed silver-rimmed glasses high on a well-defined nose and extracted three pens from his inner jacket pocket, placing them on the table. Without looking up, he produced a legal pad from the bottom of the stack and flipped past a dozen ink-filled pages. At the other end of the table, Aubrey could make out mentions of Missy Flannigan's name, orderly lists, and paragraphs of notes. It did occur to her that no one present had done such comprehensive homework. Finally, after settling on a blank page, Levi acknowledged a room full of stares. "I assume everyone remembers me." He nodded at the table of reporters. "Ned . . . Bebe . . . Gwen . . . uh . . . "

"Kim."

"Kim," he said, pointing a pen at her. "Still using that better byline?"

She dove into a flurry of pseudo note-taking while answering, "I am."

A wave of unease traveled the room. Everyone recalled Levi's memorable introduction to the *Surrey City Press*. Kim had been a new hire, only on the job a few days. At Levi's first staff meeting, he'd loudly noted that her byline—Kimmy Jones—made it sound as if she were writing for the school newspaper, which she had been only months before. Adding insult to injury, Levi had handed Kim back a redlined piece she'd done on the 140th anniversary of Benjamin Franklin Savings Bank. From there he'd remarked, "If you rewrite the lead, find a quote worth using, and back off the superlatives, it might not sound like a college student wrote it." And that was the beginning of Levi St John—expert at handling a newspaper agenda, disturbingly dense in the area of personal communication.

He moved on from Kim, wagging a finger in Aubrey's direction. "Ellis." Positive it would be their only exchange, she forced a pleasant, "Hello, Levi." The remaining salutations were polite but not warm. Levi's dark eyes gazed around the table and Aubrey wondered if he noticed the chill.

"I was about to get into the particulars of our breaking news," Malcolm said. "Since Friday's bombshell, I want to make certain everyone is up to speed. Unless you have a suggestion as to how you'd like to pursue things . . ."

Levi held up his hand. "Not at all, Malcolm. It's your newsroom. I'm just here to do the job I was assigned."

Their editor in chief opened his own folder. "Good. In that case, my gut says to start at the beginning."

"Absolutely," said Ned, determined to stake his territory. "We'll need detailed police reports from Friday, when all hell broke loose at the Byrd house. It's not every day a skeleton comes tumbling out from behind a wall."

"Excuse me . . . but actually," Levi said, pushing the glasses up again, "I take 'the beginning' as the original investigation. The one that took place twenty years ago."

Ned dug in. "Sure. We'll need to look at the history of the case. But Surrey readers want to know the current state of things."

"But the current state of *things* is going to greatly affect the past and future. Particularly when it comes to Frank Delacort." Levi reached for the folder that sat due north. "Not only do you have a brand-new suspect in a homicide this town declared solved twenty years ago, you have the compelling story of an all-but-demonized military veteran." His hand moved twenty degrees east, opening a thick folder. "If Delacort's adamant cry of innocence has suddenly turned into fact, it's going to rattle a lot of cages . . . politically, socially, ethically."

"And I suspect it's going to get his cage opened," said Gwen.

"Most likely." Levi thumbed through his notes. "I don't doubt that Delacort's lawyer has already filed a motion to have his conviction overturned. That alone is something we'll need to follow."

"True," Bebe said. "But isn't the headline here Missy Flannigan's killer, which now screams Dustin Byrd?"

Levi thrummed his fingers on a thinner folder set in a westerly direction. He took a breath that seemed languishing, like this was slowing him down. "Look, this story isn't one note or one headline. It's certainly not going to be told in one week." He motioned at the folders. "It's multidimensional, and we're at the tip of the investigation. It's critical that we deconstruct the history of the Missy Flannigan story before plunging headlong—"

"Levi," Malcolm said, raising his hand from his end of the table.

He returned the gesture. "I didn't mean to take over."

"I'm sure you didn't," he said. "The need to approach this systematically is evident."

"And that's fine," Ned said, standing his ground, "but we still have a newspaper to put out tomorrow and it's going to need a headline."

"There will be a paper tomorrow." Malcolm paused, sighing at that morning's edition. "But Levi is right. We can't go at this from last Friday forward." Levi's gaze dropped, returning to his notes. "This is why I've already created a detailed assignment list—for all of you," Malcolm said. Their editor in chief waited, his cloudy blue stare cutting down the table until Levi looked up again. From there Malcolm went on to run his newsroom, doling out assignments—everything from new interviews to retracing the first investigation. Aubrey felt a swell of pride for her boss's steady control.

As she listened, the Harper Street listing sheet grew warmer under her palm. Malcolm conducted his Missy Flannigan business and Aubrey proceeded to go about hers. She exchanged text messages with the Harper Street realtor, Alana Powell. The realtor was quick to respond, thrilled for Aubrey to tour the house that morning. The home portrait feature, which showcased for-sale properties, didn't carry the weight of hard news, but it was popular with readers, even more so with realtors. And on occasion, Aubrey's job, her presence, was also vital to the specters living inside the houses.

Despite Surrey's shocking headlines and the intrusion of Levi St John, Aubrey's day would resume. She was thankful for the luxury of routine activity—such as it was. Gathering her things, she anticipated Malcolm's dismissal.

"So if everyone is clear . . . unless, of course, you have something to add, Levi."

With a succinct click, Levi retracted the point of his pen. "Sounds fine, Malcolm."

"I'll bet," Ned said, nudging Aubrey. "He left the meatiest part of the story for Joe Pulitzer, here." Aubrey smiled but was more focused on a fuzzy photo of the Harper Street split-level.

"My one concern is Surrey itself." Levi reached for the most southern set folder, which was anemic compared to the rest. "I did a thorough overview, but I could only grasp so much of Surrey. Knowing the lay of the land, the people, is what maintains our advantage over national media outlets. I don't want to be the reason that's jeopardized."

"I appreciate your candidness," Malcolm said. "And I raised the same point when I spoke with Carl."

"Did you?" The bodies around the table collectively leaned in. "Glad to hear my potential stumbling blocks were part of the conversation."

"The smallest part. But yes. However, I did come up with a solution that Carl was on board with. I hope you'll be amenable."

"I'm listening," Levi said, surely prepared to hear about the app that would bring him up to speed on the nuances of Surrey. "I'm open to ideas."

"Good to hear. My idea," he said, smiling, "is Aubrey."

"Ellis?" he said, pointing.

"Me? Wait. What are you talking about, Malcolm? Home portrait features are my job. And it has nothing to do with Missy Flannigan—or him," Aubrey said, pointing back.

"The home portrait section is flexible enough, Aubrey. We'll work it out." He glanced around his table of reporters. "You all can get moving. We'll finish up here." Ned bumped her arm, chuckling under his breath. Bebe, openly bemused, shook her head as she and the others exited.

"Malcolm, seriously. Ellis just isn't . . . I don't see how bringing her—"

"On the contrary, Aubrey is a perfect fit. Her daily interaction with Surrey gives her a unique perspective. She has all sorts of contacts and knows this town inside and out. The two of you can work the assignment details however you like. Consider it a partnership," he said, turning to Aubrey, "with Levi in the lead."

"Malcolm," Levi said, channeling a monotone protest. "I appreciate the thought, and I'm sure Ellis knows all the best shopping and schools, no doubt the best neighborhoods, but this is serious journalism."

"What's that supposed to mean?" Aubrey fired back.

"No offense, Ellis. I've read your stuff. It's actually quite readable—if I were in the market for a three-bedroom colonial with a view. But your job, your skill set, has nothing to do with investigating or reporting hard news."

"Another thing, Levi," Malcolm interjected, "Aubrey is well liked. She's popular with the community and readers, not to mention this newsroom. To be perfectly frank, it was my assertion that her skill set might enhance yours."

"Okay . . . fine," he said. "But shouldn't the bigger picture be the point? Ellis writes advertorial pieces, she's the Sunday sweetener. She doesn't know the first thing about pursuing a story of this magnitude. I don't agree. Suggesting that—"

"But the point is I have suggested it. Rest assured; I've watched Aubrey work for some time. She's up to this. I wouldn't propose it on a whim."

"And if I respectfully decline?"

"I imagine you can respectfully do whatever you like, Levi. Your presence here wasn't offered as an option. I have to trust that the folks in charge know what they're doing in assigning you to the *Surrey City Press* and this story. Perhaps you could offer me the same courtesy."

Levi, who'd made it all the way to his feet to make his argument, succumbed. He sank back into his chair, producing the most irritated smile Aubrey had ever seen. It revealed a deep dimple that surely he hated. Aubrey shared his dislike for Malcolm's idea but she couldn't verbalize it. She was too blindsided by the disturbing directive of her beloved editor in chief. The one who'd unknowingly assigned Aubrey her worst nightmare—a fast-pass, all-inclusive ticket to a murdered girl's past.

CHAPTER
THREE

Aubrey had followed Malcolm out of the conference room and into his office where she continued her argument. But her objection to working on the Missy Flannigan story was thin. She was unable to articulate a reason beyond "It's not what I do." Apparently, starting today, it was. Malcolm had been puzzled, remarking how excited he was for Aubrey to have the opportunity to work on the story. It caught her off guard. Aubrey wasn't aware that she was looking for a better career path. It had taken years to find the home portrait feature, which Aubrey also saw as a gift. The job had allowed her to write for a newspaper while, occasionally, intervening on behalf of the dead. But Malcolm had persisted, reiterating the universal benefits of her involvement. "Just give it a try, Aubrey . . . I'd consider it a personal favor."

Having lost the battle, Aubrey packed up her house-touring gear and drove to the property on Harper Street. Hurriedly exiting the Mass Pike, she pulled up to a house marked with Alana Powell's for-sale sign. The morning sun backlit the exterior, keeping Aubrey from getting a good look. Her phone rang, Alana's number popping up on the screen. "Hi, Alana. I'm at the house. Where are you?" Aubrey glanced around the working-class street. "Sorry I'm late. Seems my day just took a hard left."

"I'm calling to apologize. My home inspection was bumped up an hour. I can't meet you until after lunch."

Aubrey shielded her eyes, still dodging the sun to get a better look at the house. "That's too bad. This may be the only free minute I have for the foreseeable future."

"Believe me, there's no way I'm losing this spot. An Aubrey Ellis feature draws too many potential buyers. How about this? You're already there and so is the lockbox. If you don't mind, why don't you head inside and take the tour without me?"

Aubrey smiled. "If you don't mind, I think I will."

"Wonderful! My seller is over the moon about the feature. It's the homeowner's daughter—Kitty Stallworth. She moved her parents into assisted living about a year ago. Jerry Stallworth, the dad, he died last spring, lifelong smoker. Anyway, you know Sunset Gardens, beautiful but pricey. With Kitty's mom still there she's desperate for the cash, plus she could use a break. Maybe you didn't hear, but Kitty's husband left her for a twenty-something college intern."

Second to endorsing commission checks, realtors liked gossiping. "No, I hadn't heard. I don't even know Kit—" Cloud cover floated in, shading the sun, and Aubrey got her first good look at the Stallworth house. "Alana, how much did you say the house is listing for?"

"A firm 375K. But just wait until you see the whole thing. It's perfect for first-time buyers, close to major routes, cute-as-a-button—*cozy!*"

"Uh-huh," Aubrey said, cutting off the engine. "Don't you think the asking—"

"I have got to run, honey. My buyers will hang me high if I'm not sewn to this inspector's shadow. Thanks again for featuring it. It's such a darling property."

After Alana gave Aubrey her lockbox code, she grabbed her satchel and headed up a cracked concrete walk. Along the way, Aubrey translated realtor code for "darling property." *Cracker box that needs work, from which you can hear the Mass Pike.* Upon closer inspection, the house revealed a passé shade of red, trimmed with white aluminum awnings veined in rust. There was a mediocre attempt at landscaping: fresh mulch, parched fall mums, and a new welcome mat. Okay, not every house sparkled with curb appeal. She'd focus on potential, maybe a unique interior element. Aubrey rang the doorbell out of courtesy. When no one answered, she punched Alana's code into the lockbox. The key popped out and Aubrey inserted it, forcing a sticky deadbolt over.

In the tiny entry, aromas circled like wagons—the bitter scent of cigars colliding with minty Aqua Velva. It was pungent, though probably not as striking to everyday visitors. Smells were a roadmap for Aubrey. She inhaled deeply, quickly ruling out the rancid stench of wickedness. Aubrey always made that determination while near an exit. She'd encountered the odor rarely, and not once since taking this job. But the lingering prospect was enough. That kind of smell was worse than rot; it was a state of being one tick past dead. Mercifully, today, her home portrait streak of luck continued. While there was death, there was no evil in the house on Harper Street. "Hello? Anybody home?" There was no reply.

Split-levels were an architectural train wreck that demanded an immediate choice: up or down? Aubrey chose up, the short flight of stairs delivering her to the main living area. Alternating between her camera and notepad, Aubrey took photographs and jotted down the obvious: hardwood floors, original windows, a working kitchen you couldn't turn around in—never mind seat a family of four. It was all complemented by harvest-gold appliances and green speckled Formica. Ridiculously dated but clean. And in that scoured kitchen, on the back of Aubrey's palate, the taste of Thanksgiving returned. It was stronger than earlier, although, not being much of a carnivore, she didn't relish the meaty zest of sausage stuffing.

She tried to swallow down the flavors while moving on to the living room. It showed off tired pleated drapes, heavy and mauve, complemented by yellow smoke-stained walls. The asking price was a stark contrast to the visuals, a hundred thousand over what the house was worth. Unless Aubrey's story mentioned buried treasure, they'd never sell it. She continued on, snapping photos, making her way through three closet-size bedrooms that shared a pink-tiled hall bath. She stopped, reviewing the captured images. They depicted what the average eye saw—too much furniture in too small of a space. But in the last shot Aubrey saw what she was looking for. An orb. It was something the average eye would perceive as a photographic malfunction. It also drove the paper's head photographer, Blake Munroe, crazy: "Aubrey, these lights in your pics are so weird . . . random." Interestingly, she was surprised to see only one orb; the aura indicated an entity strongly attached to the setting.

Aubrey glanced at her watch. If Levi hadn't managed to talk his way out of Malcolm's suggestion, he'd be looking for her. She moved onto the lower level. There was a decent size laundry room, which connected to an empty one-car garage. It was filled with the strong odors of motor oil and grass clippings. But those smells were external, attached to things present and tangible. She quickly shut the door. Passing by a half bath sporting an avocado commode, she headed for the room at the end of the hall. Aubrey opened the door and stale air rushed past her as if on a mad dash for the exit. The combination of cigarette smoke and Aqua Velva clung like an anxious child. Aubrey stepped inside and closed the door. Split-levels were stingy about direct sun and she flipped on bright track lighting. In response to the stabbing light, there was a gasp from across the room. A man sat in a crushed-velvet recliner, blinking as if she'd aimed a spotlight at him.

"Who . . . who are you?"

"Aubrey Ellis. I'm from the newspaper. I'm sorry to startle you, Mr. . . . "

"Jerry. You might as well call me Jerry—everyone in that elderly asylum does. No respect."

"I was starting to wonder if you were here."

His gaze was focused out the window. "I might as well not be." She arched a brow and kept the truth to herself, making a quiet approach. "What do you want?" He appeared to wrench his body higher in the fat recliner. His wheezing, only audible to Aubrey, fought its way in, then out.

"I'm from the *Surrey City Press*. We're doing a home portrait feature on your house. You know it's for sale, right?"

"Yes, my home. Mine since the Nixon administration—though, what's the point? I've gone from homeowner to homebound . . . to feeling homeless. They take it all away without even asking. It's not fair."

"Mmm, I don't suppose it is." Aubrey took a quick inventory. The space seemed to be his domain, the place where Jerry Stallworth belonged. There was a wood stove and a paneled bar set to the rear. It was surely the man-cave from which he hosted all the Sunday games. "I'm sorry this happened to you." She sat across from him, her eyes lingering on the blue veins that laced through his face. Aubrey plucked the listing sheet from her bag and placed it on a narrow coffee table. The warm pages felt like fire. It always amazed her when they didn't smolder—but she also understood the sensation of heat was hers alone. She leaned forward and glanced at the information. Homeowners: Jerry and Betty Stallworth. "I . . . um, I'm not just here for the house, Mr. Stallworth . . . you know?" Sometimes they did. Sometimes they didn't, and she treaded carefully until determining any spirit's state of mind. The elderly could be particularly distrustful. Jerry turned back. His face and hands were dappled with dark fleshy spots, like rotting fruit. He dragged crooked fingers through tufts of white hair—perhaps more of it sticking out of his ears than on his head. "Your daughter . . ."

"Kitty," he said. "That's her. Her and her no good ex-husband." Jerry Stallworth took shaky aim at a large framed portrait. Aubrey saw a typical family: a man looking uncomfortable in a photo-op suit and a wife with a broad toothy grin, the kind where the gums showed. Two teenage children, one gummy like Kitty, one not, and a gray golden retriever posed with them. "What are you gonna do? Can't erase the son of a bitch from the photo." The conversation stalled as a chest-rattling cough almost dislodged him from the chair. She waited. "God . . . damn . . . cigars . . . cigarettes," he sputtered. After a few starts and stops Jerry continued. "Can't do nothin' about that husband of hers. But Kitty can quit her job now, find a better one . . . take a vacation—twenty years at the DMV, can you believe that? I . . . I can help. I'm better prepared than Kitty knows."

"Twenty years at the DMV. Wow." Aubrey inched closer. "Tell me how you can help, Mr. Stallworth."

"Betty, my wife. You . . . you're not married?"

"I, um . . ." The question rattled the normally centered medium. "No, not anymore . . . almost, anyway." He waited. Aubrey hadn't anticipated discussing her love life. "It didn't work out."

"Yeah, that's what happened to my Kitty. Best twenty years of her life wasted. My Betty and me, we were different. She watched my back. I watched hers. Trust like that, it's everything. You'll see . . ." A skeptical hum pulsed from Aubrey's throat. "My Betty—she took care of it all after I ended up with goddamn rotting lungs . . ."

"Emphysema."

He nodded, still in a struggle with life on this side. "Two, maybe three packs a day, Lucky Strikes . . . midshipman through mid-level corporate America. A favorite cigar. Back then, who knew? Any . . . way, I just didn't expect . . . expect," he said, fighting for what he perceived to be useful air. He captured a breath and spent it telling Aubrey the rest. "Who the hell thinks about somebody as smart as Betty ending up with Alzheimer's? Who would have thought she'd slip so fast that she wouldn't tell Kitty about the money? If she'd left it alone, it woulda been fine. Kitty's smart; she would have found it. But then Betty started squirreling things away—my inhaler in the microwave, her rosary in the cat box . . . the oxygen tank near the wood stove."

"And that's when Kitty moved you both to assisted living." He gasped for air, maybe a breath of dignity. "You need to tell me where it is, whatever it is I've come for, Mr. Stallworth."

His faded blue eyes narrowed, sinking into creped skin. Specters could be stubborn. To him, Aubrey was no more than a stranger. He needed a sharper picture.

"You know, this can be better. All of it. Concentrate. You'll see that your reality isn't clear."

"What would you know about reality?" he snapped. "I worked my whole life to own something, and for what? Just for Kitty to end up in a mess, owing more than she's got. More than this damn house is worth." His tired lungs couldn't keep up, ragged sounds grating from his chest.

Aubrey pressed on, moving him beyond the physical. It was a wall that he couldn't yet see past. "Tell me something, Mr. Stallworth. How did you get here?"

"How did I . . . I drove, I'm sure. They've probably got a search party going at that *home*."

"No, you didn't drive."

"Don't tell me. I've been driving longer than you've been alive."

"I was just in your garage. There's no car. There wasn't one in the driveway. Nobody's lived here for months. There's no food in the kitchen, no mail on the counter." They traded stares. This would only take a nudge. "Betty, she's still at Sunset Gardens, isn't she?" The blue in his eyes pooled. "She's going to be there for some time. She'll need a lot of care."

"She will, won't she?" His chin quivered and he brushed at a tear. Then Aubrey watched him take a breath that was fuller than any before it. His eyes widened at the ease with which he inhaled. He'd want another breath. He'd have to accept his death to get it. Jerry Stallworth would want to move onto a place where everything was better.

Aubrey reached out, palms upturned—from here she could help him.

Slowly, his wrinkled hands came across, steadier now. He placed them in hers. His lungs seemed to fill and everything lightened. A smile he'd forgotten spread into the basins of his cheeks. "That's . . . um, that's so much better." She offered an encouraging nod. He took a long delicious breath. "Oh, God, that's . . . that's good. I'd forgotten . . . Thank . . . you . . . You make those damn doctors look like idiots."

"We all work with what we're given," Aubrey said. "A year ago, you would have been grateful for a doctor over me."

"Thank you for that, for coming."

"You're welcome, Mr. Stallworth. I'm glad I could help."

"Behind the bar," he said, cocking his chin. "There's a false panel in the liquor cabinet—hides the plumbing. You'd never know it was there, unless you did. Betty did. I guess she thought it would be safe."

"Probably." Aubrey let go of his hand, walking toward the dimly lit, 1970s bar.

"Miss Ellis?"

"Yes," she said, ducking behind the bar.

"You tell Kitty she's better off without that no-good husband." He laughed, which hadn't been an option moments ago. "She can get herself a makeover, take a cruise . . . redecorate her house."

Rummaging through the old paneled cabinets, Aubrey first found a splinter, hissing, "Son of a b—" Then she located the panel he described. She stood, biting down on a bloody index finger, a sizable sliver of wood lodged deep under her skin. With the opposite hand, she dumped the contents of an envelope onto the bar top. Inside were Kitty Stallworth's baptismal certificate, a grocery list, two dryer sheets, and an annuity for $750,000. "I think Kitty's going to be just fine," she said, blinking at the sum. "In fact, I'd say she's going to be"—Aubrey shook her smarting hand and looked toward an empty recliner. It rocked gently, the room bright with false light. Through the low picture window a gust of wind rose and rattled the mulch and mums, sweeping energy across Jerry Stallworth's front lawn.

CHAPTER FOUR

By the time Aubrey returned to the newsroom, her index finger was puffy and still splinter-filled. Instead of the hour she promised Malcolm, she'd been gone two, having left the house on Harper Street on a hunt for Alana Powell. Aubrey located the realtor at her home inspection on Halifax Drive. There she turned over the annuity, along with an unremarkable explanation about its discovery. Coming down the newsroom's main corridor, Aubrey saw Malcolm in his office; he looked busy, not particularly engaged in looking for her. Levi was nowhere in sight. Good. Maybe he'd talked his way out of deputizing her as his sidekick on the Missy Flannigan case. Aubrey shuddered at the prospect and headed for her cubicle.

Rounding the corner, she dropped her satchel on her desk. The injured digit caught her eye. With the opposite hand, she felt the half-moon scar on her chin. On her left forearm were deep pockmarks—bites. Today's splinter was an accidental consequence of her Jerry Stallworth encounter. Aubrey's old injuries were something else entirely. The scars represented the always lingering and potentially threatening unknowns of her extraordinary gift, and Aubrey had no desire to tempt evil.

She went about her business, unpacking her camera and notes and worries when Bebe turned up at the entrance. "Clearly, disinterest should have been my pitch during Malcolm's meeting."

"Pardon?"

"Your blasé attitude. You couldn't be less interested in Surrey's big news, and yet you managed to walk away with the story. Not to mention the bonus perk in from Hartford this morning."

"Levi?" Aubrey pressed the skin around the splinter, trying to force the wood out. She hissed at the pain. "You guessed it, Bebe. That was my strategy all along." Aubrey gave up on the splinter and folded her arms. "I'm bubbling with excitement, can't you tell?"

"I don't get you. Why someone who claims to be a reporter would rather *showcase* properties for sale than cover the hottest news to hit Surrey since . . . well, since Missy Flannigan disappeared. It doesn't make sense."

"And here's the really good part. I don't have to explain it to you." Aubrey returned to her Harper Street notes but then the rest of Bebe's remark registered. "What do you mean by 'the bonus perk'?"

"Ah, more strategy. Fine. Play it coy. But it was obvious to me. Levi may be headstrong and particular, but I can think of worse things than having to work a story with him."

Really? Could you name one? But then Aubrey smiled, recalling old gossip. "You know, last time Levi was here, he mentioned a girlfriend. Now, how is it I know that? Oh, right," she said, wagging her red swollen finger at Bebe. "You were having a moment, stunned that Levi preferred his girlfriend to your invitation for drinks . . . dinner . . . whatever."

Bebe rebutted with a slim-shouldered shrug. "Hmm, and what a vague tidbit to recall. Especially for a woman so recently back in circulation."

A retort teetered on Aubrey's tongue. Bebe wasn't worth the energy. Aubrey exited her cubicle, passing by Gwen Trumble. "Hey, Gwen.

Have you seen Levi?" she said, scanning the newsroom floor. "I ran late at my property. I was kind of hoping he'd gone on his way."

"I wouldn't count on that. He came out of Malcolm's office looking more irritated than on his way in. I think he set up shop in one of the empty offices in the back," she said, pointing. Dark and defunct, the offices sat in a glass-walled row, a daily reminder of the grim state of newspapers. But the one on the end showed new life, its lights on, a whirl of Levi St John's energy pulsing from inside.

"Thanks," Aubrey said, heading in that direction.

"Good luck," Gwen called after her. "Look at the bright side, it's not forever."

Aubrey pirouetted and offered a mock salute to Gwen. She took two more steps and paused. The energy differed—something other than the intensity of Levi's personality. She shut it down. But ten feet from the office the smell of salt air invaded her lungs. If not for the carpet squares under her feet, Aubrey could have sworn she stood on a beach. The air was reminiscent and vivid—filled with beach-goers, beach noises. She glanced gingerly around the newsroom. This was a sanctuary, a place where she'd been allowed to make a deal with the dead. Specters didn't intrude here—not unless their realtor brought them. Mental fortitude and years of a practiced life were on her side. Salt air retreated like the tide, replaced by the spicy scent of Ned Allegro's Ramen noodles. *Just a fluke*, she thought, perched at the edge of Levi's new office. She waited, then cleared her throat. Levi looked up, but her presence didn't seem to register and he reverted to his work. When she didn't dissolve from his peripheral glance, he dropped his pen and looked at her. Aubrey shrugged. "No luck with Malcolm?"

"Not so much."

"So I guess we're . . ."

"Working this story together."

She stepped inside and Levi's arms encircled the folders and notes on the desktop. Brooding looks and body language suggested a kid unwilling to share his toys. But the folders faded into a manila haze. The silver rim of Levi's watch caught her eye.

"*Time is not the point . . .*"

The voice echoed in her ears and Aubrey took a step back. Her glance traveled the office interior. Levi must have said her name more than once. The only thing she heard now was clear frustration. "Ellis. Are you coming or not? According to Malcolm, you have a contact there."

"Sorry," she said, blinking. But it wasn't until Levi stood and pulled on his suit jacket, the watch disappearing, that Aubrey was able to focus. "I didn't . . . What did you say?"

"I said I've been waiting for you to get back. What took so long? If you're going to work on this, Missy Flannigan has got to be your priority."

"Something unexpected came up with my home portrait piece."

"Like what? It's a house. You walk through—take a few notes, some pictures. Unless it was being burglarized . . ."

"Yes, that's it. I had to wait for the coast-is-clear signal." A sound of irritation pulsed from him. "I was obligated to my assignment before Malcolm's fabulous idea this morning."

"Whatever. Can we get going now?"

"Where?"

"To the medical examiner's office." He gathered select folders and notes. "I want to poke around and—"

"The ME's office?" A shiver wove through Aubrey. "The morgue, where they have Missy's body—or Missy's alleged body?"

"Do you know of a more appropriate location for skeletal remains?" Levi pocketed his keys and looked at his phone. His watch glinted again. "Malcolm mentioned you had some kind of six-degree connection there."

At the morgue? Forget six degrees . . . How about a direct line? Aubrey couldn't begin to fathom the connections. It wasn't so much the current bodies they might encounter. The freshly dead weren't well-versed in connecting. In fact, they were quite poor at it. But a building filled with lingering souls . . . That was an unknown. "Uh, Malcolm's right," she hesitantly admitted. "One of my realtors—her daughter is an administrative assistant to the chief medical examiner."

"That's a start. And it's more than we had five minutes ago." He brushed by and into the newsroom. "I assume you know her well enough to initiate a conversation?"

While lying seemed sensible, she answered with the truth. "I went to her baby shower last week."

"That'll work." Levi moved toward the exit.

"Wait," she said. "You want me to use a friend . . . or the daughter of a friend to facilitate your investigation?"

"Appalling, I know." He did an abrupt about-face, arms and folders flapping through the air. "You'll adjust, Ellis. And starting now, it's *our* investigation." Levi held up his hand. "Hold on. She's still there, right? I mean, she didn't have the kid yet, didn't go out on . . ."

"Maternity leave?"

"Right . . . that."

"No, you're safe. Priscilla has a month or two to go."

"All right then."

"Why? What is it you hope to learn?"

"Right now we have a skeleton presumed to be Missy Flannigan—which the world knows. But if a manner of death were evident, that would tell us something nobody else has. And I like being in that position." Reluctantly, Aubrey followed him through the newsroom. Levi glanced over his shoulder. "Any chance you want to drive? As noted, I'm not familiar with Surrey terrain."

Aubrey barely heard him. The dead were part of Aubrey's life, but purposely seeking out a murdered girl crossed every boundary she'd managed to construct. Her pulse thrummed in her ears and the inside of her mouth turned to sand.

When she didn't reply, Levi pivoted again. "Is there a problem, Ellis? Don't tell me you have an aversion to the dead."

"No, not so much an aversion. More like it's a subject that gets under my skin."

"Well, it's not as if Missy's going to give you an exclusive."

Shows what you know . . . Aubrey's stomach rolled on a punch of trepidation as she followed him to the exit.

◆ ◆ ◆

By the time they made it to the highway, she guessed Levi had added *poor driver* to his list of Aubrey's debatable qualifications. She'd nearly hit a dumpster while backing out of the parking lot, so preoccupied with the thought of visiting the morgue. Levi flipped through his notes, which gave Aubrey time to further mull over their destination. Short of feigning illness, there was nothing to do but trust in her practiced technique. The silence grew palpable. With the exception of her index finger, she couldn't ease a ten-and-two grip on the steering wheel. She was curious if the bead of sweat on her upper lip was noticeable. She sensed Levi glancing in her direction. There wasn't even the speed of highway traffic to distract them, as a road-maintenance crew slowed them down considerably. Conversation might have lessened the knot in her belly. But Aubrey couldn't think of a starting point—not with him. As she reached for the radio, Levi's voice cut through the quiet. "What happened to your finger?"

She tapped the swollen digit against the steering wheel. "Part of the delay at my property. I ran into a wet bar with serious dry rot. Not to mention a stubborn homeowner. An older gentleman, Jerry Stallworth. Nice man, but he . . . he didn't want to . . . *go*," she said, skirting along the truth.

"I hear that. Old geezers are tough. My father is one of this hemisphere's most belligerent."

Guess that apple didn't fall far from the tree . . .

"Looks like it hurts," he said.

"It's a nasty sliver of wood. I didn't have time to get it out. You were in such a hurry."

"Was I? Still, you should have tended to it before we left."

She tapped her finger again. "It's not going anywhere. I'll take care of it when we get back."

"It's, um . . . it's a habit of mine."

"Habit?"

"Going about things full force. Particularly things like the Missy Flannigan story. You should bring it to my attention if I do that. I mean, especially if you're, uh . . . wounded."

Her head ticked toward his. "I'm not *wounded*," she said, bristling at his placating tone. "Look, Levi, I realize our situation isn't your first choice. And it's certainly not mine . . ."

"Because?"

"Excuse me?"

"Why is that? Back in the conference room it was unclear if your objection was covering the Missy Flannigan story in general—which makes no sense at all—or covering it with me."

"So if my objection was you, that would make sense?" His arms rose in a vague gesture. Aubrey felt empathy, but not that much. "A good dose of both."

"Fair enough," he said, nodding. "Though, from what I recall, I thought we got on fine when I filled in for Malcolm."

"Sure, it was fine. Right up until you openly referred to my home portrait features as 'house porn.'"

He was quiet for a moment. "Did I say that?"

"More than once."

"You have to admit, Ellis, your features are a sure thing. All written with a positive slant. It's not exactly objective reporting."

"So now you're defending what you said?"

"Logically, not every house you walk into can be all that great. And yet, to hear you tell it . . ."

She rolled her eyes, thinking about ploughing onto the median to access their destination. It might get her arrested, but at least she could get away from him. "The positive slant is there for a reason, Levi. Realtors who spend big bucks on advertising, which is more critical than ever to newspapers, might not be so inclined if I trashed their listings."

"Fine . . . fine, I get it," he said. "It's a necessary . . . *aspect* of newspapers today."

"Evil," she said, turning toward him. "You were going to say, *necessary evil.*"

He met her full-on gaze. "I said *aspect.*" She snorted a laugh. He couldn't even hide his tone, which distinctly said *evil.* "And yes, I make no apology for being old-school when it comes to journalism. I believe in factual reporting backed by irrefutable proof. Gut instinct is a cliché and soft reporting does not serve the reader. Is there any reason you'd object to that?" Aubrey's mouth opened and closed. "However, for what it's worth, *house porn* was not a great choice of words."

"Don't hurt yourself with an apology."

He wasn't going to; road crew jackhammers were the only sounds in or out of the car. "So that's my take on this story, or any. What's yours?" Her silence baited the reporter. "Like I said, I've read your stuff. Slant aside, you're a good writer, Ellis. Why the reluctance to abandon the home portrait feature for real news?"

Aubrey tilted her neck against the headrest. In the dead-stopped traffic she closed her eyes. The question and his astuteness were equally annoying. A career as an investigative journalist had been her goal. But like everything else, Aubrey had tailored life to fit her own special needs. "I . . . it's complicated."

"How complicated could it be? Why don't you want to work on this story?"

Blurting out her objection was tempting. It might be worth the look on his face. Of course, it would be all he needed to take back to Malcolm. "*You do realize Ellis is delusional . . . That she thinks she speaks to the dead . . .*" She couldn't imagine anyone less inclined to accept her gift than Levi. "Is it necessary that everyone in journalism possess a desire to cover hard news?"

"Yes. Otherwise, where does the passion come from?" The word *passion* hit her ears just as *maternity leave* had hit his, an awkward topic that she didn't want to discuss on any level—not with him. He offered a reprieve. "Are you from Surrey? If you are, it should broaden your scope of contacts."

"No, I'm from . . ." There was no single answer. "I moved around a lot as a kid."

"Did you? Curious. I thought for sure you were at least fifth generation."

"Hardly. This past year is the longest I've lived anywhere—except for college, if a dorm room counts."

"Army brat?"

"Definitely not." She hesitated. "My grandmother, Charley, raised me." Aubrey stopped there. Levi waited. "My parents . . . they died."

"I didn't mean to—"

"It was a long time ago. I was five." Being the object of his laser-like focus wasn't appealing. But the clip of conversation eased Aubrey's current worries. The bead of sweat had stopped and she kept going. "My grandmother was in the carnival business. We traveled most of the year. It's seasonal work."

"Seriously? The carnival business?"

"Seriously. In fact, she owned the carnival. Charley inherited both halves from her ex-husbands, Oscar Bodette and Truman Heinz." She caught his sideways glance. "Apparently, the divorces were as amicable as the marriages."

"Odd. The amicable part, anyway." At least he'd moved on from passion to cynicism. "Carnival life. Sounds like feature story material, not something you hear every day."

"No, I guess you don't. It's different. People don't get it. A good carnival troupe is like family." Aubrey felt her nerves ease. "There's comfort in a nonconformist world. Nobody has to worry about blending. We wintered in warm spots, covered the East Coast circuit in the summer . . ." she said, rambling. "Although we avoided Florida. It's tough for traveling acts to compete with the big black ears."

"The black ears?"

"Mickey Mouse . . . Disney World . . . *ears* . . ." Aubrey tucked a length of crow-colored hair behind her ear. She tugged on the lobe, showing off four little studs that ran in a traffic-jam pattern on the outer edge.

Levi tipped his head, examining more closely. This was easy to read. She'd be willing to bet anything other than classic pearl studs fell outside his lines. "Disney, right, I get it." But his gaze continued to say *odd*, gliding down her bright pink blouse and gauzy turquoise skirt. Surely, to him it was a disconnected blurb of color. For Aubrey it was a critical tool. And like an artist, over time, she'd mastered the technique of color. Bright hues were a conduit. Of course, today she'd dressed in anticipation of a specter in a for-sale house. Not the group setting of a morgue. Either way, her clothes were a complete contrast to his conservative navy suit. The two of them most likely differed on everything from politics to books to dietary choices. Levi persisted, now in full interview mode. "How did you attend school?"

"Carnie life can be erratic. I can't argue that. But like I said, they're family. I was home schooled. Our master of ceremonies also had a master's degree in education. Before joining us, Carmine headed a disturbingly tough high school in Detroit. One day he reached burnout point and—"

"And he what?" Levi's dimple was full and evident. "Ran away and joined the circus?"

"It happens." She didn't smile back. "And it's a carnival, not a circus. There's a huge difference. It wasn't any *Water for Elephants*. We don't believe in animals as acts. It's mostly theme rides, games of chance, a few

Ripley's-type attractions . . . contortionists, magic acts, the usual. We did have a petting zoo for a couple of years, but the goats kept escaping."

"The goats." He nodded deeply. "That's almost unbelievable, Ellis."

"I can hook you up with a good sword swallower if you need irrefutable proof. But I get it. I'm sure it's worlds away from your Norman Rockwell upbringing. Let me guess," she said, recalling Levi's penchant for proper dining—he'd once asked if La Petite Maison, a place with unpronounceable entrees and a genuine French chef, was seriously the best restaurant in Surrey—"your childhood was anchored to widely attended family holidays, Mom with three kinds of pie, and the most prestigious private schools."

There was silence from Levi's side of the car, the kind that said she was so off the mark it was unanswerable. "One out of three," he finally said. "And the private school wasn't that prestigious. Certainly, my father would have preferred military prep." Levi shuffled his folders, checking his watch. Sunlight glinted off the metal rim, the effect so intense that Aubrey had to turn away. "Ellis?" She blinked fiercely, seeing Levi point to a gap in the traffic, which had started to move. "It wasn't my impression that you'd lived such a colorful existence. Last time I was here you struck me as . . . *withdrawn*."

"I, uh . . . It was a difficult time. My husband and I were having problems."

"Huh. You never . . . I didn't know you were married." Levi's focus stayed on the steamrollers paving the highway. Aubrey stared too, considering the one that had rolled over her marriage. "Are you . . . Is that . . . *resolved?*"

Aubrey tapped the bare ring finger of her left hand against the steering wheel. It felt more pronounced than the one with the splinter. "If you're concerned that personal drama will interfere with Missy Flannigan business, it won't. We couldn't work it out. The divorce is nearly final." Aubrey eased the car onto the exit ramp, making the quick left that led to the coroner's office. Levi was busy writing as she parked the car. He had oddly elegant handwriting for a lefty, Aubrey thought. Her gaze trailed farther right, dead-ending on his watch. In her outlying glance, a few raindrops hit the windshield. There hadn't been any sun, no rays to make metal glint. Levi gathered his folders and got out of the car. Aubrey inhaled deeply.

"Coming?" he said. Reluctantly, she followed. Between Levi's watch and whatever awaited her in that building, it was shaping up to be the kind of day where Aubrey wished she'd stayed with the carnival.

CHAPTER
FIVE

Aubrey and Levi were about to enter the coroner's office when her phone rang. "Charley, hi. Hang on a second." Aubrey pointed her phone toward the glass doors. "You go ahead. I'll be right there." Levi went inside, leaving her behind. She was grateful for the delay, though it only lasted long enough for her grandmother to say that a repairman had come and gone, having adjusted the automatic stair lift. When Aubrey and Owen formally separated, Charley had moved into the house, her arthritis having progressed to a point where she required assistance. Aubrey had been grateful for the company. "Okay, glad it's fixed. I'll see you tonight . . . My day? Let's just say we'll have plenty to chat about at dinner."

Aubrey considered waiting there for her new partner, safe on the sidewalk. Why not? She'd only be a cog in the Levi St John wheel of investigation. *Or interrogation* . . . Leery, Aubrey peered through the glass entry, looking for things only she might see. She felt like a tight-rope walker without a net. Conscience won out. It would be unkind to subject a pregnant Priscilla Snow to Levi without a buffer. Aubrey moved forward and busied her brain with Levi adjectives—aggressive, inflexible, *bullheaded*—picturing him beside the dictionary definitions for each one. Her assumptions were soon validated, seeing him firing questions at a fidgety Priscilla.

"Aubrey!" Priscilla came toward her—a darting waddle. Aubrey tried to relax, form a smile. But her senses were on high alert, waiting for a smell or sound, the taste of Missy Flannigan. Maybe it would come in the form of peppermint gum or the smack of a mixed drink—the potent kind a girl of twenty-one might favor. There was nothing immediate, only the faintest hint of chai tea, which Aubrey had drunk that morning. Sounds were equally pedestrian: ringing phones and piped-in instrumental music. Aubrey's brow knitted, and she listened for ethereal noise. "How are you, Priscilla? You look absolutely . . ."

"Fat?" She giggled and glanced toward feet she surely could not see.

"I was going to say . . . glowing." But the fill-in word was a struggle, Aubrey's mind not on their conversation. "You're just glowing. Isn't she glowing, Levi?" He didn't encroach on their exchange and poked at his phone instead. Aubrey's eyes flicked around the office space. Ordinary visitors wouldn't suspect any signs of the dead—oddly, neither did she. "You've met Levi."

"I did." Priscilla leaned in, whispering, "I thought maybe he was new. He's intense . . . *hot*, in a branding iron sort of way." She giggled again. "Hormones!"

Aubrey caught Levi's uncomfortable shift. He stayed put, still poking at his phone. "Levi and I are working the Missy Flannigan story together. Normally, he's the city desk editor at the *Standard Speaker* in Hartford."

"Oh . . . anyway, like I told him, I don't know much more than you guys, except they did move Missy's remains to the coroner's office in Sandwich yesterday." Aubrey closed her eyes. Missy Flannigan wasn't even in the building. The relief was overwhelming and she pressed her fingertips hard onto the edge of Priscilla's desk.

"Ellis, you okay?" Levi asked. She nodded, swallowing down saliva that offered no unusual taste. "You're pale as a ghost."

A baseless cliché, Levi, but never mind that . . . "I'm fine. Moved her. Why . . . why did they do that?"

"I have no idea. But they had me fill out a TRF yesterday, which to be honest I didn't really appreciate, being as it was a Sunday and all."

"A TRF?"

"Transport Remains Form," Levi and Priscilla said simultaneously.

"I assumed it was because of all the inquiries," Priscilla said. "Can you believe Fox News called and the people from the Nancy Grace show showed up here—with cameras? I think the powers that be wanted the remains somewhere with more security. Can't say I was sorry to see her go. I mean, poor girl and all, but it was just too much for me, especially at the moment." She rubbed her round belly and smiled at her visitors. "It's pretty quiet around here. Our usual crowd, they aren't big talkers, you know? As it was, Missy was our only . . . *guest.*"

"Huh," Aubrey said, sighing, "that explains a lot."

"How so?" Levi said.

"Never mind. So other than the transfer, there hasn't been any additional Missy Flannigan information since the story broke?"

"None that's passed by me." Priscilla made her way around to the inside of her desk and lowered herself into the chair. Aubrey noticed a pile of baby-themed catalogs and half-written thank you notes on the desktop. The only item relevant to the medical examiner's office was a sign-in sheet. "But if I knew anything good," Priscilla said, winking at Aubrey, "I wouldn't mind being your source." She looked at Levi. "I can't tell you how many realtors think the world of Aubrey, my mom included. She does some pretty amazing work at those houses."

"I couldn't agree more," Levi said. He grinned wide, full dimple, and backed away. "Around the newsroom, Ellis here is known as the Joan Didion of the real estate beat."

"Is she?" Priscilla said. "Huh, Joan must be with Century 21. I don't know her."

"It was a pleasure meeting you, Priscilla. And congrats on your baby." As the woman was replying, Levi moved fast to the exit, like his work there was done. In the midst of their abrupt retreat, Aubrey shot him a suspicious look. "What?" he said, getting in the car. "I can be social in the right situation."

"Uh-huh, and what situation is that? Priscilla didn't offer much."

"The medical examiner's headquarters is located in Boston. They took the remains to Sandwich—on the Cape."

"Meaning?" she said as they settled into their seats.

"Last year a prominent Connecticut resident turned up dead in Massachusetts—shot to death. The story was mine. So I happen to know that the Cape ME office specializes in homicides relating to firearms. They study ballistics. The facility specializes in state-of-the-art testing and has a highly trained staff. If a body is transported there, you can bet it's because the victim died from a gunshot wound." Levi's supposition spilled over and Aubrey retrieved her cell, thinking she too might have made a connection. "What are you doing?"

"I'm curious about a name I saw on Priscilla's sign-in sheet. She did say that Missy's supposed remains were the only body in house. So who . . . Damn," she said, her puffy index finger impeding the Google search.

"Here, give me the phone."

"Clayton Hadley," Aubrey said.

A moment later, Levi turned the phone toward Aubrey. "I'll be a son of a . . ."

"Oh my gosh, Clayton Hadley . . . former federal agent, firearms expert," she said, reading the result.

"Good catch, Ellis. I completely missed any sign-in sheet."

"You had to be willing to look *at* the baby catalogs to get past them."

"True," he said, nodding. "So if we put it all together, we can infer that a manner of death was evident, at least to the ME. Missy Flannigan died from a gunshot wound."

Levi dropped the phone back in her hand, the edge smacking against her splintered finger. Aubrey jerked her hand back and the phone fell from her grasp. "Enough. Let me see that." Levi fished in his pocket, coming up with a Swiss Army knife. Aubrey leaned harder into the car door. "Come on, Ellis. You want it out, don't you? If I can't get it on one pass, we'll go from here to the emergency room."

Reluctantly, she held out her hand. "I don't need an emergency room."

He opened the multi-pronged knife, exposing needle-nose tweezers. "Hang on a moment." From his jacket pocket he produced a lighter.

"Do you smoke?" It seemed more likely that he'd indulge in karaoke.

Levi ran the flame over the tweezers until they glowed red. "No sense in taking out a splinter only to end up with something worse."

"Are you always so prepared?"

He retracted the flame. "Yes," he said, his dark eyes jumping to hers. "Finger, please." She eased it closer and Levi slipped his glasses to the end of his nose. A low whistle hummed out from him. "You really did a job here. What were you doing poking around a bar? Isn't the idea to paint the big picture of the house for the reader?"

"Like I told you, the homeowner—Jerry Stallworth—he was a nice old man but stubborn. He didn't want to sell. We, uh, we got into a conversation. I accidently rested my hand on the bar. Anyway, Jerry . . . Mr. Stallworth, he just needed somebody to listen to him. I'm sorry if that's not something you can appreciate."

Levi probed with the tweezers, arching his eyebrows over the frame of his glasses. "I might appreciate it more than you think, particularly the stubborn part."

"Right, you said that. Your father?" Aubrey assumed he'd passed.

"Yes, my father," Levi said, hesitantly. "They don't come more tenacious than him. But the older he gets, the more he just wants somebody to listen."

Huh . . . So the senior St John is alive and well . . . "Tough, is he?"

"Tough on the outer layers. Pure titanium at the core. Your homeowner . . ."

"Jerry Stallworth."

"Right. There might have been malleability to Jerry. There's too much old soldier in Broderick St John." Levi continued to nudge at the splinter.

The circumstance left Aubrey with nothing to do but employ everyday senses. His chestnut-colored hair smelled of medicated shampoo—although, admittedly, it was thick and kind of lush. Bebe had once remarked that Levi had Kennedy hair. In the close quarters, Aubrey studied the outline of his face and clean-shaven jaw. She imagined the buttoned-up Levi to be clueless about stubble being in vogue. Stifling the physical observations, she said, "So he's in the military, your father?"

"Uh, yes—was. British intelligence, military."

"Really? He's English then." The idea fit like a glove on Levi's stoic nature. She looked back at the splinter. Conversely, the gentleness with which he probed didn't fit at all. "That's almost as intriguing as carnival life. How very James Bond."

"He wouldn't look very intelligent if you quizzed him on that. He'd consider it nonsense . . . make that *rubbish*."

"Takes himself seriously, does he?" Aubrey rolled her eyes in a gesture Levi could not see. "But you didn't grow up in England. I mean, you don't have an accent."

"No. I've lived in Connecticut since I was eight. Before that, California. It's where my mother's from."

"Really? So you were a surfer dude?" she said, distracted by the unlikely imagery.

The tweezers didn't move. "No. Not me."

"So then who—" The tweezers pinched and a zing of pain forced a hiss through Aubrey's teeth.

"Stay with me, Ellis. I've almost got it."

But his hand, the sense of touch, began to elicit something else. There was a muddled vibe circling, hovering, pressing in, another breath of salt air. "Tell me about them, your family."

"Tell you . . . ?" Levi looked at her as if no one had ever ventured to ask. "Why would you . . . Uh, my father," he said, focusing on the splinter, "is retired. He divvies his residence between London and here. New England weather feels more natural to Pa."

"Pa?" Aubrey inched back. The word hit her ears with a whisper of déjà vu.

"Pa. It's an upper-class British term for *father*. It's what we called him."

"We. You have siblings." And on the back of Aubrey's neck came the annoying itch of wool, so coarse it made her squirm in her seat.

The statement hung there for a moment. "A brother," he said. "Ellis, stop moving." It sounded more like *"Stop talking . . ."* The tweezers paused and so did Levi. He pushed his glasses up again. "I prefer not to talk about him." Aubrey felt the itch of wool retreat like a weak front line. "When my parents divorced we relocated with my father to Connecticut. End of story."

Aubrey nodded, hearing Levi's deep desire not to discuss his personal life. She shrugged. "So why did you live with your father?"

Even with his head tipped downward, she saw the forced dimple. Curiously, a blank expression rose to meet hers. "It was an unpleasant divorce. Saying my father is inflexible is a gross understatement. His mind operates solely in military measures—first the Cold War followed by the Falklands War. Of course, that was nothing compared to the war with my mother on every conceivable front. Although, you have to hand it to her . . ." He hesitated.

"Hand it to her . . . ?" she prompted.

"Nothing. They were a total mismatch. Age, lifestyles, decisions . . . habits. My mother was an actress . . . a model of sorts." Aubrey watched his fingertips whiten around the Swiss Army knife. "A drunk," he said. "Saying she was a drunk would be her understatement."

"I, um . . ." Aubrey gulped. "I assumed . . . I didn't get the impression that . . ."

"What?" he said, insisting she hold his gaze. "That there was an open bottle of vodka in my Norman Rockwell painting?" Her probe into Levi's life halted the one into her finger.

"I'm sorry. I shouldn't have pried."

He returned to her injury. "It's irrelevant history." Rain on the car's roof was the only sound, turning into a downpour. Levi held up the tweezers, a slice of wood pinched in its grip. "That's it. We're done."

In the time it took to blink, Levi put away his lighter and his life, fading into his all-business persona. Aubrey sensed anything but irrelevant history. But she pushed it and a circling entity away. Zoning in on any being connected to Levi was absurd—disbelief would be his understatement. She moved on, doing the prudent thing and minding her own business. "So, Levi, based on our new knowledge, what's our next Missy Flannigan move?"

CHAPTER SIX

Aubrey hauled a stiff armless chair out of Levi's office and maneuvered in a bulkier one with more cushion. Everything surrounding Levi came with a sense of heavy lifting. He proved her right, continuing with weighty facts before her bottom could make contact with the chair.

"Somewhere in these files, there is information about Dustin Byrd and guns. And now that we have a manner of death," he said, sifting through his research, "we might be able to turn a dotted line into a solid one."

"What's the basic 4-1-1 on Dustin Byrd?" Aubrey scooched closer to his desk.

Levi opened a thick folder and spun it toward her. "Byrd is the director of Surrey Parks and Rec, or at least he was until they put him on unpaid leave after Friday's little discovery. The only press items are town council meetings where Byrd talked about new soccer-field zoning and sewer drainage. Not exactly germane."

"Or interesting." Aubrey looked at the old press clippings, but she didn't touch them.

"Clearly, there's nothing that connects Dustin to Missy. On the surface that makes sense. He was sixteen years older. It's not likely that they shared the same social circle. As far as we know, no one in Surrey ever alluded to Dustin and Missy in the same sentence."

"Is Byrd, or was he ever, married?"

Levi flipped between two pages of legal pad. "Uh, no. Your point?"

Aubrey shrugged. "Most people do marry eventually."

"I suppose." But his agreement was weak, as if he found the argument less than valid. "Regardless, their personal lives don't intersect. Byrd's been married to the town of Surrey since he graduated high school. He never left home, never really moved on. Missy was a college student at Surrey State." Levi turned a page of orderly notes sideways, reading what looked like a miniature rubric in the margin. "'See hobbies folder' . . . Right. That's where I saw it." From his briefcase, Levi retrieved a thick accordion folder.

"Further preparedness?"

"I like facts at my disposal. And yes, if you want to stay ahead with this story—"

"I get it," she said, picturing Levi's color-coded, season-separated sock drawer.

"It's a straightforward process, Ellis. The things that align go in a subject folder—Missy, Frank Delacort, Dustin Byrd, Surrey points of interest, etcetera. The spare parts," he said, searching the compartments, "live here until I figure out where they belong."

"And does the answer to everything always fit neatly in a folder?"

He glanced past the rim of his glasses and over the desk. "It does when I'm through with it. Here's an excellent example." Levi produced a *Surrey City Press* news clipping. "Six years ago, the paper did a feature on gun enthusiasts." He held out the clipping. It showed a paunchy middle-aged Byrd in a flak jacket, posed next to a fully stocked gun cabinet.

She didn't touch it. Like her real estate listing sheets and other objects, heat was a barometer of ghostly entities, a possible pathway. Aubrey wasn't about to take that chance with Missy Flannigan. She hesitated long enough and Levi dropped the news story in front of her. "My, Surrey's director of parks and rec takes his Second-Amendment rights seriously," she said.

"Serious enough to own a gun collection that earns the Charlton Heston seal of approval."

"Add to that the body falling out of your basement wall and it does make Missy's murder look like a no-brainer." Her hand hovered over the news clipping. "It certainly makes you think Byrd is the guy."

"Why do you say it like that, Ellis? Like it's too easy." Levi picked up the story before she did. "What are you thinking?"

She was surprised he'd want to know. "Actually, I was thinking about Frank Delacort. Is his file handy?" Aubrey wasn't familiar with the specifics of the twenty-year-old case, but everyone in Surrey knew the basics: Delacort was the Surrey drifter who brought jurors to a lightning-fast verdict in the presumed murder of Missy Flannigan. "The stories I've heard, it sounds as if Frank Delacort didn't exist until the day he was arrested for Missy's murder. What came before that? I'm just wondering."

Levi thumbed through other notes. "From the gist of it, prior to Surrey, Delacort served about a decade in the military, mostly abroad."

"Army, right?"

"Yes. Delacort's detailed military record remains classified. There's only a mention of the unit he was deployed with in Kuwait. His rank, sergeant. However, there's plenty of documentation that speaks to unstable behavior, which eventually got him booted from the army."

"What sort of behavior?"

"Anger management issues mostly. And it's not just that." Levi rifled through military and courtroom documents, arriving at a page that differed. "Here, an old police report. Delacort had a stateside wife who'd once called the cops on him. Police responded to the domestic violence call, but charges were never filed." He flipped back to Delacort's army troubles. "Nice. I missed this." Levi tapped the page as he rocked in his chair. "During his exit psych evaluation, Delacort shoved his army psychiatrist, a Dr. Sonya Harrison, into a steel door."

"Charming. And they still cut him loose?"

"Apparently so." Levi leaned in and dropped the page in front of Aubrey, who skimmed the details. "Delacort turned up in Surrey right after that. Witnesses testified that they saw him talking to Missy Flannigan on more than one occasion. But in my research, the thing that really swayed the jury was the blood evidence."

"Blood evidence?"

"Ellis, you really need to get up to speed on this."

"Maybe keep in mind that until a few hours ago, I didn't know this was going to be my priority. Otherwise, my preparedness wouldn't be a question."

"Fine," he said. "I get your point." She narrowed her eyes as Levi filled in the blanks. "There was blood evidence found in the room Delacort rented." He shuffled past a few more pages. "A place called the Plastic Fork. Do you know it?"

"Yes, absolutely," she said, glad for a speck of knowledge he didn't possess. "May I?" Aubrey pointed to his laptop. He turned it toward her and she Googled the Plastic Fork. The webpage showed off a quaint two-story building with striped awnings, located on Surrey's main thoroughfare. "It's a landmark of sorts. Mick O'Brien and his wife . . . um, Irene, I think. They've owned it for years. It's a gourmet deli, hot and cold takeout."

"Apparently, it also has a room for rent. That's where Delacort was staying and it's where the blood evidence turned up on some sheets, a towel in the bathroom. In addition to that, Missy's hair was also found in his room. More specifically, in his bed. Delacort claimed Missy badly scraped her leg while jogging and that he offered medical assistance."

"That's plausible. Especially if they were acquainted, which we know from witness testimony."

"And it even sounds like reasonable doubt until you factor in Missy's fifty-dollar bill."

"Missy's fifty-dollar bill?"

He sighed, a sound that was clearly marked: *Be tolerant, St John.* "Missy vanished on the twenty-ninth of September," he said, hitting recitation mode. "Her twenty-first birthday would have been October first. Frank Delacort used a fifty-dollar bill to buy a ham sandwich and a pack of cigarettes at the Plastic Fork the day after Missy disappeared, the thirtieth. At that point, our victim had just made local headlines—standard missing persons report. At the Plastic Fork, the owner's wife . . ."

"Irene."

"Right, Irene," he said, pointing at the computer screen. "She noticed the margin of the bill, which said . . ." Levi peered at his notes and quoted: "'Happy 21st Birthday, Missy! Love, Aunt Jan.' Missy's father, Tom Flannigan, even produced the envelope postmarked the twenty-eighth."

"So the jury had proof of a window of opportunity. Add to that a suspect prone to violent outbursts, women being a documented target. The same guy who ended up with Missy's birthday money in his pocket, also has her blood and hair in his bedroom." Aubrey chewed on a thumbnail, thinking. "A preponderance of evidence. Geez, based on that . . ."

"You might have voted guilty?"

She nodded.

"It added up. Collectively, it all sounds damning, particularly the time-stamped money linked directly to Missy."

"But then, twenty years later, out of nowhere . . ." Aubrey flexed her fingers and reached toward the folders.

"Out of nowhere," Levi said, scooping up the one marked *Byrd*, "Missy's remains fall out of the wall in Dustin Byrd's basement."

"Making a man completely unrelated to the case the new prime suspect."

"Making Byrd the prime suspect and turning a convicted murderer into a martyr."

"Assuming you can make it all fit neatly into a folder."

"Assuming . . ." Levi tossed the Byrd folder onto the desk. "So are you game, Ellis? You were intrigued enough to notice a random sign-in sheet back at the coroner's office. You're curious about Frank Delacort. Does getting to the bottom of this suddenly make the home portrait beat look a little . . . uninspired?"

Aubrey stared at the Byrd folder, her emotions equally mixed. Aubrey didn't want any part of this story. Yet she was wildly tempted by the idea of telling it. She snatched up the Byrd folder. Aubrey opened it, her fingertips flying over the gun story as if it were braille. Pressing the pages hard between her hand and lap, she braced for the sensation of heat. There was nothing, only a smudge of newsprint on her thumb. The newsroom had settled into normal sounds and smells, stale coffee and the buzz of co-workers behind them. She closed the folder. "Huh . . . that's almost unbelievable."

"What's unbelievable? You didn't even read it."

"Levi, what do you know about Missy Flannigan?"

Employing a tad more tolerance, he offered the facts. "According to her parents, Tom and Barbara Flannigan, Missy was a typical college junior—quite attractive, for whatever that's worth. She lived in Surrey her whole life."

He opened Missy's folder. On top was a color photo of a blue-eyed blonde, upturned nose, and a sweet smile—most definitely homecoming-queen material. But even from Aubrey's upside-down angle, a wallop of recognition pulsed through her. She'd seen this girl before. Aubrey shook her head, trying to jar a memory that wouldn't come. Levi moved the color photo aside and the sense of recognition faded into common déjà vu. Underneath it were facsimiles, black and white versions of the same photo seen in the *Surrey City Press* and on *NBC Nightly News*. Any conscious being would feel a connection to Missy's photo.

"To the best of our knowledge," Levi said, "Missy's life was unremarkable. The most outstanding thing was her disappearance."

"At twenty-one most people haven't lived lives that make headlines. Disappearing probably *was* the biggest thing that happened to her."

"Possibly," he said. "Still, the stories about Missy weren't terribly in-depth. More like an homage to the victim. They might as well have read, *'In addition to being a Surrey doer of good deeds'*—apparently, she liked to volunteer—*'Missy Flannigan loved puppies and poetry . . . sunsets and campfire sing-alongs . . .'* There has to be more."

Aubrey read the bylines. "Malcolm wrote those stories."

"Yes . . . he did. It wasn't a criticism."

"Yes it was."

Levi removed his glasses, tapping the rims against the information in front of him. "It was." The movement ceased and he laid his hands flat on the desktop. "Listen, I've spent days separating facts from Surrey folklore. It was a tragic story when Missy vanished at the hands of a rogue drifter—the bad-things-that-happen-to-good-girls stuff that you warn your kids about. But now . . ." he said, putting the glasses back on. "Now it all seems more questionable than ever."

Aubrey wrapped her arms tight around herself, crossing the sleeves of her bright pink shirt. Her hand rose to her chin and she felt the half-moon groove. It was a symbol, a tattoo, courtesy of evil. Self-preservation and instinct said to stay away from the things on Levi's desk. At the same time, his desire to uncover the truth drew her in. "Now you think there's more to the story."

"I think," Levi said, looking over the collection of questionable facts and new evidence, "we haven't scratched the surface of the unremarkable life of Missy Flannigan."

CHAPTER
SEVEN

Surrey, Massachusetts
Twenty Years Earlier

Church bells rang. Missy sat in a pew, spellbound by the chime of a hymn she could not name. Eyes closed, she felt the solidity of the pew beneath her bottom and the airier promises that surrounded her. Incense dusted the sanctuary and a wide wood ceiling protectively spanned the space. It made Missy feel at peace. The church, she thought, was a place where forgiveness could be granted by showing up.

As the chiming came to an end, so did the window for Missy's quiet thoughts. She'd given up on calling it *prayer* years ago. Prayers were meant to be answered. So far, Missy's had not been. But her eyes remained shut as her mind absorbed the fading tendrils of solitude. She heard the heavy creak of the vestibule doors and felt sunlight spread across her back. It penetrated, refreshing her like baptism. A smile curved around her lips. Missy favored the idea of being born again. She heard Father Frederick, the dedicated priest who oversaw the sinners at Our Lady of the Redeemer. With him were two members, Mick

O'Brien and Ed Maginty. Missy slid into the shadow of the pew. She recognized each man's voice best with her eyes closed.

Moments later Missy slipped out a side door, hurrying from the church to Surrey's ball fields, a few blocks away. Spring was a busy time and she arrived ready to volunteer at the Surrey Boosters' Snack Shack. Inside the wooden structure, she wriggled her nose at a vat of steaming hot dogs and inventoried rows of packaged snacks. There was a cashbox left in her care with a few small bills, enough to make change. According to the town's volunteer call list, Heather Dixon was supposed to be there too. Missy's hands settled onto her slim hips, guessing the even slimmer girl wouldn't show. Heather excelled at sports and academics, but in addition to those notable qualities the girl was also bulimic—one of many Surrey secrets Missy kept. No, the food would be too much for Heather. She wouldn't show.

Missy was on her own as the Surrey Phantoms baseball team prepared to take on the King Phillip Knights. It was fine. Along with being a solid keeper of secrets, Missy was a hard worker, someone who powered through off-putting tasks. She pulled her long blond hair into a ponytail, ready to get to work. The Snack Shack didn't present much of a challenge. That was good. It would make it easier to multitask. Volunteering had led to other opportunities, like babysitting, which had springboarded into even better paying positions. Over time, those jobs became steady employment, providing a reliable income. Missy had managed to save most of her money. She considered her earnings as her gaze panned Surrey's wider boundaries. The town's spring fields glowed green, meeting with a dome of blue sky. On one edge, painting a foul line, was Dustin Byrd. While the distance was too far for eye contact, Missy knew he was looking at her. She stared back, though it was the dome's horizon that had her attention.

"Missy . . . did you get my order or not?" Missy's gaze snapped back to Ed Maginty's bald head, a disturbingly familiar point of view. "I said it twice. Come on, would you? Little Ed's going to miss the first pitch."

She looked at *Little* Ed, who wasn't so little anymore. She hadn't seen the boy since she last babysat for the Magintys, a year ago. He'd grown to mirror his father's large-headed look. It made Missy despise the child on sight. "Mr. Maginty. I didn't see you there."

"How could you not see me? I'm standing right in front of you." A sigh heaved from his gut. Missy knew the sound, which could represent both satisfaction and annoyance. "For the third time, we'll have two hot dogs . . . *please*."

"Coming right up." Missy did as she was asked because . . . well, because that's what you did for paying customers. She cradled two steaming tubes of beef in buns, placing them in cardboard carriers. Missy took Ed Maginty's money. She hovered near the cashbox with his crisp bill in hand. She glanced back at Ed and Little Ed. They were absorbed in the first pitch. Smiling, she said, "Here's your change." The batter popped up, leading to a rousing cheer from the crowd, the Magintys included. He didn't hear her and Missy spoke louder, "Mr. Maginty . . . your money." He turned, snatching up the cash. "Can I help you?" she said to the next customer in line.

Ed Maginty turned back. "Hey! I gave you twenty. This is change for a ten!"

"You must be mistaken."

"No. I gave you a twenty." He dropped the change onto the counter. There was unlikely eye-contact as Ed Maginty lowered his voice. "I see what you're doing, Missy. But I know the bill I used to pay for two dollar-fifty hot dogs. I want my seventeen dollars."

"You gave me a ten. I don't even have a twenty." She showed him the cashbox and its smaller bills. Ed Maginty peered inside. The man behind him looked too, peeking around Ed's fat bald head. A glance passed between the man and Missy, who smiled as if they shared a secret.

"See here, Missy, I had a five and a twenty. Here's the five. I wanted to break the twenty, so I gave it to you!"

"I'm sorry, Mr. Maginty, but you gave me a ten. I'm certain of it."

"I could take my complaint to the booster committee. Doug Dixon, the president, is a friend. I've been doing his taxes for years. You don't want that kind of trouble. Doug would see things—"

"Hey, maybe it was two tens. Is this yours?" The man behind Ed bent down and came up with a ten-dollar bill. "You must have dropped it."

A flustered Ed blinked. Missy blinked wider. "Uh, thanks. But I just came from the bank. My teller knows what kind of bills I like—crisp twenties, not crumpled tens." His voice bore down on Missy. "As a CPA, I'm aware of what kind of bill I gave you."

"Dad, we're missing the game," whined Little Ed.

"Kid's missing the game." The man gave the boy's hair a tussle. "Why don't you give Missy here a break? You got your money." Pinched between two dirty fingers, the man held out the worn but usable ten dollar bill. Ed Maginty grabbed the cash and plodded toward the field with his son.

"Thanks," she said.

"Welcome . . . *Missy.* Is that short for something?"

"No. Just Missy."

"So, Missy, this seems like a pain-in-the-ass job for one person."

"Ed Maginty's the pain in the ass." Her glare softened, ticking back to the man. She couldn't place him, not in Surrey. "I used to babysit for him and stuff. He gypped me more than once."

"Gypped you, huh?" He looked from the hot dogs to her.

"He'll tell you it was a miscalculation. But I know what I get an hour." Looking him over, Missy tallied thoughts about the stranger. "Anyway . . . that was nice of you, to give him the money."

"It had to be his ten, right? Besides, the guy seemed like a prick. Like he was bothering you."

"I can take care of myself." Missy wondered if the same thing could be said about the stranger. The air was chilly, and he'd come to the game wearing a thin army jacket. He was thirty or so, thin in the face, his cheekbones jutting at a sharp angle. His tightly shorn hair was dark and his face stubbly. His unshaven look didn't strike Missy as intentional, more like the result of circumstance. The crowds had drifted and the line dwindled. In the quiet Missy swore she heard his stomach growl. "Did you want to get a hot dog?"

"I, um . . ." He patted his pockets. "I don't seem to have . . ."

Missy plopped a hot dog in a bun and held it out. "On the house. Their accounting system sucks. They count the cash, not the inventory." The grin pushed into the hollows of his cheeks—average looking, she thought, but with a dazzling smile. He accepted the hot dog, gobbling it down with the grace of a hungry animal. "Want a Coke to go with that, maybe a bag of chips?" He nodded, half the hot dog already history. Missy turned for the cooler, discreetly shifting a crisp bill from her back pocket to her front.

Hours later, Missy didn't recall asking the man to stay. But she also hadn't objected when he hung around, telling her that his name was Frank Delacort and saying that he wasn't from around there. Eventually, army-jacket Frank worked his way inside the Snack Shack. He proved useful, doling out snacks and restocking the cooler. In turn, Missy looked the other way as he scarfed down four more hot dogs. They worked side by side until the spectators waned, trickling down to one chunky girl who bought three homemade Rice Krispies treats and a package of Red Vines. On her last pass, after she asked for a bag of Cheetos, Missy informed the girl that they were closed. She shooed her away, telling her she'd end up as fat as a house if she didn't change her diet.

"Are you always so direct?" Frank asked, putting unused buns back into the bag.

"I guess I am. There's less confusion if you say what's on your mind."

"Yeah, I been told I could benefit from that—sayin' what's on my mind." He went back to work, throwing leftover sauerkraut into the trash can. "It's just not my way. Sometimes I react first, think later."

After that short exchange Frank didn't say much else. With a score of twelve to one, the Surrey Phantoms prevailing, Missy locked the cashbox and scooped up the leftover donated treats. She tossed them into a trash can and watched Frank's eyes follow the target. "Hey, um . . . would you mind taking this to the dumpster?" she asked.

"The dumpster?"

"It's on the other side of the parking lot. It's kind of dusky that way."

"Uh, sure. Did . . . did you want to toss the leftover hot dogs too?"

"No. Leave them for now. That trash bag looks like it's going to burst."

He nodded, dragging the full can out the rear door of the Snack Shack. Missy stared until a voice drew her attention.

"It warms my heart to see how you're so invested in Surrey. It speaks well of you, Missy." She turned. On the counter, in Missy's face, was a giant ceramic cat. For a split second, she thought it had done the talking. Her confusion eased as Violet Byrd's round face and gray mop of curls peeked from behind. "Most college-age folks forget about town activities by now. It's lovely to see you volunteering like this."

"Hi there, Mrs. Byrd. I didn't know you were here."

"I came by to deliver the goodies from last week's Paint and Party. I tell you, honey," she said, hugging the cat, "your idea to switch to ceramics, call it a wine party, was brilliant. Stay-at-home moms jump at a night out. Why, I'm so booked, I had to cut back on my own volunteer hours at the Purr-fect cat shelter, plus give up my gym membership."

"Oh my, that is busy!"

"The cat shelter I feel bad about, but I can keep up with my workouts at home. Anyway, I wanted to thank you again."

"I'm glad it helped. And the Paint and Party idea wasn't so brilliant, it was more about figuring out what people want."

"I can't say I wanted a ceramics business, but I was never going to make a living with real sculpture, even pottery. Who knew so few people would be interested. But all that bric-a-brac . . . Now, there's a hobby people sign up for. Toss in some wine, and voilà," she said, stroking the cat. "Thanks to you, I'm in the black!"

Missy beamed at sweet-faced Violet Byrd. Maybe next time she'd suggest a trip to a day spa, or maybe just a box of hair-color from Walmart. Violet didn't go for fancy. "What's with the fur ball?" Missy said, tilting the Cheshire-like cat. "Pink . . . isn't it?"

Violet laughed. "Pearl finish in bubble-gum pink, thank you very much. Wendy Abbott painted it for her daughter, but she's not here. Irene O'Brien said her younger two, the twins, have a stomach bug." Violet continued to pet the cat as if it might purr. "Good thing I like pink—and cats. I'll probably be stuck with it!"

"Why's that?" Missy said, stroking the cat too.

"Moms love to socialize. Paint and Party, right? They don't care too much about collecting their projects after the kilning process." She shrugged, picking up the cat. "That's why I started making deliveries. Dustin lets me know when there's a game or other town gatherings. Otherwise, my basement would be filled with everything from trivets to an army of giant pink pussies."

Missy bit down on her lip, trying not to laugh. "We wouldn't want that."

"Definitely not. Dustin mentioned the game today, so here I am." With the cat in one arm, Violet reached out with her other and gave Missy's hand a squeeze. "Have you seen him this evening? I know he was looking forward to seeing you."

"Uh, no. Not yet. It wouldn't have been a smart idea. It was a big crowd."

"It was," Violet said, looking toward the emptying field. "And you're right. Good thing one of you is a smart thinker. Maybe after everyone clears out."

"For sure." Surrey's ceramics matriarch went on her way, passing by Frank.

"All set," he said, standing in Violet's place.

"Thanks. I can take care of the rest myself."

"You sure?" he said, his breath catching on cooler air. Frank's attempt to shove his hands in his jacket pockets was futile, the fabric bulging with discarded Rice Krispies treats. "I don't mind helping."

Missy hesitated. "Yes. I'm sure," she said, weighing guilt and good deeds. "I'll be fine." He nodded and turned, not for the parking lot but the open field. It led to a wooded cut-through that met with train tracks. Missy looked behind her, at the primitive but sheltered Snack Shack. She yelled toward Frank's fading frame. "The ice has to be dumped from those coolers." He did an abrupt about-face. "I hate to ask. I'm sure you have somewhere to be."

"A thousand places," he said, already on his way back. Frank fished cans of soda from icy cooler water and Missy emptied the popcorn machine.

"Hey there, Miss Missy. Who's your new friend?"

"Dustin. Hi." Missy abandoned the popcorn machine, making a beeline to the outside of the Snack Shack. "I didn't see you there."

"I was fixing sprinkler heads on the opposite side of the field." Overhead lighting glinted off stray candy wrappers. Missy widened the gap between herself and Dustin by picking them up. "So . . . who's this?" His round shoulder nudged toward Frank.

"Mr. Delacort?" Missy said, as if she'd referred to him that way all afternoon. "He's visiting." Frank stood, his real-life army jacket contrasting against Dustin's Sears-purchased camouflage pants. Dustin folded his arms over the paunch of his belly, crunching into the slick vinyl of a town-issued jacket. "Mr. Delacort's moving here from . . ."

"From Western Mass," Frank said.

"He, um . . . he came to get a taste of the local atmosphere. We've been talking about schools and Surrey. He's deciding between public school and Xaverian for his sons."

Frank set the icy Cokes on the counter. Then he stepped forward, extending his hand. "Nice to meet you . . . Dustin, was it?"

"Yeah . . . Dustin Byrd." Instead of shaking Frank's hand, his index finger underscored the name on his jacket. "Deputy Director of Surrey Parks and Rec."

"I see that." The unrequited handshake morphed into a pointed finger. "Great jacket. Everyone knows who you are. That and you don't ever have to worry about forgetting your name."

"Uh-huh," Dustin said. "Moving here, you say?" He looked Frank over. "You married?"

"Married? Sure. My wife's home with the boys. I drove up on a fact-finding mission."

"Over."

"What?

"If you're coming from Western Mass you would have driven *over* . . . west to east." Missy watched as Dustin gestured north and south.

Frank picked up one of the cans, tapping it on the counter. "I came from my new job. It's in Worcester. That's southwest of here, right? That's why we're moving."

"Guess it makes sense." Dustin's knuckles brushed over his mustache before cinching up his pants, eyes on Frank the whole time.

"Anyway," Missy said, "I think Mr. Delacort was leaning toward Xaverian, since it's a private school . . . all boys."

Frank glanced at Missy. "Yeah, that's how I was leaning."

"So you'll be going—" A fuzzy buzz from Dustin's walkie-talkie interrupted. "I read you, copy that, central. I'll check it out," he said, still focused on Frank. "That was the police station. I'm patched right into their system. Some stragglers got bored, busted a bunch of beer bottles under the bleachers over at the football field. Now who do you suppose is going to clean up that mess?" Neither Missy nor Frank answered, and Dustin nodded. "That's right, me. They need me there right away. Missy, do you need a ride?"

"My mom's picking me up." She pointed to car headlights turning into the parking lot.

"I didn't know she was up to driving these days."

"Yes, she's been on a good stretch—the ups and downs of MS. Anyway, my car's in the shop again. I could really use a new one."

"New one, huh?" Dustin said. "That's a pricy venture. You need to think hard about what you want to spend your money on. It all takes time."

"Speaking of time," Frank said, glancing at a watch that wasn't there, "I've got to get on the road. I only offered to help because the young lady . . ."

"Missy . . . Flannigan," she said brightly.

"Right, Missy. Sorry."

"If your mom's here," Dustin said, "I'll be going." He started toward the football field, but turned back. "What kind of work is it you do?"

Missy's mouth gaped. Frank grazed his hand smoothly over his army jacket. "Guess your uniform is more obvious than mine. I've been assigned a desk job, army recruiting office." Dustin nodded, then looked twice over his shoulder as he marched across the field.

Missy offered a big wave at the waiting car. The gesture said there was no need for anyone to get out. She slapped closed the Snack Shack's cupboard doors and trotted around to the rear. Frank was on his way out. Her hand met with his chest. "You don't really have a desk job in a recruiting office, do you?"

"Is that really your mother?"

"Of course," she said, her hand still resting on him. "It makes her feel good to get out and do little things for me when she can. She . . . she's a wonderful person. Why do you ask?"

"My gut said to."

"And my question?"

"About as real as a wife and two sons. But you made up that part." She laughed and Frank's chin cocked toward the football field. "What's with the black-ops groundskeeper?"

"Dustin? Long story. He's intense but harmless."

"It's the harmless ones that will fool you the most."

"Not Dustin. He couldn't fool me if he blindfolded me." Missy leaned, peering toward the parking lot. "You don't have anywhere to go, do you?"

"What makes you say that?"

"Before, you were headed for the woods. It leads to the train tracks and the freighter that stops on the outskirts of Surrey around midnight."

"You know the freight train schedule?"

"I know every route out of this town—freight trains to ant tunnels. That train doesn't run on Saturdays. If you want . . ." she said, glancing at the Snack Shack. "It's a wood floor, but it's dry and there's plenty to eat, at least a dozen leftover hot dogs."

"Why?"

"Why what?"

"Why would you do that for me?"

"Call it returning a favor. Ed Maginty," she said, noting the man, not his money. "I've got to go. Do you want to stay or not?"

"Okay," he said. "For the night." She stepped away and Frank tugged her back. The two were nose to nose in the isolated space. Missy was unafraid, although she did think this might be it. It would be one way out of Surrey. He could knock her unconscious and drag her off into the woods. Her mother would think she'd vanished into thin air. It would be the easiest explanation for Barbara Flannigan to hear. Missy sucked in a breath. He smelled of dirt and hot dogs and desperation. His Adam's apple bobbed through a stubble-covered throat. Then Frank's grip eased. "Hey, don't forget your cashbox."

"Oh, geez, thanks," she said, taking it. The cold metal box pressed between them. "So maybe I'll see you around."

"Maybe you will. Never can predict the future, can you, Missy Flannigan?"

CHAPTER EIGHT

Present Day

"Missy . . . Missy . . . Missy . . . what do you know that we don't?" Aubrey had sat for hours, the weight of her head now resting on her hand, fingertips massaging her temple. Her elbow eased, and her arm dropped across the news stories and notes spread across her desk. She touched the archived pages of the *Surrey City Press*. Trepidation had waned days ago; none of the news stories produced a tingle of ghostly presence. Aubrey stared harder, but it only felt like more of an inner challenge—like a math equation you had no hope of solving. Yet the impulse deepened as Aubrey focused on a skill set that deviated from standard investigation. "Imagine, Missy, what a conversation with you might unearth."

Aubrey shook her head and pushed back in her chair. She needed distance. Why would she even consider such a thing? Poking a finger—or any part of her—through that kind of portal was insane. She gathered the stories and shuffled them aside. There was no good reason, certainly no obligation, to attempt to channel Missy Flannigan. Aubrey had used her gift in a positive way. She didn't squander it or capitalize on it. She didn't owe anything or anybody a damn thing, least of all Levi St John and his ambitions. Exasperated, she stood. Directly in her line of vision was an enormous flower arrangement. It had arrived earlier that day, and now the wide display was poised on a shelf that overhung her cubicle. Peering through the flora, Aubrey observed Levi.

Inside his office, he also stood. Even his posture was determined . . . *unyielding*. He wasn't going to let this story go. Not for any reason. But Aubrey was certain that her motivation was equally strong. Inviting Missy Flannigan's death into her life was foolish, even dangerous. Knowing that the girl had been shot and where her body was found, sealed behind a brick wall . . . Aubrey sighed. It was already more information than she needed. Tapping into Missy Flannigan, accidently or otherwise, meant there was every chance Aubrey would experience the victim's terror or desire for retaliation firsthand. Levi's hunt for the truth had brought unrest. The newsroom, a place that Aubrey had always deemed safe, no longer felt as secure.

Lowering herself into the chair, Aubrey thought that a good cleansing of her karma might be in order. The upheaval of her sanctuary was the latest calamity to enter Aubrey's life, but not the most glaring. That dubious honor belonged to her marriage and Aubrey's soon to be ex-husband, Owen. She sank farther into the cubicle space, wanting to hide from misfortune, which seemed like a solid precursor to failure.

Not so long ago, *bright* and *shiny* would have described Aubrey and Owen's future. She'd married the perfect man—well, perfect for her. Aside from Owen's left-of-center appearance—the long hair, lanky frame, and cutting throwback looks—Aubrey was drawn to his self-sufficient personality. Owen was determined to succeed at life on his terms. Terms that Aubrey also desired. Both wanted the traditional life they'd missed out on—years of collected Christmas ornaments, a stick of a tree grown into a mighty oak, rooms you'd lived in so long they needed repainting.

And for the first year, marriage went that way. The word *newlywed* sparkled like a diamond. But the promise of a happy life had broken, the sparkle fading to a dull finish. While there was ample blame to share, Aubrey took responsibility for her part. She'd made the terrific mistake of keeping her gift from Owen. Worse, he'd found out by accident. He'd had a harder time dealing with it than she'd ever imagined. She should have been up front from the beginning, but every time Aubrey broached the subject of her gift, she retreated. She was too fearful of risking happiness. It had been so elusive in the first place.

In hindsight, the relative normalcy of Aubrey's new job had made it easier to keep up pretenses. They'd bought a house in a picture-perfect town; the zip code to a normal, happy life was now theirs. But it all came undone when Owen finally admitted to second thoughts about white picket fences and a routine lifestyle—he couldn't let go of a freelance career that kept him on the move. By the time Aubrey's secret came tumbling out, the marriage had already reached a breaking point. Aubrey glanced at her naked ring finger, then her cell. She'd avoided two calls from her soon-to-be ex today. The final divorce papers were waiting. Aubrey was certain that was the point of Owen's message: *"What's the hold up, Bre? I'm more than ready to end this thing . . ."* She fidgeted, eyeing her phone. The thought didn't quite ring true. He hadn't called her *Bre* since the two of them agreed that a divorce was probably for the best. Aubrey shoved the phone aside. When it came to Owen, and her gift, she still lacked courage.

Charley, on the other hand, had possessed courage enough for the two of them, especially during Aubrey's younger years. She'd shown remarkable mettle, guiding Aubrey, a girl who, at times, questioned her own sanity. Sometimes, Aubrey mused that carnival life could have had that effect—insanity. Instead of being trapped in a room full of mirrors she'd been caught in a loop of random voices. It had been Charley's sense of calm that had persevered. On one occasion, she'd told Aubrey, "If you had a genetic disease, something passed from your father to you, I'd go to the end of the earth to find a cure." A barely teenage Aubrey had watched the breath move in and out of Charley as she went on, speaking about her son's death in terms of medical history. "For your father, a gift like yours was never more than lifelong misery. It's not good. It's not bad, my dear girl. It just is. We'll find our way—together. Trust me, though. This gift is part of you. We can't change it. We can't take it out of you."

"Not even with an exorcism?" Aubrey had asked.

"You're not possessed," she'd snapped. There wasn't much that startled Charley, but that thought surely had. She'd gone on to say, "Aubrey, be aware. Not every entity is about positive messages and closure."

It was a statement that would prove to be an omen.

Between the ages of four and sixteen, Aubrey had struggled to make sense of her gift—understand how to use it and how to control it. She'd made headway, not comfortable with but accepting of the dead in her life. At seventeen a singular event halted all progress, nearly putting Aubrey back to square one. A violent encounter with the cleverness of evil alerted her to the inherent dangers of her gift—dangers that had driven her father to the brink of madness.

At her *Surrey City Press* desk, Aubrey touched evil's imprint, grazing her hand over a deeply pockmarked forearm. She traced the crescent-moon scar on her chin and thought of the faint lasting marks on her stomach and legs. *Gift . . .* How obtuse. This "gift" had upended her life. It had stolen any semblance of normal. Her own father had quite possibly died from it. He'd certainly lived in fear of it. Evil was only one of many components Aubrey was required to navigate. She glared at the black and white news stories. The whole Missy Flannigan mess was a Petri dish for evil. Aubrey picked up the news clippings and, along with her cell phone, shoved them under that day's edition of the *Surrey City Press*.

Even with these things out of sight, Aubrey's thoughts about the dead girl remained a peculiar frustration. She sighed at the concealed articles. Why wasn't there so much as a whisper penetrating from the other side? Perhaps Aubrey's strict control had deadened the pathways.

Who knew? It wasn't as if you could Google the answer. Tentatively, like a child dreading a monster under the bed, she peeked under the newspaper. When nothing roared, Aubrey retrieved the room-temperature news stories—although she left the phone buried. She pressed her palm flat on top, just as she did with her real estate listing sheets. If Jerry Stallworth had stayed to bitch, it seemed like a murdered girl should have something to say. Yet no warmth radiated, no aberrant smells or tastes invaded her body. The only scent present was the flower arrangement, fragrant white lilies and sweet violet alyssum. There was nothing palpable from Surrey's most famous dead resident.

Aubrey pushed back her chair, closed her eyes, and leaned her head against the cubicle wall. The intention was to think about nothing, yet her mind raced. She was back to toying with psychic routes, curious if the right frequency required something of a more personal nature. She mumbled a mock request, "So, Levi, let's face it. Traditional reporter tactics aren't cutting it. But if we could put our . . . okay, *my* hands, on Missy's hairbrush or pillow maybe that would rattle the right cage."

"What do you want with Missy's hairbrush or pillow? The authorities already have a complete DNA profile."

Aubrey's eyes popped open. Levi was in front of her. She nearly lost her balance as the chair wobbled and she scrambled to a steadier position, cracking her knee on the desk. "Ouch! Damn it . . ."

"Sorry. Are you all right? I was passing by and I heard you say my name."

Aubrey's hand thrust to her palpitating heart. "Mind reading would have been way more useful."

"What?"

"Nothing. I was thinking out loud. That and I'm forever banging my knee on the desk." She rubbed the throbbing spot and rolled the chair forward. "Since you're here," she said, wading through her notes, "I've tracked down every viable Surrey connection to Missy. I even spoke with her high school guidance counselor, Esther Warren. Sorry to report that previous statements are true. Missy did love puppies and poetry. There isn't much here."

He surveyed her desktop, which by volume of paper if not results indicated a solid effort. "It can be slow going with something this old. Don't let the lack of progress deter you. Maybe approaching what you do have from a different point of view is the way to go."

"Interesting. I was considering exactly that." She offered a tight-lipped smile. "So far, let's just say the other side of my brain isn't offering much."

"I meant another person, as in a second opinion. If you're going to work this late on something," Levi said, waving his arm across the newsroom. "You should get a fresh pair of eyes to take a look."

Aubrey stood again. This time she saw sunset through the windows, Malcolm's office door closed, co-workers replaced by a janitorial staff. "I didn't realize the time." She looked at the wall clock. "Six forty-five!" Managing the real estate section never kept her past five. "My grandmother has help, but she'll be leaving soon and I . . ." Aubrey grabbed her satchel. Levi's satisfied expression waned. "Was there something else?"

"No, nothing. Your grandmother . . . I didn't realize. I just thought if you did want a fresh set of eyes . . . Well, I'm sort of starving. We could grab a bite and . . ." Aubrey tipped her head at him. "Contrary to opinion, I do possess human habits, eating included."

"Right. I remember. Finer restaurants only," she said slipping on her coat. "Can I get a rain check? I'm Missy Flanniganed—out for the day."

"Not a problem. But I do have a conference call with the *Standard Speaker* first thing Monday. Seems my temporary replacement can't get the gist of the day-to-day layout. After that I managed to finagle a one-on-one with Detective Espinosa, see if he has anything new. Malcolm's asked for a meeting at three, but maybe after that." Levi tapped the papers he held against the edge of her cubicle. "I meant to ask, how's the injury?"

Having collected her belongings, Aubrey stopped and flexed her index finger at him. "It's, um . . . it's all better."

"Good. By the way, that's some flower arrangement."

Aubrey looked from the massive bouquet to Levi's lingering stare. "I take it you're more a tickets-to-the-opera kind of guy."

"Depends." He shrugged. "However, my tastes would be irrelevant in any floral selection." Aubrey proceeded to button her coat, simpering at her spot-on inference. "Flower choice would strictly depend on the recipient's preferences. That's the point, correct? To please the person for whom they're intended."

Aubrey looked up, startled by the seriousness Levi applied to something as frivolous as flowers. "Uh, you've got me there. But you can't always know what the other person likes, not in every instance."

"I disagree. It's only a matter of taking an interest in personal details. For example, I've noticed that you wear bright colors now and again. That's curious, because on the whole, I'd say ostentatiousness doesn't suit you—like those flowers," he said, pointing to the arrangement. "Based on observation, I'd suspect you're more the understated, under-arranged daisy type." Levi paused at the next cubicle. "As for myself and fine dining, true enough. But I also like a good cheeseburger on occasion. In that instance, I wouldn't be looking for a Zagat-rated establishment. Just a detail."

"I see," she said, blinking at the thoughtful bullet of Levi insight.

"So a Flannigan rain check then. I'll see you Monday."

"See you . . ." On the breath meant to repeat his words came unlikely spontaneity. "So if you want to look over my notes, and you are truly starving, Inez never minds staying late."

"Inez?" he said, looking around the newsroom for the worker bee he'd clearly missed.

"Inez, she's Charley's in-home help. I could ask if she'd mind staying late."

"If it works with your schedule. Just let me know. Otherwise, I'll be in my office with my non-Zagat-rated folder of takeout menus."

CHAPTER
NINE

Aubrey was positive that Tang's Orient Express did not meet the baseline for a Zagat rating. But Levi didn't raise an objection as they talked and ate. He was analytical and inquisitive, pressing but never crossing the boundaries of reasonable Missy Flannigan theories. Levi mentioned his own update, but said that he wanted to hear Aubrey's first. She obliged, offering the tidbits she'd unearthed. "The only thing that stuck out was an observation Esther Warren, the guidance counselor, made about Dustin."

"I thought you said Warren was Missy's guidance counselor."

"Turns out, Dustin's too. Esther was quick to note her twenty-five years of service." Aubrey put down her fork and relayed the woman's in-passing thought. "When I said that Detective Espinosa anticipates finding all sorts hidden deviant behavior from Dustin Byrd—a computer full of porn, maybe a graveyard of dismembered cats in his yard—she thoroughly disagreed."

"How so?"

"Esther suggested that people . . . men who perpetrate this sort of crime are, along with twisted, usually clever and rather intelligent. According to her, those aren't terms she'd use to describe Dustin Byrd. If anything she recalled an underdog, the kind of kid who craved prestige but didn't have the goods to get there."

Levi's chopsticks deftly captured the rice on his plate. "The guidance counselor has a valid point. But," he said, pinching a bite of moo shu pork, "that sort of personality also supports other conclusions—a hair trigger detonated by years of frustration. Think about it. In today's society the kid Warren described, if that disturbed, is often the one who inflicts violent crimes on entire student bodies. What if Dustin Byrd always felt he should have a girl like Missy and one day—"

"One day he just grabbed what he couldn't have." Aubrey picked up her fork. "Plausible. Or maybe a different scenario that includes Byrd."

"What's that?"

"I've been thinking. And, mind you, I have no proof, not a shred of evidence."

"Just a theory?"

"Just an idea."

"I'll entertain it," Levi said, fluidly working his chopsticks.

"Big of you. What if there was something *reciprocal* going on between Dustin and Missy?"

"Like an affair?" The chopsticks halted. "I don't want to stereotype, Ellis, but have you seen their photos? Byrd was sixteen years older than Missy. It's like Charlize Theron dating Woody Allen, less the creative genius." Levi drew a thinking breath, a habit she'd observed. "Scratch that. Make it Grace Kelly with Martin Balsam. He was a charac—"

"He was a character actor from the 1940s, more or less the image of Byrd." She tilted her head. "How do you know that?"

"My mother. We watched our share of old movies when I visited." Levi busied himself with the chopsticks before looking up. "And you?"

"The Golden Age of Hollywood. One of a few staples in my traveling childhood." Aubrey concentrated on her white rice and noted her own Levi details. "So along with an occasional cheeseburger, you like Grace Kelly movies, and blondes—apparently," she said, hiding a smirk behind her water glass.

Levi bristled. "Back to Missy and Byrd," he said over the buzz of nearby diners, "we have no indication of a relationship between the two. A man's marital status, or lack thereof, doesn't prove a covert relationship." Aubrey's cell, which sat on the table, vibrated toward her. Owen's name lit up the screen. It was the second time he'd called since they'd arrived. "Speaking of relationships," he said, pointing at her phone, "old husband or new boyfriend?"

She dropped the phone onto the seat beside her. "I wanted to be available in case Charley called. Inez could only stay until eight. And, um . . . the first." He swallowed a mouthful of Kipling pale ale. *Add British beer*, she thought, *to a fondness for old movies, cheeseburgers, and blondes.*

"You said that was resolved."

"It is, except for signing on the dotted line. I know I said it wouldn't interfere—"

"It's not that," he said, putting down the beer. "I just thought if somebody calls twice in an hour, maybe it's important. Maybe you should answer."

Levi's personality provided a nice barrier for incoming emotion. It allowed Aubrey the courage to pick up her phone. She imagined she could hear anything Owen had to say and not flinch in front of him. "If you're sure you don't mind?" There was a gesture of indifference and Aubrey connected to her messages. Her eyes drew wide as she listened to Owen's earliest voicemail; she gripped tighter to the phone. The rather personal message ended and Aubrey listened to empty air for another thirty seconds. Putting down the phone, she looked at Levi and realized her error. Body language required an explanation. Aubrey scrambled to come up with one: *Owen was hit by a bus . . . He's moving to Peru . . . He's demanding I return his collection of U2 albums . . .* Too flummoxed, she went with the truth. "He . . . Owen," she said, pointing to her silent cell. "He says we're making a mistake. He wants to talk, work things out."

Levi nodded, his mouth curving downward, as if in deep assessment. "That's good, I guess. And probably not so surprising considering the flowers."

"The flowers?" Aubrey's stare flicked between the phone and Levi. "Oh, the flowers. They weren't from . . . Trust me when I say reconciliation wasn't in the cards."

"But it's what you want, right—to reconcile?"

"Yes . . . of course," she said, awed by her reversal of fortune. "I never wanted a divorce in the first place. I only wanted what Owen had prom—" She didn't finish the personal thought.

"So do you want to go . . . see him, or whatever? Far be it from me to get in the way of a *Beyond Tomorrow* kind of ending."

"See him. Absolutely . . ." she said, smiling. "He just caught me off guard. But that's Owen. Always spontaneous. I can grab a cab." She stood but didn't move. "Aubrey Smith." She sat again. "He starred in *Beyond Tomorrow*. Hardly anybody knows him . . . or that movie."

"If I recall, the plot had something to do with ghosts who visit the living in hopes of reuniting two young lovers."

"That's right. Charley and I watched that movie over and over because . . ." Aubrey stopped short. "It's just kind of incredible that you'd know the movie."

"I don't know about incredible. Smith was English, maybe that's why it sticks. A curious coincidence, the name and all."

"More than you know. Anyway . . ." Aubrey said, shaking off his ghostly note. "We weren't done discussing Missy Flannigan."

"Missy and I will be here on Monday. And I suspect your attention won't be one hundred percent right now. I get having a life, Ellis."

"Do you? I mean, of course, I'm sure you do."

Levi leaned forward and skimmed his legal pad. "Just . . . if you don't mind me asking, did you say you didn't want the divorce?"

In her stunned moment, Aubrey supposed she'd confessed as much. "True. It was just . . . circumstance. A year ago, divorce seemed like the only realistic solution." Levi nodded and returned to his notes. "Why do you ask?"

"Human behavior. That's all." On Aubrey's slide out of the booth Levi added, "It strikes me as curious. What moves someone to the brink of ending a committed relationship, and then turn up with an eleventh-hour desire to repair it? Of course, I'm not speaking about your situation specifically. I don't know anything about it. But overall, I see that sort of flip-flopping behavior as the epitome of *uncommitted.*"

His word choice hit too close to home. "You can't make that kind of across-the-board assumption about relationships. No matter what's happened, Owen's not flip-flop—" Aubrey's jaw locked. He could be so incredibly irritating. "You're right, Levi. You don't know anything about it. It was extremely . . . *complicated*, things between Owen and me that you couldn't possibly grasp."

"Really?" he said. There was a visual standoff. He smiled. "My philosophy professor at Brown might disagree. She was delighted when I chose to double major, writing my thesis on the fallacies of Cartesian dualism. And then there's MediaMatters. I don't think I'd be sitting here if I didn't exhibit some aptitude for getting my head around a story."

Aubrey continued to stare, eyes narrowing. She was tempted, again, by the idea of blurting out her gift for the sole purpose of rocking his neatly filed world. She glanced away. It wasn't the point. "It was never a matter of . . . Owen has a lot of integrity. If you must know, I kept something from him that I shouldn't have. It's what pushed the marriage to the brink."

"You lied to him."

"I wasn't honest."

"Is there a difference?"

"I like to think so. And you're over-simplifying. Suffice it to say my choices aggravated the problems we already had."

"So this was a happy marriage from the start."

"It was . . . for a while. It will be again," she said more defiantly.

"You seem determined. I wish you luck."

"Thanks so much." But instead of leaving, Aubrey slid back, intent on making a point. "Ultimately, the time apart will prove beneficial. The bottom line is Owen and I wanted the same things—clearly, we still do." Aubrey held out her phone as if it were proof.

"Those things being?"

She shrugged. "Nothing so out of the ordinary. A regular, normal happy marriage."

"Now who's over-simplifying," he said, continuing with his work.

"Don't be so cynical. Just because you can't see it or don't want it."

"I never said that."

"Regardless . . . Obviously there are going to be bumps in any relationship, but if two people are united—one address, one unified life grounded in routine—I don't see why they shouldn't be able to work it out."

He nodded, as if considering her take on the matter. "So at what point did Owen decide a routine life *wasn't* what he wanted?"

And irritating hit a new high. "Owen's job requires a lot of travel—abroad, the West Coast. It's very volatile, demanding. Some of it is even classified."

"He's a spy?"

Aubrey made a face. "He's a network security architect, meaning he designs secure data centers for Fortune 100 companies and select government projects."

"Computer tech expert."

"To say the least. His expertise is almost one of a kind. He couldn't very well up and abandon his responsibilities," she said, using Owen's own argument.

"Impressive. I think I get it. Owen didn't want to give up his high-octane life for a nine-to-five State Street job—even at the risk of his marriage."

"How very succinct," she said, hearing Levi file a year's worth of passionate arguments into one neat summation. "You know, on second thought, it isn't complicated. Owen's always been committed to 'us.' Maybe it's as simple as him needing time to come full circle. You know, finish living life one way before starting another—outgrow it."

Levi didn't reply and Aubrey rose. But as she exited the booth, she heard him mutter, "Here's hoping he grew into the man you were hoping for." She spun around, eyeballing Levi. "Sorry," he said, glancing up. "I shouldn't have said that. But a lot can change in a year—that's something I know a thing or two about."

"I'm amazed."

"That I can recognize change?"

"No, that somebody managed to tolerate you for that long." Levi retreated to his legal pad; it made Aubrey feel as if she was the one who'd overstepped. "Just know Owen and I will be fine."

"Noted," he said, staying focused on his work.

She was about to offer a conciliatory "See you Monday" when her phone vibrated. It was a text from Owen. *Just left a VM. Firewall fubar. Stuck in New York. Can we get together as soon as I get back? Love you.* Aubrey pocketed her phone. She supposed there wouldn't be any reconciliation that night—well, not between her and Owen. "Before I go," she said, fully prepared to leave, "so that I'm up to speed, exactly what is your Missy Flannigan update?"

"Missy Flannigan? We'll talk about that Monday."

"No. By Monday you'll be accusing me of being out of the loop, slacking. So, if you don't mind, I'd like to finish our discussion."

"If you insist," he said, placing the legal pad on the table. She dropped her coat and satchel back onto the booth and slid back in. Levi produced a new folder and Aubrey sighed. This one was marked:

Flannigan, Tom & Barbara. "Yesterday, I caught the Flannigans with their garage door open. I spoke to them—briefly."

"You spoke to Tom and Barbara Flannigan? And you're just telling me now?"

"I needed to mull it over. I'm not sure what it meant, or if it meant anything. Tom Flannigan, he was sitting in Missy's convertible—sharp little muscle machine—which they've kept like a shrine. Her father was sobbing uncontrollably, like he couldn't get a hold of himself."

"Assuming the remains are Missy's, it is the confirmation they've been dreading for twenty years. Doesn't that make sense?"

Levi was quiet, sipping his pale ale. "It should. Grief can be insurmountable. But this seemed . . . *off.*"

"Off?"

"That's why I didn't mention it. I have no proof, just . . . a feeling."

"I see. Something less than concrete facts."

"Tom Flannigan's reaction. It was outside the parameters of what I'd consider normal." Levi's thumb brushed over the face of his watch. "I've seen what that does to a person, a parent especially. Losing a child in some horrible senseless way." He looked at Aubrey and she saw emotion invade his usually staid expression. "I shouldn't judge."

The topic of Missy Flannigan slipped from Aubrey's focus. It was replaced by a pulling sensation, an urge to wrap her hand around Levi's watch. The need to reach was overwhelming, like fighting a sneeze. *Better still, Levi, if you could take the damn thing off and hand it to me . . .* Aubrey forced her folded hands into her lap. As she tried to quell the impulse, a sound pierced through the atmosphere. It wasn't the fast clip of Mandarin or clinking of dishes. It wasn't the conversation of other diners. It was a young man's voice—faint but reminiscent. A conversation Aubrey had heard before. *No. A conversation I've had before.* Aubrey saw blond buzzed hair, eyes the color of tropical water, a whistle around a neck. Fast as a heartbeat it was gone, another sense invading. Her lungs filled. Aubrey's head snapped toward Levi's. "Do you smell that?"

"What? Fried rice and spare ribs?"

"Salt air. I smelled it the other day too, outside your office."

"I'm pretty sure all you can smell for three blocks is Chinese food." His brow furrowed. "Ellis, are you all right?"

"No," she said, dragging the cloth napkin across her mouth. The heady mist of ocean receded, and on her palate came the sharp taste of whiskey. It was enough to get drunk and then some. "Levi, who—" She balled the napkin into her fist. If Levi was skeptical of his own *feelings,* conveying the prospect of a presence was absurd—probably suicidal. "I mean, yes . . . of course. Sorry. My sense of smell, sometimes it comes right off the rails."

"Uh-huh," he said, looking queerly at her. "Anyway, that's why I didn't mention anything about Tom Flannigan. Too arbitrary."

"It doesn't fit into a folder."

"Right. Not yet anyway."

"So you keep digging."

"*We* keep digging." The waiter came by and left the check with two fortune cookies. Levi was quick to pick up the bill.

"We'll split it."

"Not necessary." Before she could object, he reached for his wallet and held cash out to the waiter. "Along with accommodations, Media-Matters has been good enough to supply a modest expense account. I think this qualifies as a business dinner." Levi tucked away his wallet as he stood. "So shall we go? I assume you still have somewhere to be? . . . Ellis?"

Aubrey didn't respond. She was too distracted by a feeling that anyone else might describe as intense déjà vu. On her mind were frothy surf and seagulls, another jab of conversation: *"Stop ignoring your instincts . . ."*

The voice was so crisp it was a wonder Levi didn't hear it. She suspected he'd recognize it. "Sorry. I blanked for a second." But her out-of-place recollections and Levi's watch were enough to draw Aubrey into further conversation. She spied the fortune cookies the waiter had left.

Aubrey nudged one toward him. "Wait, we're not finished." He hesitated. Undoubtedly, fortune cookies were a waste of his focus. Surprisingly, Levi sat and cracked one open.

"It says, 'Something bright and shiny from the past will give you insight to the future.'" His wide shoulders shrugged. "That's what I like, a non-specific fortune. Lots of room for possibility."

"Don't mock. And don't cancel out the universe," she said. "Maybe it means you're going to find yourself at a bigger . . . *shinier* press than the *Standard Speaker*."

"I like that. Ambitious fortune telling," he said. "But, more likely, my old desk lamp will arrive from Hartford tomorrow—shiny chrome. I had them send it."

"Oh, did you really?"

"I did," he said, then crunched down on the cookie.

Aubrey stopped and started twice before boldly sticking a toe in the water. "So you don't believe in anything intuitive? Anything beyond hard facts, something more . . . spiritual?"

"What? Like religion?"

"Not exactly. Maybe more of a spiritual energy. Something more concrete than a fortune cookie," she said, pointing at the one on the table. "Less confining than organized religion."

"Not in my experience. I don't believe in fate. Life isn't subject to any more influence than random chance—win the lottery, get hit by a bus." Levi paused, draining the beer. "Walk away from a tragedy or die in one."

On his words salt water receded and the smell of burning wood curled in, like smoke from under a door. "That's kind of specific."

"Your turn." Levi shoved the cookie toward her.

As he did, the scents abated.

Aubrey picked up the cookie, breaking it in two. "Interesting," she said. "'You have remarkable equipment for success. Use it properly.'" Not even a fortune cookie wanted to give her a break.

"I'll translate that one. You should be covering more than the real estate beat. Even your fortune cookie agrees." Levi picked up his pen and tapped it against the legal pad. "Do you think you will, Ellis—expand your professional horizons?"

She wanted to say yes, but common sense answered. "It's tempting. But ambition isn't my only consideration."

"Are we back to the old husband?"

"It's not that. Owen would be thrilled if they made me editor in chief. I—it's, um, it's hard to explain." Aubrey stood, pulling on her coat.

"Then what? I can't imagine why someone with real talent wouldn't pursue their professional goals."

Aubrey thanked him for the compliment, but avoided a reply by heading out the door and into the parking lot. From behind her, Levi's hand grasped her shoulder. "Hey, Ellis . . ." She turned. Levi was tight on her heels, his height surpassing her five-foot-ten frame. His hand lowered and Levi widened the personal space. "Tom Flannigan, he was a laborer of some sort."

"A machinist for a tooling company. Why?"

"And Barbara Flannigan, Missy's mother. She was a substitute schoolteacher until she was diagnosed with MS. She hasn't worked in years."

"That's right. Barely middle-class backgrounds, nothing riveting. They live in a high ranch off of Beech Street."

"What do houses in that neighborhood go for?"

A contemplative hum rang from Aubrey's throat. "No more than 225K, max."

"When I was in the Flannigans' garage, their other car, it was an older subcompact model. Missy's car, it's not an Aston Martin, but it is fancy for a family of their means. Don't you think?"

"I'd agree, except the police asked that question years ago. Tom Flannigan said Missy inherited the car from her uncle."

"Damn. I guess the police would have documented that." Levi's supposition faded and they kept moving toward his car. From the driver's side, he called across, "We have that, right? Somewhere in that vacuum of court records and old interviews we have confirmation of an inheritance?"

Aubrey hurried around to where he stood. "Now that you say it, I've never seen confirmation of an inheritance. Not one piece of paper other than Tom Flannigan's word. But surely, otherwise . . ."

Levi turned hard toward her. "Otherwise, where do you suppose Missy got a car like that?"

"Who bought it for her and why?" Their stares clung to one another and the idea. Aubrey moved back around to the passenger side as contemplation followed. They settled in, their seatbelts clicking in the quiet. Levi started the engine.

"Hey, Ellis,"

"Yeah," she said, turning toward him.

"If this pans out, I'll have to put more faith in fortune cookies."

"Why's that?"

"Missy's car. Something bright and shiny from the past giving me insight to the future."

CHAPTER TEN

Surrey, Massachusetts
Twenty Years Earlier

Frank Delacort decided there wasn't a tick to the town of Surrey that Missy didn't have figured out. This was after her most recent angel-of-mercy act, informing Frank he was relocating to a small flat above the Plastic Fork. After his first night at the Snack Shack, Missy had come back the next morning. In her hands were a bacon and egg sandwich, a steaming cup of coffee, and a lifeline that, maybe, he should have seen as attached to a string. She'd handed him the breakfast while comparing him to a stray dog: "I wanted to know if you hung around or followed the scent right out of town."

He'd been called worse than a dog, and she was right to wonder. If the skies hadn't burst open he would have been gone. But thunderstorms kept him there while nightmares catapulted him from a restless sleep. His first night on the Snack Shack floor, Frank dreamed he was in a bunker on the fringe of the Kuwaiti desert. He was caught in a rapid fire exchange, one of many. Shrapnel-filled bodies lay bloodied at his feet. He looked down. Instead of seeing soldiers, Frank saw his wife, Laurel.

In the dream he felt horror, the searing pain of seeing his wife's lifeless body. But as he bent to cradle her in his arms, Frank saw himself press his Ruger pistol to Laurel's head. He needed to make damn certain she was dead. He'd lurched upright from the dream, scrambling to a corner of the Snack Shack. Awake or asleep, he couldn't change any of it.

Hours later, when the weather and images had passed, Frank peeked out the Snack Shack cupboard doors. His breath rode the cool May morning air. In the distance Dustin Byrd patrolled the perimeter. He'd been fooling with the sprinklers he'd claimed to have fixed. "Bet it's not the only hose you play with," Frank snorted, ducking back inside.

Not long into his Snack Shack sabbatical, Frank realized his only real mission was avoiding Surrey's czar of parks and recreation. It was a simple assignment. Otherwise, field visitors were scarce. A few stray kids came by to play basketball and a man and his dog jogged through at sunrise each morning. At first Missy's visits were sporadic. But soon there was a pattern and Frank was able to track her visits by the sun's movement. She'd even provided a sleeping bag, pillow, and a small radio, bringing creature comforts to the makeshift accommodations. Twenty yards from the Snack Shack was a public restroom that Dustin cleaned and stocked with toilet paper. Frank had rigged the lock to open in off-hours. He liked the idea of the puff chested, walkie-talkie-toting field grunt cleaning a piss-stained toilet courtesy of him. Even from a distance, he could see who Dustin Byrd was—a guy who craved glory and respect, but never did a real thing to earn it. Frank had plenty of time to make the study, sleeping in between, filling himself with Cheetos and Cokes while waiting for Missy. Compared to what he'd known it wasn't bad. But when the Surrey Phantoms' away games ran out, he and Missy agreed that something had to give. Frank talked about catching that freight train. Missy had countered with a different idea, a place downtown called the Plastic Fork.

On moving day, Missy led him up an exterior rear staircase, which Frank was glad about—he wouldn't have to come or go via the fancy deli shop below. It was private. Frank surveyed a room that was sunny and furnished, right down to cable TV and a VCR. But touching the soft knit blanket that covered the edge of the bed, Frank grew more wary. There had to be a catch. His leeriness intensified as new personal effects tumbled onto the bed. This was also thanks to Missy, who'd picked him up from the Snack Shack in an almost-new car. "Like it?" she'd asked, as they slid into the shiny convertible. Frank wondered what her old man did for a living, wondered if he was the kind of guy who'd given his daughter lots of stuff and little else. Maybe that explained her need to be needed. As they drove, Frank sank into the warm leather interior. But before leaving the public parking lot Missy had raised the top. It was a smart move. Her survival instincts would have been a plus in enemy territory.

Missy stood at the side of the bed, surveying the new clothes. "You couldn't move in with nothing but an army jacket and dirty jeans." She looked into his pondering face. "Mick, the owner, he would have been suspicious. I told him you were my mother's cousin." Frank's brow creased at the lie. It slipped out of her mouth as smoothly as the ones she'd told Dustin Byrd. "Oh, come on, it's nothing to get in a knot over. Just a few basics from Old Navy. I guessed at the sizes, thirty-three waist, thirty-four pant leg."

"Damn close." Frank said, touching the items, which included underwear. "Missy, I don't . . ."

"It's a couple of pairs of pants and some underwear. Don't make a big deal out of it." She folded the pants and eyed the underwear. "I guessed briefs. You didn't seem like a boxers kind of guy. I'm pretty good at that."

His gaze rose from the underwear to her. "And where'd you acquire that skill set?"

She tucked the pants tight to her chest. Frank saw a breath that rose and fell like a wave. "Nowhere in particular, just girl talk. The college version of Truth or Dare."

"Okay," he said, "we'll let that one go. Instead, explain how some guy with a vague history and no references gets the owner to rent him a room? How does that work?" While the space was bigger than the Snack Shack, its walls seemed tighter and Frank's survival instincts told him to pay attention. It was followed by a stroke of paranoia, Frank picturing a news crew and cops showing up, nabbing him for . . . well, for what?

"I needed a favor from Mick. He wasn't in a position to decline."

"But I haven't got a dime. What'd you use for rent money?"

She shrugged. "First two months' rent is on him."

"Must owe you a hell of a favor."

She turned her blond head and tight ass toward the tidy kitchenette, which was also stocked. Watching her stir ice into a pitcher of lemonade, Frank thought she ought to be wearing an apron, maybe a strand of pearls. Even her words matched the scene. "Silence is golden," she said, putting the pitcher in the refrigerator. "Mine's worth its weight and then some. I know Mick's schedule by heart. He works late afternoons and evenings, some weekends. When Mick's here, he has help—Curtis, who happens to be deaf. Mick's wife, Irene, and a small crew open in the mornings. No one will bother you. Irene doesn't question anything Mick does." Facing Frank, she tucked her hands behind her back. Missy looked as innocent as fresh snow, and he guessed she knew this. "As for money, you have an interview with Emmett Holliston at Holliston's Hardware & Feed tomorrow morning. It's just a quick walk from here."

"What kind of favor does he owe you?"

"None," she said, perplexed. "There was a sign in the window. I stopped and asked." She held up her hand to his incoming objection. "I told him you were a veteran. That's the truth, right?"

It seemed futile to argue. "Yeah, that's the truth."

"By the way, are you handy? I mean in a fix-it sort of way."

"I can use power tools. I've laid some brick. Why?"

"I think that's part of the job, local repairs and whatnot."

"Missy, why are you . . ."

"Mr. Holliston was appreciative of your military service. He was anxious to help. All you have to do is show up and speak loudly. Remind him that I sent you. He's hard of hearing and kind of forgetful."

In Frank's hands were a package of socks, a couple of T-shirts, and the underwear. She was right. They were the kind he liked. He tossed them onto the bed. "I give the fuck up. Where's the catch? I get the hot dog. I could even see the food the next morning. I started to wonder when you kept me dry and fed. Why? I have nothing . . . I am nothing. What's in this for you?"

Missy opened the refrigerator again, this time coming up with a bottle of Rolling Rock. His mouth watered—Missy had that way about her, making you feel like a man who'd wandered in from the desert. If she produced a carton of Marlboro Lights, he was out of there.

Instead, she popped the beer top on the counter edge with smooth authority. Missy crossed the worn linoleum floor. She stopped near the bed, near him. "You want this, Frank." He couldn't tell if it was a question or a statement—or even if she was talking about the beer. "I'd bet there are a lot of things you haven't enjoyed in a while." Her thumb rolled over bottle sweat, and Frank felt as if his pants would burst wide open. "You don't want to say. That's okay. I get it. Let me ask you a question. How long have you been in Surrey?"

He shook his head. Time wasn't Frank's strong suit.

She answered, "Thirteen days, two weeks tomorrow." Missy put a knee on the bed.

Frank backed up a step.

"We've talked a lot in that time, haven't we?"

The inside of his mouth felt like sand. He wanted to do something with his hands. He wanted a fucking cigarette. He nodded.

"You gave me your last dime when I took Ed Maginty's money. You know that too, right?" Missy sipped the beer.

He watched the cold brew slide down her throat as a lump flushed through his. He nodded again, wondering if the AC worked. The place felt hotter than the whole Middle East, maybe Hell . . . probably both. "You never asked me about Ed's money. You never said a word. I thought that was pretty fucking nice, Frank." He drew a short breath. "I'd done nothing for you, and you did that for me. So, actually, you were the one to do something baffling first. Tell me why you did it?"

"I, um . . . I don't—"

"Don't lie to me, Frank," she said, her lacy voice growing an edge. She took another mouthful of the beer. "Was it because you thought it might be the fast track to getting in my panties?"

His cheeks ballooned and he blew out the breath. He'd tried not to fantasize about Missy. In turn, she'd never hinted at a physical interest in him. Mostly—no, completely—the relationship was conversational. Missy had wanted to know things like the places he'd been, everywhere from Afghanistan to Altoona. For her part, she spoke about her college classes at Surrey State and how this small Massachusetts town was not her destination. Aside from her mother's struggles with MS, and how bad it made her feel, Missy didn't talk about her family. She never mentioned her father. But she did dart from the Snack Shack more than once, saying she needed to get to church.

"I think," Missy had said one afternoon, "I'd make a good nun. I can dedicate myself to a cause. I like to help people—if they deserve it. That kind of life, there's lots of things you have to do. But there's some you don't. A person would be someone else if they became a nun." Kiddingly, Frank had asked if she understood the vow of chastity. Did this appeal to her as well? Her angelic face grew troubled as she replied. "Like I said, it would be one way to change your life."

What life did this beautiful girl of twenty have to change?

Her answer had made Frank uneasy, and he found himself avoiding talk about Missy and men, women and him. He'd barely mentioned Laurel, only to say that he had been married and his wife was dead—kind of like he'd once owned a nice suit until moths ate through it. So, no. Other than a reflexive male response, Frank had played priest to Missy's dream job. He had no plan to seduce her. Of course, looking at her now, a knee sunk into the sheets, smelling good enough to make his dick ache, she seemed to have suggested the idea. He attempted an evenhanded reply. "It would be a lie if I told you that I never thought about your panties." Frank's hands caressed empty air. "But it didn't seem to be where it was going. You know?"

"Sounds like you mean that, Frank. It's weird, but it sounds like you mean it."

"Then just let me say, for the record, I woulda done the same thing about Maginty's money if you were ugly. The guy was a prick."

"I think you would have." Missy took another long sip. "I admire that. And, yes, Ed Maginty is a prick. But I did take his money."

"You said he deserved it."

"He owed it."

"You said he shorted you . . . for babysitting."

"He shorted me all right." She shifted her gaze away. "Anyway, I came to the Snack Shack every day, spent time alone with a guy who could have done anything to me. There was nobody around for miles. You know what that makes you, Frank?"

"Stupid?"

"Trustworthy. After a while, I came there because it felt safe. At first I figured I was playing with fire." Missy's strawberry lips flattened and she wrapped her hand loosely around the neck of the beer bottle. "That first night, I thought you'd knock me unconscious, drag me off to the woods, and rape me. Maybe something worse. From there, you could have hopped on the next freight train."

"Damn. Is that what you think of me?"

"I think I've never met anyone like you. Not in Surrey." Missy's gaze drifted, landing on the crotch of his jeans. "Works, doesn't it? I mean, it didn't get shot off or anything?"

"My life moved beyond a fast fuck a hundred years ago. Between war and my wife . . . it's just not the first thing I think about anymore." Frank grabbed the Rolling Rock from her and downed a long, needed mouthful. "I guess my thoughts don't fit the norm. But, yeah, it works."

She seemed confounded. Then she laughed. "I've never heard a man say that—that their life had moved beyond a fast fuck."

Frank thought about asking how many conversations she'd had on the subject with how many men, but he assumed she meant universally, as if comparing him to the standard she'd seen in movies or read in trashy romance novels. "It's not that it isn't a thought. It just wasn't my first one." A sticky silence wove between them, like fly tape. Missy peeled herself away by taking a turn around the room.

"Do you think you'll be comfortable here?"

"I'd be more comfortable if I knew what's in this for you?"

She stopped, piling her blond locks on top of her head, spinning once, and letting her hair fall. "Maybe I like rooting for the underdog. Maybe I'm anti-establishment. Maybe I'm just fascinated by a guy who doesn't fit the norm. Can we leave it there for now?"

"Is that what you want?"

"Have another beer, Frank. We'll get around to what I want."

CHAPTER ELEVEN

Present Day

The *Surrey City Press* conference room served as a mini command center. In it, Aubrey and Kim sifted through what seemed like endless Missy Flannigan files. The last box finally hit the table. "I think," Kim said, "we are on the verge of documenting that there's zero proof of Missy inheriting that car from an uncle."

"And there won't be any in this box." Aubrey lifted a bundle of bound pages. "It's the transcript of Frank Delacort's original statement."

"Why even bother looking at it? Unless, of course, nobody ever noticed that the homeless, penniless army vet mentioned buying Missy a car."

Aubrey half smiled, skimming through the lengthy statement. Kim was right. No surprises. There was only Frank's adamant insistence that he was innocent. His admission that Missy offered him shelter. The claim that she was injured and that Frank had come to Missy's aid the day she went missing. Aubrey sat on the edge of the conference room table, murmuring, "Why, Frank, do I get the distinct impression that this isn't a lie, but it isn't the truth either?"

"You and Levi really believe there's more to Missy's story, don't you?" Aubrey looked up from the transcript. "Yes," she said. "We do."

"Well, do you also agree that the source of that car isn't here?"

"Yes," she said, dropping the file back in the carton. "And I'd thought as much yesterday." Aubrey scanned the rows of vetted boxes, her next thought testing her real reporter skills. "So I made a phone call to a contact inquiring about Missy's car. It's a long shot, but an idea."

"Wow, look at you." Kim massaged her neck, stretching it from side to side. "The sleuthing reporter on a fact-finding mission. Sounds to me, *Ellis*," she said mockingly, "like Levi is having his way with you."

Aubrey wriggled her nose. "Excuse me?"

Kim laughed. "You have to admit, this is a change from your gentle home portrait pieces."

"Real estate might not be riveting, but I run a valuable slice of the *Surrey City Press*." Aubrey sat up taller, her mood bristling. "And, trust me, there's more to those house stories than makes print."

"Sorry. I didn't mean any disrespect to the home portrait feature. I just never realized your penchant for hard news." Kim waved her hand at their thorough, albeit fruitless effort. "That and you deserve a medal or extra vacation days for putting up with Levi."

"He's not so fierce." Aubrey thought harder about her reporting partner. "Maybe a little fierce. Blunt, for sure. But underneath the buttoned-up exterior, I don't think he's had the easiest go of it."

"Seriously? Unbutton him—which I think Bebe would still like to do—and I doubt you'll find anything but an ice sculpture."

"Probably." Aubrey placed the lid back on the last carton. Her gaze caught on her healed index finger. She ran her thumb gently over it. "Maybe." In between working on the Missy Flannigan case, Aubrey had mulled over the scent of seawater, the young man's voice that had rolled in on a wave. The smell of burnt wood and the disturbing taste of whiskey. None of it had reoccurred since their dinner at the Chinese restaurant. It seemed as though Levi's close-mindedness, combined with her practiced guard, was enough to ward off whoever had wanted in on his behalf. "Anyway," she said to Kim, "the sooner we solve the mystery of Missy Flannigan, the quicker we send Levi back to his usual haunt. Besides, none of this is about how famously Levi and I get along, is it?"

"No. I suppose it isn't." At the sound of a male voice, the women turned to find their subject in the doorway.

"Levi. We didn't see you," Kim said, popping to her feet.

"I gathered as much." Silence filtered through, but Aubrey didn't flinch. The thought wasn't harsh but true. Levi, of all people, should be able to grasp that. "I just spoke with Detective Espinosa. The ME's report came back. The skeletal remains are Missy's."

"Wow," Kim said, slumping back onto the table's edge. "Shouldn't be, but there's a shock factor in confirmation." She headed for the door. "I'll go man my battle station. National media will be all over any update."

"That's good thinking, Kim," Levi said. "Your work, liaising between us and national media, has been quite effective."

"Uh, thanks . . ." She exchanged a curious glance with Aubrey as she left.

"And how goes your and Kim's fact-finding mission?"

Instead of friendly co-worker, Aubrey heard stiffness, the all-business demeanor with which Levi had arrived. It annoyed her. Not so much the tone, but his ruffled feelings—or that she'd noticed them. Robotic Levi was easier to negotiate. She stayed on task. "In this room, there's nothing to confirm the source of Missy's car. Whether she inherited it or, just maybe, Dustin Byrd bought it for her."

"Not terribly surprising." Levi's meditative gaze wandered the cardboard trail, making its way to Aubrey. "What do you mean 'in this room'?"

His astuteness never faltered. "I know you're skeptical of a Missy-Dustin romance. But I had a vague lead, so I pursued it."

"What sort of lead?"

"A connection to Missy's car via one of my homeowners. Remember the Stallworth house I told you about?"

"I remember the stubborn old man who didn't want to move."

"Uh, that's right," she said, dodging Jerry Stallworth's postmortem state. "During our conversation, Mr. Stallworth mentioned that his daughter, Kitty, had a lot of years invested at the DMV. The DMV has access to all sorts of old registration records."

"So you're betting a stranger will go digging for decades-old information? Rather unlikely, don't you think?"

"Ordinarily, I'd agree. But while I was at the Stallworth house, I came across . . . I found something of value that belonged to Kitty. I returned it. She was extremely grateful. In fact," she said, folding her arms, "Kitty sent the flowers on my desk. The gesture, while *ostentatious*, was a good measure of her gratitude."

"The flowers were from Kitty," he said, his head bobbing. "Interesting. And so you took advantage of the woman's appreciativeness by using her to do some DMV fishing. Ellis, that's . . ."

She tensed. "Too underhanded?"

"I was going to say *ingenious*. What did you find out?"

"Nothing yet. I was hoping to hear something today."

"At least it keeps the ball rolling. But we do need to decide our next move. Confirmation of Missy's body will weigh heavily in Delacort's favor. A judge won't have any choice but to cut him loose, not if they intend to charge Dustin Byrd."

"But there's still no motive. No hard connection between Missy and Dustin."

"No, there's not. But imagine the headline if we could produce one. So if you hear from Kitty, let me know."

"Sure. And I can hang around for a while. I already asked Inez if she'd mind staying late."

"Sounds good." Levi glanced at his watch. This one was newer, all silver metal. No leather band. No glint. There was no reference to anything but the time. "I'll be in my office. But I can't stay too long. I have a, uh . . . thing later."

"I missed lunch," Aubrey said. "Did you want to get quick takeout?"

"Can't," he said, backing out the door. Aubrey followed. "The thing later, it's kind of a dinner."

"Fair enough. Are you courting the DA or Detective Espinosa?" Levi's work focus was nonstop. "I doubt drinks will sway Espinosa into divulging anything. But you might have better luck with Marvin Kitteridge. I hear Surrey's sitting DA is susceptible to a few libations."

"Actually, it doesn't have anything to do with the Flannigan story," Levi said, still moving. "It's a dinner date."

They both stopped. Apparently, Levi St John did have a social life. "Right . . . sure. You'd kind of said that. Sorry, I just assumed . . ."

"That I slept here?"

"Of course not. Well, maybe on weeknights."

"But if you're hungry, feel free to order something. You know where the menus are."

"Me? Nah, I'm fine," Aubrey said. "I might have plans later myself. I should hear from Owen anytime," she said, picking up her phone and glancing at the blank screen.

"I take it the marital reconciliation is underway."

Aubrey touched the traffic jam of studs that lined her ear. "We're working on it." She put the phone down and folded her arms. "Owen's just been delayed . . . business. Serious business."

"You said that he designed computer security systems."

"Right . . . designs, implements. Actually, he's kind of a computer genius."

"Is that a job description or more of a specific title?"

She rolled her eyes. "The network security he designs is super high tech, custom. It's a lot of responsibility. It also keeps him on the move."

"So you mentioned."

"Did I?"

"Yes—when you were defending him at the Chinese restaurant. But clearly I'm not the one who has to be convinced."

"I told you, Owen's hesitation wasn't about us, it was about leaving a job that also required a serious commitment."

"Right," he said, holding up a hand. "I remember. I couldn't possibly understand the issues involved."

Levi's ability to find her last nerve and stomp on it was remarkable. "You know, if I thought you had any capacity to understand the whole situation, I might confide—"

Levi's phone interrupted. "I have to take this—Detective Espinosa," he said. "I'll be here until about seven."

He left the room. It was just as well. Personal conversation had hijacked any work-related atmosphere. Again, Levi was annoyingly on point. Aubrey sighed, leaning against the edge of the conference room table. She needed to hang on to the truth: the marital rift between her and Owen had been a test—wisdom they'd pass along to their children someday, the story they'd reminisce about on their fiftieth wedding anniversary. Reconciliation was about believing that Owen was ready to commit to one job and a permanent address. And why not? From the moment they'd met, he'd seemed so sure about the life he wanted.

Owen Kennedy hadn't grown up in a carnival, but his childhood had been as unorthodox as Aubrey's. His mother was the CEO of a large pharmaceutical company. He'd never known his father. Aubrey had been amazed by that, as she at least had vague memories of her own. The story went that Owen was the product of a medical convention experiment—his mother had carefully selected the gene pool with no regard to a specific candidate. But apparently she'd been more intrigued by the idea of producing a child than raising one. She'd been a cursory parent, supplying her son with a childhood of travel and nannies and five-star hotels.

From their first conversation forward, Owen had been as committed as Aubrey to the idea of a mortgage and a landline. Buying his Boston loft was a huge step in that direction, something Owen had surprised Aubrey with a week before their wedding. But the trendy space had never felt like home. That's when she suggested a house in Surrey—a town that stood out from her own nontraditional childhood.

Owen had been wholly on board, enamored with ideas about lawn mowing and backyard barbecues, even children to fill the spare bedrooms. Fate lent a serendipitous hand when their realtor showed them the Arts & Crafts home on Homestead Road. With a little paint, it'd be perfect. And while Aubrey took a turn around the vintage but charming kitchen, the realtor also told her about an opening at the *Surrey City Press*. Owen and Aubrey couldn't have been happier. But their grounded life began to quake not long after the new paint had dried and the lawn mower had barely been used. The first hint of unrest came when Owen stalled, refusing to sell the Boston loft. It had led to loud arguments about her husband choosing to stay in the city after a business trip. "Come on, Bre. You're being unreasonable," he'd said. "It was a six-hour flight after a twelve-hour day . . . And I'm leaving again tomorrow afternoon." Part of their plan had been the mutual agreement that Owen would accept a permanent position close to home. Last she'd checked he was still living a freelance life, moving from country to country faster than a FedEx delivery.

The final straw had come for Aubrey when she'd received a message from her husband via Nicole Lewis—a like-minded assistant Owen employed when the workload got too crazy. She was polite but direct, wanting to know if Aubrey could run into Boston and grab the USB drive he'd forgotten and get it to Madrid by the next morning. When Aubrey told the girl what Owen could do with his USB drive, the shy Nicole was flummoxed, replying, "Uh, okay. I'll pass that along . . ."

Aubrey supposed Owen's last straw had come a few months before that, when he finally learned about her extraordinary gift. Her secret had tumbled out by accident, crushing them like snow from an avalanche.

Standing in the conference room now, Aubrey swallowed down the memory as if it were a bitter pill. The troupe's old master of ceremonies, Carmine, had stopped by Charley's apartment to visit, the moment innocent and impromptu. Owen and Aubrey were there as well, putting on a good show for Sunday dinner. Charley had grown suspicious as to why her granddaughter always seemed to be home alone. In the midst of casual conversation, Carmine was quick to assume that Aubrey's husband was privy to her gift. Information veered out of control before she or Charley could stop it. Owen's fair complexion blanched before turning fiery red. Aubrey was left with no choice but to fill in the blanks. She'd never seen her husband so upset—not even when defending his on-the-go life.

A shouting match had accompanied them back to the craftsman. "Are you serious?" he'd yelled. "Just make me understand how you could keep something like this from me!" Once home, he'd grabbed his pillow from the bed and a blanket from the linen closet. "I'm sleeping in the guest room. Jesus, Bre, that's just creepy . . . freakish." From there things had unraveled like a runaway spool of thread. Owen's travel schedule amped up, which was his response to dealing with the news of her gift. And it wasn't necessarily the way he'd found out—though certainly the timing couldn't have been worse. Their rift was more about his stunned reaction, insisting that his wife's need to hide the truth only proved her own farce: a normal life was never anything more than an impossible dream.

Aubrey wrapped her arms tight around herself. She felt small against the backdrop of the cavernous conference room. The irony was laughable; a gift that kept her so in demand had left Aubrey utterly alone. She needed to fix that. And now, with Owen's change of heart, it would happen. She'd been right about what she said to Levi. Owen needed time to grasp her gift, to realize what she already knew—they belonged together. Maybe, before long, Owen would move back into the house on Homestead Road. Life would go on as they'd planned. Aubrey picked up her phone, which sat on the table. She reread Owen's last text; it encouraged renewed hope. *Done ASAP, I swear. If not I'll blow my own damn firewall and pull a Robin Hood with the client's 800-mil.* Aubrey smiled, brushing her fingertip over the two hearts at the end of his message. He'd made the initiative; that was huge. For the moment it would have to be enough.

In the quiet of the space Aubrey shivered, expecting to see the breath she pushed out. Something was definitely brewing, something different filled the air. The cataloged fragments of a life interrupted, perhaps. But whether they were fragments belonging to Missy Flannigan or herself, nobody currently seemed present who could answer the question.

CHAPTER
TWELVE

Before heading to Levi's office, Aubrey cleared her Owen-filled mind by tending to cubicle housekeeping. She picked through the fading flowers on her desk, discarding dead blossoms—the wilted lilies and shriveled violet-colored alyssum. Aubrey paused on the spent flowers. Flowers of a similar color seeped into her head. She heard the crank of carnival music. She saw games of chance and a man with a dazzling smile. There was the whirl of noise that went with summers past and the vague flash of a girl who didn't speak. Aubrey shut it down and sat. Just as fast, she stood again. She reached for the bouquet and dropped the vase into the trash, abandoning the dead flowers and carnival memories.

She busied herself with menial tasks, organizing real estate listing sheets that had accumulated. Pile A depicted average homes, properties that Aubrey or any staffer could paint in a positive, thousand-word light. Pile B represented outright rejections. Aubrey might not have honed hard-news reporter skills working the real estate beat, but she'd learned a thing or two about sales people. For one, realtors would break into a smile but never a sweat selling you on the charm of their listing. She'd wised up to that after realtor Carol Vickers convinced Aubrey to cover a "darling listing" on Stimple Street. "You might want to keep that umbrella open," Carol had said, ramming her shoulder into a front door that wouldn't budge. The home's leaky roof was the least of it; the smell of smoked meat permeated the house. "Such a fascinating hobby," she'd said, holding a handkerchief to her nose. "The current owner cures all his own pork—indoors!"

That left pile C, the smallest batch of listing sheets. They conveyed something more than county tax records and approximate living space, an innate vibe lost on anyone else in the *Surrey City Press* newsroom, maybe the East Coast. Sometimes the thing that drew Aubrey to a house was the proverbial X marks the spot. Sometimes it took time to ripen. But always, when one of those sheets landed on her desk, Aubrey knew she'd be walking into something more than a house for sale.

Having tidied her work area, Aubrey checked her messages. There were a dozen calls from realtors wanting to know when her usual feature would return. For weeks, Aubrey's home portraits had been replaced by syndicated real estate stories and a sampling of DIY projects. The voicemails were interchangeable, except for one. It was from Marian Sloane. She worked for one of the less prestigious agencies, Happy Home Realty. Their listings often included properties that the more successful agencies had passed on for one reason or another.

While Marian's message was similar, prattling on about a high-end reproduction that Aubrey "just had to see . . ." there was an underlying urgency. A communication Marian Sloane had no idea she was conveying. Aubrey replayed the voicemail, sensing that this property's story had less to do with a prime location than it did a resident spirit. Still listening, Aubrey glanced at Levi's office. The voice of a young man interrupted her focus, competing with the tasks at hand. It drifted into her ears like a memory. It was the same voice she'd heard in the Chinese restaurant. It challenged Marian's message. Aubrey couldn't decipher the words, but she did know the voice was connected to Levi.

Aubrey stood ramrod straight. The spirit's audacity was unprecedented, invading space that, otherwise, was devoid of random apparitions. Her height gave Aubrey a clear view of Levi. Experience insisted she disregard the random voice and whatever message it brought. She stared. Levi was absorbed, but his focus didn't represent his usual tight buzz of energy with a phone pressed to his ear or his fingers moving like fire across a keyboard. Yet his concentration was intense, visible—his mind linked to the voice in Aubrey's head. It surpassed the energy that penetrated Marian Sloane's call.

The phone message came to an end and so did Marian's pitch, which included custom fireplaces, a marble foyer, and motivated sellers. Aubrey's inexplicable ability channeled through her; then it divided. There was far more to Marian Sloane's message and her listing. That needed to be Aubrey's priority. That was her obligation. That was the deal with the dead. But as Aubrey reached to replay Marian's message, her attention was stuck on Levi. Absently, she hit erase. "Damn it," she said, glancing between Levi and the phone. "Get out and leave me alone!" she hissed. "If you know Levi, then you know he'd never be open to hearing you."

Gathering her own folders of Missy Flannigan research, Aubrey headed for Levi's office. She was determined to be the entity in charge. But she lingered near the door, marginally recanting. Unlike most human beings, Levi's presence carried the weight of an iron anchor. Casual observers saw it as bombastic tenacity, his dogged professional nature. In truth, it went beyond that—or so Aubrey was learning. She waited, hoping Levi's brooding mood would lift and he would abandon the memory on his mind. The one that had delivered a specter to the forefront of hers.

Aubrey reined in her composure and pushed a pep talk through her head. Inside Levi's office, they would stay on topic, she thought, clinging tight to the Missy Flannigan materials. They'd concentrate on relevant business. The two of them would speak about Dustin Byrd—the procedural time line, if Delacort were cleared and Byrd indicted. Did the newspaper's legal liaison have a direct answer to that? And Violet Byrd—did Levi happen to catch her interview with Nancy Grace? Perhaps it was a mother defending her son or maybe a preemptive move arranged by Byrd's attorney. Or maybe it was just show business. Apparently, Nancy Grace was on a mission, adamant that Frank Delacort was still the guilty party. A shaken, elderly Mrs. Byrd had been encouraged to canonize her son, talking at length about her non-violent, gun-toting offspring. Taking a cleansing breath, Aubrey chose to start there.

She stepped into Levi's office. "I can't imagine what will become of Violet Byrd when her son is arrested for murder. It's a dotted line away from the main story. But maybe it's a good human interest piece for Gwen—especially since Violet just appeared on *Nancy Grace*."

Levi looked up. In his hand was a small leather-bound photo album. "*Nancy Grace* . . . ? Sorry, I wasn't listening."

Not a good sign. When wasn't Levi listening? Aubrey waded farther in. Seawater came crashing toward her, but Aubrey refused to budge. "I thought Dustin's mother might make a good filler piece. The Byrds have lived in Surrey all their lives. Violet volunteers at the Purr-fect Cat shelter and oversees the membership committee at Our Lady of the Redeemer. She runs that little ceramics business out of her house. Tons of people have been there. I think it's an angle worth exploring." Levi hummed a vague reply and removed his silver-rimmed glasses. It revealed a younger man's face.

The voice was clearer now. *"Stop ignoring your instincts . . ."*

"Shut up," she murmured. Levi's expression turned curious, the way it did after Aubrey had announced the smell of seawater in the Chinese restaurant. She smiled as if she'd said nothing, continuing on. "Violet Byrd can't even go home—not that she'd want to, not after what they found in her basement."

Levi put the photo album in a drawer. The room and waves quieted.

He eased back in his chair, producing a cloth handkerchief and polishing his eyeglass lenses. "Uh, sure. It might be worth a look. See if Violet Byrd wants to talk to you."

"I said Gwen. It might be a good story for Gwen." There was internal hemming and hawing. Empathy bubbled as Aubrey saw the lost look on Levi's face. She'd give him one chance. "Levi, is something bothering you—something other than Missy Flannigan?"

On the suggestion, his moodiness didn't just shift, it vanished. He sat upright and shuffled the papers on his desk. "You're right. Doing a piece on Byrd's mother is a good idea." Eyes on her, he said, "I'm fine."

"You seem distracted." He forced the smile that, in turn, forced the dimple. Regardless of his lack of reply, she'd cracked open the portal by asking the question. The smoky scent of burning wood penetrated the space. It was intense, probing, and Aubrey half expected the fire alarm to sound. It didn't. There was only Levi, floundering to find his footing.

"It's nothing. Let it go, Ellis."

She couldn't. The taste of whiskey burned at the back of her throat. She coughed. Alcohol mixed with an herby taste . . . No, it was a smell. Pot. Marijuana.

"Are you all right?"

She nodded, teary-eyed, pointing to her throat. "Just a tickle." Levi's cell rang; he answered. The smells and tastes retreated, vapor swallowed by space.

"Yes, Beth . . . No, sure, I saw your text." Levi stood and tapped the phone's screen, huffing. "Absolutely," he said, never missing a beat. "I'm already on my way."

"Late?" she asked as he ended the call.

He tossed the phone aside and unrolled a shirtsleeve, expertly corralling a cufflink. "I missed Bethany's text about taking an earlier train." Finished with the other sleeve, he tugged on his suit jacket, brushing at the lapels. "Date night. Not what I do best. I should have brought a fresh shirt."

"That depends," she said, tucking her stack of Missy Flannigan paraphernalia tight to her chest. "Is it a first date or someone who's comfortable with a slightly rumpled you?"

He adjusted the jacket. "Intimately acquainted with deep wrinkles. Bethany knows me . . ."

He hit the brakes at the edge of his personal life. It was fine. Aubrey didn't need to hear a litany of what Bethany—apparently the longtime girlfriend—knew. As she turned to leave, Gwen showed up at the door.

"Here you are," she said to Aubrey, a stack of papers crooked in her arm. She separated a few pages and held them out. "Your listing sheets got mixed up with my fax. Sorry, I guess I've had it for a couple of days. It's from a Marian Sloane. Fancy house. Looks like a fun tour." Aubrey extended her arm halfway before Levi's voice gave her an excuse to retract it.

"Gwen, since you're here, Ellis had an idea about a story on Violet Byrd. Maybe get with her later and work out the angle."

The features editor came farther into the office, still holding out the listing sheet. As she did, Aubrey's nose filled with different smells, something coarser than burnt wood, more pungent than pot. Then it was gone. "Fine, Levi," Gwen said. "First thing tomorrow. I do have a family."

He retrieved keys from his desk and turned off his computer. "Right. I meant tomorrow."

Hesitantly, Aubrey reached for the listing sheet. The paper hit her fingertips like the business end of a branding iron. She let go, a hissing gasp sucking through her teeth. "Paper cut!" She winced. Aubrey balled her hand tight as Gwen retrieved the wafting pages. "Would, um, would you mind dropping them on my desk?" she asked. "I'm trying not to get real estate info mixed up with Flannigan business."

"Sure," Gwen said, turning for the door.

Aubrey unfurled her hand and glanced fast. No paper cut was present, but tiny blisters had formed on her fingertips. And that, Aubrey understood, was what you got for ignoring the job to which you were obligated. She clenched her fist tight, trying to cut off circulation. Aubrey dropped the Missy Flannigan folders onto Levi's desk, steadying herself with her other hand.

"Ellis, are you sure you're okay? You've been acting odder than usual since you came in here." Aubrey struggled to come up with a reason why tears stung at her eyes. He came around the desk, drawing nearer. "Ellis?" he said again. "Geez, was it a paper cut or a knife wound?"

Neither, but thanks for the concern . . . Aubrey's watery gaze moved around his office, landing on the wall clock. She grasped at believable subterfuge. "Oh, gosh, look at the time! Didn't you say you were late for Bethany's train?"

"Uh, right," he said, glancing at his watch. "She gets in at . . . Are you sure you're—"

"I'm fine." Aubrey folded her arms with the pinch of a vise. "Low blood sugar. Remember, no lunch."

"Right, no lunch." Levi looked between her and the clock. "Maybe you should—"

"Seriously. I'm fine. Like I said, my dinner plans were up in the air. There's a chance Owen will get back to town tonight."

"Right . . . your husband." He retreated several steps. The desk phone rang and Levi kept moving, answering it. "Yes, she's right here. Hang on." He held the receiver out. "Receptionist's desk. It's Kitty Stallworth."

Aubrey took the receiver in her uninjured hand. She listened as a chatty Kitty Stallworth seized the conversation. Aubrey replied with a few uh-huhs and an "I see" as Levi looked on. "Thank you, Kitty. That is unexpected . . . really intriguing. Yes . . . You're welcome again." Aubrey nodded as the woman rambled. "Yes, the flowers were beautiful. Not necessary, but thank you again . . . It was just good timing, maybe a reporter's eye. That's all. I'm positive too. Your father is looking down, so relieved . . ." she said, repeating the woman's words. "No doubt he's resting in peace. Uh, Kitty, I don't mean to cut you off, but . . . Right. Thanks again for the information . . ."

"Well?" Levi said before she had the receiver in the cradle. "Was she able to trace the VIN number? Do we have a connection between Dustin and Missy?"

"Not exactly." Aubrey ran her fingers through her hair, the other hand still balled tight. "We have a brand new puzzle piece."

"How so?"

"Kitty, in her great enthusiasm to assist, managed to trace Missy's car back to the original bill of sale and the lot where it was bought in Portsmouth, New Hampshire—way before easy-access computer records. Portsmouth is seriously north of here. The snazzy Mustang has a history of two owners. The first was the dealership where the car was used as a demo for a year. After that it was sold one time for $15,500."

"And the buyer?"

"Missy Flannigan. She bought the car herself, Levi. Even better, according to the bill of sale, she paid with a cashier's check." Aubrey sighed. "So where does that leave us?"

"Facts," he said, taking a deep breath. "I'd have to stick with solid, irrefutable facts. We've proven Missy didn't inherit the car from an uncle. It also tells us that her father lied about it."

"Believable theory," Aubrey countered. "It's possible that Dustin Byrd gave her the money. Maybe her father was clueless and he just wanted to protect his daughter. Surely Dustin had disposable income, living at home . . . never marrying."

"Plausible," Levi said, narrowing his eyes. "But not as likely. If you're going to buy someone a car, you don't give them the cash. You give them the car."

"Point taken," Aubrey said. "So where did a college girl, from a less-than-middle-income family, get that kind of cash?"

Levi sat on the edge of his desk and sighed. "Honestly, Ellis, that information makes me ask even bigger questions. What secrets, besides the cash source for a fancy muscle machine, was Missy Flannigan keeping?"

CHAPTER THIRTEEN

Surrey, Massachusetts
Twenty Years Earlier

Missy was late. The weather was awful and she'd almost turned the car around twice. Rain thumped like fat tears on the convertible's roof as she pulled into the deserted parking lot of Watts Lumber. Along with a torrential downpour, she'd managed to hit every red light between Surrey and Leominster, several towns over. Dustin was waiting. She saw his full moon face peering down from the truck's oversize cab. It was his most practiced gaze, a look that went with his ever-growing concern. Missy took a breath and then the plunge, opening her door. The passenger side of the truck swung open. His body stretched the span, reaching to yank her inside.

"Damn, I was about to give up!" he said. "You should have met me in Surrey."

"Surrey? That's risky, don't you think?"

"Leominster isn't much better. Would you believe I ran into Randy Combs twenty minutes ago, right here in the parking lot. Scared the shit out of me, rapping on my window like the do-gooder he is."

"Randy Combs?"

"Yeah, he works for the town too, child welfare services. One of those cushy jobs, the kind where you don't have to account for your time half the day."

"I know who he is. What did he want?"

"Nothing much. Just wanted to know if I was having truck trouble, parked here like this."

"What did you tell him?"

A grin pushed into Dustin's round cheeks. "I told him I was waitin' on my girl—that I hadn't seen her all week." He leaned over and kissed Missy. "I said we were heading straight to the Red Maple Motel to have the hottest sex west of the Atlantic Ocean."

"You didn't?" she said, wide-eyed, her hand pushing on his chest.

"Of course I didn't," he said, laughing. "I told him AAA was on its way. But in just a few months I'll be telling him, and the rest of Surrey, that I plan on doing just that, with my wife, every night of the week." Dustin pulled her closer. "Anyway, why are you so late?"

"Traffic. The rain."

"Okay, but after we're married, I won't be any less concerned when it comes to your whereabouts. I hope you know that." Missy brushed the last drops of rain from her arms and smiled at him. "Truth be told, I like to think of that as the other way around." Dustin's hand trailed along the cool skin of her arm. "You waitin' on me to come home—me looking forward to a little dinner. What do you think about that, Miss Missy?"

A hum rang from her throat and she answered honestly. "I think looking forward to my cooking is a borderline fantasy."

"I'll take my chances," Dustin said. "You look cold." He didn't wait for Missy to confirm as much, producing a town-issued jacket and wrapping it around her. "As for the cooking, Mom's offered to teach you a dozen times."

"I know . . . I know," she said, gathering the jacket even though the July air was more wet than chilled. Missy's name was branded on the breast, so for now it was a garment they kept hidden in his truck. It was the anchor item to Missy's upcoming twenty-first birthday presents from Dustin: the jacket on her back, a ring on her finger, and him on her arm—publicly. "I'm just wondering how my cooking will compare to Violet's."

"You're going to be the perfect wife. Besides, Mom's a whiz in the kitchen and she'd be glad to show you." Dustin cupped his hand around her cheek.

Missy inhaled hard, wondering where the shiver of expectation had gone. She pushed past its absence. "It's sweet of her to offer," Missy said, and she did think it was. "Violet's been amazing. And you'd think by now I might have picked up a thing or two."

"Don't worry about it. You've got a lifetime to figure out all my favorites. And Mom has been good to us, keeping our secret. But I, for one, can't wait to end it—make honest women out of both of you." He pulled her into a tight embrace as he made his vow. Missy's hands were busy holding the jacket closed, making the motion awkward. Her throat thrust into Dustin's shoulder where air was momentarily cut off. "And whether you're a fine cook or we live on takeout, it won't matter to Mom," he said, letting go.

"She just wants to see us happy, doesn't she?"

He smiled. "Mom's like that—simple pleasures. In fact, it wouldn't surprise me if she thinks our wedding night will be the first time we . . . you know."

"You're kidding?"

"You have to admit, innocent follows your face." Dustin traced over her collarbone, running from the hollow of Missy's throat to her cheek. "Besides, I've never said, 'Hey, Mom, instead of going to the shooting range, I'm bedding Missy at the Red Maple Motel.' She thinks intimate exchanges occur on the couch, holding hands, while she scoots off to do her weight training."

"Now you're just teasing!"

"No, I don't think I am. Mom loves her exercise."

"I didn't mean . . ."

Missy laughed at the remark, but as Dustin spoke, his hand moved lower, running along her leg. Humor dissipated as she watched his wind-chapped digits edge under her skirt. Separating herself from this act wasn't nearly as hard as the others. Missy reminded herself to be grateful about that. "And now we're just under the three-month mark." Dustin leaned across her lap, popping open the glove box. From it he retrieved a daily planner. It was where Dustin noted important things: when the town drains needed flushing, water restriction violations, and October first, Missy's twenty-first birthday. There was a fat red circle around it, the date he'd designated. She'd actually been impressed by his plan; it was crafty and in-depth. Dustin's mantra had been clear: "Twenty-one is respectable, Missy. Eighteen invites too much speculation and sixteen . . . well, people just wouldn't understand."

"It'll be here before we know it. You're right." Missy took the planner from him, but as she reached to put it back a hard object caught her eye. "Hey, this is new." From the deep hollow of the glove box her hand gripped a revolver, fingers clasping the trigger. "When did you—"

"Give me that thing!" Dustin locked his hand around her wrist. Her fingers disengaged, dropping the gun, which he grabbed. "Are you crazy, Missy?"

She laughed. "I'm not the one with a gun in my glove compartment!"

"Remember, I told you about it—cost me a damn fortune, but it was worth every penny. Slim and fine piece of weaponry. This Super Redhawk is considered an expert firearm. In the military, they only assign them to special ops, a few sharpshooters."

"So how'd you get one?"

Dustin grazed the cold barrel of the gun lightly over Missy's arm. "Well there, Miss Missy, you just have to know the right dealer—and I do." He pointed the gun toward the windshield. "I took this Ruger baby out to the range this morning. It was the envy of every other shooter—I looked damned important just holding it." Dustin talked a lot about his guns. They were his property and he liked to let people know as much. "But the last thing we need is for you to get hurt with one. I'd have a wicked time explaining that." He tucked the Ruger into the recesses of the glove box. "Of course, maybe after we're married I might teach you how to use it."

"Right. After we're married," she repeated. "The time has gone fast, hasn't it?"

"What are you talking about? I swear, if your birthday was any later in the year I'd just take my chances—tell your parents today. I think your mom will be pleased, and your dad will come—"

"I don't give a shit about him." While she said the words, Missy's thoughts turned to the contents of the glove box. She imagined the power of pulling the gun's trigger. "But I do want him to know how much you love me . . . how normal it is. If it weren't for my mother, I'd never speak to him again."

"We've been over this. No question, your father's behavior was wrong, cheating on your mother like that when she's so ill. But—"

"Dustin," she snapped at his misconception. "There is no *but*. And you should know, my father—" She stopped. Missy gently placed the planner back in the glove box. It wasn't Dustin's fault. That was the story he knew, because that was the one she'd told him. The truth was too repulsive. "Forget it. Could we just not talk about it?" But her throat had gone tight, and a fresh knot gripped her stomach.

"All right, okay," he said, his hand swooshing over the vinyl jacket sleeve. "I know how much he upsets you. Why don't we"—his . . . glance moved between her balled fists and taut jaw—"go back to a happier topic?" He tucked the jacket tighter, as if this might help. "Hey, here's an idea crazy enough to solve everything. Let's do it tonight, run off and get married."

"Now?" Predictability was the trait that drew her to Dustin. In five years he'd exhibited all the spontaneity of a wet match. Missy deftly negotiated around it. "Dustin, that's sweet. But you came up with a solid plan for a good reason. Does it make sense to blow it now, when we're so close?"

Dustin leaned lazily into his side of the truck. "Yeah, it is a smart plan. But I'm starting not to care what anybody thinks. I just want us together. Don't you feel the same way?"

"You know the answer to that," she said, employing his rhetoric. "If your job wasn't in the public eye we could have said the heck with it a long time ago. But you still want to be the director of Surrey Parks and Recreation, don't you?" He hummed in agreement. "And we don't want our relationship to put any kind of *mark* on your integrity— no matter how ridiculous. Right?" As Missy spoke, she slipped into a practiced ritual. She caressed his bulky arm muscles, shrugging off the jacket. Damp perfumed skin brushed against his. She didn't make eye contact, also a ritual.

Men had specific smells; Dustin's was infused with grass clippings, chlorine, and security. But in the last year, maybe more so in recent months, the lure of the last one had withered like a summer flower. Missy shifted closer, trying to be good. She tried to snuff out deodorant bar soap and the sensual cotton T-shirt smells of Frank Delacort. "I've been thinking about us a lot lately," she said, which was true. "Waiting, it seemed like a lifetime when we first talked about it. Like it would never get here."

"But you're glad it's almost here, right, Missy? I mean, you're looking forward to telling everyone that I'm your guy. That it's you and me—forever."

She hesitated a second too long.

"Missy?"

"Dustin," she said, turning his question into hers. "How can you even ask that? After all the plans we've made. Tell me again how it goes." She soothed them both by nuzzling into him and an old daydream. "Please?"

He feigned irritation, a smile spreading beneath a bushy mustache. "Okay. But only if you really want to hear it."

"I do." Missy snuggled closer, willing old feelings.

"On a few acres, just outside town, we'll build a log-cabin house. It'll be rustic on the outside, but you'll have every modern convenience on the inside, including a big kitchen. You'd like that, right?"

"Sure," she said, her fingers running over the buttons on his khaki shirt. "A kitchen with a giant window that looks out over a yard with a pool." It was her favorite part of the big picture.

"Right. We'll take all the money I've saved . . . Did I tell you I crossed the eighty-grand threshold?"

"Dustin, that's incredible," she said, rewarding him with a kiss.

"Yep, eighty grand—tucked inside my bedroom safe. I definitely don't need Ben Franklin Savings knowing my net worth."

"Oh, you're being silly about that. They're very discreet at the bank."

"Sure, if you've got nothing saved but a few hundred bucks." Missy smiled and shrugged. "Anyway, our house will have four bedrooms, a huge one for us," he said, kissing her neck right below her ear. "One for guests and a couple we'll put those kids in not too far from now—maybe before your twenty-second birthday."

Kids . . . Missy's breath quivered on the exhale.

"Cold?"

"A little."

"I told you." His arms bundled around her. "Hey, speaking of the Red Maple, I thought we could see if they have the room with the Jacuzzi tub available."

Agreement hummed from Missy, but her mind wasn't on the Red Maple. It wasn't even in the truck. It was in the room above the Plastic Fork. "I'm not sure I can wait that long." It offered an excuse that would make Dustin's evening complete. Instead of touching his shirt buttons, Missy undid them, her mouth following, gliding over his hairy chest.

"Damn, Missy . . . not here. Not like this." Dustin always thought it should be in a bed. It was a mindset that had, once, so thoroughly charmed her. Missy wriggled her fingers beneath the slope of his belly, reaching for his belt buckle. "I wanted to put some dinner in you first. I thought we could go to the other side of Leominster. We wouldn't run into anybody there."

"Don't you like the pouring rain?" She kissed him. Dustin responded, his tongue flying into her mouth like a missile. "The thunder . . . the wind, the empty parking lot." She reached past him, hitting the control that moved the seat back.

There was lots of headroom in the cab and Missy stood tall on her knees, Dustin's hand sliding beneath her skirt. With the other, he rapped his knuckles against the foggy truck window. "This weather is making things private. Nobody would see us." Dustin's mischievous brown eyes skimmed her body, his fingers looping around her underwear. "I suppose it'd be okay. Watts Lumber closed at five sharp. But what's the rush?"

"No rush," she said, helping him slide her panties off. "But I do have a major accounting test tomorrow. That summer class I'm taking."

"Didn't you say that was Monday? You said that's why you had to cancel." He wrapped his hands around her ass, laying claim to Missy like he did his guns.

A sultry moan vibrated out of Missy and she bit down on her lip. It bought her a moment. He was right. She'd used that excuse to spend Monday drinking Rolling Rocks with Frank. They'd eaten chicken wings, played three hands of gin, and watched the movie she'd rented from Blockbuster. But as he undid her blouse and Missy unhooked her bra, the misstep was forgotten. Dustin was too busy shoving his pants down. Rain hammered the truck's roof. It was as rhythmic as the groans radiating out of him. Missy kissed him back the way he liked, stroking him, multitasking as she took in the truck's rear view. It wasn't as foggy as the rest of the windows. Dustin would stop if he knew that. He'd insist on the Red Maple. It wasn't where she wanted to be. But her plan moved along as Dustin's hand crooked around her neck, yanking Missy into lustier kisses. She closed her eyes and whispered something dirty in his ear, straddling Dustin Byrd and the very fine line she walked.

◆　◆　◆

At nine forty-five Missy was in another deserted parking lot. But the rain had lifted, meaning she only had to jump the puddles to the rear stairs of the Plastic Fork. One of the best things about Dustin's job was his five a.m. call. It gave her lots of free time. After having sex in his truck and a quick meal at Hobart's Barbecue, he'd yawned twice, farted once, and kissed her goodnight. In Missy's hand now was a bottle of champagne, compliments of Marty Finch, who owned Finch Liquor and supplied Missy with alcohol on demand. She never bartered for goods, making Marty the exception to the rule.

Today was Frank's one-month anniversary at Holliston's Hardware & Feed. That called for a celebration. Missy bounded up the tall, narrow staircase, her steps light and happy. This was the effect of Frank Delacort, and with each passing day she found herself wanting more. Frank was unexpected, like a punch of air in the midst of a last ghastly breath. He was mesmerizing and strong, complicated but easy to be with. He was also incredibly unique—not once had he suggested that they have sex. At the top of the stairs her thrumming heart consumed Missy. Whatever she felt for Dustin, it paled wildly in comparison to the emotions Frank stirred. She couldn't figure it out. But Missy also wondered what was so wrong with that. There wasn't time to speculate as the flat's steel door flew open, the surprise attack thrusting Missy into the wooden rail. The worn barrier bowed as the champagne slipped from her grip, going overboard and smashing onto the asphalt below.

◆　◆　◆

Frank grabbed Missy, knowing his grip was viselike. He didn't care. He hauled her inside, the door slamming behind her. "You tell me what the hell is going on!" His voice was ugly—scary—he didn't care about that either. "Right now, Missy. I'm not fucking around."

"Frank, stop! You're hurting me!" He let go. Missy stumbled back. "What is with you? Have you been smoking the fertilizer at Holliston's?"

"I want to know what game you're playing." Frank's bad luck continued to spiral. Between his dead wife and the army, he'd been on the receiving end plenty. But this was too much. "You must think I'm pretty dumb, the way you sneak over here, then take care of your real life business. I don't think I've been a bigger pawn . . . or putz—not even with Laurel." Frank didn't wait for a reply, moving fast across the room. He'd made up his mind. Laurel had played him for a fool; he wasn't giving Missy the same chance. Frank took his duffel bag from the closet and began shoving whatever life he'd accumulated into it. "Just forget it. There's nothing you could say anyway. I'm out of here."

"Frank, wait! You can't—" She rushed toward him.

He swore he heard panic. But that couldn't be right.

"Two nights ago we sat here and drank beer, watched a bad movie, played cards . . . What happened? Why are you so angry?"

Frank pulled his frame upright. Hearing the question made him aware. He recognized the same blinding rage he'd felt toward Laurel, even Dr. Harrison. He fought for self-restraint. He couldn't get hold of the rage, not entirely, but he did redirect it. Frank threw the duffel bag, tipping over a chair. He came toward her. Missy backed up until she hit a wall. He tried harder, recalling Dr. Harrison's advice. Frank imagined how Missy saw him—a wild, looming, out-of-control vine, something that could strangle the life out of her. Staring into Missy's damn damp eyes, something inside him softened. It tamped down his temper, enough that his mind could get a grip around the hot edges of anger. He backed up. He was still angry, but he'd keep it to words—they just wouldn't be very nice ones. "Your innocent act, it's really good. But you know that, right? Your never-been-bedded wannabe-nun face. But you're not so innocent, are you Missy?"

"What, exactly, are we talking about?" she said, her gaze scaling his rigid body. *"Specifically."*

"I saw you," he said, sound seeping through gritted teeth. "I watched you fuck that dick-brain, weed-whacking mastermind in his truck."

"You saw me . . . with Dustin?"

"Yeah, with Dustin! Who the hell else would I see you with?"

She didn't say anything, like there might be another answer. "How did you . . . Watts Lumber is miles from here," she said, skipping right over denial. "You don't have a car."

"Logistics?" His fists balled so tight Frank thought he'd crack a bone. "You only want to know the longitude and latitude?" For safety sake, he backed up. "Fine. Watts supplies stock to Holliston's. The old man was too shaky; he didn't want to make the drive. He told me to take the company truck and make the pickup. I was in the loading bay when you got there. I stayed to watch since I had a front row seat for the whole peep show! And I'm an ass for thinking you . . ."

"For thinking what?"

"Nothing." He refused to go near vulnerability. Instead Frank retrieved the duffel bag. "My damn fault. I thought you were somebody else." He zipped up the bag and slung it over his shoulder.

"No!" she said. "You can't leave! Where are you going?"

"I'm getting out of your way, sweet Missy Flannigan. Send up a flare to the Surrey Parks and Rec patrol unit. The dickwad can head over and have another go at it in style." Frank threw the room key onto the mattress. It bounced like a ball on the taut military-made bed. "Shut the lights when you're done."

"Oh my God, Frank." He blew past her in a whirling gust of emotion. "You're jealous."

Frank spun around; he almost swore she was smiling. "I'm not jealous. You and your sweet candy ass give yourself too much credit."

"Then why else would you get so upset or care who I was with behind Watts Lumber?"

And this was why a smarter Frank avoided women. They confused the shit out of him. They twisted words and the way he felt. Laurel, Dr. Harrison, and now her, a girl he never thought would climb into a bed, or a truck, belonging to Dustin Byrd. "I am not jealous," he said. "There's an outside chance I'm suffering from Stockholm syndrome—the way you've kept me here."

"You could have left anytime you wanted. Staying was your choice."

He still stood closer to the exit than her. He wished he could be that smarter Frank and leave. Some fucked up feeling inside wouldn't let him go.

"I can't change what you saw, Frank. But you're not being fair." She was the calmer, more rational of the two. He desperately wanted to be the one in control. "You've never even suggested . . . Well, you never even asked if I had a boyfriend."

"A boyfriend I could get my mind around—even a girlfriend. But him?" The duffel bag crunched in Frank's white-knuckle grip. "Why him, Missy?"

"It's a long story. I . . . ." Missy stared at her hands. They wrung together in a way that said the explanation was just as twisted. "Dustin was in the right place at the right time. That's . . . that's the most basic answer I can give you."

"How long?"

"How long what?"

"How long have you been . . ." Frank dragged his hand over his crew-cut and rushed through the rest of the thought. "How long have you been doing that with him?"

Her hands unknotted and Missy's arms moved to self-comfort. Frank saw her finger dig into her flesh. "Almost five years." She looked everywhere but at him. "Since I was sixteen."

"Since you were . . ." The duffel bag hit the floor. "You've got to be kidding me. What kind of man goes after a sixteen-year-old girl?" Frank shoved his hands in his pockets. It would force him to be still and think. "All right, I can see you making a mistake at that age. But why are you still with him? Byrd's a puffed up know-it-all who doesn't know a goddamn thing. I could make him piss in his county-issue boots in a heartbeat."

"Don't make me defend him. Dustin's not a bad person. Sure, maybe a little false ego, but he's been good to me. Don't hate him for that."

"Okay, how about I hate him for having the scruples of any predator?" Frank was right about Dustin Byrd being an asshole. He'd just undershot what the dickhead could accomplish. "I would never go near a girl that age. It would take incredible circumstance to consider . . . *you*, at twenty."

"Is that why . . . why you've never . . ." Missy tipped her head toward a bed that they'd treated as if it were invisible.

"There's lots of reasons why I've never . . . gone there."

"For a while now," she said softly, "you and I have talked about everything under the sun. We got drunk and still you never even hinted . . . Do you know how surreal that is, Frank? Do you have any idea how that made me feel?"

"Unwanted?"

"Unbelievable. You chose to spend time with me, *just me*. The thoughts in my head, talking . . . listening. That must sound small and 'so what' to you, but it was a first for me."

"Glad to be your novelty, Missy." His focus moved from the untouched bed to the moonless sky outside the Plastic Fork. "But I get it now, why you weren't interested in more."

"No," she said, which sounded like confirmation to Frank. He wished he were as emotionless as the army had intended. "You don't get it at all." Missy's chest heaved, her sweet façade cracking under utter honesty. "A little more than a month ago you stood right by that bed and asked me what I wanted. Do you remember?"

"I remember you being a cocktease then turning it off like a faucet. I took that as an almost-twenty-one-year-old *girl* who wasn't ready for anything more." Frank stared into her watery blue eyes, thinking he'd made the smarter choice that day. That maybe he'd even been looking out for her. "Guess I was wrong."

"Not entirely. Please, Frank," she said, "just keep listening." His stance was tense but stationary, at ease but not quite. "When you asked me that, I had this brand new idea. But it was all so strange, different from anything in my life. At first I just reacted the only way I knew how—I guess that was the cocktease part."

"And that's changed how?"

"Because I changed. And before you turned up at the Snack Shack, I didn't think that was possible. I thought being with Dustin was more than I could hope for. I never imagined things could change so fast over a few buckets of chicken wings and some bad video rentals."

"Missy, what are you talking about?"

"You. I'm talking about you, Frank. It's the way you ordered mild wings when we both knew you liked hot. It was you telling me to pick the movie and asking what card game to play. It was Frank Delacort wanting nothing from me but to be with me. From the time I was nine years old," she said, her voice shaking, "nothing has been about what I wanted—not with Dustin, certainly not before him. Not with anybody."

And despite whatever his uneven life hadn't delivered, Frank thought this was the emptiest, saddest thing he'd ever heard. A punch of pride drove through him. He, Frank Delacort, had made something better for her. Frank moved past the duffel bag, righting the chair he'd knocked over. The toppled object was indicative of his temper and he needed to erase that. It didn't go with the man she claimed to see. He stood a foot from her, staring at her soft skin, admiring her altered out-look. "I'm sorry about the champagne you brought."

"It was just cheap champagne. Today is one month at Holliston's, you know? Missy's hand brushed against his. "I wanted to celebrate. I thought we could see if grilled-cheese sandwiches go as good with champagne as they do Rolling Rocks."

"I guess the champagne isn't going to happen. Neither is the beer, I'm fresh out of Rolling Rock."

"That's too bad," she said, their fingers linking. "Got any other ideas how we can celebrate?"

"Maybe. As long as it's what you want."

"I want you. I want out of this town, out of this life." He saw a tear at the edge of her eyes. He brushed it away. "I think, Frank, that maybe you're the answer to a prayer."

Frank squinted through the giant picture window. He didn't know about that. But he did know he felt something good standing there with her. "Missy, I don't want to talk about him anymore, but if we start something here . . . You should know, I'm not into community property. If there's an *us*, there can't be a *him*—not for any reason." He looked back at her. "Do you understand what I mean?"

"There. You just did it again. That's the nicest thing anybody's ever said to me," she said, her mouth bowing.

Frank didn't want to think about right or wrong, but he felt sure this was more honorable than what Dustin Byrd had done. He pulled Missy close. Residual anger melted as she hugged him. Frank closed his eyes, not kissing her. Not yet. He needed to find his center. Calm was at the center. It was the one good piece of advice Dr. Harrison had given him before he'd thrown her into a steel door.

"Wait," Missy said, bobbing out of his reach. He almost lost it; he almost grabbed. It gave him confidence when he didn't. Maybe she could fix that part of him, like whatever it was he'd done for her. "You could sell tickets with this window." Missy pulled down the yellowed shade. "Just roll it back up tomorrow; the spring doesn't work."

"Will do," he said, mesmerized, as she glided back to him. Frank helped her discard the blouse and unsnapped her denim skirt, which slid to the floor. He stripped the undergarments from her body unceremoniously. He didn't want to think about where her clothes had been. She pulled off his shirt, Frank shuffling out of his jeans. Doubt vanished as they fell onto the bed and Frank realized how much she wanted this. He wanted to make her come, and there was an encouraging moan almost as soon as he made the effort. Everything whirled as Missy kneaded tighter to him—he liked that. But he wanted her to look at him, tell him. Frank straddled her, but he couldn't get the words out. *Goddamn it, tell me you won't fuck him again?* It was weak . . . needy. He hated both.

She saw the question on his face. "What?" she said, breathless, her hands running hard over little scars and used skin. He rose over her, kissing her. She kissed him back.

"Missy, this . . . this is supposed to happen to us, right?"

"God, I hope so," she said as he thrust himself inside her. "I was beginning to believe *this* was nothing but a means to an end."

CHAPTER
FOURTEEN

Present Day

On the coffee table were a large tin box and a bottle of wine. Aubrey stretched out her legs and rested her feet on the table too, flexing her aching arches. As far as Missy Flannigan was concerned, it had been a satisfying, forward-motion kind of day. The rest of the evening wasn't proving as productive. Aubrey swallowed a mouthful of red wine and dropped her cell phone beside her. "That was Owen."

"I gathered as much." Charley clicked off the television, sitting stiff in her wingback chair.

"He's stuck in New York longer than expected. He sounded really disappointed."

"And you?"

"Of course I'm disappointed! Everything changes in one phone call and we can't connect long enough to tear up the divorce papers." Her brow wriggled at Charley. "If it weren't for all this Missy Flannigan business, I'd get the car and drive down there myself." She picked up a throw pillow and gave it a punishing toss into the sofa. Charley was silent, not encouraging the option. Aubrey changed the subject. "I was thinking," she said, gliding her glass past the comfy, casual furnishings. "If I recall, that chair of yours had a mate. What became of it?"

"It's in storage. It doesn't fit in your house. I should probably get rid of it. Sometimes," Charley said, sipping her tea, served nightly with a shot of whiskey, "it makes sense to let go of things when they no longer fit into your life."

"And yet," Aubrey said, smiling, sensing an uptick to the conversation. "It might be wiser to recognize the value in keeping what you already have. I mean, the chairs do go together."

"Perhaps. At a glance. But the supposed mate, it hasn't shown the same constitution, lived up to expectations," she rebutted, resting her head against the back of the tall chair in which she sat. "Of course, I appreciate the remorse in discarding a once-meaningful thing. But sometimes one has to make the more practical choice."

"I don't see that as practical," Aubrey argued. "It could be that the chair is entirely repairable. Chances are you'll never come across two chairs quite like those again." She put the wine glass down and focused on Charley. "Obviously, they were meant to be together."

"You could be right." She breathed deep, surveying Aubrey's eclectic choice of furniture. "Yet, I feel a duty to mention that recently, upon closer inspection, I learned something about the banished chair."

"What's that?" Aubrey said.

"The so-called mate isn't a match at all. In fact, it's nothing more than a cheap knock-off."

Aubrey picked up her wine. "Well, lucky for me it's my house . . . my life. I get to decide what . . . or *who* fits."

"Why, of course," Charley said, patting her hand against the firm arm of her chair. "I was merely talking about furniture."

Aubrey narrowed her eyes. It was all so easy for Charley, with her revolving rotation of husbands. Why fight for marriage number one when a second or third held so much possibility? Aubrey leaned deeper into the couch cushions, her big toe nudging the latch on the tin box that was shaped like a small treasure chest. "Seriously. You ought to get together with Levi. I believe you'd find common ground."

"Do tell? Your odious partner in reporting is aware of your personal affairs? I didn't realize you'd bonded."

"Clearly, I should have just taken the bottle to bed." Aubrey sat upright and refilled her glass. "We most certainly have not *bonded*." She took an unladylike gulp, her foot brushing over the tin. "But . . . *odious* is a strong word. I'd say Levi is stubborn, direct . . . ambitious—which, in the right light, might mimic *odious*."

"In the right light, I wonder if he'd favor a young Gregory Peck or perhaps Rock Hudson? Though I didn't get a—"

"No, definitely Gregory Peck. Levi has a longtime girlfriend."

"Interesting. I've always found that term vexing. I hear *longtime girlfriend* as *not that interested*."

Aubrey laughed. "In Levi's case? Quite possible. I can't imagine him overly interested in anything but his work. Wait. How do you even know what my reporting partner looks like?"

"I Googled him." Aubrey's curiosity segued to a disapproving glance and Charley returned to her tea. "I needed to put a face to the person you've been chattering on about for weeks. Whatever his ticks, the man has moxie. He's certainly made his mark—editor of the *Brown Daily Herald*, MediaMatters City Desk Editor of the Year, Reporter of the Year—twice."

"My, did your homework, didn't you?" Aubrey's big toe continued to fondle the latch on the tin box. It squeaked like a tight gate as she raised and lowered it. "As noted, I'm sure Levi likes his 'longtime girlfriend,' but ambition is his true love."

"Seems to fit. But I also Googled him because I needed to know if Mr. St John's face matched the man in my dream."

Aubrey's alarmed look shot from the tin box to Charley. "Did it?"

"Is there a reason it should? Is there something about Mr. St John, other than his newspaper moxie, that you haven't shared?"

"Maybe." Aubrey took another gulp of wine. "Yes," she confessed. "There's someone—a young man—looking for Levi. But I can promise you one thing; I won't be brokering that exchange."

"For what reason, may I ask?"

"Uh, where to begin? For starters, Levi would be as open to the idea as he would be to"—she picked up her glass, sweeping it by Charley—"well, marrying his longtime girlfriend."

"Set in his ways, is he?"

"Imagine the conversation: 'Levi, FYI, for the past few weeks, someone's been hammering my brain on your behalf. Salt water and burnt wood, a bit of a pothead from what I can gather . . . There's this wicked itch of wool—and that damn watch of yours, the one with the leather strap. Does that hodgepodge mean anything to you, other than ideas about labeling me a mental patient?' No thank you."

"That's an intense host of signs, Aubrey. You don't think he'd recognize the specter attached to them?"

Aubrey thought for a moment. She sat upright and her knuckles knocked against the tin box. "I don't want to be that involved in Levi's life."

"Because?"

"Because Levi's here to do a job—that's all. Because I don't allow random entities to push me around my newsroom—there are rules." She set the glass down, a splash of cabernet spilling over. "Because I have enough going on with sizzling listing sheets and blistered fingers," she said, holding up her hand. "Not to mention a damn dead girl swirling two inches from my head."

"I thought you said the only Missy Flannigan progress you've made is the generic investigative sort."

"It has . . . it is."

"Then I don't see how she factors in . . ." Charley stopped, struggling to straighten her crooked posture. "You're considering it. You're thinking about making a concerted effort to connect with Missy Flannigan. How stunning."

"Would you be that shocked?"

"I've known you a while now, dear, and I dare say it would. Can I ask why? You've never been open to using your gift proactively. Spirits seek you out, not the other way around."

"I'm thinking out loud. It's just talk."

"Careful what you talk about, Aubrey. You never know who's listening." Her grandmother's blue-gray gaze focused on Aubrey's crescent-moon scar. In response, Aubrey pushed down her sleeve, covering her pockmarked arm. "If you were to take up ghost hunting, a murdered girl would not be the place I'd like to see you start."

"I agree—completely. Yet . . . I'm curious," she said. "When this began, I thought I'd be fighting a Missy Flannigan insurrection . . . resurrection. The fact that her presence is as cold as most of our leads . . . it's disconcerting, that's all."

"Ah, I see. Something like a genius stumped by the equation."

"I don't know about that, but if I did make an effort, it might speed things up. It could lend a hand in substantiating Dustin Byrd's guilt or Frank Delacort's innocence—or the other way around. We'd be done." Aubrey picked the wine glass up again. "And Levi could go back to where he belongs."

"Ah, so we've circled back to Mr. St John. Why is that?"

Aubrey offered a deadpan stare. "Because he's freaking me out a little, okay?" Once more, she touched the tin box. "Levi's intense physical presence, coupled with his reeking . . . noisy . . . itchy . . . *bossy* past."

"Oh my, that adamant of a specter, is it?"

"Enough so that Levi turned up in *your* dream. Charley, what . . . what, exactly, was Levi doing in the dream?"

"As long as you ask . . . He was sitting on an airplane, reading a newspaper. I couldn't tell you his destination, he was definitely *returning* . . . flying east. He was so focused . . . complex. Um, virile, if I had to pick a hands-on word."

"You don't." Aubrey bristled at the footnote. "But that does sound like the Levi in our newsroom."

"Of course, none of that was the curious part."

Aubrey heaved an irritated breath. "What else?"

"There was a boy seated next to him, eleven or so, I'd say. Handsome fellow in a Rhodes scholar sort of way. Too big for his age . . . glasses. He had a book in his hands—*Treasure Island*, but he wasn't reading it. More like he was clutching it, hanging on to it for dear life. The dream drifted into a feeling of horror, regret. The intense guilt emanating off the boy was powerful—I woke feeling terribly sorry for him. He was clearly . . . *tormented*. But Levi, he simply ignored the child."

"Again, sounds like Levi behavior—impassive, closed off. I'm surprised he didn't ask the flight attendant to change the kid's seat."

"Perhaps. If it hadn't been for one thing."

"What's that?"

"The child was also Levi."

Aubrey waved her hand in the air. "Enough! I don't want to hear anymore. I'm not playing psychic Sigmund Freud to Levi and his ghosts. It's not my problem." Aubrey grabbed a throw from the sofa back. She curled into a ball and covered herself. "And forget any ideas about me attempting to connect with Missy. I swear, I had everything under control. *This* was not my life. Not until a skeleton fell out of Dustin Byrd's basement wall and Levi showed up, upending everything. I don't need this right now—not with Owen."

"Life has a nasty habit of doing that, not going according to plan." Charley stared at Aubrey, her grandmotherly side showing. "Fine. We'll move on. Tell me about your standard reporter progress. You said something about solving a piece of the puzzle via Mr. Stallworth's daughter."

It would be like Charley to point out the living via the dead. "Kitty Stallworth," she said, perking up from her balled retreat. "It was marginally helpful—another chunk of blue sky in a million-piece puzzle. But I don't know that the information puts us any closer to knowing Missy Flannigan's whole story." Aubrey reached for her wine glass. But her line of vision stayed with the tin box.

"You don't take it out very often. I was surprised to see it here."

Aubrey's blistered, bandaged fingers circled the wine glass rim. "Not half as surprised as me," she said, staring at the box. "It . . . it was just there, on my mind all day. I guess that's why I got it out of my closet."

"Is it your plan to open it?"

She shrugged. She sat up, discarding the throw. Aubrey took a last sip of wine and flipped open the lid. Years later and she still imagined pink smoke rising or that fairy dust would twinkle through the air. More to the point, she thought a pop-up Pandora should simply explode in her face. Inside the box were mementos. The curious items left by the other side. Some screamed *ghost gifts*, but others were random keepsakes with which Aubrey could never make a solid connection to the dead. She began to sift through the tokens. A number of items looked as if they belonged in a scrapbook while others appeared destined for a trash can. Logically, it looked like a box of junk. "This one is still my standout *souvenir*." Aubrey held up a crinkled bag of Skittles, its sell-by date long past.

"Your first visual encounter. How could I forget? That boy, I think he nearly scared you to death."

"Almost," Aubrey said, recalling the ginger-haired boy at a rest stop in Jim Thorpe, Pennsylvania. "I was so naïve," she said, shaking her head.

"You were barely twelve."

"But I didn't even suspect. At that age—sometimes I didn't know if I was talking to the living or the dead. It took a while. Anyway, all I knew that morning was I'd spent three hard-earned dollars trying to get a box of Junior Mints out of a vending machine."

"Remind me. How many bags of Skittles came out?"

"Three. Eventually, I gave up, figured I was stuck with the Skittles—which I still hate. I will never forget how the air stopped me cold. We were surrounded by sweltering asphalt and exhaust fumes and all I smelled was that hospital. It was so dense and disinfected."

"Anybody else would have high-tailed it to safety, Aubrey. It took a lot of courage for you to follow it and approach that woman."

Did it?

At the time, Aubrey felt sure she'd only followed the young boy out of pure fear. A few feet beyond the vending machines, she spied a woman on a bench. She'd captured Aubrey's attention, not because she looked at the twelve-year-old Aubrey, but by the way the woman stared into the sky—like she wanted to climb inside. Other sounds muted. They were there but in the background. The closer she got to the woman the more vivid the specter became. "The boy . . . it was like being inside a bubble with him."

"What was his name?" Charley said, as if caught in the same memory.

"Matthew . . ."

"That's right. I'd dreamed of his mother a few nights before. Gingies, both of them."

"Mmm, redheads with freckles," Aubrey said. "Matthew was so adamant, standing on the bench, pushing on my shoulders. He kept telling me to sit and talk to her."

"And how wonderful that you did. What a gift you gave her, Aubrey."

She smiled, then didn't. "I never imagined handing someone a bag of candy could be so meaningful . . . the way she reacted."

"What better symbol could the boy have chosen than the treat his mother brought him in the hospital—his favorite candy."

"Lucky for him they had them in the vending machine."

"And the boy's message . . . I remember you telling me afterward how clear it'd come to you. That you'd actually spoken with him."

Aubrey nodded, repeating the message that went with the favorite tale. "'Matthew says he loves Skittles . . . and you. He says you shouldn't worry about him. Nothing hurts anymore.' And then he was gone. The woman . . . I never even asked her name." Aubrey's eyes were teary. She looked back at her box. "I wish I'd been more careful. I'd get so upset or startled by an encounter I'd just throw the ghost gift in the box and slam the lid. I should have written Matthew's mother's name on the Skittles bag, the date . . . some kind of record."

"It doesn't matter, Aubrey. The important thing is the gift you gave to her, the message from her son."

"I suppose," she said, shrugging. "That day at Jim Thorpe. It was the first time, you know?"

"First time what?"

"The first time I thought I could be something besides Heinz-Bodette's next big attraction." Aubrey put the Skittles back in the box. "Of course, not every encounter went as smoothly," she said, opening her hand to reveal two marbles.

Charley's expression soured. "George Everett—an ass who didn't deserve the privilege of your gift."

"In George's defense, I wasn't terribly composed about the whole thing." She hesitated, the marbles rolling around her hand. "I get it. Lots of people aren't wired that way."

"Like your Mr. St John?"

"He's not . . . I was thinking about Owen."

"Owen is disturbed by it, Aubrey. I don't know that he'll ever understand. Deep inside, you know it's the reason you never told him. Brilliant as Owen may be, he doesn't possess that kind of . . . *moxie.*" Aubrey's hand shot up in a defensive gesture, and Charley pursed her lips tight. "Moving right along . . . What brings the box to the table? Perhaps a confession from Missy's killer?"

"I wish," Aubrey said. She plucked more random items from the tin treasure chest. Onto the coffee table, Aubrey laid a teething ring and matchbooks, coins from Turkey and a thimble. Next to them she placed an envelope. Inside were the violet-colored flowers that had wilted in Aubrey's hand. She remembered them turning up at the duck-shooting booth that she'd worked with Yvette late one season. There was also a shiny gold key, a glass butterfly, and a plastic bag full of beach sand. While these last items were undoubtedly ghost gifts, Aubrey never could connect them to anything but a curious moment in time. Staring, she found herself drawn to the sand. Unlike the other items, which had been delivered to her, Aubrey had gathered the sand herself. It made it different than the rest of the ghost gifts, perhaps less meaningful. Still, she picked up the plastic bag, shifting its weight like a Slinky, one hand to the other.

"Aubrey? Is there some . . . Is the sand significant? If I recall, it came from our mid-season break, after our Connecticut-Rhode Island stops."

"I think that's where I got it. Mystic, maybe?" She shook her head. With so much travel, physical and metaphysical—like Matthew's Skittles—Aubrey wished she'd better labeled her ghost gifts. Levi would be appalled by her slipshod filing. "I was what? Maybe fifteen?"

"No, sixteen, I believe. And it wasn't Mystic," Charley said. "Not that summer. They had a terrible jellyfish infestation, so we went up the coast a bit."

She looked at Charley. "You're right. I'd forgotten that. What was the name of the beach?"

"Oh my, it was outside Old Saybrook. I remember because it's where Katharine Hepburn lived. I thought it might be fun to look her up! You'd disagreed—profusely." She smiled, pointing a crooked finger at her granddaughter. "Rocky Neck, that's where we were."

Aubrey nodded. "Rocky Neck. I didn't remember that. I should have marked the bag . . . and the flowers," she said, touching the envelope. "My teenage years . . . Most of the time I was just trying to keep from throwing up."

"True," Charley said.

"But now that you say it, the sand did come from Rocky Neck. I don't know if it's our whirlwind travels or my whirlwind encounters, but I don't recall what motivated me to gather it."

"Rocky Neck is only a few hours from Surrey. Is it possible that the sand connects to Missy Flannigan?"

Aubrey wanted it to connect; she held tight to the bag. Moments later she felt nothing but frustration. "If it does, I have no idea how."

"Give it time, dear. You never know how or when something will clarify." Charley rose from her chair, heading to bed. As she did, Aubrey pulled the coarse twine that secured the bag. She stuck her hand inside and bit down on a breathy gasp. Charley didn't hear, motoring up the stairway. The theory felt cold, but the sand filtering through Aubrey's fingers was warm. It felt as if the grains had been scooped seconds ago from beneath a blazing summer sun.

CHAPTER
FIFTEEN

Thoughts stirred like a potion in Aubrey's head. She'd tugged on a nightgown and brushed her teeth, all the while unable to escape the bag of sand. Its meaning was no longer abstract, but confusing and present. How did a bag of sand connect to Missy Flannigan? It was utterly removed from any theories they'd formulated. There was Missy in her paid-in-cash convertible. Missy the college co-ed. They knew of a benevolent Missy, the girl who'd offered Frank Delacort shelter and volunteered at Surrey town activities. Nowhere was there speculation about Missy and the beach. After going to bed, Aubrey tossed and turned until tomorrow became today, until she'd concocted a scenario by which Dustin Byrd dragged Missy over state lines and to the beach, shooting her before drowning her. Or perhaps Nancy Grace was correct, and it was Frank Delacort who'd carried out the devious plot. Hours later, Aubrey sat upright, the antique bed squeaking as she hurled a pillow at the wall. It collided with her earring tree. The tinkle of metal was the only sound that resonated as jewelry scattered across the hardwood floor. "Damn it," she said, flopping flat onto the mattress.

Frustrated and out of reasonable ideas, Aubrey lay awake for a while longer. Her last thoughts were of Levi. How he'd kept his conversation with Tom Flannigan to himself, not able to make sense or use of the information. She'd do the same. The sand was like that, something that had meaning but didn't fit. A weary breath escaped her lips and Aubrey murmured sleepily, "Sand in a bag . . . Sand from Rocky Neck . . . Sand doesn't have a damn thing to do with Missy Flannigan . . . But sand and Levi . . . Levi grew up near Rocky Neck . . ." A bright sun rose over the fact as the sound of seagulls circled. It pulled and churned until a whirlpool surrounded Aubrey, its strength drawing her inward. She couldn't get out; she couldn't fight it. Her bedroom seemed to fill with salt air and smoke. In the distance she was aware of a lifeguard—a whistle around his neck, light glinting off his watch. His hair, she thought, was blond and buzzed. She might be right or wrong about these tangibles. The beach was too sunny and distant to know for certain. But as Aubrey drifted to sleep, a memory came wrapped in a dream. She saw a young man, a lifeguard. He appeared, so it seemed, dead on arrival.

◆ ◆ ◆

Cone-shaped light stretched east, blanketing Rocky Neck beach. The Heinz-Bodette Troupe was on a July retreat, a respite from routine heat and grind. Aubrey had risen late, indulging in the nuances of being sixteen—a motel room and cable TV. Now she walked along the beach, looking for her grandmother. Shuffling through the sand, Aubrey appreciated her growing ability to control random spirits. She immersed herself in an inventory of physical elements, a device she'd nearly perfected. Real beach-goers came with endless sights and smells, particularly noise, the squawk of circling waterfowl aiding her efforts. The listing of tangible things enhanced normalcy. It made it safe to be there. Ordinary mothers tended to children while fathers rammed umbrellas into sandy earth. Breathing in sticky salt air, Aubrey continued to tally earthly items, separating the living from the dead.

She paused, mentally sorting one family's beach kit: towels, beach balls, buckets, shovels, Cheese Nips, water wings, maybe peanut butter sandwiches for lunch. She listened to the impatient mother who gave directions about not drowning. Three . . . no, four boys. The oldest wasn't close to Aubrey's age. The father buried a cigarette butt into the sand and moved on to man things, tuning his radio to all-day sports talk and camouflaging his cooler cans of Bud Light. The mother basted her four little ducklings with sunscreen so they might brown and not burn. The second to the youngest, maybe three years old, stood out from his brothers. He possessed a greater presence and Aubrey was transfixed. She shook her head, forcing her attention away. After sunscreening the infant, the mother plunked the slimy baby near the father. He mumbled something about keeping an eye on that one.

Poised at the narrow tip, Aubrey looked into the widening cone of brightness; the crowds were growing thick. She spotted Charley. Her grandmother was hard to miss in a flamingo-colored bathing suit. Aubrey glanced back at the family. The burdened mother, fringe father, and loud boys moved on with their beach day activities. The oldest one was deep into directing the "pirates" with orders about castle building and treasure hunting. "No prisoners, aye? Just cut their throats when you spy 'em, matey!" His brothers growled spit-and-vinegar replies. They pushed past Aubrey, who murmured, "Reckless . . ." Instinct hummed. She should keep an eye on the boys, especially the one with personality. But Aubrey didn't make an effort. Instead, she trudged deeper into the light.

"Here you are!" Charley's gregarious voice jumped out as always. "Thought maybe a third day with an old fat woman and her leathery tan was too much for you!"

Aubrey dropped her tote onto the blanket. "Charley, your tan is not leathery, it's bronze and warm."

"So's a good saddle," she said, patting the chair next to hers. "Were you taking in the sights?"

"Just getting my bearings . . ."

Charley nodded, her silver hair bobbing at her shoulders. "Ah, object counting." She twisted as best she could, glancing at Aubrey. "All's clear, I take it?"

Dropping to her knees, Aubrey didn't reply. Instead, she dug through the beach bag for sunscreen. "Here, put this on."

"Oh, go away with that stuff. I may take a swim later. In all probability that will result in a stroke or shark attack. Then it's just a waste of sunscreen."

"Charley, don't be difficult." But as she smeared a greasy handful onto her grandmother's back, Aubrey's gaze hooked on to the horizon. For a second, it was all she saw—the luring sparkle of water, brighter than it should be. Her belly gurgled, cinching to a cramp. Aubrey took a deep breath and tried to relax as nothing but intense salt air hit her lungs.

"Aubrey . . . you didn't answer me." Charley gripped the arms of her beach chair, forcing her body harder toward her granddaughter.

From the corner of her eye, Aubrey saw her grandmother's painful turn. Her expression collapsed the looming sense of the surreal. "I'm fine," she said, grasping on to her grandmother's shoulders "I'm fine," she repeated as Charley faced forward.

"If you're sure . . ." Her grandmother opened a magazine and Aubrey put the sunscreen away, not bothering to apply any to herself. She wasn't sure how much time had passed—moments, maybe minutes—when the poke of a magazine met with her knee. "Here . . . they had a new Time *at the newsstand. I bought the latest* Glamour *too. If you don't want it, Yvette will flip through and . . ." The magazine nudged Aubrey again; then it dropped onto the blanket. In one concentrated effort, Charley heaved herself up from the chair. She turned her back to the ocean and faced Aubrey. The sudden movement, which defied the woman's size and arthritic bones, drew Aubrey's attention. "What do you see?"*

"A lifeguard . . ."

Charley turned toward the ocean. She shielded her eyes with her hand, then scanned the beach. "Me too . . . Blue shorts and swimsuits, one man, two girls . . . women, whistles around their necks."

Aubrey stood and sweat trickled down the back of her legs. A wave of nausea rolled through her stomach. She swallowed, tasting a mouthful of salt water, a hint of alcohol. "No, two girls . . . and two men. But one is wearing orange shorts—he's different. He's been here a while, watching over the crowds . . . He's an excellent swimmer." The thought had filtered into her head and out of her mouth—not an observation but a fact she suddenly knew. "Athletic . . . so very determined . . . and . . ." she said, looking at Charley. "Utterly dead."

Aubrey closed her eyes for a moment. She opened them, concentrating on tangible items: umbrellas, volleyballs, coolers, books, people layered like seals . . . An airplane flew overhead. The crowd and Aubrey looked up. A banner trailing behind: "Brewsters, half-price drinks, shrimp by the pound, $4.99 before 5 p.m." The plane pushed on and Aubrey realized her mistake. She was left with nothing but empty blue sky. The blank space allowed enough room for the singular lifeguard—the one in the orange shorts—to push his way in. "Damn it . . ." she said, heaving a breath. His energy connected with hers, adamant and unyielding.

"We'll go," Charley said. "That's enough beach time . . ."

She shook her head. "He's so insistent. He's been waiting so long . . ."

"Let him wait a little longer. Give it a few years; surely another medium will be along." Charley looked toward a man she could not see. "Tell him you're on vacation."

Aubrey squinted, hearing beach noises that had turned tinny. He'd won, nodding in Aubrey's direction. "I can't," she said, feeling oddly responsive. "It has to be me."

"Aubrey?" It was a struggle to look at Charley. "You don't have to do this."

"I think I do."

Moving toward the lifeguard's growing presence, Charley's voice waned, saying, "I'll be right here . . . watching . . ."

Aubrey slogged forward, the solid edges of beach paraphernalia and people dimming. It was like looking through dark sunglasses at everything but the lifeguard. There was a rush, the topsy-turvy sense of being turned upside down in that saltwater sea. A few yards away, the lifeguard appeared glassy against the mottled glint of ocean, neither here nor there—part of the sunlight, part of the earth. A flotation device rested around his shoulders, a whistle on his neck. On his wrist was a leather-banded watch. His swim trunks, she guessed, were an older version of the lifeguarding uniform for Rocky Neck—this was definitely his beach. Aubrey gave in to the feathery feeling unearthing her. "Shit," she muttered as he smiled.

As eerie and dead as the lifeguard was, Aubrey felt his heart flutter; he was so anxious to communicate. Cool little waves washed over her toes, and Aubrey curled them into muddy silt. It figured. There was nothing solid here to hang on to. The smell of sea air mixed with smoky scents, marijuana and burning wood. She tasted booze. She didn't know what to make of any of it. Like the napalm that had wafted off George Everett's Roy, smells and tastes often played an undefined role. On the upside, at least vomiting wasn't imminent. Yes, she was better at this than a few years ago, and hopeful that she could steer the exchange.

"Hello," he said. Ordinary etiquette forced Aubrey to make eye contact. "Finally. I've been waiting for days . . . longer, I think."

Aubrey motioned at the horizon, forcing her glance to follow. "From what I can gather, it's all about timing. What do you want?" she said, practicing the art of control.

"At first I was confused. I thought it was your grandmother."

"It's not. Not like me. Sometimes she dreams of people . . . family members, loved ones."

"I can imagine. She's very spiritual. There's a strong energy—but it's not like yours. I think it was her swimsuit. The pink. Color, it's like a phosphorous trail."

"*I know. Hence the dark swim suit.*" *Aubrey grazed her hand down her long frame and dull navy suit.*

"*But color would make it so much easier to find you.*"

"*And I would want to make it easier because . . .*" *Aubrey rolled her eyes.* "*Never mind. Can we cut to the chase? What is it you need? Did you have a fight with your girlfriend, leave things unsaid?*" *Aubrey looked over her shoulder. It could be that one of the giggling, bikini-clad girls behind her belonged to him. She supposed he was handsome enough, with his shiny lifeguard muscles, eyes the color of fallen sky.*

"*What's the hurry?*" *He smiled, his aura more California surfer, less specter—though Aubrey had the distinct impression he'd been in his current state a while. The sun sparkled off him, matching the twinkle of ocean. It made for a seamless blend.* "*Why are you so determined to avoid me? I've watched you count things for days. Tasks won't help. You know you can't ever stop it.*"

His demeanor was frustrating. Usually spirits were more anxious to deliver their message. This one was perplexing, like he had all the time in the world—on the other hand, maybe he did. "*Fine. So now that you have my attention . . .*"

"*Brody,*" *he said.* "*My name's Brody.*"

"*Brody,*" *she repeated. Aubrey glanced over her shoulder, curious if his family was nearby—a mother, maybe a sister.*

"*I'm going to West Point in the fall.*"

Aubrey smirked and her gaze dropped to her muddy toes. A muddled past, present, and future was telltale. They often confused time. Some apparitions had no earthly idea where they belonged. "*Quite an accomplishment, West Point,*" *she said, playing along.*

"*Yeah, you'd think that.*"

"*You don't want to go.*" *Aubrey was struck by the disconnect, as his easygoing manner seemed naturally opposed to marching and weapons.*

Brody shrugged, his square chin bucking up toward the deep sea. "*I'm used to it. I went to Valley Forge Military Prep. I hated it, but Pa, he expects . . . I can't disappoint him.*"

The smell of smoldering wood overtook the salty sea. Then a blast of heat hit her that had nothing to do with the sun—it was more like a roaring fire. "Even if that's not what you want?"

"Doesn't matter what I want. You know how parents are—fathers in particular."

"Not really. Both mine are gone."

"My mother's dead. It was Pa and me until he remarried."

"Wicked stepmother?" *Perhaps this was the problem. Clearly, no blood relative was present, and Aubrey now assumed it reasonable to rule out a girlfriend.*

"J.C.? That's what I call her . . . Jacqueline Claire. Nah," *he said shaking his head.* "She's cool. Squirrely but cool. Blond, curvy, tall, big boobs." *He laughed.* "She used to be a Playboy Bunny." *Aubrey shrugged. When you lived in a carnival, Playboy Bunny didn't seem so off the grid.* "J.C. and Pa, it went like this: USO tours London. Military hero attempts to reinvent life." *His face sobered.* "The only thing they invented was my brother. I . . . I haven't seen him in a long time, my brother . . ." *As he spoke his frame dimmed, like a bulb on the fritz.*

"A brother?"

"Half-brother," *he said, brightening—literally.* "We're flying out to California to visit J.C. Pa doesn't trust her, not after last summer."

"What happened last summer?"

"My brother almost drowned. The gardener pulled him out of the pool. Pa went nuts. But it wasn't all J.C.'s fault. My brother told me he'd gotten bored, decided to dive for pennies . . . But kids do stupid stuff, right? Pa says it's a good idea if I tag along before . . . I go."

"To West Point?" *He didn't respond but waded farther into the water. With her arms crossed, Aubrey traced her long toes through fine sand and tiny shells.* "So it's nice chatting, but there must be a reason you dropped in on my seaside visit?"

"No," *he said, smiling.* "There's a reason you dropped in on mine."

"Like what?"

His appearance grew more vague. "If only you didn't fight it so hard . . ."

Aubrey looked directly at him. "Thanks, but I don't need advice from you, ghost. You worry about your side of things. I'll take care of mine."

"Okay, but it's your own fault. Had you responded sooner, there'd be more time. As it is," he said, "you'll have to run."

"To what? Where?" she said, her head whipping from side to side.

"To the family. The one with the boys. Earlier, you ignored your instinct to help. You shouldn't have."

With a clear direction in mind, Aubrey turned hard to the west. "The baby?"

"The toddler. The older brother, he's not paying attention. Frankly, he's a little reckless."

"That's what I said! But when?"

He looked at his leather-banded watch, the sun beaming off the rim—like it was real. "Soon . . . High tide, it can catch you off guard here . . . One minute it's a pond, and the next . . ."

"The tide?" she said. A jogger veered wide, staring at Aubrey. She started toward the tower chair, but the lifeguard's warning and a stronger intuition stopped her. She pivoted in the muddy shore. "Wait! I don't understand. You don't know those people. You're not here because of them!"

The lifeguard's toned body stood firm—as if he had mass. Larger waves crashed around him, creating the illusion of substance. "Geez, I am a life-guard. This is my stretch to patrol. And you're not being very grateful. I went out of my way to show up, help you out."

"Help me?"

"Think how awful you'd feel if that kid drowned. Stop ignoring your instincts. Keep that in mind—because now, you owe me." She couldn't tell if he was joking. Just what she needed, a specter with a sense of humor. "You said it yourself, timing is everything. He'd never listen right now. He's got too much of Pa in him. But next time . . ."

She sloshed backward in the surf. Aubrey turned toward the family. Though the matter was urgent, Aubrey spun back once more. "Next time?" she said. This was about closure. Specters didn't pencil in return engagements.

"Next time . . ." he said. The smell of fire was doused by salt-covered air. The incoming swell was harsher. It crashed and claimed him like a bubble. Aubrey was left with no choice but to take off running, full charge, down the beach.

CHAPTER SIXTEEN

Present Day

Aubrey sat up sharply, panting and squinting into darkness. Her heart fluttered like a moth trapped in light. At three a.m., caught in a feverish sweat and tide of nausea, most people would have called a doctor. In her case, medicinal intervention was moot. She stumbled to the bathroom in search of a cool cloth. Aubrey gripped the porcelain sink and closed her eyes, aiming for deep gulps of air. The vision had left her with memories of a younger Aubrey, blindsiding her. It had been some time since the presence of the dead felt so overwhelming.

Like the old days, she lost the battle and heaved over the toilet. Aubrey crumpled onto the tile floor, feeling the grouted seams and cold penetrate her knees as she retched again. She flushed and wadded up some toilet paper to wipe her watery mouth. By the time she righted the queasy feeling, Charley was in the doorway. "Something you ate?" she asked. Aubrey shook her head and slumped onto her rear end, the edge of the commode lending support. "See someone you recognize?" She nodded hard, the nausea pulsing again.

"The sand . . ." Aubrey swiped her hand across her mouth.

"From Rocky Neck."

"It belongs to a lifeguard."

"And the lifeguard, does he belong to Missy Flannigan?"

"No," she said, spitting into the toilet. She peered up at her grandmother. "He belongs to Levi. It's his brother."

They talked for a few minutes before Aubrey insisted that Charley go back to bed. There was nothing she could do. A short time later, shivering from the sweat and implication, Aubrey retrieved the tin box from the living room. She climbed the stairs and got back into bed, but she didn't open the box's lid. What for? She'd gotten the message. The question was what to do about it. Aubrey might have endured a month's worth of fever and nausea for a portal to Missy Flannigan. Having to invest that much of herself in Levi's ghost wasn't as welcome. Yet, between the adamant dream and a persistent presence, she saw no choice.

Shortly before four a.m. she settled on a plan—direct and simple. Aubrey would start at the beginning, explaining her box of ghost gifts. From there, Levi could take it or leave it. She even went as far as to text him:

4:08 Can you come by my house in the a.m.? Need to tell you something.

Levi texted back almost immediately, and Aubrey muttered, "Jesus, do you ever sleep?"

4:10 What's up?

4:12: Long story. Needs to be in person.

4:13: Something about Missy?

Aubrey thought for a moment. Missy might very well be the only temptation to which he'd respond. No, even a white lie was not the way to win Levi's confidence.

4:16: Not exactly. But important. Will you?

Several unanswered minutes went by and Aubrey did wonder, in a four a.m. sort of way, what Levi was doing.

4:27: OK. Beth's got a conference call at 8. Is 7:30 good?

4:29: Sure.

She thought a moment longer. Curiosity and the need for a little more clarity about Levi prodded one more text.

4:30: You never said, what does Bethany do?

4:31: Works in publishing, acquisitions editor. Why?

4:32: No reason. Just wondering . . .

She didn't anticipate another text from Levi and was surprised to see one more:

4:34: I'll bring coffee. See you then.

Aubrey laid the tin box beside her bed. In a few hours, all would be resolved. Levi could connect with his brother—or not—and they could move on with what mattered. Aubrey reached over and stroked the tin lid like she would a house cat. She closed her eyes. Even a little sleep would be a good thing. But her eyes felt spring-loaded, popping open. Who was she kidding? Aubrey had thought it herself earlier. Levi wouldn't see anything more than a box of junk. She sat back up. He'd insist she was certifiable. The reporter credibility she'd earned would be ruined. He wouldn't want her anywhere near the Missy Flannigan story. It also wouldn't satisfy Brody, who she suspected would not be dismissed. No specter had ever visited twice, and Brody had waited years. Clearly, tenacity was a St John family trait—like red hair, or that damn dimple. Neither brother would vacate Surrey or Aubrey's life until they got what they'd come for. Aubrey abandoned the box and picked up her phone. She'd cancel.

While clicking through her messages, she saw earlier texts from Marian Sloane. They were pleas, really, almost begging Aubrey to find a spot on the schedule for her high-end reproduction on Acorn Circle. Aubrey's thumb rolled over her bandaged fingertips. Singed skin. It was a sure sign of her neglected home portrait features and the specters that went with them. She chewed on her bottom lip, wondering if she might kill two ghosts with one stone. It just might work. Shortly before five, Aubrey texted Marian.

4:50: Good news. I've had some space free up. Let me know if 8:30 will work for a tour.

Apparently, realtors and ambitious newsmen were primed and ready before the crack of dawn. Marian also replied immediately. Eight thirty would be just perfect. "All right, Levi," Aubrey said while texting confirmation to Marian, "you're a 'show me' kind of guy. So that's what we're going to do. Come for a ride with me. First I'll show you. Then I'll tell you."

◆　◆　◆

Before seven thirty Aubrey was pacing her living room, showered, dressed, and having already shared her plan with Charley. Her grandmother sat in the dining room, which was more of an alcove. She ate grapefruit and toast while watching her granddaughter stride back and forth. "Aubrey, have you factored in the time it will take to explain the trench you're standing in?"

Aubrey stopped, the long, bright red sweater she wore swinging like a cape. "What?"

"You've about worn a hole in that floor. Why don't you sit, have a cup of tea?"

"No, then I'll just have to pee. Besides," she said, pacing again, "Levi said he's bringing coffee."

"You don't drink coffee."

"I know," she said, shrugging. "That's mostly what I'm worried about." They traded wry glances, Aubrey veering off course enough to glance out the living room window.

"And it's your belief that the spirit on Acorn Circle will be open to putting on a convincing show for Levi? It's a risk, wouldn't you say?"

Aubrey considered the heat emanating from the listing sheet, the subliminal message in Marian's voicemails. "Normally, yes. But with the vibe I'm getting off this house, I don't think Helen Keller would miss it.

It should be obvious enough to make my point, start a conversation." She peeked around the curtain again. "Damn. He's here."

"I must have misunderstood. I thought that was the point." Another droll glance passed between them, Charley's morphing into a worried gaze. "Aubrey, you don't have to do this. If there's no chance he's going to be open to it, I don't see the necessity in subjecting yourself. Whatever the brother may want, you have no idea about Levi's past. What you might be dredging up."

"True. It could be my gift is the far lesser thing Levi has to face today."

Charley secured a wedge of grapefruit, though her spoon stopped midair. "Regardless, keep in mind that your well-being is my main concern. You don't owe Levi anything." The doorbell rang and Aubrey sighed in Charley's direction.

"No, apparently I owe his brother." At the door, she hesitated. Never once had Aubrey set out to prove her gift. "Nothing like starting with a Herculean challenge." She swung the door wide. "Hi," she said too cheerily.

"Uh, hi." A freshly shaven Levi, carrying a tray of coffee cups, opened the craftsman's wooden screened door. Aubrey had been certain a sea-soaked flood of his brother would arrive with him, but there was nothing. "I brought . . ."

"Coffee," she said as he made his way into the living room. "Levi, this is . . ."

"Charley," he said, nodding. "El—your granddaughter's mentioned you."

"You as well. How fascinating . . . You're exactly as I pictured."

"Am I?" he said. "I brought an extra coffee in case . . ."

"How very thoughtful. Aubrey didn't mention that."

Aubrey flashed a terse smile at Charley. "Levi's work ethic tends to overshadow his social graces," she said, taking the cardboard tray. "But thanks. This was . . . *thoughtful.*"

"Oh, right," he said, staring at the cups. "You don't drink coffee."

"It won't go to waste. Charley's good for several cups." That was where the conversation dead ended, and Aubrey watched as Levi took a short turn around the living room.

"So, this is home." He looked at Charley. "I was having a little trouble picturing it."

"Owen has a loft in Boston," Aubrey said. "We lived there before buying this. We never sold it before he . . ." Aubrey shut up. "I've lived here for a while now."

Charley made a difficult rise from the table, grasping her walker and placing one of the cups in an attached holder. Shuffling across the hardwoods, she stopped. She reached out, touching Levi's arm. "I could see where you'd have trouble picturing the house. That's the thing about my granddaughter. She doesn't fit into a set mold. You'd do well to keep that in mind." She patted his arm as if they were old friends, then shifted her grip onto Aubrey. "Are you sure, dear?"

"I don't see another way."

"Well, good luck to both of you. Yvette phoned. Said she'd like to come for a visit. I believe I'll call her, set a date. It was lovely seeing you again, Levi."

"Again?" he said to Aubrey, as Charley exited via her chair lift.

"Uh, the arthritis. She gets confused now and again."

"What does arth—Never mind." He busied himself with the coffee and Aubrey searched vainly for a foothold. "Ellis, is something wrong? You look tired . . . paler than usual."

"Thanks. I didn't sleep much. What I have to say, it kind of kept me up." His tall frame loomed, the angles of Levi's face growing more perplexed. "Did you have a nice evening?" she asked.

"What?"

"Your date . . . with Bethany. Your longtime girlfriend, right? That's what you said . . . what I'd heard around the office. Not that I was prying, just gossip, you know?"

"Actually, it wasn't all that great. It's, uh . . . it's become more of an on again, off again thing."

"On again, off again? In what way?"

He sighed; she waited. "We met a few years ago when I was on assignment in New York. Last winter Bethany took a job abroad with her publishing house. She . . . we ended things—something about me not making our relationship a priority. Except for returning a Brooks Brothers sweater, things seemed . . . *over*. Then she came back, literally showed up at my door in Hartford while I was packing to come here. Beth said she wanted to try . . ." A breath huffed in and out of him. "Ellis, is my personal life the reason you summoned me, because—"

"I was just making conversation."

"I thought that's why I was here, because there was a point to a conversation."

"There is. I'm getting to it," she said, glancing at the mantel clock. "It's not that simple."

He also looked at the fireplace. "Your parents?" he said, pointing at the double frame photos.

"Yes, Peter and Ena Ellis, a few years before they died."

"Except for the eyes, you favor your mother—the bone structure," he said, pressing his glasses tighter to his face.

"Bet you don't favor yours at all," she said, recalling Brody's description. At four a.m. the contrast between Levi and his mother hadn't registered. Now, the Playboy Bunny thing did seem like a wildly curious talking point.

"Not even a remote resemblance." Levi checked his watch—Brody's watch—against the clock on the mantel. "Runs slow sometimes."

It was a good opening for a leading question. But the eerie absence of Brody St John stopped her and Aubrey stuck to her house plan. "We have an appointment shortly . . . at a house, one of my home portrait properties."

"Ellis, I don't really have time for house hunting. If we could, I'd rather get to the reason you asked me here."

She patted at the air between them. "Levi, if you could just give me some leeway."

He nodded, but she knew it was under duress. "I heard that Delacort's lawyer is pushing for his conviction to be overturned. If the DA wants to move forward with a case against Byrd, something like that will have to happen first. I was watching the wires all night. That's the trend."

"Funny, huh? How *wire* translates into *Twitter* nowadays."

"I meant wire—well, Internet. AP got a leak out of the DA's office—that's what I was reading when I saw your text this morning." She nodded at the information. "I'm also hopeful a military connection that my father has comes through."

"Comes through?" Aubrey said, hearing vernacular that fit more comfortably in her world.

"Yes, he's made plenty of contacts over the years, high ranking in most instances. If it pans out, we may shed some light on Delacort's classified service record."

"I see," she said, hands wringing.

"With all that in play, it's going to be a busy day." Levi set his coffee on the table. "So come on, Ellis. What's going on? You're acting quirkier than usual. You're not ill, are you?" She shook her head. "Is it something more . . . *personal?*"

Aubrey's mouth opened and closed. The conversation was going in every direction but the intended one. "Levi, come for a ride with me. Either this will all make sense, or by lunchtime you'll be insisting Malcolm replace me with Bebe." Aubrey grabbed her satchel and headed for the door.

"Doubtful. Not even you could drive me to—"

As Aubrey opened the door she shuffled backward, shuffling right onto Levi's feet. "Owen! What in the world . . ." She glanced over her shoulder. A single page of the *Surrey City Press* wouldn't fit between herself and Levi. "Sorry." She said, inching forward and focusing on Owen.

The last time she'd seen her almost ex-husband, he'd been wearing his go-to-court clothes, which were vastly different from his everyday look: jeans and a leather jacket, fists punched into the pockets. Rock musician, biker, undercover cop, guy chased by undercover cop—at a glance, anything seemed more plausible than computer genius. She blinked at his everyday appearance, the one to which she'd been so drawn. "You told me you were stuck in New York for a few more days."

"I was . . . I am," Owen said. He pulled sunglasses from his face, revealing pale-blue irises. He smiled. "Maybe Steve Jobs would have been less of a jolt."

"Today, of all days . . . maybe. But I'm just surprised. That's all."

"There's a systems glitch with a Boston client. It requires an onsite fix. Nicole couldn't handle it." Owen's curious look shifted to Levi. "Of course, I didn't think I'd be the one in for a surprise—particularly pre-breakfast."

"What?" Aubrey glanced over her shoulder at Levi, who remained inside the house, holding the screen door open. "No. This isn't what it looks . . . You don't understand." Aubrey stepped out onto the porch.

"Ellis," Levi said, "if you need to catch up here, I can always head to the office."

Her gaze jerked between the two men. "Uh, no. That won't work. It's fine. Owen, this is Levi St John. I've mentioned him. We're working together on the Missy Flannigan story. He just got here . . . we were just leaving."

"Really?"

"Really," Levi said, extending his hand.

Owen's lanky frame stood stiffly, fists still punched in his pockets. "Kind of early for newspaper business, isn't it?"

Levi withdrew the greeting and Aubrey felt his tenacity dig in. "Guess you're unaware. News never sleeps."

"Guess I'll have to keep that in mind when I move back into my house." Owen gestured toward the living room. "Anyway, Aubrey, the tech support staff I'm meeting isn't in for a few hours. I was hoping we could grab breakfast, talk. I have to go back to New York tonight." His gaze moved to Levi. "But I shouldn't be more than another day or two."

Aubrey held tighter to her satchel; inside was a folder, the heat of the Acorn Circle listing sheet seeping through. "I would love to . . . really. But I have more than a few"—she glanced fast at Levi—"urgent matters to take care of this morning."

Owen glanced over Aubrey's long red sweater. He stepped back. "Is it, um . . . Sorry. I should have called. Old husband habit," he said to Levi. "You know how that goes."

"Not so much."

"Whatever. I know you're busy with the Missy Flannigan story. I just thought we could . . . We have a lot to talk about."

"We do," Aubrey said, smiling. She pointed over her shoulder. "Did you want to wait here until your meeting?"

Owen leaned, peering inside. "Charley still bunking here?"

"Of course . . . yes. You know she moved in after—"

"Thanks, I'm cool—especially if you're not here. I have to swing by the loft quick anyway. I'll call you later." He ducked in fast, kissing her on the cheek. "I'm meeting with a realtor, putting it on the market."

"Are you?"

"Again, Ellis," Levi said, interrupting, "I can just catch you—"

"No, it's fine," she said, her smile floating to Levi. "I'm coming."

They parted ways on the porch, Levi and Aubrey a few steps ahead. As Owen turned for his car, Levi bumped her shoulder. "Sounds like Owen doesn't relish the idea of spending time in his living room alone with your grandmother."

"Different tastes in furniture," she said, stepping in front of him. "Get the car, Levi. I'll drive."

CHAPTER
SEVENTEEN

A PowerPoint would have been the efficient way to go, a bulleted, dia-gramed presentation of the remarkable life of Aubrey Ellis. Levi could take notes, ask questions. Ideally, there would be an analytical intellec-tual discussion phase. He could start a file. In lieu of that option, and since they were short on time, Aubrey went with the next best thing. She began by asking Levi to hang on to the folder that held Marian Sloane's listing sheet. Then she treaded carefully, prefacing what, besides high-end amenities, the house on Acorn Circle might offer. "Levi," she said as they drove. "Do you remember me asking you if you believed in anything spiritual, something other than organized religion, more than wishful thinking?"

"At the Chinese restaurant."

"That's right. You said you don't believe in faith or fate; that the world runs on random chance."

In her peripheral glance, she saw Levi look toward her. "When you say it like that it does make me sound . . . unyielding."

"A perfect example. Overall, *unyielding* might not be the best word choice, right? Not the most accurate portrayal of you," she said, navigating the curve in the road and the conversation.

"Depends on the topic, I suppose."

"Okay. But it could be *shortsighted*, like describing my home portrait features as 'house porn.'"

Levi looked out the window, watching suburbia dwindle, replaced by acreage and custom homes. He turned toward her. "Ellis, is this payback for trash talking your home portrait pieces? Because I thought I'd apologized . . . that we'd gotten past it. To be honest, I thought we were . . ."

"We're what?"

He hesitated. "That we're working well together, making a solid team . . . reporting team."

"I'd have to agree," she said, surprised by her own conclusion. "And no, that's not what this is about. I was just asking if you really do see life as random, nothing but cause and effect."

"I'm not sure what you're driving at. Do you want to know if I think life is influenced by more than what we can see?"

"Yes. That's exactly what I'm asking. Is there any circumstance where you might consider the idea?" Aubrey turned onto Acorn Circle then followed a circular drive until it met with an opulent house. She thrust the car into park and twisted toward him. "Would it sway you if there were some level of proof?"

His fingers thrummed the folder. "Ellis, I'm not really up for a philosophical debate." Levi tipped his head toward the sun and house, an overdone colonial, flanked by huge columns and a rotunda entrance. "I certainly have no idea what I'm doing here—at Tara," he said, hoisting his hand toward the property. "But if there's breaking Delacort news, or any other significant event, and I miss it because—"

"Levi," she said, loud enough to shut him up. "The timing here is not perfect. I also realize what I'm about to say is going to sound . . . *out there*, to you in particular. So I need to know what I'm up against.

If there's anything inside you that's open to the idea of more . . . more than just *us*," she said, her hand circling the confines of the car.

"Like aliens?" he said, his expression going straight to annoyed.

Aubrey took a deep breath. "I was thinking more about spirits, apparitions . . . specters."

"Ghosts?"

"Yes," she said, cutting the engine. "Do you think that's possible?"

He jerked back in his seat. "You're asking if I—"

"Yes, I'm asking if you think it's possible. After we die, can a part of the soul remain here? Or is it unequivocally ashes to ashes, dust to dust? Lights out, game over."

His fingers slid up under the frame of his glasses, rubbing hard. "Figures. The moment I admit to an amicable working relationship . . ." He addressed Aubrey, using the same spark of conviction with which she'd spoken to him. "No, Ellis. I don't believe in ghosts . . . or spirits . . . or karma . . . or the need to have my chakras cleansed. It's absurd—all of it."

"Believe me, your chakras are another mess entirely," she said, clenching the steering wheel. "So I suppose asking you to consider the idea that I can communicate with those who have passed would be totally off your radar."

His voice was quiet and dull. "Or any rational person's radar."

"St John one, Ellis zero." Staring at her bandaged fingers, Aubrey tried a different approach. "Levi, remember yesterday, in your office, when Gwen handed me some papers? It happened to be the listing sheet to this house," she said, pointing toward the front door. "I dropped it, right? I said it was a paper cut. But my reaction didn't fit a paper cut, did it?" He didn't reply, reaching for his cell phone, instead. "What are you doing?"

"Calling a cab."

Aubrey sucked in a breath as he asked to be connected to the closest taxi service. She was committed now. "You were concerned . . .

surprised. You even asked if it was a paper cut or a knife wound. Do you remember that?"

"Yeah, hi. I need a cab at . . ." He made brief eye contact. "Where the fuck are we? Never mind." He opened the folder, plucking out the listing sheet. "Uh, 312 Acorn Circle . . ."

"Levi, look at my fingers." Aubrey peeled off the Band-Aids, thrusting an upturned palm under his nose. But the redness had dulled, the blisters not as prominent as yesterday.

"Yes, it's in Surrey . . . I think."

"This is what happened when I took the listing sheet from Gwen. I've been ignoring my usual job for weeks. The need to visit this house has clearly become urgent. The properties I visit, Levi, they're not always run-of-the-mill colonials with ordinary histories. Sometimes it's more than the people who currently live there. Sometimes there are circum—"

"Right, I'm still here." His angry glare flicked between Aubrey's hand and her face. "No, I didn't realize the address is beyond your service zone. I'll pay an upcharge. Can you just send somebody—now!" He clicked off his phone and she folded her hand into a ball. "I don't know what you're selling, what you're smoking, or what you're into, Ellis. But I don't want any part of it."

"Levi, if you would just lis—"

"No," he said, reaching for the door handle. "I'll wait outside for the cab."

Frustration surged and Aubrey smacked her palm against the steering wheel. "I swear, you are the most infuriating man I have ever met!"

"At least it's a rational fact. Here," he said, shoving the listing sheet at her.

Reflex forced Aubrey to take it. She yelled as the sensation of grabbing a boiling pot rushed through her. "Goddamn it!" she said, smacking the paper back at him. Halfway out of the car, Levi turned back.

Aubrey shoved two bloody blisters in his face, her palm bright red. He blinked wide and his jaw slacked. "Your next line of defense will be that this is carnie sleight of hand. I get it, Levi! You think I'm crazy or a con, probably both. All I'm asking you to do is walk through this house with me. It will take at least that long for your cab to get here." He didn't speak, his head shaking. "In the past few weeks I thought we'd established that much camaraderie and respect."

"Why? Why are you doing this?"

She didn't have an answer—not a quick one. Levi was still so far from listening. Marian Sloane saved her from a round of doomed persuasion. The realtor pulled up behind them, her horn honking.

"This is ludicrous. You know that?"

"Don't think I haven't considered it."

Levi opened the door again.

"Do this much and hang on to the listing sheet . . . please." Begrudgingly, he complied, picking the paper up off the car floor. He exited the vehicle, examining the sheet front and back, perhaps looking for the secret panel.

"Hello . . . hello!" Marian said. "Sorry to keep you waiting."

"No problem. Marian, this is Levi St John. He works with me at the newspaper. He's riding along this morning."

"How serendipitous! Wonderful to meet you, Levi." She never stopped moving or talking as she headed toward the front door. "I just love that sweater, Aubrey. So bright and cheery." She glanced over her shoulder. "And I'm glad you've brought a friend, because I should mention, I can't stay."

"Oh?" Aubrey said.

Marian stopped short; the three of them huddled on a marble slab entry. "It completely slipped my mind." Her fingers flitted through a fine layer of bangs. "I have an anxious buyer who wants to see a property clear on the other side of Surrey. Naturally, I didn't want to lose the home portrait spot, so it's wonderful that you'll have company!" She fumbled with the lockbox as Levi checked his watch. "I've been mean-ing to bring a different one. This box gives me such a time." She smiled eagerly, punching the code in again.

"Odd architecture for around here, isn't it?" Levi said, touching a huge fluted column. His glance crossed paths with Aubrey's, who squeezed her freshly blistered fingers into a fist.

"You're a sharp one," Marian said. "It's a Southern colonial repro-duction."

"So, not old?" Levi retrieved a cloth handkerchief from his pocket and absently held it out to Aubrey.

"Correct. Just meant to look vintage. It was built in the late nineties."

On Marian's third attempt to open the lockbox, Aubrey intervened. "How about I give it try?"

"Uh, sure. But I doubt you'll have better luck." She stepped aside. "The code is 12-25-65 . . . my birthday. Christmas Day baby." The woman nudged Levi. "But the box is defective. I should really replace—"

"There we go." The box popped open and Aubrey retrieved the key, handing it to Marian.

She slid the key into the lock and pushed open double doors. Marian motioned toward the entry and her tone hit perfect realtor pitch. "Please, go right in." Marble floor continued into a grand two-story foyer. It met with a turned staircase that was a fine match to Levi's Tara remark. "It's, um, it's been empty for a while. The owners built a new house up past Boston, on the North Shore."

"Without selling this one first?" he said.

"They, um . . . they just wanted to move on. No one imagined it would still be on the market, not at this price."

"I can see why." Levi's gaze moved between the grand square foot-age and listing sheet. "Even a price in the low seven digits seems like a bargain."

"You've got an eye all right!" Marian squeezed Levi's arm. "The real estate market can be so finicky! It's such a bucolic piece of land . . .

picturesque. There's even a barn out back, running water, electric. Just perfect for a pony!"

"If you need a pony." Levi paused, peering out a window and looking for his cab. A faint pinging noise emerged and his attention was drawn from the view to the curved staircase.

Marian stayed on point. "While it's obviously gorgeous, it's just not what people in this part of the country are used to. I'm certain that's the reason it's still on the market."

"Is that right?" Aubrey spoke as the two women moved clockwise around the foyer. She ended up at the bottom of the staircase with Marian at the door. As Aubrey neared the stairs, the pace of the ping increased.

"Absolutely," Marian said, her hand on the knob. "Uh, let's see, you won't want to miss the reproduction elements throughout, though there's new granite in the kitchen, updated appliances, executive home features that can be hard to come by in Surrey—"

"Serino." Levi looked up from the listing sheet. "The homeowner is Bruno Serino."

"That's right," Marian said. "Also, there's a custom cherry library, five-hundred-bottle wine cellar on the lower level, along with a maid's suite, and—"

"Who's Bruno Serino?" Aubrey asked, fanning the small flame of curiosity she heard from Levi.

"Just the owner," Marian said. "A well-to-do businessman."

"Family," Levi said. "The Serino family is more of an American dynasty. You've never heard of them?" Aubrey shook her head. "Bruno Serino is the head of the East Coast faction of Serinos. They own a pro sports team and racecars, a successful brewery in St. Louis, a chain of ski resorts in Europe—true American jetsetters." He looked at Marian. "But that's not why the name is sticking out for me. There's something else."

The realtor shrugged. "My only interaction with the Serinos is the listing of the home."

Turning in a tight circle, as if the answer might be behind him, Levi glanced up again. The pinging continued to sound from the stairwell—tinny and rhythmic. Aubrey was quiet, her attention on the rising noise. It was Levi who asked, "Is there somebody else here?"

"Here now? No, of course not, just us chickens!" But Marian finally did look toward the staircase. "It's probably the heating system."

"Did they go as far as to fit their reproduction home with steam heat? Otherwise that doesn't sound—"

"My heavens!" she said, holding the key out to Aubrey. "Just look at the time! I'll have to fly to make it to the other side of Surrey. You know how to lock up properly, don't you, dear? We did experience a little vandalism recently."

"Not a problem." But as Aubrey spoke an odor tickled her nose. She swiped at it with Levi's handkerchief. "We'll be fine."

"Beautiful! Take your time, take the grand tour. Be sure," she said, halfway out the door, "not to miss the his and her bathrooms in the master suite. You're a love for doing this, Aubrey!"

Aubrey crossed back to the front door and pushed it shut behind Marian as Levi noted, "Isn't that unprofessional, just leaving you here?"

Aubrey turned and leaned her weight against the door, tucking the key in her sweater pocket. "In some situations realtors don't like to hang around. And I'd be willing to bet," she said, her head tipping toward the steady sound, "Marian Sloane hates showing this house more than she does splitting her commission."

"Why?" He held up a hand. "Right. She thinks it's haunted too." Aubrey didn't reply as he glanced out the window for his cab once more. "So what is it we do now, Ellis? Draw the drapes, light a candle, hold hands around a card table? Shame you didn't bring a Ouija board."

She made a face. "Foul, grossly exploited conduit. I wouldn't touch one if you begged me." Aubrey coughed, the tickle in her nose traveling to her throat. She kept going, pointing toward the second story. "You hear the ping, right? That's fairly . . . typical. Sounds are one—" Aubrey stopped again. An odor seeped in, redolent—more remarkable than the ping. Aubrey covered her mouth with the handkerchief. It tamped down the smell as Levi offered a rational theory.

"Like Marian said, it's a reproduction. The Serinos probably did install steam heat. It explains that sound. Eccentric for sure, but something you get, right, Ellis?" Aubrey remained tight against the door and Levi looked toward the adjoining living room. "What is it about that name, the Serinos? I can't put my finger on it." Aubrey cleared her throat hard, trying to dislodge the insistent tickle. He turned back. "Allergies?"

"Um, no, not allergies. Just something odd in the air." She took a harder look around the empty foyer. "It happens."

"Like when you thought you smelled salt air in the Chinese restaurant."

Beneath her feet, through her shoes, Aubrey sensed a disturbing wave of heat rise from the marble floor. "Yes, like . . ." Aubrey looked at Levi's perplexed face; he was squinting at her neck.

"Are you sure you're not having an allergic reaction? That rash around your neck looks . . . itchy."

The odor dissipated and Aubrey took a deep breath. She ran her hand over skin that had begun to prickle. She told herself it was nothing more than the intense rush of having ignored her job. She pushed forward. "Why don't we just take the tour?"

"Do I have a choice?"

"You have at least another ten minutes until your cab arrives." He lingered behind and Aubrey glanced over her shoulder. "You won't find it."

"What's that?"

"A note on the listing sheet about this house having steam heat." Double doors opened to an elegant library. It was surrounded by custom built-ins, a coffered ceiling, and sleek Brazilian cherry flooring. Levi moved forward; she could see where the aesthetics would appeal to him. Aubrey stayed near the library entrance. The odor faded, but things weren't following their usual pattern. A spirit was evident, but it wasn't reaching out. It was hovering, and this made her uneasy. The obvious explanation was Levi. Negativity was influencing an otherwise fluid process. Her quest for proof was losing traction. Aubrey wondered if the house on Acorn Circle would produce nothing but a rash and barren square footage. Levi moved to the far end of the room where the reporter in him lent a hand.

"What happened in here?" He stood in front of French doors that opened to a patio. One side of the door was covered in plywood, its glass gone. "Looks like somebody tried to break in."

"Marian mentioned minor vandalism. When a house is empty this long it happens."

"Yes, but I wouldn't call this minor."

"Welcome to the rose-colored world of real estate," Aubrey said, glancing around.

From the intact side, Levi examined the damaged frame, his gaze moving on to the view. "Might as well look at this while we're here. I assume, in addition to your extracurricular activity, you are doing a story on the house."

She didn't reply. Instead, Aubrey's glance flicked about the room, the way it might if a bee were buzzing through.

"Marian was right about one thing. It is the perfect spot for a pon—Wait . . . this doesn't make sense."

"What doesn't make sense?"

Levi's sightline moved from the outdoor space to the glossy hardwoods beneath their feet. He pointed to the exterior. "If somebody tried to break in, shouldn't the glass be on the inside?"

Aubrey moved fast to where Levi stood. Scattered across the patio was an angry splash of glass. She looked from the shards to Levi. "Unless something was trying to break out."

He stepped away. "You can't be serious."

"Something harboring an awful lot of angry energy," Aubrey said, more to herself than him.

"That's ridiculous, Ellis."

"Is it?"

"Yes. More like someone swept the glass outside and just didn't bother to pick it up. Marian didn't strike me as the most industrious realtor."

She looked at the floor. "Maybe. But there's not a mark on these hardwoods. There's also not a stick of furniture in this house. That's thick glass, Levi. It would take a lot of force to shatter it."

"Or the vandals brought a crowbar."

Instead of rebutting, Aubrey drew the handkerchief to her mouth. Her eyes pinched as tainted smells and an unwelcome aura bled into the physical space. Her heart fluttered; then it began to pound. "You know what, Levi? Let's just go." A miserable cold sweat burst through her body and Aubrey headed for the library door. "This was a bad idea."

"Which part? Wait . . . what are you talking about?"

"I changed my mind. Coming here was a mistake." She hurried down the hall, her senses piqued in the marble-clad entry. She felt Levi and someone else follow. Both were on her heels. A hand closed around Aubrey's arm, and she could not swear it was Levi. Near the staircase, a terrific force spun her around. She felt a shred of relief as she stared into Levi's unyielding face. "I shouldn't have brought you here. Forget what I said. I . . . I'll drive you back to town."

"Not so fast. I want to know what the hell is going on. You drag me to the middle of nowhere with some cockamamie story about ghosts . . . or seeing ghosts . . . or speaking to ghosts—doesn't matter; each is more unbelievable than the other. And while I'd like to say you're a total fruitcake or off your meds, I—that's not been my perception since we started working together, Ellis. So," he said, letting go, "I want an explanation."

"No!" she said, moving fast to the door.

"No?"

"No!" she repeated, pirouetting in a shaky three-sixty turn that got her nowhere. "Levi, understand that you're not the fiercest force in this house, and I need to get out of here." She was racing now, the taste of blood rushing through her mouth. There was no approachable spirit, only the feel of death—a horrid death. Smell. Smell was the most aberrant sense. The stench returned, saturating real air. Aubrey knew that stink. She'd smelled it before. The night she'd ended up with scars on her chin and arm. Aubrey gagged, pressing Levi's handkerchief to her mouth. She reached for the doorknob. It wouldn't open and she began to yank on it, pulling at it like the madwoman Levi described. Large hands came from behind, covering hers. She calmed a sliver and together they tried the door.

"Where's the key?" he asked when it didn't budge.

All forms of communication malfunctioned and Aubrey jerked her hands out from Levi's, banging her fists against the door's solid wood center. "Just . . . I need to get out of here! Please!" With Levi's hands alone on the brass knob it moved. He opened the door a crack. Aubrey revolved in his arms, cloaked by his frame, and stared at him. Since he'd come to Surrey, she'd made an incidental study of Levi. The way he looked at the world and what was in front of him. This face she had not seen. But she could also imagine her own expression, her breathing staggered and fearful. Her neck felt like fire—rope burn. She shuddered under the cover of his body, sweat mixing with tears. On her palate were stifling tastes, her ears were filled with the hollow screech of a lost soul. It was inbound, reaching, with Levi as the only entity standing between her and it.

"The Serinos," he said. "I know who they are . . . why I remember them."

"Let me go . . ." Aubrey's trembling hands clutched his jacket lapels. She peered over Levi's shoulder and into the foyer. A mewl rose from her throat as the pinging resonated. He heard that much; she was positive. But dangling before her, in the elegant marble foyer, was a vision he'd never see. "Please," she said, eyes going wide. "Just let me the hell out of this house."

Levi opened the door and stepped back. Aubrey spilled like a bucket of red paint onto the white marble entry. She clung to a pillar, the regal column serving its most basic purpose by holding her up. Relief, the kind you might feel if the airplane suddenly pulled up from a nosedive, rushed her. Levi followed. The massive doors remained open, framing the foyer. "Tell . . . tell me what you remember."

"A few years ago the Serinos were in the news. A story made the Hartford papers—not Connecticut news but sensational enough for us to follow. The Serinos' teenage son . . . he hung himself here."

Her head tipped upward, a gaze sweeping across the vast space. "From the balcony rail."

"The parents were away, at one of their European resorts. There were a lot of questions about their absence, their negligence. They found their son when they finally did come back. According to the medical examiner, he'd been dead for days. We . . . the *Hartford Standard Speaker* picked up the wire stories."

Aubrey held tight to the pillar, its mass grounding her fears. "Do . . . do you want to hear the rest?" she asked.

"A story you remember from the papers?" She shook her head. His Adam's apple bobbed deep. "Then how . . . What else do you know?"

Aubrey squinted into the foyer. The distance granted her an advantage. The spirit inside the house couldn't get out. "Eli was the son's name. He wanted to scare his parents more than anything else—he, he was a very troubled kid . . . teenager. His parents. They weren't very good ones." They both quieted, hearing the ping. Levi perceived cryptic noise, but to Aubrey it translated into an angry rash of words. "Eli was expecting them home. He didn't mean to go through with it. It was an accident. He slipped. The garrote . . ."

"Your neck," he said, pointing.

She reached up, touching indentations at the base of her throat. "Eli was testing his theory. He never thought it would hold. He dangled there—" She motioned toward a foyer that told no such story. "The phone rang twice while he twisted. He could hear his mother's voice. She said they'd changed their plans. They weren't coming home. It was a miserable, slow death—incredibly alone." Her eyes moved from the house to Levi. Tight breaths pulsed in and out of him. "The mother, *Suzanne* . . ." Aubrey tipped her head, straining to hear. "She erased the phone messages. She just wanted to erase everything. And Eli, and he's still so . . . so very angry."

"This is impossible. A few minutes ago you said you didn't know who the Serinos were. How . . . how do you know all that?" The burning sensation eased and Aubrey patted the handkerchief to her neck. It came away showing flecks of blood. Levi looked away, then back, as if this might change what he saw. "What do you mean, 'He's still angry?'"

"I can feel it." Aubrey closed her eyes, still dangling too close to a place she truly feared. "Eli Serino's wrath . . . his anger. It's everywhere inside that house. I can taste it, the blood. He, um, Eli, bit his tongue, severed part of it." Aubrey's hand brushed over her mouth and she was grateful not to see more blood. "The force of the drop, the pull."

"There's no way you could know that. No media outlet would report anything so specific. The ME wouldn't release that information."

Aubrey's stare ticked past the foyer of the house on Acorn Circle. She stopped on Levi's stunned face. "Eli told me. It's what I said to you earlier in the car. I know you don't believe it. But they can hear me, Levi. I can hear them. Eli, he's, um . . . he's in there . . ." she said, pointing. "His neck is broken. Everything about him is . . . broken. I see him." Aubrey shrugged, a shiver moving through her. "He's beside the staircase, where he killed himself. He wanted me to come here." Levi spun on his heels. The angry spirit offered a token validation, the foyer's crystal chandelier swaying slightly in an absent breeze.

CHAPTER EIGHTEEN

On the outskirts of Surrey, Levi turned into a dusty café parking lot. "We're stopping," he said. Aubrey had handed him the keys in the driveway of Acorn Circle, taking refuge in the passenger seat. She pressed her head to the cool glass of the window. "Questions," Levi said, thrusting the car into park before twisting toward her. "I need to ask you questions."

"Fine, as long as the only thing moving is your mouth." With her arms wrapped tight around her belly, Aubrey leaned forward and shot him an ill-feeling glance. "Think of it as the queasy aftermath to the carnival ride you wished you'd skipped."

If a person could storm out of a car, that was how Levi proceeded. She was taken aback when he appeared on her side and opened the door. Aubrey shed her bright red sweater and lagged behind Levi as he marched into the café. She spent a few minutes in the ladies' room pressing a wet paper towel to her face and fishing fresh Band-Aids from her satchel. A glance in the mirror revealed a ragged Aubrey, though her neck showed only faint red marks. She swung the bathroom door open, prepared for what was bound to be Levi's hardnosed inquiry. Sliding into a booth, Aubrey saw the disbelief on his face. Levi's fact-finding nature would not acquiesce, and his first line of defense was to be expected: she'd staged the whole scene, going into the house with a full knowledge of its history.

"Sure, I suppose I could have," she said hoarsely, thinking, *"Yep . . . you're onto me . . . you win, Levi . . . "* Still woozy, Aubrey guessed it might be the fastest way out for both of them. The thought was sidelined as a waitress delivered hot tea.

"He said he didn't know if it was milk or lemon, so I brought both."

Aubrey blinked wide at Levi. But a thick Cockney accent barged in, spiriting her attention away. *"Florence . . . Florence . . . Florence . . . "* It was not the voice Aubrey expected—not Brody's voice. But in the aftermath of her morning, everything, earthbound or otherwise, seemed off. Inside the café, Aubrey battled to keep other spirits at bay, her topsy-turvy state of mind reeling. She felt like her teenage self and Aubrey drew an unsteady breath as she reached for the milk.

"Ah, I knew she was a milk gal," the waitress said. "Good for you, sweetie. It appalled my husband, Virgil, to see Americans take lemon with their tea." She served Levi his coffee. "I'm Flo. Shout if you decide you want breakfast." She sashayed away, mercifully taking Virgil with her.

"Did you want something to . . ." Levi said. Aubrey waved him off, stirring the milk into her tea. She took a deep breath and pushed up the sleeves of her cobalt blouse. Levi stared at the indentations on her forearm.

"Yes. The scars are part of it. I'll explain them if you want." Aubrey pushed the blouse sleeves back down. "For now I think the house on Acorn Circle is enough to deal with. It, um . . . what we experienced was more than I anticipated." He sipped his coffee casually, as if to dampen pointed curiosity. "What you suggest, me staging the whole thing, it's plausible." Aubrey looked toward the gravel-covered parking lot. "It's not even terribly clever, right? I embellished the same news stories you recalled—the pinging sound was a nice touch, a little theater blood on the handkerchief." She eyeballed him. "Damn. I am friendly with the secretary at the ME's office—insider information. I didn't even think about that."

"I did."

"Of course you did. So maybe that's where I got my facts. *If* I was putting on a show."

"Which is what they do in carnivals."

"Which is what we do in carnivals," she agreed, nodding. "It all makes for a great gaslight effect. But to what point? Why would I do that, Levi?"

"Because . . . well, because you believe it. Maybe you're completely sold on your own . . . "

"Psychosis?" He didn't object. "Wow, scammer to psychotic in .08 seconds. That might be a new record."

"Sorry, Ellis. But either seems more rational than your explanation."

"Yes, because sitting here while you decide between *crazy* or *liar* is such an appealing way to spend my morning." Aubrey's back thudded against the booth, and she folded her long arms. "Newsflash, Levi, you're not the kind of person carnies try to hustle. Can we agree on that much?" His attention turned toward the same parking-lot view. "You're so sure it's a story of sorts. Work the angles," she suggested. "Go for it. Align pieces the way you do all tales that come with helter-skelter parts, things that don't make sense to the average eye. Where would you start?"

He looked back. "The glass from the door in the library."

"Good choice. Biggest most undeniable evidence first—kind of like a skeleton falling out of a brick wall. What did you see aside from the obvious?"

"Aside from glass being where it didn't belong . . . I saw your reaction. That's when you got *spooked.*"

"You're right. When you pointed out the glass, that's when things started spiraling out of control. That house, it was a mistake. I assumed its urgent draw was me neglecting my job. Turns out the specter inside had an ax to grind, desperate for a conduit to move its energy. Nobody tried to break in, but a very specific entity was trying to get out. The French door, the pinging, which Marian aptly ignored . . ."

"Shed some light on that. Have you ever discussed the house in *that way* with Marian Sloane?"

"Not a word. Ask her if you like. But you saw it yourself, her nervousness and quick exit. I'd imagine Marian's experienced things she really doesn't want to know any more about. And why do you think the homeowners vacated without selling? Trust me; nobody wants to be in that house—the Serinos or Marian Sloane."

"Isn't that illegal? Don't they have to report something like that?"

"To who? *Ghostbusters?*" Aubrey offered him a confounded look. "Careful, Levi, you're starting to make an argument for the other side." She paused to sip her tea. "Just FYI, in the state of Massachusetts realtors are required to disclose homicides that took place on a property but not suicides, certainly not suspected ghosts. Whoever ends up with that house is in for a time. Until, of course . . ."

"Until what?"

"Eventually Eli Serino will make his way out. The parents can move all they like. But in my experience you can't ditch the spiritual world by changing your address. Eli's issue isn't with a house—though he appears stuck in the one where he took his own life. It's strange . . ."

"You think?"

"Eli Serino is not my first encounter with someone who committed suicide. There's an irony to their presence. People who take their own lives come to me surrounded by a different energy. Their ability to move on is weak, but their link to *here* is ferociously strong."

"So, purgatory?" he said, rolling his eyes.

"That's not a word I've ever heard from them. I don't know that it defines their state. It's more about the fallout from an unfinished life. Suicide's a messy business. In most instances, there's so much left unknown . . . unsaid."

"Okay, enough psychological . . . theoretical analysis," he said. "Back to the house. You know I heard the pinging. I saw the glass. I'll even go as far to admit that a two-hundred-pound chandelier rattled despite an obvious catalyst. But what did you mean when you said you *saw* Eli Serino. Like what . . . like a vision?"

"The stronger the entity the more vividly my gift translates it. Sight is probably the sense I rely on least. Most specters don't harbor enough energy to create a visual presence, but the one living in that house. It was incredible . . . and *evil*."

"Evil."

Aubrey touched the scar on her chin. "Not every soul is looking to send a positive message, make amends." She cocked her head at him. "The *Long Island Medium* never mentions that, does she?"

"The . . ."

"Forget it. To answer your question, yes. I saw Eli Serino." Aubrey pushed herself hard into the vinyl-covered seat, her shoulders arching. "My particular ability exceeds the boundaries of most clairvoyants. It runs in the family," she said, deadpan.

"So what you're telling me is you see—"

"If you're about to say 'I see dead people,' I'm so not continuing this conversation."

"But that's what you're telling me, that's what you're asking me to believe."

"That's what I'm telling you. Believing it is strictly your call."

Levi rubbed his fingers across his forehead as if trying to straighten the twisted thoughts. "Look . . . even if I were inclined to buy into what you're saying, there's got to be a more logical explanation." It was a standoff stare, his hole-burning, hers more that of a passive trial witness.

"Levi, taking you to that house was a first. I don't give on-demand performances. I don't do this for profit or recognition, not even in my carnie days."

"You've never deliberately told anyone in the newsroom . . . Malcolm, Kim . . . Ned?"

"Not even Bebe."

"And Charley is aware . . ."

"Of course she knows. My father . . . As I said, it runs in the family. My father had the same gift . . . affliction, whichever. Trust me; growing up in a carnival was the less colorful part of my childhood."

His forehead knotted. "Color."

"What about it?"

"You were wearing that long, bright red sweater. On the days you visit houses, I've noticed . . ."

"I wear bright colors—very observant, Levi," she said, genuinely impressed. "They're drawn to color. It's not so far removed from nature. Animals with dull coats are less noticeable. Earthy tones help minimize the effect of . . . well, of me. It's one of many coping mechanisms."

"Coping mechanisms? Such as . . ."

"Mmm, that's a long conversation. Most of it is internal . . . abstract. It's about keeping myself grounded, having a stronger will than whoever is looking for a way in. My job at the newspaper was a big turning point. I don't have an answer for everything. I don't know why I was suddenly given a course of action. Unbeknownst to MediaMatters, my gift seems to be the reason they hired me for the home portrait fea . . ." Verbally, the thought petered out. Aubrey drew the conclusion in her head: it seemed the dead, Missy Flannigan and Brody St John, were responsible for delivering her and Levi to the same place. "As I was saying, with the exception of today, it's been a workable plan—for both sides."

"The Stallworths."

"What about them?"

"The first time you mentioned them, it was a conversation with Jerry Stallworth. We talked about how stubborn he is, and how my father is the same way. You said that's why you ran late that first morning—you were *talking* to Jerry Stallworth."

"That's right," she said, stirring the tea again.

"Then yesterday . . . when you were on the phone with Kitty, you said her father was 'resting in peace' now."

"Did I?" she said, smiling at her error.

Levi leaned back. "I brushed it off—because we were busy with Missy Flannigan or because I thought I'd misunderstood."

"You didn't. Jerry Stallworth died last April." Aubrey placed her spoon on a napkin, her fingers folding like a prayer. "The day you arrived at the *Surrey City Press*, Mr. Stallworth's spirit was present at his house on Harper Street. Kitty was willing to help research Missy's car because of what I found in the house and what I returned to her—an annuity for close to a million dollars."

"Excuse me?"

"Jerry directed me to a piece of paper so squirreled away in the wet bar with dry rot that no one would have ever found it. Once Jerry was able to communicate that, he moved on . . . at peace, just like I said to his daughter."

Levi's hand ran rough over the back of his neck. "That's . . ."

"Thank you so much for not saying crazy."

"Hard to fathom."

"I'm sure it is."

"And your ex . . ." he said, working another tangent. "Owen. What's his take on this?"

Aubrey sat tall and tighter. She hadn't thought about including her personal life in an explanation to Levi. "Owen knows now. I didn't tell him before we were married . . . He, um . . . he found out accidentally."

"So, on some level, that would make you . . ."

"A liar?"

"Yes."

"On some level. On the other hand, that *lie* was almost our final undoing. Breaking up isn't what I wanted, which would make it illogical for me to confess to something so untrue."

Levi drank more coffee, his dark eyes scanning over her. "Aside from the big picture, here's what makes even less sense. Why? Why are you telling me any of this? The person least likely to believe that you can . . . do what you claim." Aubrey's gaze, slow and deliberate, drifted to Levi's leather-banded watch. His hand flew protectively over it. "No!"

"No what?" *Good, keep going, Levi, connect the dots . . . You come up with the reason . . . Say it!*

"I don't know how you know . . . but this is total bullshit!" Levi lurched from the seat, throwing a ten-dollar bill onto the table. He didn't look back, bolting for the parking lot. But since they came in Aubrey's car, she knew the rational side of Levi would prevent him from leaving. She watched as he stood there, his arms pressed stiff into the car's hood. It was as if he was trying to get unwelcome emotion to drain from his body.

Watching from the café window, Aubrey sipped the last of her tea and said to herself, "That went well." She considered pushing the point, telling a slightly vulnerable Levi what she knew. His brother had been waiting years, dropping a breadcrumb trail onto her path for weeks. If Levi were willing to hear her, she might just spell it all out. Then she considered Brody's reluctance. He wasn't going to show until his brother was ready to listen. The ghost demanded more. The task fell to her. "Bully for St John tenacity," she said, setting down her cup and exiting the café. On her way out, Aubrey heard the disappointed pleas of anxious specters. Her nose filled with rose-scented bubble bath, scones, and fish—trout maybe, cooked over an open campfire. On her palate were a myriad of tastes, so many that they were impossible to discern. She forced it all away, ambling into the bright sun of the parking lot. Here, empty space greeted her. Levi leaned against the car, his face shadowed with skepticism.

"What happened to your parents?"

Aubrey shuffled to a stop. There was a plain breeze, and on it scents and tastes faded to October air and tea. "I'm fine now," she said, ignoring the question. "I can drive back to the newsroom."

"Are you going to answer me? Surely, at this point, you can't think it's none of my business."

Halfway around to the passenger side, Aubrey turned back. "It will only complicate what you refuse to acknowledge. That and it has nothing to do with—"

"I want to know. I already know that they're dead. How did they die?" Aubrey's glance cut across the car. This was Levi St John, compiling information, arranging facts, steering the interview. "You claim your father was like you."

"Like me . . . but not like me." His face looked perplexed. "Sorry, I don't mean to confuse what you already can't grasp. My father . . . Peter Ellis, he was never able to negotiate his ability. It haunted him, much like Eli Serino haunted that house. Ultimately, I believe my father's *gift* cost him and my mother everything . . . everything in this life, anyway."

"She knew this about him? She believed it?"

"My mother knew. She accepted it. But with me . . . I think the same gift scared the hell out of her." Aubrey dropped her satchel onto the hood, guessing Levi wasn't unhappy about a two-ton vehicle separating them. "Some of my earliest memories are of having conversations with people in my bedroom."

"But you weren't talking to stuffed animals or a make-believe friend."

"No. Not from the look on my mother's face. I remember her holding me . . . rocking me, pressing her hand to my head, saying, 'Stop, Aubrey, just stop . . .' I didn't understand. It all seemed perfectly natural to me, like learning to read. But watching my parents, how my father suffered . . . Even at four or five, I grasped the idea that there was nothing normal about it. Eventually"—she paused and waited for a couple of patrons to pass by—"my father ended up in a sanitarium."

"A sanitarium."

It was the "Ah ha!" he'd been waiting to hear. "Yes. The place where they put you when your mind doesn't fit the norm. Feel better?"

"Not particularly. Keep going."

"Ironically, it was the worst possible place for someone *like him*. My parents were living abroad at the time, in Greece. That's where my mother was from. I don't think she knew what else to do. But she couldn't bear it, couldn't stand to see him so . . . haunted. He couldn't cope with this." Aubrey grazed a hand downward, as if offering herself as evidence. "My mother was afraid he'd injure himself, or worse . . . me. Peter Ellis couldn't escape it. He couldn't learn to live with it. The way Charley tells it, the sanitarium was worse than the in-between life of the ghosts who visited him. In time, enough was enough and . . ."

"He killed himself."

"No. If he had, I believe things would be different. When I was five, my mother checked him out of the sanitarium. She took him to live in the country. She thought distancing him from people might be the answer. Apparently, it didn't help. That summer Mother packed up everything I owned and sent me to the states, to Charley. While I was gone . . ." Aubrey paused, examining the surrounding scenery, always curious if her parents might be listening. Then she looked straight into Levi's eyes. "My parents went for a drive into the mountains. It was a treacherous road in good weather. The day they went, there were torrential downpours, even mudslides. According to the police, the car skidded off a hairpin turn at a high rate of speed."

"An accident?"

"It's the most logical answer."

"But nothing about this is logical." She was quiet, forcing Levi to draw the conclusion. "You think something . . . or someone besides bad weather caused the accident."

"Conceivably. But according to the police report my mother was driving."

"Do you think it was intentional?" He dragged in a long breath. "You believe your mother drove the car off a cliff?"

"I don't know, Levi. An accident is the most rational explanation. But I've heard Charley talk. I *appreciate* how desperate my mother was to help him." Aubrey's bandaged fingers ran along the scar on her chin. "I know the place my father couldn't escape. I stood on the edge of it today. I can't imagine it being my daily destination. The cause of their demise doesn't matter. It's more about accepting that their physical existence here has come to an end."

"That . . . that's an incredible story, Ellis."

"But from what point of view?" As she spoke, the wind kicked up in a rousing swirl. "I've missed my calling and should be writing novels, or insanity is inherent and that's all you need to know."

His stare was probing. He silently got into the car and Aubrey did the same. Levi started the engine. "Despite what I believe or don't believe, I'm sorry . . . very sorry about the way your parents died."

Aubrey smoothed the fabric of the red sweater, which lay in her lap. Tightness swelled in her throat. It was the renascent pain that went with talk about people who you'd loved and lost. Sometimes Aubrey forgot that, having been so young, so distanced from her own loss. "Thank you. I've had plenty of time to be angry about it, question it. I certainly can't change it." A sideways glance darted toward him. "That said, there's only one conclusion I can draw. They must be at peace."

"Why do you say that?"

"Because I've never heard from either one of them." Their gazes tangled. Levi hesitated, as if he couldn't mentally retrieve how to shift the car into drive. "In the right circumstance, it's an incredible gift to be offered, Levi. Enviable, really. The opportunity to communicate with someone you loved. Someone you never thought you'd have a chance to speak with again. I'm only suggesting—"

"No . . . just no." He found reverse and backed recklessly out of the space. "Absolutely not, Ellis." Shifting into drive, Levi made solid eye contact before hitting the gas. "Do not bring it up to me again—ever."

"Why? Because you don't believe me?"

"Partly."

"And the rest of it?"

"Because I'm the reason my brother is dead."

CHAPTER NINETEEN

Aubrey wasn't sure if Levi's reaction was about shutting her down or an innate ability to compartmentalize. After a silent ride back to the newsroom, he disappeared into his office with Gwen. Aubrey openly eavesdropped. Their discussion focused on Gwen's Violet Byrd feature. Apparently, the woman had been willing to talk about her son, though Gwen was concerned about the toll any feature would take on his elderly mother. In turn, Levi was steady and pragmatic, helping Gwen fine-tune the angle she'd chosen for the piece. Listening, you'd never guess that Levi's last conversation was about an offer to broker a visit with his dead brother. Aubrey walked toward her cubicle, running into Malcolm along the way. "There you are, Aubrey. I got a call from my source at the DA's office. Delacort's conviction has been overturned. They're not saying when exactly, but he'll likely be a free man by dinnertime."

"Seriously? Levi said he thought it would go that way, but I really didn't think . . . Have they issued an arrest warrant for Dustin Byrd?"

"There's hubbub, but no official word," he said with a spark Aubrey liked to see. "Legal says a judge wouldn't cut Delacort loose without compelling evidence against Byrd. You know, I've been acquainted with Byrd for twenty years. Something about him always rubbed me the wrong way."

"So you never believed Delacort was guilty?"

"I wouldn't go that far. But, twenty years removed, and I'd say my reaction to Delacort's conviction was like the rest of Surrey—glad a killer was off our streets. Glad it wasn't one of us."

Aubrey looked long down the corridor. "Does Levi know about Delacort's exoneration?"

"No, I was on my way to tell him. Unless, of course, you want to. It is your story."

"Uh, that's okay. I'll let you deliver the news."

"Because?" Malcolm said.

"We had a bit of a blow up earlier. I don't think Levi is interested in sharing breathing space with me at the moment."

"I had the impression you were getting along better than expected."

"We are . . . we were," she said, fidgeting. Details would be difficult to convey.

"Is there something I should know? If he's being overbearing or difficult . . . I won't have Levi bully you. I don't care if he is Carl Toppan's . . . make that Carl Bernstein's personal protégé."

"It's not that," she said. "Things got off track. Levi and I, we ended up in a . . . situation I never anticipated."

"Then I will speak with him—"

"No, don't, Malcolm." Aubrey lightly touched his arm. "It was my fault," she said, realizing it was. "I . . . Things were said that were way outside Levi's comfort zone. I have no complaints about the way he's doing his job."

"That much is good to hear, if not a tad unexpected."

"Believe me. A lot of things about Levi are unexpected."

It was hard to detect a furrow in the wrinkles of Malcolm's brow, but that's what she saw. "Would, uh . . . I don't mean to pry, but would this conversation . . . this *situation* be something of a more personal nature—not newspaper or Missy Flannigan related?"

Aubrey's gaze, which had dropped to her wringing hands, shot back up. "Yes."

Her editor in chief nodded gently. "I see. That is surprising." Her own brow knotted in reply. "Clearly that wasn't my intention when teaming the two of you up. But I know firsthand that sometimes these things just happen."

"What things happen?"

His hand brushed Aubrey's arm in what felt like a fatherly gesture. "Even an old geezer like me knows chemistry when he sees it. I'm sure it will work itself out. In the meantime, I'll inform Levi about Delacort, maybe offer him some sage man-to-man advice."

"Chemistry . . . sage advice . . . ? Whoa, Malcolm, that's not what . . ." Aubrey spun around but it was too late; her boss had already turned the corner. "Oh, for the love of . . ." Aubrey thudded a palm to her forehead.

Continuing down the corridor, she smoothed out the notion by reminding herself that Malcolm was old school—married to Norma, a secretary he'd met forty years ago at the *Surrey City Press*. And while he might not plot an office romance, surely he could envision one. The story went that during the heyday of newspapers and stenography, cub reporter Malcolm had asked "Will you marry me?" in Pitman shorthand. Then he asked Norma to transcribe it. She did, having the print room mock up a *Surrey City Press* headline that said: *Yes!*

Malcolm's romantic ideals didn't fade from Aubrey's mind, but followed her all the way to her desk. Tucked into the private space was a fresh bouquet of red roses. For the briefest second, Aubrey perceived the flowers as a peace offering from Levi. She shook her head at the ridiculousness. *How absurd. Besides, Levi would never send red roses . . .* She touched the velvety petals. *If Levi sent flowers, he'd send daisies . . .*

Damn, he'd told her as much. Aubrey plucked the card from the bouquet's center. The fact that he'd be correct, that she happened to love daisies, was completely irrelevant. She cleared her throat, tearing open the flap, reading: "Just a token to show you how much I want us to work. Love, Owen." Aubrey smiled at the flowers, snatched her cell from her satchel, and dialed. "Hey, thank you," she said breathlessly. "I got your flowers. That was sweet. You didn't—"

"I wanted to," Owen said. "I was sorry this morning didn't work out. I wanted a more romantic statement than 'I'm selling the loft.'"

"Selling the loft *is* romantic . . . It puts you back in our bed."

"It does. Okay . . . so along those lines, how about dinner tomorrow night, someplace . . ."

"Romantic?" she said, laughing.

"Definitely. Maybe La Petite Maison?"

"You don't usually like anything so fancy. We don't have to—"

"Nope. It's perfect. Meet me there at seven? That's about as quick as I can make it back from New York."

"Seven sounds great."

"And Aubrey, I have a surprise for you. Something I think you're really going to love."

"A surprise? In addition to fine dining, studio for sale signs, and roses? I'm intrigued."

"Good. Stay that way until tomorrow."

"I will. And Owen, I . . ." Aubrey's call waiting beeped in. She glanced at the phone. The name Priscilla Snow lit up the screen. Friendly, yes, but the secretary to the medical examiner didn't make a habit of calling Aubrey. "Owen, there's a call I need to take, can we . . ."

"Right, sure. I've got to get back. I'll see you tomorrow."

"See you then." She switched to the incoming call. "Priscilla. Hello, how are you?"

"Overly pregnant and on complete bed rest until the baby comes. Funny, by now I thought I'd burst from excitement!"

Aubrey laughed. "I bet there's nothing like it . . . motherhood." She sat on the edge of her desk, touching the red roses again. Perhaps, before long, she and Owen would be having the same conversation. Children had been another topic that didn't fit into his on-the-go life. Aubrey breathed in the scent of flowers and the future. "What can I do for you, Priscilla?"

"I think it's what I can do for you. I'm doing paperwork from home—a person can only binge-watch so many episodes of *Sex and the City* and *Grey's Anatomy*, you know?"

"I imagine bed rest would get tedious."

"So I was actually thrilled when the boss sent over some work. I called because I came across something interesting. Are you and . . . oh, I forget his name. The intense, stone-chiseled reporter guy . . ."

"Levi." Aubrey turned her back to the bouquet.

"Right, him. Anyway, I told you I'd let you know if there was anything new on the Flannigan case. And, well, there is."

Aubrey whirled like a top off the desk and landed in her chair, notebook open. "Absolutely, Priscilla. Anything you've got."

"It's a big enough deal that my boss asked me to add the info to our closed file. I'm sure I shouldn't be sharing. But what the heck, being a bit stir crazy will make you gab, right?"

"I suppose. What, um . . . what did you learn?"

"They called in some firearms expert . . . a, uh, Clayton Hadley. He was able to match the bullet lodged in the skeletal remains to a specific type of gun. It's a . . . Oh, hang on." Aubrey heard papers rustling. "A Ruger handgun. Now, generally speaking, Ruger is a fairly common name in weapons—you can probably pick one up at any gun show. But here's what differed. The bullet taken from Missy is linked to a Ruger Super Redhawk, much rarer. According to Hadley, the ammo and weapons were limited military issue. So that's interesting, right? But here's the part that will make your headline."

"What's that?" Aubrey said, the pencil poised on her notepad.

"Because they're so rare, the Ruger Super Redhawk's real claim to fame is with collectors. I guess it's like having the Pink & Pretty Barbie from the eighties. Gun enthusiasts pay top dollar for one. You'll never guess who had a Super Redhawk in his collection?"

"Dustin Byrd." Aubrey said, the tip of her pencil snapping off.

"Dustin Byrd," Priscilla confirmed. "Paperwork in our file includes the list of weapons confiscated from Byrd—among his firearms was a Ruger Super Redhawk."

"Talk about a smoking gun."

"That's what I said! I think it would make such a cool headline, don't you?"

"Pretty close. No wonder they exonerated Delacort."

"There you go! I knew it was a big deal. And now you know before the rest of the world does."

"Absolutely, Priscilla! Thank you so much."

"Hey, no problem. My mom said she owed you. Your real estate stories have helped her move more than one property."

"Glad she feels that way. But I'm the one who owes you. Listen, I've really got to run with this."

"I hear you. Hope it helps with your newspaper stuff."

"It may turn out to be Surrey's scoop of the century." Aubrey glanced down, seeing the scrawl from the blunt tip of her pencil. She hadn't realized her hand was moving. "Sophia . . ." she said, the name almost forced from her lips.

"Sophia? How did you know . . ."

"Know what?"

"That we're naming the baby Sophia. Nobody even knows it's a girl."

"Oh, uh . . . you must have mentioned it when I saw you at the ME's office."

"Gosh, I don't think so. We want to surprise everybody. My mom will be thrilled—that was her mother's name. And that's the only sad part. My grandma died about a year ago. We were very close."

"I'm sorry to hear that, Priscilla. But something tells me your grandmother is very excited . . . even if she's not *here*." Aubrey's hand continued to move without conscious effort. *"Un regalo dal cielo,"* she said, reading the unfamiliar words.

"You speak Italian?"

"I guess. A little . . . on occasion. Why?"

"That's exactly what my grandma used to say to me. It means *a gift from heaven*."

"And she will be."

◆ ◆ ◆

Aubrey moved like a bullet but stopped dead at the edge of Levi's office. Misfiring would be easy under the circumstance. He was on the phone and taking notes. Levi glanced up, inhaling deep and averting eye contact. "Yep, incredible info, Major . . . No, I appreciate your effort— absolute confidentiality. You have my word." He hung up and scanned the top of his desk, finally forced to meet her gaze.

"You heard about Delacort's exoneration?" Aubrey said.

"I heard." Levi didn't say anything else. Left up to him, Aubrey was sure that she'd no longer be part of his circle of privileged information. She ignored the sting. There was still a job to do. She'd be damned if Levi was going to stop her. "I just got off the phone too," she said, sticking tight to newspaper business. "Priscilla Snow called. She had the reason they exonerated Delacort."

"Really? And what was that?" Resigned to her presence, he pointed to a chair. Aubrey closed the door and sat.

"Priscilla called to tell me the gun used to kill Missy was a Ruger, a rare Super Redhawk," she said, glancing at her notes. "The bullet lodged in the skeleton set it apart. Clayton Hadley, the ballistics expert, concluded that the ammunition was a match to that particular gun. Most importantly, the gun was found in Dustin Byrd's collection." Levi's stare flicked between his notes and Aubrey. When he didn't interject she continued. "So . . . I'm assuming that makes it a slam dunk for the DA, hence Delacort's release. You've got the uncommon murder weapon, the bullet, and the owner—all under the same roof where the victim's remains fell out of his basement wall. It looks like Surrey did rush to justice." She waited, inching forward in the chair. Levi's face remained puzzled, never nearing the look of *eureka* she'd anticipated. "Levi, don't you see this as significant? Don't you think we have our headline?"

He leaned back in the chair. "We've got a hell of a lot more than that."

"Meaning what?"

There was a contemplative rock to the chair as Levi looked at his notes. She could almost see the gears grind in his head. "I just got off the phone with Major Floyd Henderson in D.C. He's a high-ranking officer with the DOD. He has access to just about any sealed record you'd want."

"The friend of your father."

"Uh, yes . . . my father. It took some finessing. Due to the volatile nature of high-value targets, the records I wanted to know about were classified—highly classified twenty years ago. But being as the file was old and the information no longer germane to national security, the major was willing to shed some light on facts that weren't in play. Not until a few minutes ago." Levi pointed to the notepad, his finger tapping against it.

"What kind of facts?"

"Specific details regarding Frank Delacort's service record. Before being booted from the army, Frank achieved the rank of sergeant."

"Right. We already knew that."

"We did. What we didn't know was his precise role in the military. Delacort was a sniper, an expert marksman, Ellis." Levi picked up the piece of paper he'd been writing on and held it up for Aubrey to read. "Here's a list of weapons with which Delacort is intimately familiar. Just to note, marksmen are generally proficient in rifles. Delacort's expertise varied. It included other weapons. Take a hard look at the last one."

Aubrey focused on the listed items. Most were large weapons—machine guns, high-powered sharp-shooter rifles. The list dwindled to less impressive firearms, a marksman insignia Beretta and other handguns. Some Aubrey had heard of; others she hadn't. At the bottom of the list an asterisk marked the last weapon cited. "Oh my God. What . . . what does the asterisk mean?"

"It means that in addition to all the weapons on that sheet of paper, Frank Delacort was a certified marksman with one handgun—a Ruger Super Redhawk. A perfect match to the gun that killed Missy Flannigan." The notepad dropped onto the desk. "So what do you think our headline is now? Because I'd say there's a fifty-fifty chance the state just let a murderer walk free."

CHAPTER
TWENTY

Surrey, Massachusetts
Twenty Years Earlier

Missy hadn't seen Dustin since breaking things off. Everyone in Surrey banked at Benjamin Franklin Savings Bank, except for him, so she was sure she wouldn't run into Dustin there. The fact put Missy at ease as she glided across the bank's marble floor in her tennis whites. Missy was doubly glad to see Ginger Imai working the end teller booth. It was closest to the safety deposit box room. Missy liked Ginger Imai, finding the forty-something Japanese woman helpful and discreet. When they did talk, Missy's intuitive nature assured her that Ginger's was genuine. She also appreciated the woman's self-sufficiency. The unmarried Japanese immigrant made a living by using her head for numbers. Missy liked to think she did the same thing—except for the Japanese part, and the physical services rendered to secure those numbers. But that no longer mattered. Missy had closed up shop the moment Frank latched on to her idea about the two of them leaving Surrey together. Finally, a prayer had been answered, and soon Surrey would be her past.

"Missy. Good morning. How can I help you?" There was a slight bow from Ginger. The cultural nuance made Missy think their stories had something in common. Perhaps Ginger had been a geisha. Maybe she fled Japan to escape the same life Missy prepared to abandon. She smiled at the unspoken camaraderie, explaining to Ginger that she wanted to visit her safety deposit box. "Do you have a tennis match?" she asked, leading the way.

"No, just a lesson. Last one." Missy shrugged. "I paid for them earlier in the summer—my plans were different then. But I guess I just want my money's worth, like everyone else."

Missy had come to the bank for two reasons that morning. The first was to make a pragmatic assessment of what was inside the rectangular metal box. Ginger delivered it to her, leaving Missy alone with her possessions and thoughts. She wanted to peruse the random bits of paper and photos that she'd had the forethought to save. Their potential worth was intriguing. Money was the only thing holding up her plans with Frank, Missy having spent the bulk of hers. Theoretically, the items in the box were like insurance policies and the idea of cashing them in was tempting. Missy chewed on her lip, thinking. Not everyone would fold like Mick O'Brien.

A few months back, when she confronted the proprietor of the Plastic Fork with unsavory photos, Mick had nearly shit his pants. The married father of three had a proclivity for *acting out*, posing with his accessories, wearing his mail-order Dom gear. At the time, he'd been carried away by the kinky fun, uninhibited because of the joint they'd smoked, not caring how many pictures Missy took. Now, if the photos were to go public, Mick's marriage, his business, and his life would be ruined. Who in Surrey would frequent the Plastic Fork after learning about the lurid acts going on over their head while they ordered a tuna salad sandwich? So Missy saw it as reasonable when she informed Mick that her continued discretion would only cost him accommodations for a homeless veteran. After Mick's panicked reaction, Missy began to reevaluate her safety deposit box. But sitting in the quiet room, having unlocked the box, Missy realized its contents were also volatile, the possible fallout an unknown. Missy didn't like unknowns. She let the idea go for a moment and switched gears.

She retrieved two leather-bound diaries from her tote bag. It was the second reason she'd come to Ben Franklin Savings that day. Missy tucked them underneath the other items in the box, wanting to bury the diaries in the same dark place as her past. When Frank agreed to leave town, her intention was to burn them. Maybe she still would. There was time to decide, money to be secured. For now, life had changed so much that Missy wanted the damn diaries out of her sight. She closed the lid and locked it. "I'm all set," she said, opening the door.

Ginger returned, bowing again as she took the box from Missy. "You certainly like to admire those pearls and whatnot. Don't you ever wish to wear them?"

"I'm not much for trinkets and baubles. I'd rather have the cash any day." Missy stood, smoothing her tennis whites, brushing a hand over her Neutrogena appearance. Then she looked into Ginger's puzzled face. "But my grandma sure did love them. It makes me feel close to her to come and sit with them now and again." While her reminiscent smile was not attached to a real memory, she did like the imagery she had produced. Perhaps, one day, she and Frank would have grandchildren. Perhaps her life could be something other than what she had expected.

"That is sweet. I had a grandma too—she lived in Hokkaido, an island off Japan. I did not see her for many years at a time. How special yours left you something so meaningful."

Missy hummed along. Her agreement was appropriate acting, but really aimed at her absentmindedness. Ginger had commented before on the supposed jewelry, and Missy meant to sneak in a few costume pieces. It would make sense to show off pearls if, indeed, that's what was in the box. But Missy had trouble with small-scale lies, regular girl thoughts. She did not blame herself for this, guessing she hadn't processed a normal thought in years. Not since an October night, the day after her ninth birthday. That night Missy woke with a start, finding her father's hand in her underwear and her point of view forever altered.

Missy stared at the box, tucked safely in Ginger's arms. But it was as if she could see right through the metal. Missy heard the dairies' heinous captured words about Tom Flannigan. From that first night forward, normal thoughts had bled into darker ones, Missy negotiating one strange circumstance after another—like the motivation for getting the safety deposit box in the first place.

That came two years ago, after catching her mother trying to flip the mattress in her bedroom. Mercifully, her illness made it an unachievable task. The hiding place for Missy's clients' keepsakes was the perfect irony, a spring-coiled homage to the common tool of her trade. Now Missy shuddered at the memory. Not only would the flip of a mattress have killed a healthy income, it might have killed Barbara Flannigan. Although, not as painfully or swiftly as the truth about her husband. Missy was determined to keep this much from her mother. Physically, with her MS, the woman had suffered enough. It was that and the idea that exposing Tom Flannigan would only lead to unsavory opinions about Missy. How could it not?

Until Frank, men wanted her for this—only this. Not one ever wanted to help or asked how sweet Missy Flannigan ended up the best little trick in Surrey. Even Randy Combs, who worked for child protective services and had a flexible schedule, never questioned it. He just acted as if fucking Missy were an off-site seminar with hands-on research. They all wanted what they'd paid for and to get on with their lives— whether it was going home to their frigid wives or taking their kid to a ball game. Missy had earned a solid five digits meeting their needs. The key, the payoff, had been turning their advantage into hers.

On the way out of the safety deposit room, Ginger stopped to talk to a co-worker. While Missy waited her mind vacillated over the box's contents. Her clients were everyday men who would pay to keep Missy's mouth shut. Hell, they'd paid enough for her to open it. They were the type of men who probably couldn't believe what they were doing, though that hadn't stopped them either. In the heat of their twisted passions some had foolishly allowed their pictures to be taken in poses that would turn their wives rabid. Others had hastily tucked motel receipts in their pants pockets, only to have Missy confiscate them the moment their backs were turned. Dumbest of all were the forget-me-not thank you notes that read like signed testimonials. Yes, when it came to the simple offering of a physical act in exchange for cash, men could be completely stupid. Among their most grievous errors, however, was underestimating sweet accommodating Missy Flannigan. She glanced pensively at the box, considering the payoff and the risk. It would be messy, it would take time. There was no guarantee. It could backfire. Both Frank and Dustin might find out that neither of them was Missy's best kept secret. She needed to think harder.

Missy thanked Ginger Imai. She was one step away from the revolving door when Dustin came spinning toward her. Wearing camouflage shorts, work boots, and a safari style hat, he looked more prepared to tame the jungle than Surrey's public grounds. Missy shuffled to a stop, her tennis shoes squeaking as she broke from the door's path. She hadn't seen Dustin since leaving him teary-eyed near the defunct rubber-processing plant. She'd barely gotten the image out of her head. He'd had the most dazed expression on his round face—like his world had ended. As Missy's message finally sank in, his mustache quivered and his head shook uncontrollably. There was nothing she could do. And whether it was because of Frank Delacort or the unavoidable passage of time, it didn't matter. It had to be done.

Distracted by the memory, Missy wasn't thinking. She definitely wasn't moving fast enough as Dustin spied her, a startled gasp heaving through his thick chest. "Missy."

"Dustin." She was glad for the bank's Main Street location, a setting where they excelled at being acquaintances. "What . . . what are you doing here, inside the bank?"

Over his heart, he patted the pocket of his cotton shirt. "Mom asked me to deposit some checks for her."

"Oh. How . . . how is Violet?"

"Violet?" he said, as if he couldn't place the proper noun. "Uh, fine. She's fine. She's going to the carnival this weekend. She goes every year."

"Right. Me too. And, um, you?" she asked, hopeful that he was taking a date.

"Me? I'm not . . ." His gaze skimmed over her all-white attire. "I'm going fishing." She nodded, waiting for Dustin to proceed with their scripted, around-town dialogue: *Missy Flannigan . . . I haven't seen you in ages . . . remind me again where you're going to school . . . ?*" They'd had a code for everything. *"I haven't seen you in ages,"* equaled *"Call me as soon as you can,"* and so on. But Dustin didn't say any of that. Instead he said, "I miss you."

It wasn't expected and it gutted her response. Missy nearly panicked at his wavering words. He didn't look well. There was no mischievous twinkle to his dusty-brown eyes, just circles underneath. His slight second chin was gone, like he hadn't eaten in a week. "I'm sorry," she said, feeling like maybe she was.

He took a step closer, closer than he'd ever come under Surrey's watchful eye. "You look . . . amazing."

"I have a tennis lesson."

"I miss you," he said again, as if what she'd done had rendered him a babbling idiot.

"I have to go, Dustin."

"Did . . . did you hear? I got the promotion, Miss. I'm going to be the director of Surrey Parks and Recreation."

"That's, um . . . that's wonderful," she said, backing away. "But I have to go."

"Wait!" He grabbed her arm; Missy's gaze ripped around the bank's cold stone interior. "Can I . . . could we please just talk?"

"Dustin, what are you doing?" she said in a hissing whisper. "People will see."

"Do you think I care about that? Missy, how can you do this now? I got the promotion—we're there, baby. Maybe you think waiting like we did meant I was ashamed to tell people. But that's not it at all. I was protecting you."

"Do you think you're protecting me now?" He let go, and Missy rubbed her arm. The grip was unlike Dustin, angry as it was desperate. "Talking won't change it. You didn't do anything wrong. It's just me . . . and what I want . . . and this town . . . and . . . and things you couldn't possibly understand!" She felt an unlikely rush of emotion. "I have to go." Missy heard him call her name as she dashed out of the bank, rushing around the corner. She ran headlong into Frank who by instinct, if not collision, wrapped his arms around her.

"Hey, fancy meeting you here. I thought you had a tennis lesson."

"Frank . . ." Missy welcomed the embrace before realizing the public setting. She broke from his hold.

"What's wrong?" His hand grazed her shoulder, like he wanted to hug her again. "Missy?"

She couldn't tell him the cause of her upset. Frank wouldn't get that, nor would he want to hear it. So she went with what he would like to hear. "I ran into Dustin. It was horrible. He was just awful to me."

"Seriously?" he said, looking down the street. "Maybe now's a good time for that little weasel prick and I to have a talk."

Her hands boldly bumped his chest. "What? No! You can't confront Dustin."

"Why not? If you think I'm leaving this town without calling out that cradle-robbing asshole . . ." Frank's dark eyes were wildly intense. "Missy, you dumping him isn't the only consequence he should have to face. He's a predator. He works around young girls all the time. Do you know Randy Combs? He comes into Holliston's now and again. He works for Surrey's family services and I've got half a mind to tell him—"

"What?" His depth of local knowledge was wholly unexpected. "You can't do that!" She sucked in a panicky breath. It felt like the entire town was under a dome, air quickly dissipating. They needed to get off that sidewalk. They needed to get out of Surrey. She was one wrong conversation away from an avalanche of fateful discoveries. "Where are you headed?"

"To the post office," Frank said, a few letters poking from his breast pocket. "If old man Holliston doesn't pay the bills right away, he forgets. He's fuzzy like that. I have to remind him to write me a check on Fridays."

"After the post office?"

"I'm repointing bricks over at a house on Sherman Street. My sharp-shooter skills aren't much use to Holliston, but my handyman services are making him a buck." Frank's agitation faded. "'Course, now that I think about it, Holliston won't realize if I'm gone for an hour or all afternoon."

◆ ◆ ◆

Frank rolled away from Missy's naked body, heavy breaths heaving out of him. God, but she knew her way around a bed full of sheets . . . or in a shower . . . or bent over a chair . . . or . . . Damn, he'd yet to suggest anything that Missy wasn't willing to do. Relationships weren't his strong suit, but that part of this one seemed to be on autopilot. The sex was astounding. Although he did notice that Missy rarely made eye contact, and afterward, her disposition drifted to unsure. The first few times they were together, she'd slipped from the bed and dressed before he could get rid of the spent condom. While Missy wasn't innocent to the act, she did seem confounded by other things. The *after things* that, in Frank's experience, women liked better than sex. Laurel certainly had.

His desire to spend time with Missy perplexed her as much as his initial hands-off behavior. His stomach wrenched imagining that Missy's behavior was the effect of a long and inappropriate relationship with Dustin Byrd.

"Where are you going?"

Frank heard a touch of fearfulness in her voice. He turned back. "Just getting something to drink. Do you want anything?" he asked, stopping by the bathroom. She said no and he got a glass of water. On his way back, Frank turned the air conditioner down a notch. "I don't think this thing works too good."

"Soon you won't have to worry about it," she said, only covering her feet with the sheet. Missy didn't have much modesty.

Frank put the glass on the nightstand and straddled her, his teeth nipping her soft pouty lips. Jesus, she had the greatest fucking mouth. *Literally* . . . He fought a sly smile and addressed the simple subject. "Probably not. I guess fall gets here before you know it."

Her hands pushed hard on his shoulders. "What do you mean fall?"

"The season after summer. Blond moment?" he teased, easily leveraging his weight to kiss her again. "September will be history and I won't need the AC. It's not worth complaining to O'Brien. Of course, with as hot as things get around . . ." He stopped, abandoning his straddled position. "What?"

"We have a plan, Frank. We're leaving Surrey, the two of us."

"Sure. In time."

"What do you mean, 'in time'? We said the beginning of the month, right after my birthday. You promised, Frank. We planned it. You said we could go to your sister's in New Jersey. That we could stay with her until you find a job. Then I'll write my mother, tell her about us, and . . . Frank?"

"Uh, yeah, we can probably do that." He picked up his cigarettes and lit one. True enough, Marie had asked Frank to come and stay with her after the psych hospital released him. It wasn't a lie. But he wasn't too sure about showing up with a girlfriend, both of them unemployed. "Missy, I've been thinking, maybe we'd be better off saving some cash before heading out of here."

"Absolutely not!" She sat up like a spike. "We can't do that! If cash is the problem, I have a solution that comes with a healthy payoff. I was just thinking through the details this morning."

"Yeah, what's that?" he said, taking a deep drag.

"I, uh . . . we can sell my car."

He laughed. "Then what? Hitchhike? That's crazy." He flicked ashes into a soda can. "Besides, I, uh . . . I figured the car was a gift. I'm not sure whose name it's in—yours or his. I didn't think it was my business. But I guess now it is."

Missy folded her arms stiffly across her chest. "I bought the car, Frank. And not only did I buy it, but I paid cash. So let that go to show that I can pull my weight." She relaxed, touching his arm. "Together, the two of us, we could make it."

"I didn't realize . . ." He wanted to ask how she'd managed to save that kind of money. But then Frank thought better of it. He needed her to listen to reason. "Still, if we took our time. What's the rush? Surrey's a sweet little spot—hey, I even hear the carnival's coming to town this weekend. I thought we could go and—"

"A carnival. Your mind is on a carnival?"

"Uh, no. I guess not. There were some flyers at Holliston's. I just brought one home," he said, touching the glossy paper that sat on the bedside table. "That's all. The point is I don't mind Surrey, and I have a perfectly respectable job."

"But I don't—" and her blue eyes began dripping tears. "I don't want to stay here, Frank! You have no idea how much."

"Why? If you think Dustin's going to cause a problem . . . Missy, he's the one who needs to worry—a thirty-three-year-old guy screwing around with a sixteen-year-old girl."

"He was thirty-two at the time," she corrected. "And it's not Dustin."

"Then what? If he opens his mouth, he'll be looking at statutory rape charges. Byrd will need every dime of his fat house down payment for a lawyer." Missy had confided this too, Dustin's safe full of cash. From the sound of things, the asshole had all but promised to have her barefoot and pregnant before her twenty-second birthday. Frank sucked hard on the cigarette, thinking about payback. Byrd had something coming other than a promotion—another piece of information he'd overheard at Holliston's. "If we stayed in Surrey, went public, it would get old Dustin right in the nuts." Frank narrowed his eyes, taking another drag. It wasn't enough. In the past, he'd taken out better men for less reason. Frank smiled as his fantasy progressed, imagining the terrified look on Byrd's face. Oddly, it seemed to match the one on Missy's.

"Listen to me," she said, her fingers squeezing into the muscle of his forearm. Frank tried drawing the cigarette to his mouth, but her grip was too firm. "I am not . . . *I cannot stay in Surrey*. Not another week—barely another day. I don't want a log-cabin house, tennis lessons, or a side trip to the carnival. There's enough circus in my life. I want out of here. If money is all that's stopping us then I'll come up with the cash. But if your plan is to stay in Surrey, it won't be with me. Please, Frank . . ."

The cigarette smoldered between his two fingers, and her nails nearly scored his flesh. He eyed the burning butt. She let go and he snuffed the cigarette out. "I don't get it. What the hell's here that's got you so spooked?"

Missy ran her hands up his sinewy arms. She scooted her bare ass along the sheet and burrowed tight to him. A wild thump from her chest pounded into his. "Frank," she said, her voice gritty and tense. "I need you to listen to me. I need . . . I need to tell you something about my father."

CHAPTER
TWENTY-ONE

Present Day

"I appreciate the desire to put Surrey behind you, Mr. Delacort. But talking to us might give you closure." Sitting at Malcolm's desk, Aubrey switched the phone to her other ear, as if this might make her more persuasive. "The *Surrey City Press* would really like an opportunity to hear your side of . . ." She picked up a pen, following the urge to doodle on a notepad. "Yes, I completely understand how you feel . . ." Absently, she watched the pen move, swirling strokes of blue ink on the yellow paper. "Um, no, I've never been incarcerated for twenty years unjustly, but . . . Right. I'm sure all sorts of media outlets want to talk to you." Aubrey began to shade in the object she'd drawn. She listened, reaching for plausible reasoning. "Personally, Mr. Delacort, I think there's serious poetic justice in talking to us first." Aubrey's gaze moved from the drawing to the five pairs of eyes opposite her. She hoped Frank Delacort couldn't hear the collective breathing. "Yes, I can see how the idea of being whisked from state prison to the set of *Good Morning America* is tempting . . . I agree. Room service is pretty sweet too." Aubrey forced the pen down and picked up the notepad, swiveling away from Ned, Kim, Gwen, Bebe, and Malcolm's anxious stares.

Levi had made initial contact the day before, talking to Delacort's attorney. But when today's phone call came in, her news junkie colleague was nowhere to be found. Aubrey took the call, surprised to find a freshly released Frank on the other end of the line. He'd been contentious at first, saying he only wanted a chance to tell the *Surrey City Press* to go fuck itself—the newspaper that had all but cheered on his guilty verdict. Yet Frank had softened as Aubrey spoke. It left her unsure about his motivation for continuing the conversation. Was his willingness to talk based on her persuasive arguing, the fact that she was a woman, or perhaps, she thought, glancing at the notepad, something else? "Aubrey Ellis, that's correct. Your attorney has all the relevant numbers. Just give it some thought before deciding." Aubrey turned the chair around and picked up the pen. "I understand that coming back to Surrey isn't appealing. Again, we'd be glad to come to you. Thank you for speaking with me, Mr. Delacort. I hope to hear from you." The phone hit the cradle, Aubrey exhaling the breath she'd been holding. "We'll see."

"Aubrey, that was stunning," said Gwen. "It sounded like you really connected with him."

"Mmm, connected. Good choice of words," she said, looking at the drawing. It was a sketch of tiny leaves in a wreath-like pattern. But how it connected to Frank Delacort she had no idea.

"Personally, I don't get it," Bebe said. "Why would he even consider speaking with you . . . *us*, instead of one of the larger media outlets?"

"He hasn't yet," she said. "And, admittedly, I'm surprised too."

Ned peered out the windowed office and into the newsroom. "I shouldn't say it, but if Delacort agrees to this, I wouldn't mind seeing Aubrey get the credit instead of . . ." He wrenched his neck a little farther. "Has anybody even seen St John today?"

"He's working from home. Speaking of which," Malcolm said, "don't you all have assignments? If there's more to know about Delacort,

I'll keep you informed." They dispersed, leaving Aubrey alone with Malcolm.

"Gwen's right. That was good work. And I don't mind mentioning, you don't look half bad in that editor in chief chair."

"Let's not get ahead of ourselves." Aubrey relinquished the seat, taking the page from the notepad with her.

"Well, I can't go on here forever. Anyway, keep me up to speed," he said, taking her place. "After what you and Levi uncovered with Delacort's claims and the info on Byrd's guns—damn, the headline could be epic. Anything from: *Byrd Found with Smoking Gun* to: *State Exonerates Killer*."

"I agree. It does feel like it could go either way. But the next move is up to Delacort." She examined the paper filled with a circle of leaves, curious how it connected to Frank—concerned that it might link to Missy Flannigan. Aubrey thought about her more recent episode with Eli Serino. The idea of encountering Missy remained a disconcerting prospect. Aubrey breathed deep and tried to will away the dark thought. "About Levi, is he really working from home?"

"Actually, I haven't heard from him. I just didn't need them to know that. I thought perhaps you . . ."

"No, I haven't seen him since yesterday. He disappeared not long after we spoke about Byrd and Delacort in his office."

Malcolm looked as if he was on the verge of handing down an ultimatum about Levi. Aubrey cut him off. "I'll handle it. I'll find Levi and we'll get this story right. You don't have to worry, Malcolm, about anything but newspaper business."

"I hope not, Aubrey. I'm counting on you both."

◆ ◆ ◆

Before leaving the *Surrey City Press*, Aubrey stopped by human resources. On a different notepad, she scribbled an address. Ten minutes later, she was circling the parking lot of Green Hills at Surrey. She spotted Levi's car and parked, making her way up a mum-lined front walk. Green Hills was an affable condo complex—golf course, club house, year-round exterior maintenance. Aubrey had covered more than one for-sale unit there. They were pedestrian home portrait visits, the condos containing nothing but mirror-image floor plans and anxious sellers. Apparently, MediaMatters leased one annually. It accommodated out-of-town corporate types, and currently provided housing to a reporter on loan.

She rang the bell, boldly peering in the sidelights. On the second buzz she heard footsteps. The door opened and Aubrey stepped back. Levi without a tie. To her, it seemed as revealing as Levi without pants. Her impression didn't ease as her gaze traveled downward, from his open dress shirt, undershirt beneath, past his very-there pants, and onto his bare feet. She pulled her gaze back up and squinted into his blood-shot eyes. "Not a great moment to decide to take a Jimmy Buffett vacation day, you know?"

"What do you want?"

"What do I want? Uh, Levi, we're kind of in the middle of a major unfolding story—the pieces of which nobody has but us—and you choose not to show up?" He walked away from the door. Aubrey was marginally surprised it didn't slam in her face. "Will you stop and talk to me?" she said, following. "Malcolm has no idea where you are, and if you don't think that the entire newsroom is wondering why ace-reporter, Levi St—"

"I'll call Malcolm." He turned from the middle of the living room. "As for the rest of them, I could give a . . . Never mind. You fill in the blanks."

Aubrey saw a silk scarf hanging over a chair and on the table was a cosmetics bag. "Is, uh . . . is Bethany still here?"

"She is and she isn't." He picked up a coffee cup, though Aubrey spied a bar nearby. She guessed the open bottle of scotch and half-empty glass explained his evening. "She went to visit an old college roommate in Salem. You have any *contacts* there?" She tipped her head, offering an unamused stare. "I told her I had some things on my mind. That I was running late this morning."

"And she just left? Even though you're clearly upset."

"I'm not . . ." He sucked in a breath. "I'm working through it."

"Looks like the only thing you're working through is a bottle of scotch."

He walked to the bar and screwed the cap on. "I had a few drinks last night. Is that a problem?"

"We both know that's not the problem. Did you talk to Bethany about the Serino house or anything we spoke about yesterday?"

He turned toward the bar again, as if vacillating between the coffee cup and scotch. He chose the coffee, gulping it. "No. I didn't go out of my way to share my day with Bethany."

"Of course not," she said, taking a turn around the room. "Why share your feelings, especially when filing things away comes so naturally?"

"That's another thing. I really wish you'd stay the fuck away from my feelings."

"Tempting. Perhaps you can tell me your secret for so deftly ignoring them." An even trade of glares passed between them. Aubrey backed off. "You were . . . you are upset. I just thought someone to talk to might not be an awful idea." She placed her satchel on the table and her hand on her hip.

"Ellis, I hate to be rude . . . No I don't. If I wanted to talk, you wouldn't be my second . . . or even last choice."

"Yeah. I got that, Levi." She felt remarkably alone in the room, thinking *now* might be a great time for Brody to show. She stalled, opting for the other reason she'd turned up on his doorstep. "I thought you might be interested in a Frank Dela—"

"I'm handling Delacort from here." He picked his cell up, glancing at the screen. "I'm waiting for his attorney to call."

"Catch up, Levi. I spoke with Delacort."

"You spoke with . . ."

"Frank Delacort. Correction, freshly exonerated Frank Delacort who's busy being courted by countless media outlets."

"According to his attorney, the *Surrey City Press* was pretty much Delacort's last choice. In fact, I think that message was the only reason he returned my call. So what happened to spur that communication?"

"I, um . . ." Aubrey slipped her hand into the pocket of her skirt, touching the paper from Malcolm's desk. A ghostly vibe via Frank would be the last thing Levi needed to hear. "Why Delacort chose to call, I can't really say. But I did have a fairly decent dialogue with him. He's considering giving us an interview."

"You're kidding." Levi narrowed his bloodshot eyes. "You know, Ellis, maybe that's for the best. I should just head back to Hartford. Sounds like you and the rest of the Surrey team can take it from here."

"Malcolm doesn't want the rest of the team. He wants you on this story, Levi. He wants us to handle it."

"You have the scoop on Delacort. You'll figure it out. If he agrees to talk," he said, finishing the coffee and blowing by her, "you and Ned can handle it. He's been champing at the bit from the start."

"Levi, wait!" Aubrey braved his gust of anger and followed, not really thinking about where they were going. "I'm not comfortable handling this with Ned. Don't let what I said about your bro—" Her discomfort struck a new high. Inside his bedroom were an unmade bed and a tangle of sheets. Aubrey's gaze jerked from the furniture to the ceiling fan, unable to avoid seeing a puddle of silky black nightgown that lay on the carpet. "You know," she said, ignoring the scenery, "between your last trip to Surrey and this one, I've thought a lot of things about you. Not all of them pleasant."

"Great," he said, punching a pillow onto the bed. "So in addition to unearthing my past—which is none of your business—you want to give me a personality assessment?" He moved on to the closet, hauling out a suitcase. "Thanks, but I'm aware of areas that need work from my annual review."

"What I was going to say is that it takes a while to get to know Levi St John. A person may even have to *want it*. So I've thought a lot of things—some off-putting and some pretty damn amazing. Either way, in all of that, I never thought you were a coward."

Levi took a step toward Aubrey, his hand wrapping so tight around the spindle of the four-poster bed she swore the wood cracked. "You don't know what the hell you're talking about."

"I know more than you think."

"Don't start, Ellis. I repeat, I have no idea why my past has become your present-day trivial pursuit, but I won't let you do this. I won't let you sully what good I have left. Disrupt the peace I've made with it."

"Bull, Levi. You haven't made peace with any of it. You couldn't even tell your longtime girlfriend about something that had you so upset you dropped a bombshell story and ran from a job that—from what I can gather—is the only thing keeping you alive."

He opened a dresser drawer, thrusting boxers and T-shirts into the suitcase. "Hey, why don't you give Suzanne Serino a call? According to Aubrey Ellis lore, it sounds like she deserves a little torture from beyond the grave!"

"Eli Serino wasn't interested in communicating anything positive. But your brother, Brody, he—"

Levi froze, fists clutching underwear and T-shirts. "What did you say?"

"Brody."

"I never told you . . . I never said his . . ."

"No, you've never told me his name. I know a few things about your brother. He was a lifeguard, a place called Rocky Neck. It's on the south shore of Connect—"

"I know where the hell it is." Levi dismissed the revelation and returned to the task of packing.

Aubrey stepped farther into the bedroom. "I also know your brother attended Valley Forge Military Prep. He was supposed to go to West Point. But he didn't want to, did he, Levi?"

He abandoned the suitcase, striding toward her. "Absolutely correct. But it's still information any good reporter could uncover. There was a nice piece in the local paper about the scholarship the town gives out in his name. Of course, there's also Brody's obituary. Current circumstance makes me choke on it, but your big reveal only proves one thing: you are a damn thorough reporter."

"Thanks. But I really didn't come here fishing for a compliment."

"Good, because I really didn't mean to offer one." He slammed the suitcase shut. "Although, I didn't think dogged aggressiveness was in your wheelhouse. I stand corrected."

"I have a job to do, Levi. We have critical information on the Flannigan story that could blow this whole thing wide open—whether it's Byrd's connection to Missy or information about Delacort that was totally missed the first time around. But without your input, the story will only be half as good." Aubrey was determined to stand her ground, and her height aided the effort, so she nearly met him eye-to-eye. "And so we're clear, to my dismay, that *was* a compliment."

Levi backed up, and ran a hand through his hair. The gesture seemed like a reluctant admission. Walking away from the Missy Flannigan story was not in him.

"However, we also have something more personal, just as important, to settle first."

"I told you, I'm not interested in discussing my brother."

"Great. That makes two of us—if it were up to me. But it's not. Seems I'm the one without a choice." Aubrey paused as the briny smell of sea washed ashore, the cutting taste of whiskey burning at the back of her throat. She was relieved. Brody wouldn't stand her up. He was there. Even more forceful than taste or smell was a wallop of incoming emotion, a rare occurrence in Aubrey's experience. She'd felt it in Jim

Thorpe, between the ginger-haired mother on the bench and her son. She'd recognized it as similar to the connection she shared with Charley. But this bond, it belonged solely to Levi and his brother. "Brody's waited a long time for this chance, Levi. So much so that he's visited me before. Do you have any idea how improbable that is?"

"You mean more so than the idea of communicating with the dead, period?"

"I was just a teenager—on *your* beach in Connecticut. That day— in addition to saving a young boy's life—Brody assured me he'd be back. At the time, I had no idea what he was talking about. But I do know it's something more than your precious random chance. Do you really think it's coincidence that you and I should end up in the same news-room years later?"

"So now he planned it?"

"Planned it . . . knew it would come to pass . . . understood that one day he'd have this exact opportunity. Look at it any way you need to. Don't confuse my gift with an ability to explain the universe," she said. "I'm not that special."

Levi's expression remained vague, looking as if he were unde-cided—possibly about what she was saying, more likely about how to get rid of her. It was a battle of wills, and Aubrey understood that she was out of pleasant approaches.

"Just go. I don't want you here," he said, toneless. "I'll come into the office shortly. We'll work the Flannigan story . . . *just* the Flannigan story. If we can keep it to that—"

"I can't." Aubrey slumped onto the footboard of the bed. "I get your skepticism. I really do. Believe me. You are far from my first trip to that rodeo. It's one of many reasons I don't want this," she said, her arm cir-cling empty air, "to be my life. I know the things I've said about Brody can be attributed to good research. For instance, I—"

But Aubrey stopped, distracted by a voice. It was clearer than in recent weeks, nearly as vibrant as that morning on Rocky Neck beach.

She skimmed her gaze downward, her mind focused on the words—Brody's words. Tiny waves of explanation began to wash toward her. Levi's hands were thrust to his waist; his watch was at her eye level. Aubrey looked up. "The scent of salt water and the smell of burning wood. They don't go together."

"What are you talking about?" Levi said.

"Some things are mutually exclusive. Brody was a lifeguard on that beach in Connecticut, but he didn't die there. He died three thousand miles away . . . in a fire."

"That's it! We're done." He grabbed Aubrey's arm, yanking her off the bed. "I want you out of here, now!"

Levi hustled her toward the door, his will and size moving them out of the bedroom and through the condo. Aubrey continued to talk, the sound of Brody's voice supplying her with a steady stream of information. "You were visiting your mother. You've never told me much about her."

"Sure I did. She was a drunk. Still is, for the most part," he said, all but dragging her through the living room. "If you did some in-depth Googling, you probably even discovered that she starred in a soap opera back in the day." They came to an abrupt halt in the hall. Levi's grip tightened, yanking her toward him. "If you can tell me the name of it, I'll give you bonus points and politely open the door, which, believe me, is not my first instinct."

Aubrey pulled her arm back, the two of them caught in the narrow condo hall. "Actually, I have no idea about that. But here's a lesser-known piece of Levi St John trivia—your mother, she was also a Playboy Bunny. That's how your parents met. She was part of a USO tour."

Levi's mouth pursed to a hard line. He sounded like a bull snorting a breath. "A minute detail, but not impossible to ascertain—especially if you've seen the April '77 issue of *Playboy*. My mother looks amazing on deep-pile shag. Did you happen to catch the heart-shaped mole on the inside of her left thigh?"

"Afraid not. Brody didn't mention anything like that about J.C."

On the breath meant to deliver more cynicism, Levi stopped. "J—"

"J.C.," she said.

Emotion crept onto Levi's stone-carved face.

"That's what Brody said he called her. It stands for—"

"I know what it stands for." His wide dark eyes turned to slits. "I know my mother's . . . I just . . ."

"You'd forgotten that. Or you haven't thought about it in years, what Brody used to call your mother. It's also not something I would have learned via the most scrupulous research." There wasn't any rebuttal, just a startled look. "They had a good relationship, Levi. That made you happy. Brody liked your mother, he was even a little envious that you had one . . . despite her flaws."

"An astute guess." But his tone had weakened. Levi shook his head. It was involuntary, more like he was fighting her for the mental edge. "So beyond a few facts, this is a well-honed craft, strategically placed guesses. A parlor trick, a Vegas show . . ." But Levi didn't move, his body almost pressing into hers. His mouth opened and closed. He held his arms stiff to his sides and his hands curled to fists. "Prove it, Ellis. Tell me one thing . . . just one thing that no one on this earth could possibly know."

"I'll tell you two." Aubrey breathed deep, the scents of seawater and burning wood marrying together. "Brody went with you to California because you almost drowned in the pool the summer before. The gardener pulled you out." Levi's jaw slacked, his eyes so glassy Aubrey saw her reflection. "You confided to Brody, and I sincerely doubt another living soul, that you'd been diving for pennies."

Levi stepped away, his back to the wall. His glare glanced off Aubrey and into the corners of the narrow entry. He looked down as her hand came up and boldly wrapped around the watch on his wrist. "And the other thing?"

"It's about the night he died. That's why Brody's here. It's why he's waited all these years for this chance."

"So this is the same as what Eli Serino wanted," Levi said, swallowing hard. "Tell me, Ellis, is part of your job description to deliver vengeance?"

"What?" she said, her head shaking.

"I told you, I'm the reason my brother is dead. What could Brody possibly want other than . . ."

"Levi, listen to me." Aubrey's voice fell to a hush, the soft tone filling the generic entry hall. "Talk to me. *Trust me.* I swear to you. It'll be all right—all of it." She tugged on his arm. To her surprise, he allowed his hand to be drawn into hers. Aubrey felt compassion, startled by his need for human comfort. "Tell me what you did. Explain to me why your brother's death is your fault."

CHAPTER
TWENTY-TWO

Thousand Oaks, California
1994

"Dear God, my sweet boy! I swear, a foot—you've grown an absolute foot! Let me look at you!" Her soft hands squeezed Levi's face. They smelled of a cottony lotion and a trace of lime. Dreamy blue eyes, unlike his, stared at him. Looking into them, Levi felt as if his eyes were open under water. "Handsome . . . just to-die-for handsome!" She made no mention of the glasses, which were new since he'd last seen her. But she was right about the height. Last summer his mother had also crushed him at the door, holding Levi to a safe line well below her bosom. This year he smashed directly into it—then it was like trying to breathe under water. She didn't seem to notice that either.

"You're suffocating him, Jackie. Let the boy go," his father said, gripping Levi's shoulder.

"And you're being ridiculous as ever!" Levi cued to the high-pitch of false pleasantries, which he often thought was part of their divorce settlement. He caught his father's impatient glance and his mother's tense smile as she clung to what he assumed to be her court-ordered civil tone. "What's the matter, Rick?" His father hated to be called Rick. "Does my show of affection have you in a blue-blood knot? I swear," she hummed under her breath. Her long nails glided through Levi's hair. She loved his hair. This made no sense to Levi, since he had his father's thick hair. But what between his parents did make sense? "It'll be all I can do to show the child enough love while I have him."

"Yes, and if you like, we can review why your time with him is limited." The stroking stopped and her fingers pressed into his scalp. She let go and smiled at her son, less tense. But it was followed by another flip remark, and Levi was drawn to her lipstick-covered mouth. He'd watched his mother paint her whole face, kind of like a human paint-by-numbers. She could even do it with a cigarette in her hand, though she repeatedly insisted it was her last one. Levi was awed by the finished face. Everyone was. He knew his mother was beautiful. Not just pretty, the way all the kids in his fourth-grade class thought their mothers were pretty. But the kind of beautiful they put in magazines. Levi had confirmation of this on his last visit, having found a carton of Virginia Slims and an old issue of *Playboy* in her nightstand drawer. Miss April, 1977. He'd made the mistake of looking through the magazine, not fully prepared to find his mother with a staple through her stomach. Levi was fairly sure this staple was different from the ones she talked about having after he was born. He'd seen most of her anyway; bare body parts didn't faze her—clearly. But Levi concentrated on his sandals, reminding himself not to open drawers while he was there.

Jacqueline was busy rebutting his father's remark about visitation. "*Limited* because you had the judge in your back pocket, Broderick." Levi stared harder at the floor. He didn't want to be the cause of this and yet, he was. From his lower point of view, he saw porcelain fists rise to his mother's narrow hips. In turn, his father's hold tightened around his shoulders. He almost panicked. His father could do an abrupt about-face and take him back to Connecticut. He might, no matter what any custody agreement said. Levi hoped not. He had to pee and he loved the pool. Of course, he would use the bathroom first.

"Enough, Jackie," he said, yanking Levi closer. "We agreed that exchanges would be diplomatic."

"Then maybe you should have brought someone from the British embassy with you." The jab would likely incite the war his parents had never finished fighting. For some reason, Levi had the stupid idea that a divorce would mean a truce. Nothing like that had happened. Levi looked up, his mother's pool-water eyes connecting with his. He watched her stand down. She broke eye contact and looked across the room. "Hey, you," she said, her voice bubbly. Her blond head bobbed around his father's strapping frame, looking toward Brody, who hadn't said a word since they arrived. His brother was like that lately, so quiet you could forget he was there. "Cat got your tongue or what? You planning on stayin'? I sure hope so, 'cause I got fun on tap for three!" Levi and their father moved out of the foyer and into the sunken living room, making way for Brody.

"Hey, J.C., it's nice to be here. Thanks for inviting me." Brody waited, not yet at ease, his hand wringing around his watch. It was a new habit, as it was a new watch, a graduation gift from Levi. His father had helped him pick out the military timekeeping piece. Brody seemed far happier with it than the first edition encyclopedias of war, which was Pa's gift—at least that's what his brother had called them. Levi had never felt there was much he could do for his big brother, so it pleased him to know Brody was so taken with the watch.

"Your father thought you tagging along was a good idea, and for once I couldn't agree more. I hope you brought your trunks. I know you're an excellent swimmer."

"Yes ma'am. First place in the five-hundred-meter freestyle this year."

"And mind you," Pa said, "he forfeited his last weeks' lifeguarding to super . . . to *visit* here with Levi." His father stepped back into the foyer, retrieving one of the suitcases. As he brushed by his mother, Levi heard his accented mumble, "At the very least, I have some assurances my younger son won't drown while in your care." She had no snarky reply.

Levi guessed that was the cause of the latest tension and the reason he hadn't visited over the Christmas holiday. Last summer, pennies tossed in the deep end of the pool were deeper than Levi thought. The side was suddenly a mile from his outstretched arms. The gardener had pulled him out as a flood of water rushed up his nose. But it was his mother who'd scared him more. She'd cried hysterically as he coughed up chlorinated water, covering him in salty tears and kisses, her breath heavy with the stuff that she kept in the bar. His father would never have been the wiser. Even at ten, Levi knew better than to relay a story like that. But on the return trip to California to collect Levi, his father ran headlong into the gardener. Emilio felt it was his duty to explain his heroics. Levi supposed this was most of the reason that Brody was there. It also explained the tangled mess of roses in the front yard.

The rest of the reason took a little more thinking, and that's what Levi had done on the long flight, having finished *Treasure Island* and *The Red Badge of Courage*. Naturally, Levi had known his parents all his life, but he always felt as if he had known Brody longer. His half-brother was seven years older. Brody's mother was American too and had died of something awful that nobody wanted to talk about. According to their father, American heritage was the only thing Rosalee St John had in common with Levi's mother. Levi often thought this is what he and Brody had bonded over—absentee American mothers. That and Pa, a man for whom fatherhood seemed a greater mystery than *The Count of Monte Cristo*. Fair or not, Brody had been thrust into the middle of Levi's broken home. And instead of siding with their father, or worse, taking his stepmother's side—a woman Brody openly liked—he'd done his best to protect Levi from the fallout. When it came to his parents, Brody was Switzerland. Even so, and despite the pool incident, Levi was surprised that his father had agreed to the terms of the visit. Somewhere over the Grand Canyon, Levi thought maybe that had more to do with Brody and Pa than it did his mother and him.

Levi had always had a good memory, recalling clearly—from the time he was little—his parents fighting: his mother stumbling in from somewhere she wasn't supposed to be, late at night, and the sounds of the violent outbursts that followed. Smashed crystal marring the library paneling and silent meals where clinking cutlery was the only sound. But even clearer than this, Levi remembered what Brody was going to be. Brody was a soldier, away at military school most of the year. He came home on breaks, although just about the time his peach fuzz hair grew out and his posture looked anything less than rigid, he'd have to go back. Valley Forge Military Academy was an important place; Pa said that all time. Brody was destined to march in their father's military footsteps. It was an unchangeable fact, like Brody's eyes were blue and his thumbs double jointed. But over the last year, the things surrounding those facts had changed. Anger, between his father and brother, had invaded their orderly lives once again. It was something Levi had never remembered hearing from Brody before. Then, a few weeks ago, when Pa was out of town, he left Brody in charge.

At first, things were fine—the two brothers breaking the rules by eating in front of the TV and not brushing their teeth until noon, if at all. But Brody strayed even further. Levi had noticed a lingering odor coming from his bedroom. It smelled like oily burning herbs, the scent hanging in the air longer than his mother's cigarette smoke. When Levi questioned it, Brody shrugged it off, blaming it on unwashed salt-water swim trunks. "Give me a break, kid! Pa's not here and Valley Forge isn't breaking my balls anymore. I've got two months until the West Point crap kicks in—so fuck a little stink and mess." It wasn't the unlikely show of temper or even the untidiness of Brody's room. Levi also appreciated the reprieve from spit-spot. It was more about defiance, something he'd never witnessed from the always cooperative Brody. Days later, after Pa had returned, Levi swore the same saltwater, swim trunk smell had moved into the garage.

Lost in thought, Levi barely felt the poke to his shoulder. Brody was handing him a glass of lemonade. "It's fine, drink it," he said. He leaned over, whispering, "Don't worry, J.C.'s on her best behavior." This was a reminder of the spiked punch she'd once accidentally served them. Levi had been six at the time.

The foursome stood in the square living room like mismatched chess pieces. The shag carpet tickled Levi's toes, and the piped in rock music—the kind his father hated—seemed to be playing louder than it should. Levi was the only kid at Foxxmore Academy who knew every word to the *Rumours* album. He peered toward the pool. If it weren't for Brody, he guessed his father would have insisted it be drained and backfilled. It wasn't that he felt unsafe with his mother. But compared to living with Pa, the need for instant decisions could be . . . well, life or death. No matter what the upset in Connecticut, Brody wouldn't let anything bad happen to his brother.

"Brody, you're in the room at the end of the hall upstairs. I thought you'd like the extra privacy. Levi likes the one right next to mine. Or at least you did last summer," his mother said, shaking her head at his height. "You can bunk closer to your brother if you'd rather, sweetie."

"No, it's okay, wherever," he said, sipping the lemonade.

"So, Rick, should I put your things into the maid's quarters? I don't have live-in help—so if you dare . . ." She swept her hand past the front door and toward the rear room.

He glanced at his watch. "Do not tempt me, Jackie. Though I truly doubt either of us could stomach it for long. I'll be off. I'll be staying in town one night. Brody has the number of the hotel."

"What's the matter, Rick? Afraid a few days in the sun might crack your exterior?"

"You truly feel a mere fifty-six-hundred-degree-Celsius object could accomplish this after surviving you? Unlikely. Brody, you have the number?"

"Yes, Pa." Brody's hand slipped into the pocket of his seersucker shorts. It was the third time Pa had checked since they'd gotten on the plane. It was always odd to see Brody in street clothes, like today's lightweight shorts and polo. Levi had two distinct visions of his brother—one in full dress uniform, a wool thing that had to have been suffocating on graduation day weeks ago, and his orange town-issued swim trunks. Brody was always more himself in the swim trunks, his staple summer uniform as he patrolled freedom and Rocky Neck beach.

"I'll call you at nineteen hundred, as we arranged, son."

"Seriously?" his mother said, shaking her head. "Thank heaven your other son was spared." She moved toward the door. Levi guessed Pa was supposed to follow. He did, but not without a warning glance at Brody—short code for the operational tactics he'd laid out at dawn: "Know where Levi is at all times . . . Do not be duped by that woman's light-hearted manner . . . And never allow your brother near the pool without you . . ." For any other eighteen-year-old it might have been a big responsibility. But it was a small mission for the military-savvy, certified lifeguard Brody.

♦ ♦ ♦

After the initial settling in, Levi and his mother were off to a good start. Her casual lifestyle was a jolt to the system, but it wasn't long before Levi's bed went unmade and he rested his feet on the coffee table without a care. A week into the month-long visit, she'd taken him to every nearby tourist attraction. One trip included a movie studio, where Levi saw the sets to some of his favorite old westerns. There was something about the steadiness of John Wayne that he preferred over the brawny overkill of Arnold Schwarzenegger. Disneyland was a longer day, and Levi was unable to muster his mother's enthusiasm for the crowded theme park. But it seemed like it would crush her if he was less than elated, so he smiled and went on every ride twice. In between her friends came to visit—lots of them, a revolving door of pretty people. The women tousled his hair, remarking, "My God, he's going to be a heartbreaker! Say what you want about your ex, Jackie, but that *Seven Brides for Seven Brothers* brawny frame will suit your son. So, exactly how old is the brother?" His mother laughed with the women, and sometimes men, who asked, but she always answered, "Not old enough. Hands off!"

Since Levi's last visit, his mother had started acting in a soap opera, which accounted for most of the new company—although there were others, including members of a punk rock band. The lead singer was a rough-looking guy named Reese. He wore metal through so many pieces of flesh that Levi imagined unhooking them would cause the punk rocker to fall apart. But mostly Levi was mesmerized by his accent. It was British, but incredibly different from his father's. It made him pay attention when Reese talked, which was a lot. Levi was also amazed by how many ways someone could use *fuck* in a sentence. Reese lived with one of the women when she wasn't on the soap opera, which he liked to joke about. "Yeah, mate, she's fucking the fucking bloke all day, then she's got to come home and fucking fuck me!"

Levi had little idea what a soap opera was, but he guessed it was something more than "a preposterous excuse for real employment," which was the only description his father had provided. His mother seemed to feel differently, beaming over her new job. One afternoon she insisted Levi watch. "Here, baby, just see for yourself. It's hard to explain. Kind of like a dramatic movie that never ends." After that she disappeared into the kitchen to talk on the phone and sneak a cigarette. From the opening scene, *Santa Barbara* delivered the drama his mother promised. She—or "Brianne," her name on the soap opera—was in the midst of a fierce argument with a guy who called her a slut. They lived in a fancy house, and apparently the two of them argued violently all the time. Then, right before a commercial break, "Brianne" downed two drinks. It made Levi wonder if it was the reason she'd gotten the part. But when *Santa Barbara* resumed, Jacqueline St John's true talent became evident as "Brianne" shed more clothes than Levi imagined was possible on television. She proceeded to kiss a different guy, and the two of them got into bed. Levi watched the TV bug-eyed as his mother came back into the room. "Isn't that neat, baby—seeing your mama in her first big part?" She didn't seem bothered by the activity, her TV persona and the man rolling around in the bed, kissing and breathing heavy.

Somewhere in between, Brody had also entered the room. His face looked as screwed up as Levi's insides felt. "Uh, hey, J.C., I promised Levi serious pool time this afternoon. Now seems good." He nudged Levi's back until he stood. "Do you want to come with us?"

"Oh sure . . . the pool." She looked hurt that Brody hadn't suggested a bowl of popcorn, while the three of them cozied up on the couch to watch the rest of *Santa Barbara*. "No, you boys head out. I have to learn my lines for tomorrow anyway."

"Yep, no problem," Brody said, opening the slider. "Come on, kid. You can watch TV later." Levi slipped under his brother's arm, which was locked around the sliding glass door. He heard his voice make that angry sound. "Ten days left of fun in the sun. Better get yours while you can. Pa will be back before you know it."

As their return date to Connecticut drew nearer, Brody's mood worsened. That's what Levi was thinking as he cannonballed into the deep end of the pool and his brother plopped hard onto a lounge chair. He took off his watch, laying it on a side table. But Levi knew he'd be lucky if Brody spent ten minutes in the pool with him. Levi thought the trip would be a longer version of those rare instances when Pa went out of town. But things hadn't gone that way. Except for the fights with Pa, Brody was even quieter than the weeks before they'd left for

California. When they went places, like studio tours and amusement parks, Levi's mother had to coax him into coming along. And in many instances he didn't. The only time Brody seemed happy was when his mother's friends came by. He liked Reese in particular, and all of them openly smoked the stuff that was clearly not wet saltwater swim trunks.

Happy turned into something else entirely when Brody added cans of beer to the routine. He could down a whole six pack while smoking the tiny rolled up cigarettes that they passed from person to person. It was confusing. But it was also the only time Brody smiled or laughed, and Levi wasn't sure how that was a bad thing. The herby scent made its way into Brody's bedroom, which didn't seem to faze his mother. Levi thought maybe it should. He almost said something after finding a snoring Brody and a bag of the stuff they used to make the little cigarettes. Beside his slumbering body was an open bottle of Johnnie Walker. But Levi chose to keep quiet. He didn't want Brody or his mother to get into trouble. There was no gardener—no one except Levi who knew—and that meant his father would never find out.

Levi figured it was a waiting game. In another week the visit would end. He and his brother would return to Connecticut and normalcy. Not long after that Brody would head off to West Point. His brother was blowing off steam; that was all. He guessed West Point would be a lot like Valley Forge Military Prep, maybe tougher. And Levi focused on that logical procession of events. He'd nearly convinced himself that the moment would pass as he headed up the stairs from the solarium. The afternoon sun was too hot and Levi retreated to his bedroom to finish the Jules Verne novel he'd started that morning. Levi got halfway down the upstairs hall and a mumble of conversation turned into clear dialogue. Brody was in his mother's bedroom, the door half open. An uneasy feeling stopped Levi. Instead of going in, he slipped behind his own bedroom door and listened.

"I feel for you, honey, I really do. Believe me. No one knows better than me how difficult your father can be."

"And still, you won't talk to him."

"Oh, Brody, it's not that simple. And talking to him isn't what you're asking me to do. Think about it. You want me, a woman Broderick St John all but loathes, to tell him that A, you're not going to West Point—an event that's been on his calendar since the day you were born. And, B, there'll only be one son returning on the flight home with him. Sure. That'll work."

Levi thought the remark was odd; the custody agreement was iron-clad. There wasn't any way he wasn't going back to Connecticut next week. Brody cleared up his misconception. "I need backup, J.C., and there's nobody I can ask but you. I want to stay here! He's going to flip about West Point—"

"Brody, that's crazy talk and you know it. He'll kill us both! Correction. He'll kill me and drag you straight to West Point."

"You don't understand how serious I am about this. Whether you help or not, I'm not going to West Point! I hated the six goddamn years I spent at Valley Forge. I'll hate that place even more. I talked to Reese. He said he'd give me a job as a roadie with his band." This statement caused Levi to take a step back. Broderick St John's son working in a punk rock band? You might as well announce you were defecting to the enemy.

"I know it seems tempting, even glamorous—Reese talks a good game. I can see how it's appealing, especially compared to a place like Valley Forge. But it's not that simple. As much as I disagree with your father on just about everything, I can't fight that battle for you. I just can't."

"Why? Why won't you help me?" Brody's voice carried a pitch of desperation. "You hate him as much as I do! Shit, you probably hate him more." Levi's eyes widened. Disagreements, fine, but hearing Brody say he hated Pa made his insides clench. "How could you not? He took away your own damn kid!"

"And that's exactly why I can't talk to him. Listen to me, honey. Broderick did his best to make sure I see as little of Levi as possible.

That's true. But we both know I gave him plenty of ammunition. And after last summer, you can bet I'm lucky that all I lost was Christmas. Imagine what your father will do if I put myself in between the two of you. Just think about it."

"What? What could he possibly do? You're already divorced from him." There was a growl from Brody, guttural and tense. "If I stay here, he'll take it out on you. And if you try to help me, he'll find some way to make sure you never see Levi again. Won't he?"

"I love that boy, Brody." Levi heard his mother's voice swell. "I may not win any prizes for mother of the year. Nobody's ever going to cast me in that part. Given a choice between the two of us, Levi might be better off with Rick most of the year. But he is my son, and I can't do anything to risk the time I do have with him. I certainly can't do something that your father would see as a direct attack. Can you understand that?"

There was quiet, then Brody's voice. It sounded so lost. "I guess . . . Yes, I do. I just don't know where that leaves me."

"You'll figure it out, sweetie. You're a smart kid. Maybe you're making more out of it than need be. Think of all the months you'll get to go without your father hovering—that's something. And if it's not what you want to do with your life, it's not forever. You're young. It's not like he's sending you off to prison."

"My life has been nothing but a fucking prison since the day I was born."

"Brody, come on, you're starting to sound like a *Santa Barbara* storyline! Let's just try to enjoy the rest of your vacation. What do you say? We're having a get together later, some of the gang from work—even Reese. There'll be plenty of party favors. At the very least, it will take your mind off things."

Brody laughed, which didn't sound funny at all. "Right . . . sure. I ought to grab ahold of freedom while I can." As Brody came out of his mother's room, Levi ducked behind the door. Brody walked past and into his room, slamming the door shut.

Levi peeked around the corner and inched into the hall. From the edge of her open bedroom door, he saw his mother sink onto the bed and reach for the drawer where she kept the magazines and cigarettes. She took out the whole carton. But instead of smoking one, she threw the carton to the far side of the room, packs of cigarettes spilling everywhere. "Broderick St John, you are a miserable son of a bitch. That poor kid," she said, hands covering her face. Standing in the hall, Levi didn't know what to do, which direction he should go.

CHAPTER
TWENTY-THREE

"Eventually, I chose to go into my mother's room. What I didn't know was that a few hours later that same decision would cost Brody his life." Levi and Aubrey had forgone furniture, and instead had sunk onto the condo floor. As he sat in the narrow entryway, Levi touched the timepiece, the way a blind man might feel what he couldn't see. Scooting forward a few inches, Aubrey also made contact with the watch. He didn't pull away. Levi's stillness said he was ready to listen.

"We're up to that night. I need . . ." Aubrey ruffled her fingers through her hair. Then she focused on the solid white tile floor. "Brody wants you to tell me all of it, everything, exactly the way you saw it."

"Brody wants . . . ?" She nodded; Levi half laughed, shaking his head. "I guess if nothing else we can label it *shock therapy*. I don't know if I . . ." There was a look on Levi's face, an expression completely removed from the man Aubrey knew. "I've never spoken about it."

She smiled. "Brody says it's time . . . Time to stop, Levi . . ." Aubrey listened harder, repeating words that made no sense to her. "He says you're not Mr. Z?"

"Mr. Z." He looked hard into Aubrey's eyes. Again, she saw her reflection, maybe slightly less doubt. "Mr. Zablouski," Levi said. "He was a science teacher at Valley Forge. Brody had him three years in a row. I was an inquisitive kid, maybe relentless. Brody used to tell me I was the only person who ever asked 'why' more than Mr. Zablouski."

"The early makings of a reporter. So report the rest, Levi. Tell Brody and me what happened that night—at least what you think happened."

His voice was reluctant, his hand raking over his pained face. "If I'd made a list of a million things I thought I'd do while I was here in Surrey . . ."

"I know. This wouldn't be a million and one."

"No," he said, shaking his head at her. "It wouldn't." Levi took another deep breath. "It started out like every other night. Everyone was partying, the music was loud. It was a bigger crowd than usual. At some point, Brody came downstairs. He seemed different . . . settled, even calm. I was surprised. His conversation with my mother had upset me. Everything seemed better and I let it go. I had no answer, that's for sure."

"You were eleven."

"Not having an answer wasn't an excuse—Pa drilled that in from early on. But I didn't say a word to Brody, nothing. I acted as if everything was fine. It was the same feeling of relief I had about Valley Forge—our family's spin on don't ask, don't tell."

"Meaning?"

"Pa shipped Brody off to military prep when he was nine. Here I was, eleven, and he'd never said a word to me about going. I never asked him why because I didn't want to know. I just assumed Pa thought I couldn't hack it. That's what I thought until I was . . . I don't know, sixteen or so."

"But that wasn't the reason."

"I suppose Brody told you that?"

"No. It's my own opinion."

"Eventually, my mother explained that the stipulation was part of their divorce settlement. If she left, if she agreed to visitation only, my father agreed not to ship me off to military school and he had to stay stateside with me."

"Tough point to negotiate."

"He's a stubborn, difficult man. She, on the other hand, makes decisions without considering the consequences." Levi rose and Aubrey watched as he disappeared down the hall. She heard ice hit a glass. She followed, seeing Levi pouring scotch. "Yes . . . I'm stalling."

"Okay. Seems we have nothing but time since Delacort has us in a holding pattern." Aubrey cocked her head; she listened. "Brody doesn't agree. He's done waiting. He . . . he says 'Move, soldier.'"

Levi turned, facing her. "That's, uh . . ." He downed a mouthful of the drink and stared. "*Move, soldier* was household code for *Get it done before Pa catches up with you.*" He sat and put the drink on the coffee table, his hands running rough over his thighs. "The party went on late into the night. Brody hung out with Reese and my mother's other friends—all kinds of drinking, smoking, and snorting. I must have fallen asleep on the sofa. It was about three in the morning, maybe a little after. Normally, Brody would have made sure I went up to my room, but he didn't that night. It's a twisted irony."

"Because?"

"Because if I'd been upstairs, I would have had a better chance of saving them. They were too out of it to hear the smoke alarm, but I would have heard it. Those few extra seconds, going from the sofa to the stairs, who knows? As it is, my choice, it's a huge part of what I've never been able to get past."

"Go on," she said, not particularly sympathetic to Levi's perception of happenstance.

"Like I said, the smoke alarm woke me up. I was confused, everything was hazy. Then I realized the haze was really smoke. I started calling for my mother and for Brody. Nobody answered. I went toward the stairs, and the smoke got thicker. I didn't think," Levi said, standing. He picked up his drink and paced the room. "I just ran up the stairs. Then . . . then I had to pick a direction. The smoke was coming from my mother's bedroom. There were these little stadium lights here and there, they were still working. I got down on my hands and knees and crawled into her bedroom, screaming for Brody. I . . . I was amazed he didn't hear me. She was out cold on the bed. The far side of the room was burning, the curtains, the furniture."

"The direction she'd thrown the carton of cigarettes."

"Exactly. My mother later said there was a bottle of nail polish remover on the vanity, lots of tissues. She might have lit some candles while she was getting ready that night—she couldn't remember. Over the years, she's reiterated the accident scenario. Insisted it wasn't the result of drugs or alcohol—not directly.

"She wouldn't wake up. I pulled her by an arm and started dragging her. By then I was glad for that foot I'd grown. I dragged her right down the steps. It was just minutes . . . it couldn't have taken more than two minutes. I flung open the front door and hauled her out onto the lawn. Right about then the glass from her bedroom window burst. Flames started shooting out of the house. It . . . it looked like a movie set. She coughed. I could see she was breathing. I ran back inside, back up the stairs. I was near the top. The stadium lights had gone out. It was pitch black. God, the heat coming from my mother's room . . . It was hot, so incredibly hot. But Brody's room was in the opposite direction. There was still time. I fell twice. It was so dark and smoky, I was disoriented. The second time it felt like someone pushed me and I slid right to the bottom of the stairs—I remember repeating that to the police, like it was my excuse for not saving him. But I also got back up. I wasn't leaving that house without Brody."

Levi put the drink down and scrubbed a hand around his neck. "I tried again. I didn't make it very far. I didn't know flames could move like that. From nowhere they consumed the top of the stairs, the hall—like a back draft. I had no choice . . . I . . . I couldn't get to him. Not without going through fire." He stared past Aubrey, his eyes wide and wet. "I left my brother there to burn to death."

She moved toward him and Levi retreated. "I don't want sympathy," he said, holding up his hand. "It was my parents' divorce, my mother's house, my fault—not Brody's. If it wasn't for me, Brody would never have been there in the first place. Even in a tragic accident, people are culpable, Ellis."

Aubrey kept moving and eventually the two of them stood in the bright light of an arched window. "Levi, listen to me. It wouldn't have mattered if you got to him. It was—"

"I know. I've heard all the rational speculation. The smoke got to Brody before I ever could. As it was, the fire was so intense it took hours to put it out. But if I'd been quicker, if I'd chosen Brody over my mother . . ." Levi plucked the glasses from his face, swiping at his eyes. "I've thought that for so long . . . I thought about nothing else on the plane trip back from California, my brother's bones in cargo, in a casket." Levi's eyes pinched shut and a visible shudder ran through him. "You know, Ellis, you really know how to bring out the fond memories."

"Sometimes the memories aren't exactly as they appear. Keep going . . . *please.*"

"It . . . it was a miserable choice to make. So many years later and the decision doesn't feel any different, any more manageable."

"Levi, I swear to you, a different choice would not have mattered."

"How can you say that?"

"Because . . ." Aubrey pulled in her own deep breath. On the exhale came the words that had been pounding at her ears since Levi started talking. "It wouldn't have mattered because your brother was dead before the fire ever started."

◆ ◆ ◆

There was no choice but a direct one. She'd never encountered such a determined specter. But perhaps this was the strength needed for Brody to make good on his seaside promise. It had never been Brody St John's intention to communicate before this moment, and Aubrey understood why. From that night in California until today, it had taken the time in between, and a series of recent occurrences—Missy Flannigan's fate included—to get an ever-logical man to this place. Aubrey waited, watching Brody's confession sink into Levi. She could feel the looming impatience of a specter.

"What . . . what did you just say?" he said, his expression twisting.

"Maybe we should sit." Levi was too dazed to argue and the two of them sat on the pinstriped sofa. Oddly, it was the scent of Chanel that seized Aubrey. It wafted off a delicate cashmere sweater that lay across the arm. Aubrey cleared her throat.

"I'll get you some water . . . unless you want something stronger," Levi said.

"No, it's fine." Aubrey shifted the sweater to a chair. "I don't need you to do anything but listen." The sexy scent of the sweater was crushed and carried away by a wave of salty sea. "May I?" she said, looking at Levi's watch. A snort of laughter rumbled out of him. He undid the watch, surrendering it. There was a sense of liberation as it hit Aubrey's palm—thoughts flowed freely. "Brody left his watch by the pool earlier that day. That's how it survived the fire." Levi pulled in a deep breath. It was another tiny piece of his past that she could not have known. The draw from the watch was magnetic, her hand folding tight around it as signs and symbols clarified. The watch's real job had been to tick away time until finding its way to her.

"It's so warm," she said, rubbing her thumb over it. "But in a very positive way."

"One of the firefighters found the watch. He gave it to my mother. She gave it to me. She was so completely devastated."

"From the story you tell, your mother made a lot of precarious choices. But she's not responsible for Brody's death. He very much wants you to know that."

"Did he overdose? Did that punk-rock prick give him something? Is that why he's dead? Because if it is, I strongly disagree. In fact, I'd finally side with my father—who's at least been charitable enough to blame my mother in my presence."

Aubrey reached for the upper part of Levi's arm. She could feel the intrinsic strength, a solid line connection between Levi and his brother.

"You're right about the drugs—a combination of . . ." She paused. "It doesn't matter. Brody says it didn't even all come from your mother's friends." Aubrey paused, navigating the giant secret being whispered in her ear. Her brow crinkled and she let go of Levi's arm. The watch dropped into her lap. "Oh my God. How did I not see that?"

Aubrey squeezed her eyes shut. Her hands pressed together like a prayer and she drew the knotted fingers to her mouth. What an incredible oversight, the reason a dead brother had remained here for so long. Aubrey opened her eyes. She needed to tread carefully. "Levi, there's something you don't know . . . Something about the night Brody died. It's going to be so very hard to hear . . . harder to believe." Instead of touching the watch, Aubrey reached over, gripping his hand. "Your brother didn't die of an accidental overdose. Brody took his own life. He killed himself."

"That's a lie!" Levi tore his hand from hers. He lurched off the sofa as if Aubrey had jabbed him with a needle. "I knew my brother, Ellis. And that would never have happened. I don't know who the hell you're communicating with, but there's no way Brody killed himself."

Aubrey's demeanor remained opposed, and Brody's presence was as concrete as the two of them. "He did, Levi. He planned it. The story you just told me. Think about it. Even an eleven-year-old sensed how desperately unhappy he was. You said it yourself. When Brody came downstairs that night, he seemed 'different' and 'settled, even calm.' It was because he'd made his decision."

"That's absurd. Brody could have packed up and left if he was that determined not to go to West Point."

"Could he?"

Levi, who was pacing in a small circle, stopped.

"He couldn't go against an order . . . that's what I'm hearing. He'd been trained to follow orders his whole life. Your father's, the prep school . . . His conversation with Jacqueline, it was a last frantic attempt. In the end, he could only see one way out. He . . ." Aubrey listened. Conveying disconcerting facts to a stranger was one thing. Bringing this kind of news to someone she . . . Brody wedged his way into a deep flutter of emotion, insisting that she stay on task. "He'd been considering *how* for some time. The concept of death, it wasn't new to Brody or even frightening." Aubrey pressed on, gently offering each word. "He says it was the upshot of military school—they'd prepared him for the possibility. It was Brody's plan to swim out into the ocean, just far enough not to make it back. Then the trip to California came up, and for him, the time had come. He's . . ." She shook her head. "My God, it's such a frantic whirl of energy . . . He's . . . he's showing me a photo in a black frame." She smiled, the warm gesture slipping into the anguished air surrounding them. "You and Brody, there's a British flag hanging behind you . . . I'm not sure if you've gone on a trip . . . maybe to England? He's definitely referencing a plane." She smiled wider. "I know that look, Levi. Your serious face, you had it perfected at what . . . seven or eight?"

Levi didn't respond. He walked to a desk, opening a drawer. From it, he removed a black-framed photo. With zero expression, he crossed to where Aubrey sat and handed to her. "Six, actually. I brought it from Hartford. I . . . I guess I wanted it with me, but I didn't want to look at it."

"I see," she said, examining the photo, which depicted Levi with the face she'd described. In the photo was her lifeguard with his little brother, the St John boys posed in front of a British flag. It was attached to a small airplane, the two-seater kind. "So you weren't traveling . . . Sorry, it's not an exact science."

"Maybe not. But that's pretty damn amazing. We were at an air-show in Washington. The plane on hand represented the Royal Navy. My father was ecstatic—delighted when the pilot offered for Brody to fly with him. I wasn't allowed to go. I was too young."

"Too young both times, Brody says. You were too young for a sim-ple plane ride when you were six . . . And five years later, you were still far too young to understand the complexity of Brody's pain or how to help him. And for that, your brother insists he's sorry."

A ragged breath vented out of him. Levi stared, the messenger unap-preciated. "What the hell am I supposed to do with this, Ellis? Brody was tough and smart and caring. My brother always protected me, whether from the fallout of my parents' marriage or a swimming pool. He would not have done that to me. Not all those years ago, not today."

"His death wasn't senseless, Levi. It's also something Brody didn't even realize would happen in the days leading up to it. Will you sit with me again . . . please? He very much wants you to hear the rest." He did, though Levi's reluctance was evident. "The fire was an accident—an unfortunate, horrific accident, exactly what Jacqueline said. Exactly what the fire personnel and police concluded. There was no stopping it. He . . . Brody wants . . ." Aubrey listened harder, wanting to get the message exactly right. She clung tight to the watch. "Could I have a piece of paper?" From under several fashion magazines, Levi produced a legal pad, and then handed her a pencil. With the watch in her left hand, Aubrey pressed the pencil to paper. For a few seconds there was nothing. Then she wrote hurriedly, speaking the words out loud. "'I stepped away from my pain and the fire began. Then I understood why. It was easy . . . willful,'" she said and wrote, "'and necessary. Otherwise . . . my reckless selfish choice would not have mattered.'" The pencil dropped like a weight, a wave of exhaustion feeling like it could take Aubrey under. "The last physical thing your brother experienced was his own pain. The smoke and heat, it was coming, and he was at peace going by his own hand."

The impressions in Aubrey's head gathered one at a time, like raindrops forming a puddle. In the reflection of the water came the message a brother had waited so long to convey. "If Brody hadn't already been . . . *dead*, he would have been passed out in his room, just as you thought that night. You would have gone after him, Levi. You would have made it up those stairs the first time. And the two of you would have never made it out of there alive. Brody was destined to die in that house that night . . . and so were you," she said, a swallow rolling through her dry throat.

"How can you possibly know that?"

She shrugged. "I don't. I'm only relaying a message. You said you fell, not once, but twice on the stairs."

"I was disoriented. It was dark, smoky."

"Maybe. You also said it felt like someone pushed you down the stairs. Your words, Levi. You said it to the police all those years ago. You just said it to me."

He sank back into the sofa as if someone had pushed him again. "Brody? He kept me from . . ."

"And that burst of flames you described, the ones that consumed the hall and the stairs."

"But how could he . . ."

"Remember the noise at the Serino house? The movement of the chandelier and the glass in the French door?" Levi nodded, having witnessed the power of phantom persuasion. "I suspect in your case that was the energy of somebody who loved you hard at work. Brody made certain you didn't get back up those stairs. His life had ended, but he was determined to make sure yours didn't. Your brother's death, while tragic, had a greater purpose, Levi, and that was to keep you alive."

CHAPTER
TWENTY-FOUR

Aubrey's desire to stay felt natural, the ease with which she and Levi spoke even more so. But altering the past came with a present-day learning curve. In that regard, Aubrey saw signs of fatigue in an always self-possessed Levi. He'd asked more questions, listening intently to answers. As they talked, the stream of information shifted tributaries, moving from Brody to herself. Eventually Levi's brother faded from view. Aubrey said that she doubted he would return.

"Not every being is accessible, Levi—at least not to me. More often than not, a spirit's connection brings the living solace, eases pain. That's a wonderful thing. What's harder to comprehend is the more compelling peace that a soul passes on to. We don't want them to go. But if that's the case, I believe *here* pales in comparison, maybe it's even a moot point." She'd handed him back the watch and he brushed his thumb over the cool glass of its face. "Of course, rare is the individual left to mourn who appreciates that perspective."

Their conversation continued until Bethany called. It alerted them to time and the tangible people in their lives. Aubrey took the interruption as her cue to leave. "Thank you," Levi said at the door, touching her arm. He retreated fast, shoving both hands in his pockets. "That and I'm sorry for being so . . . so . . ."

"So Levi St John?" She smiled. "How could you be anything less?"

"I know I can be . . . *unyielding*. I don't accept everyday things at face value, never mind something like . . . well, what happened here."

"I understand."

"Most people don't. I know that. But if my orderly, probing tendencies bother other people, I don't mind it about myself."

"There's a lot to be said for being comfortable in your own skin. And you're not the only one who came away with something today. Connecting with Brody was a hugely different experience for me. Sublime and fulfilling," she said, absorbing the unusual poignancy of the encounter.

"I would have thought those adjectives dulled years ago—kind of like the star athlete scoring his millionth touchdown. Why was this different?"

"I'm not sure. In my life, people on both sides have expressed gratitude, definitely fascination at my ability. And there can be tremendous satisfaction in healing and helping. Don't get me wrong. What's the saying? 'It has its moments.' But serving as the connection between you and Brody, it's never felt so . . . *personal* for me."

A lone dimple eased into the hollow of Levi's cheek. "I'm glad to know this wasn't a one-sided affair."

◆ ◆ ◆

Driving home, Aubrey fidgeted and fiddled with the radio. She clicked off a hypnotic ballad. She felt decidedly displaced. Surely her mood was a reasonable aftereffect. Aubrey had shared a life-changing experience with someone she cared about—and yes, she'd come to care about Levi. But what she was experiencing felt more . . . *covetous* than rewarding. By now, surely Levi's longtime girlfriend had arrived on the scene. Bethany was there to listen and to help. Aubrey chided herself as she drove. "You're being ridiculous. You did your part. Let his girlfriend do the rest." At a stoplight, Aubrey looked in the rearview mirror. Blue-gray irises showed an unlikely flex of green. "What are you, twelve?" she said, eyes narrowing. "Be glad he has someone who cares about him."

Even if I am the person who righted his entire world . . .

Stepping on the gas, Aubrey moved on, but only down Route 30. She wondered what Levi might confide to Bethany. An in-depth explanation would require specific details. And while Aubrey hadn't stipulated, she felt as if it was understood—Levi would keep her gift to himself. She was sure of it. He'd trusted her with his past. She trusted him with her gift. Perhaps Levi and Bethany's evening would be typical. Maybe he'd choose to keep the events of that day between the two of them. Aubrey didn't know if that was right or wrong, but it was how she thought it should be. Pulling into her driveway, her subconscious settled on a scenario: Levi at peace, poring over volumes of Missy Flannigan files. Bethany absorbed in her fashion magazines. Opposite ends of the room.

At home, Aubrey worked on distancing herself from the day, particularly in light of her evening—a long-overdue date with her husband. Aubrey climbed in the tub, thinking a warm sudsy bath would wash away the Levi cobwebs. But after rerunning the water twice and pruning her skin to a lovely wrinkled state, thoughts of him still wouldn't go away. Levi's vulnerability, his honesty, his willingness to face things that had haunted him for so long stayed at the forefront of Aubrey's mind.

Wrapped in a towel, she stood in front of her closet, perusing a wardrobe that looked as if it belonged to two different people—half earth tones, half brilliant hues. After the complexity of the afternoon, color was the last thing Aubrey wanted to bring to the evening. She searched the duller side of her closet, on the hunt for something that might complement the occasion—the start of the rest of her life. Taking a deep breath, Aubrey concentrated on Owen and the powerful ways he'd so thoroughly captivated her. He was a man who could explain the universe in code. She understood none of it, though Owen did— because he lived it every day, because that was how his brain worked. Aubrey saw their equally odd minds and improbable gifts as the bedrock of their renewed relationship. But it was more than that, things like the softer side of Owen and an attraction that had clicked on a whole other level—about thirty thousand feet to be exact.

The first time they had sex—which was the first time they'd met— was in the airplane's lavatory, halfway through a six-hour flight. She'd been wearing a comfortable wraparound dress that had lent itself to the unexpected event. Aubrey pursed her lips, thinking about it, still a bit stunned by the fact that it had happened. She'd never done anything so impetuous. She'd never even thought of it. Of course, she'd been lucky; it surely could have been reckless misfortune instead of the start of a life together. Thinking about that, Levi slipped to where he belonged—the back of her mind.

Aubrey touched a silkier dress she rarely wore. *I wonder if Owen remembers the beige sheath dress. It could be construed as sexy, or at least I've always thought so . . .* Aubrey had worn it to work a week or two ago. She'd caught Levi doing a double take. He'd been forced to say something like "Wow. That's, um . . . different." Whatever *different* meant. Aubrey rolled her eyes. "Would you just get out!" she said out loud. She shoved the dress to the right. Who gave a damn what Levi thought? "Even when you're not being annoying, you're being annoying." But a few moments later Aubrey returned to the dress. Huffing, she yanked the figure-hugging beige garb from its hanger. With no time to spare, she grabbed a silky black wrap from the top of her closet, making certain the dress read as sexy, as opposed to *different*.

Twenty minutes later, Aubrey and Owen arrived simultaneously at La Petite Maison. They'd always had good timing. He hurried across the parking lot, meeting her more than halfway. His embrace was familiar and the first thing Aubrey noticed was that he smelled like her husband, the scent of patchouli ingrained. Owen said he wore the offbeat, beatnik aftershave because people who didn't know him figured he'd just finished smoking a joint anyway. He kissed her like her husband too—passionately. More like he'd done in that airplane lavatory and on the floor of their craftsman living room the day they'd moved in. But instead of responding, Aubrey felt a rush of mixed emotions. She detached from the intimate moment, tucking back a wave of flaxen hair that had slipped from his signature ponytail. His arms stayed tight around her. "Sorry," she said, wiping a smudge of lipstick from his mouth and glancing around the busy parking lot. "It's kind of public out here."

"We can fix that later. Did you have a busy day?" he said, retreating to generic conversation.

"Busy is an understatement."

"New Missy Flannigan developments?"

She'd answered without thinking. A busy day required details. "Uh, kind of a dotted line story off the main story," she said. "I meant busy in that I was out of the office all day. Levi and I were chasing down . . . extraneous information." She didn't want to lie, but sharing Levi's deeply personal experience seemed even less appropriate. "You look nice," she said, changing the subject. Owen wore an open button-down oxford over a tight T-shirt, a trendy leather sport coat over it—it was a look that complemented his slender frame and Bohemian lifestyle. His hand moved lithely over her back, then caressed the nape of her neck. His light irises seemed to smolder, and she guessed the last place Owen really wanted to be was a fancy French restaurant. Before he could suggest "Let's get the hell out of here," Aubrey tugged on his hand. "They won't hold a reservation five minutes in this place."

The hostess checked Owen's jacket, but Aubrey chose to hang on to her wrap. Leading them through the dimly lit restaurant, the hostess seated them in a high-backed booth toward the rear, a private spot. A waitress enhanced the date-like atmosphere, lighting a candle and bringing Aubrey a glass of wine, Owen a bottle of Bud Light. His easygoing habits wouldn't be swayed, not even by La Petite Maison's award-winning wine list. She shuffled her wrap on and off, hesitating, looking for a segue into conversation that usually came naturally. Owen darted ahead.

"I just want to say . . . the way I reacted to . . . *everything* . . . It was immature, unwarranted. I'm sorry, Bre."

The nickname hit her ears like forgiveness. He hadn't said "Bre" in nearly a year, not since the parting scene in their living room. "Owen . . ."

He held up a hand. "Just let me get this out. I even practiced on the drive from New York." She smiled at his cautionary thoughtfulness. "When I found out about your . . . *gift*, it was a knee-jerk reaction. The perfect excuse for me to be angry after I'd already reneged on what I'd promised. Being so pissed off, it was an easy out."

"Yes, but the timing couldn't have been worse. I should have told you before we were married—that one's mine," she said, staring at her glass of white wine. "All mine. I'm sorry I didn't." She looked up at him. "But Owen, now that you do know, how do you feel about it, my gift? A year ago your reaction was so negative. It almost seemed like . . . well, it seemed like it frightened you."

"I wouldn't say frightened as much as stunned." Owen downed a long mouthful of beer, then tapped the bottle on the table. "Maybe it did make me uncomfortable," he admitted. "But more than that, it hurt, Bre. You didn't trust your own husband enough to confide in me. That part did make me reconsider a few things."

"Like what?"

"To be honest, I spent time these past months wondering if we'd rushed into things in the first place."

"And did we?"

He didn't hesitate. "No. We didn't. The time apart . . . the space, it proved that to me." Owen reached over, taking her hands in his. "Our relationship was whirlwind and spontaneous. But you also *got* me, Bre—totally. Like no one else ever has."

"Okay. But do you get me? Can you accept what you know, live with it? Deal with it?" Owen let go of her hands. She hadn't meant to say it like that—not in an accusatory way. Aubrey wasn't sure she was ready to hear the answer. "I . . . I'm going to the ladies' room." She stood, leaving the silky wrap on the seat.

Once inside the restroom, she peed, though she didn't really have to, and washed her hands. She dragged a brush through her hair and fussed with the front of the dress. The color was conservative, though the dress was cut low—enough to reveal a hint of lacy camisole. Sexy was not a look on which Aubrey relied, but the suggestive edge had its place tonight. Maybe it could help bridge any angst Owen had about his wife and her gift.

Seconds later, Aubrey's take on sensual overtures was doused. A woman came into the restroom: blond, petite, and head-turningly pretty. She wore sexy like a layer of skin. She also wore the quintessential little black dress. It fit her smartly, stiletto heels maximizing the chic ensemble's appeal. If Aubrey wore heels like that, she'd tower over most men. But the woman appeared affable, flashing a smile of solidarity at their reflections.

"Men," she said. The blonde rolled her eyes, pulling a powder compact from her clutch. "I'm starting to wish I swung the other way . . . you know?" She glanced at Aubrey via the mirror and laughed a little. "In a day, mine's gone from his usual brooding behavior to outright vague. God only knows what's eating at him now." She took out her phone, texting frantically. A friend, Aubrey thought, a confidant savvy to the saga of the blonde's love life. Aubrey felt a touch of envy. She'd never had many close friends.

"I suppose they all come with their challenges." Aubrey pushed the restroom door open, thinking she'd just have to do better at negotiating hers. She walked back to the table and sat, seeing that Owen had ordered more drinks. Moments later the blonde glided past and disappeared into the booth behind them. Still, she continued to draw Aubrey's attention. Most likely it was a spirit seeking an opportunity. It was odd. Aubrey was on her game, if not her guard. She could be immune to strangers if she chose. Aubrey focused on Owen, who was talking on his cell. She could tell from the techno-chatter it was Nicole.

"Right, just apply the new policy rules and that should allow the VPN to work from the branch locations. Tell them the system should be up and running for the international sites by tomorrow afternoon." He listened for a few more seconds. "Okay, call if it's a major meltdown and you can't handle it. Otherwise"—he smiled at Aubrey—"don't. Sorry," he said, ending the call. "New York project, last stages. I left Nicole to finish configuring the firewall."

She smiled back and sipped the wine. "I'm glad you have someone who so clearly understands what you do."

"When it comes to tech support, Nicole was a find for sure." He drank a mouthful of the beer. "Handy, to say the least."

"That's not so easy in my line of work, so to speak."

"Should I take that as a direct question? The one you avoided before running away to the bathroom."

"I realize not telling you was huge. Maybe part of my concern was that you wouldn't be able to get your mind around my gift. While I see similarities," she said, pointing toward his phone, "like the average person's inability to grasp how your brain works, I also see differences. At least I do now. Your abilities, they're tangible. Mine . . . not so much. Not everyone can deal with my gift," she said, prepared to give him room to articulate his concerns.

Owen leaned back into the booth. His moment's hesitation felt like forever. "Look, Bre . . . I can't argue how the world at large perceives your gift. But being here, wanting to put our marriage back together . . . I hope that tells you what you need to know about us. That and I assume *it* . . . your gift won't be at the center of our lives. I mean, you did do a damn good job of hiding it from me."

"And is that what you'd expect? If we're back together I'd hide it from our life?"

"Not so much that. I just wouldn't expect it to be the focus. I thought you'd see that as a plus. I mean, it's not like you'd ever consider hanging a shingle out front and offering up psychic readings."

While he was going for humor, the visual struck Aubrey as anything but. She shook it off; she was being hypersensitive. "Of course not. But I do need to know if my gift is something you can understand."

"How about this," he said, taking her hand in his again. "Instead of me trying to convince you, how about I prove it to you? I want to tell you about my surprise."

She'd almost forgotten he'd mentioned one.

"Remember Sky Secure Technologies?"

"The tech conglomerate you've done work for in the past."

"That's right. They've been trying, for forever, to get me to come on board full time."

"Have they?" she said, unaware of previous offers.

"This time, in an effort to make good on my promise to you, I went to them. I made it known that I was ready to settle into one job. One place. They jumped at it."

As his surprise sank in, Aubrey realized she'd been right all along. It was precisely what she'd said; Owen only needed the time to catch up with the concept of her gift. "Jumped at it, as in offered you a permanent position?"

"Not any position. Vice president and chief network architect of their software development. It's all my freelance work rolled into one awesome scenario and then some. I couldn't have designed a better position."

"Owen, that's fantastic. And you think you'll be happy with this—one job in one place, no more travel."

"I want to be honest. It wouldn't be zero travel. Some here and there. Sky Secure has a large net, worldwide clientele. But as the chief architect, they'd be the kind of trips you might want to take with me—Paris, New York, an occasional stop back here. You can see Charley."

She sat up taller. "Back here?"

"Yes. Sky Secure is headquartered in Seattle. You knew that."

"Oh, I'd forgotten, or I wasn't thinking about . . . We'd have to move." Aubrey shuffled the wrap on and off, reminding herself that she hadn't tacked a non-relocation clause to Owen's promise of giving up his freelance life.

He shrugged. "True. But it would be for a great reason, and it'd be the last one—I swear. You wanted roots, Bre. Seattle can do that as well as Surrey."

She smiled at his enthusiasm. "That all sounds wonderful. It's exactly what I wanted." She cleared her throat. "But what about my job?"

"I've considered that," he said, clearly proud of having anticipated her concern. "The brass at Sky Secure has offered an assist. They've communicated to me that making an introduction at the *Seattle Times*, for the wife of the VP of network securities development, would be their pleasure."

"Owen, I can't—"

His hand rose to her incoming objection. "Nothing handed to you. It would be an opportunity to have a conversation—that's all. With your work on the Flannigan story, I'm sure you'd be hired solely on your own merit."

"Maybe. But—"

"Bre, come on. You can't tell me you're that attached to the *Surrey City Press*."

Aubrey pulled the wrap tighter around herself, too sidetracked to formulate a response. Her job. That was the point. But instead of seeing a newspaper, the masthead and Times New Roman font, she saw a face—even a dimple. "The Missy Flannigan story has been a huge change for me. Since I've been working it, I've realized some things about my career, maybe what I want or can accomplish."

"Okay, if you've broadened your horizons, wouldn't a paper like the *Seattle Times* be a step up? No offense to the *Surrey City Press*, but seriously, Bre. Tell me one part of this plan that isn't perfect for us. So what I need to know . . ." He gathered her hands tighter into his. "Is if *we're* still what you want."

Aubrey glanced up from her wine glass. A loud pulse of conversation erupted and she looked beyond Owen's impassioned plea. The voices coming from the booth behind them stonewalled her reaction.

"Bre," Owen said again.

Her hand went up, halting him. Conversation penetrated. The sexy blonde was thoroughly annoyed. The man with her was equally agitated. Aubrey listened to his serious tone; his voice was recognizable—even brooding.

CHAPTER
TWENTY-FIVE

"It's not you, and I am not doing it again!"

"The hell you aren't! I let it go the past two nights," the blonde said. "But I didn't come all the way from New York to be ignored. Seriously, if you're hyper-focusing on what you told me earlier . . . There you go again, over-analyzing everything—including the absurd! I told you how it sounded—crazy, just plain crazy. Of course, if there were a shred of truth, a tell-all book might be the way to go. Let me know, my house pays big bucks for the right biography!"

"Lower your voice. And I wasn't thinking about that. Clearly this isn't going well. It's my fault. I was distracted. Why don't we just . . ."

"What?" Owen said.

Aubrey's hands balled into two tight fists. The sting of betrayal made her dart from their booth, pouncing on the one behind them. She couldn't believe her gift had become fodder and the basis of an argument for the two people sitting behind them. "Are you kidding me?"

"Ellis . . ." Her name came out guilt-coated from Levi's mouth.

"I thought you preferred casual dining." So furious she didn't know whether to scream or cry, Aubrey felt completely exposed. Forget a little black dress. She should have just showed up to La Petite Maison in her underwear. "It's not what you're thinking," he said.

"Come on, Levi, it doesn't take a psychic for someone to understand that their ears should be burning. You must be the longtime girlfriend," she said, not caring if it was inappropriate or rude.

"Uh, yes, I'm Bethany Grey. How do you know Levi?"

"I'm Aubrey Ellis. The 'crazy' you just heard tell of. But don't be too hard on him. The trauma of me tends to excuse all sorts of reactions." With her hands on her hips, she shot Levi a searing look. He put his napkin on the table, rising. "You know, for somebody who looks for positive channels with the dead, the living manage to keep right on disappointing! Did your girlfriend even make it home, or did you call her the second I was out of earshot?"

"Levi?" Bethany said, shrinking back in her seat. "Who is she and what is she talking about?"

"You see what it gets you. She thought everything I told you was insane. Or maybe she's like you and needs hardcore proof. Why not? Everybody loves a sideshow demonstration. Actually, Bethany, I got a hot vibe off you earlier. Maybe it'll pan out. You'll be convinced and then you can take it all back to your big city publisher. Let them decide if it's worth a hefty advance or just a good laugh."

"Ellis," Levi said, reaching for her arm. She wrenched it back, unsure if the gesture was meant to soothe her or protect Bethany from the batshit-crazy woman Levi had reported.

"How could you do this? I trusted you. I thought you understood."

"Ellis," he said again. His voice was so calm she wanted to slap him. "Beth and I were talking about the Flannigan case. I mentioned the newest information we have on Frank Delacort. I probably said more than I should have."

Bethany smiled, shrugging. "That's a definite possibility. When Levi cares about something, he's hopeless. He can't let go. But I'm afraid he's wasting his energy on this one. I'm with the DA and team Byrd. I don't care what you think you have on Delacort. A body falling out of your basement wall can't be explained away. Byrd's your killer."

"What you heard was Bethany being sarcastic. She said if there was a Delacort connection, something really outrageous, I should write a tell-all book. *About the Flannigan case*—nothing else." Aubrey looked from Levi to Bethany to Owen, who'd joined the commotion.

"I'm pretty astute with these things," Bethany said. "They like that in publishing. Call it a sixth sense. Anyway, I guess I'm not really on my game tonight, because I'm still wondering who you are?"

"I um, well . . . right now I'm somebody who wishes the floor would open up and take a big gulp." Aubrey wallowed in a deep pang of embarrassment, accentuated by the sympathetic expression on Levi's face.

"Ellis is on staff at the *Surrey City Press*. And this is my fault." Levi glanced at Bethany, but his focus stayed with Aubrey. "I shouldn't have shared information about Delacort. It should have stayed between us. Ellis is right to be upset."

"Yes, but she was talking about talking with dead people. What does that have to do with—"

"Guess I didn't mention that part," he said. "Somebody came up with the idea that we should bring in a psychic."

"A psychic?" Bethany picked up her glass of wine, half-heartedly hiding a smirk.

"Right, that was my first reaction too. Ellis here, she offered a surprisingly convincing argument."

"Levi, you can't be serious? You, of all people, were willing to entertain ideas about psychics?" Her pouty mouth frowned at Aubrey. "If that's true, then you must share your secret. I can't imagine Levi sitting still long enough to listen, never mind calling that sort of nonsense convincing."

"I, um . . . It took some doing," Aubrey said.

"Honey, if you were able to—"

"Let it go, Beth." Bethany and Levi traded a look; she shrugged but was silent. "Ellis must have thought I was being disrespectful to her ideas. I wasn't." His stone face softened. "I swear."

"I'm sure . . ." The words caught in her throat. "I should have known better."

"And any mention of facts about the Flannigan case was an anomaly," Bethany said. "Levi's stubborn nature is only surpassed by his honesty."

"I know," Aubrey said, damp lashes blinking. "I mean, that's become apparent in the time we've worked together. I should have realized . . ."

"No worries." Bethany moved her glass in a *cheers* motion, Chanel wafting off her arm. The scent was as intense as an ardent specter. "If anything, what you heard was me being silly. Levi and I, we're negotiating the hazards of a long-distance relationship. Truth be told, I was upset with him. Turns out, he stayed home all day while I visited a friend."

"I told you, Beth. I had a ton of work to do on the Flannigan case. You would have been bored silly. I . . . I just needed to work in the quiet."

Bethany's manicured hand stretched out, capturing Levi's. "Hey, baby, maybe you should take this whole misunderstanding as a sign to rethink suburbia, even Hartford." Aubrey stared at their tangled fingers. The term of endearment sounded louder than the rest of the remark. Bethany's smile turned broad and blinding. "I've been trying to convince Levi that when this story is over, he should apply to a New York daily, maybe even the *Times*. You can't duplicate someone like Levi. Anyone would be crazy not to snap him up in a heartbeat."

"Great. Sounds like you two have a plan," Owen said, inching his way into the tight exchange. "Bre, why don't we go somewhere else?" She glanced at their table, seeing two twenties. "We can finish up our conversation someplace more private."

"Don't do that," Levi said. Aubrey's eyes went as wide as Bethany's. "What I mean is why don't you join us for dinner? Both of you."

"But Levi," Bethany's voice was soft but tight. "It's supposed to be just the two of us. There's, um . . . there's even *homemade* dessert . . . *at home.*"

"Really," Aubrey said, reaching for her wrap, "I wouldn't dream of intruding."

"Thanks for the invite, but no." Owen closed his hand around Aubrey's arm. "My wife and I have other plans. She'll see you tomorrow."

At the coat check, Owen turned to Aubrey. "I thought you said you were working with him all afternoon?"

Aubrey hesitated, her white lie sounding more like a full blown one. "Uh, that's right. That's what I told you."

"You said you were out. But you didn't say you were at his home."

"It's not. It's MediaMatters', they have a corporate condo. It . . . it just worked out that way. It wasn't a big deal."

"Enough of a deal that Mr. Honesty just lied to her. She thought he was alone."

"Owen, I was with Levi, but we weren't working on the Flannigan case." He took a giant step toward the dining area. She grabbed his arm. "It's not that. It's not what you're thinking."

"Really? Because standing near the guy, first while he's in my living room, then as he oddly objects to you leaving, that's not the vibe I'm getting."

"You're reading into it. It's not like that. Not at all. Levi, he's . . . It's just absurd to think about him that way, if you knew him. Work is his entire life."

"Seriously?" he said, thumbing over his shoulder. "Did you not get a good look at her?"

"Okay, that may be a slight overstatement. But it's also another great point," Aubrey said, still holding tight to his arm. "Bethany is his longtime girlfriend. For God's sake, Levi will probably move to New York just to be with her, just like she said, just as soon as the Flannigan story is over. He doesn't have anything to do with us."

"Then do you mind telling me why the hell you were with him all afternoon?"

"Actually . . ."

He stepped back, blinking wide. "You do mind."

"It was personal—for Levi. I don't know that it's my story to tell."

Owen's expression looked as disturbed as it did a year ago. "I take it this is where your gift comes in, somebody dead from his past came a-calling."

"In short, yes."

"I guess it would have to be 'in short,' since the details are none of my business."

"Owen, what happened today with Levi was complicated and the outcome unexpected. It . . . it was painful to hear, difficult to deal with."

He was quiet for a moment. "So I guess you had no problem confiding your gift to him. A guy who's . . . what to you, exactly?"

"You're twisting things. It wasn't about confiding my gift to Levi. It was about offering him long-awaited, badly needed closure."

"Damn. I'm so glad you could be there for him."

"Don't take it that way. It wasn't even a friend helping a friend."

"Again, I'm not liking the alternatives."

"It was a message that no one but me was in a position to offer. I wasn't some shoulder to cry on. That's not Levi. That's not what happened."

"Good to know he's such a rock." With his keys in his hand, he spun the ring around his index finger, grabbing them into a clenched fist. "Fine," Owen said, exhaling hard. "I get it. This is the part you were concerned about. The *things* I'm going to have to get used to. Sorry, Bre, but you picked a bad place to start."

"Owen, listen to me. I can control my gift. But I can't ignore it— not when it's that important. I'm sorry this particular incident was about Levi. I'm sorry that upsets you, but I don't choose spirits. It's the other way around." She could see him struggling with multiple issues— her gift and the fact that it suddenly involved Levi.

He shook his head, making eye contact with everything but her. "Could you give me the courtesy of a learning curve?"

"Of course," she said. "It's taken me a lifetime. I don't expect you to completely understand. Not that easily."

The hostess handed Owen his jacket and he tugged it on. He looked past Aubrey and into the main dining room. His expression soured. "You've got to be fucking kidding me."

"I don't mean to interrupt," Levi said, walking toward them.

"Then don't," Owen snapped.

"It's important," Levi said as Aubrey turned. He held out his cell. "Delacort called. Could . . . could we speak in private?"

"My wife is off the clock," Owen said. "Share it with your girlfriend."

"It's the break we've been waiting for," he said, ignoring Owen. "And it really can't wait."

"Can't it?" Owen narrowed his eyes at Levi. Then he softened. "Do what you have to." He kissed Aubrey on the cheek, whispering, "I can deal. We have the rest of the night."

"Why don't you get your car?" she said. "We can leave mine here for now. I'll be right out."

Owen started for the exit but turned back. "On second thought, take your time. I'll call over to Trapeze, see if they have any champagne on hand—or at least that organic wine you like. It's low key, but more our style."

"Sure. I haven't been since . . . Sounds fine, Owen."

He nodded, eyeing Levi as he left.

"Celebrating, I take it."

"Owen's been offered a job. A really great job in Seattle. He wants me to go with him."

"Congratulations . . . I'm happy for you, Ellis . . . Have you started packing yet . . . ?" Any one of those responses would have been appropriate, but Levi's only reaction was a deep swallow. In the uncomfortable quiet, Aubrey stood taller, the wrap draped loosely around her arms.

Levi turned his head, rubbing his fingers hard across his brow—erasing something, recalling something. "Delacort," he finally said. "He's willing to talk tomorrow afternoon—to you."

"Me? You're kidding. That's amazing."

"I thought so. But we'll need to review your approach, get all the questions in order." The suggestion was met with more silence. "I guess you're unavailable the rest of the evening."

"I don't think that would be a great idea." Aubrey glanced at the restaurant exit. "But if Delacort is asking for the afternoon, can we discuss things tomorrow? Early." She considered tossing a length of fabric over her shoulder; it seemed like the kind of confident gesture that would shore up her position. Instead, Aubrey found herself apologizing. "Levi, while we're here . . . I'm sorry about the way I behaved in there. I'm sorry I doubted you."

"I can see how you'd misconstrue what you heard, how it looked."

"I just assumed . . . The truth is I never asked you not to tell Bethany, so even if you had—"

"It wasn't appropriate to share it with her—for a lot of reasons." The swallow rolled through again. "Protecting you was one of them."

"Protecting me?"

"It's hard to articulate. But I found myself strongly opposed to the idea of anyone putting you through what I did. Hypocritical? Yes. Shamefully so."

"Thank you." She smiled softly. "That means a lot."

"I'd never share your gift with anyone. Not unless you wanted me to. I can appreciate it now. But I also see the burden. For what it's worth, I like to think loyalty is up there with honesty—especially when it comes to . . . *friends*."

"Friends," she said, nodding. "That sounds like an official upgrade from *colleagues*."

"I guess it is."

"Still, Bethany must think . . ."

"Don't worry about what Beth thinks. She'll be off on another tangent by the time I get back. She doesn't dwell."

Aubrey stared into the dining area, which offered a good view of Bethany. "Is that why it works between the two of you? She's easygoing, and you're . . ."

"Definitely not?" He hesitated, adjusting his glasses. "For a long time, Bethany was a buffer between me and myself. She kept me from tumbling too far from . . . well, life. In turn, my driven nature seemed to anchor her. Bethany's clever. I don't know about a sixth sense, but she's good at what she does. Good at being resilient in impossible situations."

"You being one of them?"

"You have to counter honesty and loyalty with something."

"You're a challenge, Levi. But hardly impossible." Aubrey looked toward Levi's longtime girlfriend again. Bethany seemed oblivious to them. She was texting someone and as Aubrey watched, her imagination tumbled forward into the conversation:

Break in the action. Levi being Levi. He's conferencing with a coworker.

Who?

Some woman he's working the Flannigan story with—a high-strung head case, apparently. Can you believe he invited her to have dinner with us?

No way! Levi's on your time. You're his ltgf. (Aubrey envisioned bath towels with the acronym for longtime girlfriend.)

Yes, but I'm not that kind of ltgf. Levi's a complex man. I understand him. What could she possibly mean to him?

Nothing.

You got that right.

OK, call me later . . . After you fhbo.

Aubrey squeezed her eyes shut, squashing the hand-towel acronym: *Fuck. His. Brains. Out.* Tugging at the wrap, she folded her arms. "How nice that you and Bethany complement one another so well."

"We did once. Relationships change. Usually because the people in them change."

"Sometimes . . . I'm sure." Silence edged back in. "Goodnight, then." Aubrey got as far as the door. She turned back; he hadn't moved. "That last remark. Why do I get the impression it wasn't about you and Bethany?"

"I don't know. Is there a reason you should take it another way?"

Aubrey cinched up her shoulders. "No. Of course not. Owen and I . . . we're going to be fine. Better than fine. My life isn't going to be a parade of marriages, not like my grandmother, or even the tragedy of my parents."

"Good," he said, nodding. "Because Seattle's a damn long way to go find out otherwise." Levi moved fast to where Aubrey stood. "I'm not saying you shouldn't go—if that's what you want. But I also don't see the need for a snap decision."

"How do you even know . . ."

"I didn't say a word to Bethany about you, but I did overhear your entire conversation."

"My entire conversation?"

"With Owen. It was an accident at first. Obviously, I didn't know you were there, behind us. I heard your voice, and . . . and then I just kept listening. Could I . . . Can I offer an outsider's opinion about what he said?"

"Do I have a choice?" she said, sure it was rhetorical.

"Speaking strictly from a career perspective, the *Seattle Times* is a fine paper. But you've got one hard news story under your belt. You'd be better off staying here, at the *Surrey City Press*, building a portfolio that's weighted toward hard news."

"So you don't think coverage of one complex murder and two-hundred clips of home portrait pieces will sway anybody to give me a city beat."

"I'm not saying you don't have the talent—clearly you do. Your descriptive powers are enviable and your work on the Missy Flannigan stories is exemplary. Hell, we'd hire you in a heartbeat at the *Standard Speaker*. I'm just offering a perspective from someone in the field. Your *husband* seems to feel he has it all worked out." Levi waved his hand toward the door. "But I'm not sure he realizes how fierce competition is for newspaper jobs."

"He might not."

"So you agree. Three thousand miles is a hell of a long way to go with no guarantees, just to find out . . ."

"Find out what?"

"That it's not what you want . . . any of it."

She hesitated. "My job, right? We're talking about my job?"

"Your job . . ." He took a deep breath. "Your life."

"My life." Aubrey stared. His image was strikingly altered from the buttoned-up, hard-nosed reporter who'd ploughed into her life as the Missy Flannigan story broke. "I understand the job part. But why are you so concerned about my life?"

"I'm not."

"Okay then." She turned for the door.

"Your grandmother."

Aubrey turned back. "What about her?"

"She was nothing more than a footnote in Owen's shiny new plan. Are you really going to pack up and go—just leave her here?"

"One thing Charley's used to is moving. She'll come with us."

"To that damp climate? In her condition? That'd hardly be in Charley's best interest."

Aubrey nodded. "She'll be touched by your concern." She turned for the door once more. It almost felt like an aberrant force spinning her back around. But it was only Aubrey who was compelled to ask, "Why don't you want me to go?"

Levi came closer, his hands shoved in his pockets. "Owen's a persuasive talker. Not necessarily what one expects from a computer genius. But I don't think he gets you—not like you need him to. He spent more time talking around your gift than he did trying to understand it."

"Owen is trying to fix our marriage. I'm sorry if his approach isn't analytical enough for you. But you don't know him. Spontaneity, big gestures—that's his way. Another thing, he's not solely to blame for our problems. Keep in mind, Levi, if I hadn't hid my gift from him, it wouldn't be an issue at all."

"Are you sure about that?"

"You're a fine one to judge. You didn't exactly respond with positivity when I was trying to convince you. As I recall, you tried to throw me out of your condo."

"It was an extenuating circumstance. You were relaying something more than the existence of your gift. Surely you can see that."

"I see that doubt and disbelief was acceptable behavior for you, but damn anybody else who has trouble grasping it—Owen in particular."

"This isn't about me, and they're not comparable situations," he shot back. "To start with, when you told me, I wasn't already married to you!" It shut them both up, Levi's hands thrust to his waist and his gaze to the floor. Bethany looked up from her phone, tipping her head in their direction. He lowered his voice. "That, um . . . that came out awkwardly." Levi's hand rose as if he might touch her. He didn't. "I only meant to offer an objective opinion. That's all."

"Fair enough," she said, her tone softer. "But whatever happens between Owen and me . . ." She shrugged, a glassy gaze veering toward the bar, landing back on him. "Levi, listen to me. With any luck, soon we'll get to the bottom of the Missy Flannigan story. Surrey and everything connected to it will go away. *I'll go away* . . . You'll go back to Hartford or move to New York, whatever the future holds. And truly,

I hope it's with less burden than before." She looked once more toward Bethany. "But other than Missy Flannigan . . . Other than the amazing few hours we shared this afternoon, I'm not sure why the idea of me moving to Seattle has you . . . so concerned about my life."

The statement seemed like too much of a challenge, even for an articulate Levi. His chin cocked toward the parking lot and her husband, whose car idled at the curb. "Just . . . just whatever you do—or don't do—consider all the angles. That's all I'm saying. Would you do that for me . . . *Aubrey?*"

Her gaze flicked to his, the sound of her first name sounding intimately subliminal. The honk of a horn intruded, but it did nothing to disrupt Levi's focus. He reached out. With a steady hand, he took the fallen edge of her wrap, and gently draped the fabric across the low-cut front of Aubrey's dress. He didn't touch her physically, not even grazing her skin. The subtle gesture made Aubrey's breath shake, a flutter rising from deep inside, something complicated and sweet. "I guess, right now," he said, "we both have obligations, other places to be."

CHAPTER
TWENTY-SIX

Most people perceived speaking to the dead as a mind-rattling, soul-shaking experience. Driving west into a waning sun, Aubrey thought the description mirrored her feelings about speaking to Frank Delacort. "Honestly, given a choice," she said to Levi, whose focus was steady on traffic, "I think I'd rather go back to the Serino house."

"No, you don't."

"No. I don't." Aubrey bit down on a thumbnail and returned to her notes. After she'd arrived at work that morning, neither had spoken about last night. There wasn't time or space with Malcolm on hand, the three of them strategizing the Delacort interview. They'd spent the drive role-playing, rehearsing the carefully crafted questions. It was a litany that read like an olive branch—offering subtlety that budded with leading questions that would, hopefully, get Frank to talk. But foremost on Aubrey's mind was the fact that she'd have to go it alone: no other reporters, no photographer. "I'll talk to the lady reporter. That's it. I'm not even sure why . . . But I'll fucking do it." That had been the message from Frank to Levi. Aubrey had an idea about the why, shifting her notes aside and running her thumb over the tiny ring of leaves she'd drawn on the notepad. Their meaning was still an unknown.

If Aubrey had doubts about a successful interview, she assumed Levi did too. It was understandable. It was a stretch: storybook home portrait reviewer to hardcore investigative reporter. That morning, her first glance at Levi hadn't helped. Anyone would have thought he'd spent the night in his office. The trash can overflowed with empty coffee cups and his face was unshaven, his permanent-press looks decidedly wrinkled. His disheveled appearance added to her angst. But Levi remedied that before they left the office, disappearing and returning clean-shaven, wearing a fresh dress shirt. It was marginally comforting. Her partner looked prepared, on his game, and Aubrey was compelled to do the same.

"The main thing is to keep an exchange going. Do not allow Delacort an opportunity to hijack the conversation." Levi checked the time. They were on pace to arrive a half hour early. Nothing would be left to chance, including Mass Pike traffic. Frank had requested they meet at an obscure diner a good distance from Surrey. "Don't rush," Levi said. "Think about how you phrase things and watch for any weaknesses on his part. That's your opening. Finesse your way into his military history. Double jeopardy, the fact that he can't be tried for the same crime twice, may lower his guard and lure him into revealing a secret he's kept for twenty years."

"And if I do all those things right, we'll get what we're after?"

There was a sideways glance from him. "Okay, honesty time. This is one part skill, one part luck, and two parts crapshoot. The odds aren't really calculable—but don't tell anybody I said that."

She smiled at his candidness. "We had a decent dialogue when we spoke on the phone. A friendly tone might be the best way to unearth information."

"I agree. There's no harm in leading Delacort to believe that we're on his side. If he didn't kill Missy, then he should be as anxious as the DA to prove Dustin Byrd did. But I also think . . ."

"You also think there's a chance he did do it."

Levi rapped his knuckles against the steering wheel. "That's one reason I'll be sitting, discreetly, as close as possible."

"Is the other because you don't think I can do this?"

"What?" Levi looked surprised, his glance weaving between her and the traffic. "Why would you even say that?

"I don't know about you. But it's occurred to me that I might not be the best candidate to pull this off—even in a crapshoot."

"On the contrary, I think someone less jaded has a better shot. Imagine Delacort's guard if I were the one asking questions. Besides, I have confidence in your skills. You should feel the same way." They drove in silence for another mile.

"There is one thing I am concerned about. When you talk to Delacort . . ." He paused. "Since I now know . . . *everything*, we are talking about a murdered girl here. There's a chance you could be sitting down with her killer. With anybody else, that would be the sole apprehension. With you . . ."

She nodded deeply. "You're starting to think about the dead in a whole new light."

"Much to my amazement—and concern. That's the reason you didn't want to work on this story in the first place, isn't it?"

"My true objection might have thrown Malcolm just a bit." Aubrey smoothed the pages she held on her lap. "Initially, my impression was a dead girl who surely had a whole lot of anger to convey. Maybe a score to settle." She looked from the papers to Levi. "To be honest, when Malcolm suggested I work on this story, it scared the hell out of me."

"And so far . . . ?"

"Are you asking if Missy's shown up, rattled a chain?"

"Yes," he said. "That's what I'm asking. I want . . . I need to be prepared."

"And so you will." Aubrey cleared her throat. "Here's what I can tell you: A public setting makes any connection more difficult—there's lots of interference. It's also my practice not to let it in. We have that on our side. Most important, so far, I haven't had one thing indicate Missy's presence." She laughed softly. "Not even a trace of Midnight Fire."

"Midnight Fire?"

"Missy's perfume. It was mentioned somewhere in all those files. About a week ago, I went by a boutique downtown where they still sell it."

"And?"

"And nothing. Nothing other than it smelled like the kind of stuff a twenty-year-old would wear, cotton-candy sweet, sexy around the edge."

"So you've been concerned, curious about how and when Missy Flannigan will turn up in all this?"

"How could I not be?" Aubrey gripped harder to her notes. "Levi, we are in uncharted territory. Never have I gone looking to channel someone who's passed—not like this. We're talking about a girl who had her life snuffed out, her body sealed behind a basement wall. Clearly, it was an *unpleasant* death."

Levi followed the curve of the exit ramp, and Aubrey saw him take a deep breath. "And if you were to encounter Missy, it could be the same, or worse than the anger you felt in the house on Acorn Circle . . . from Eli Serino?"

"That's been my assumption. My apprehension. But a part of me wants to know why . . ." Aubrey stopped, shaking her head at the taboo thought.

"A part of you wonders why Missy hasn't come looking for you."

"Makes me some sort of masochist, doesn't it?" The GPS answered, announcing that they'd arrived at their destination. In front of them sat the dingy Exit 43 Diner, framed by a tired asphalt parking lot.

"I think," Levi said, backing into a spot away from the main entrance, "it makes you a solid investigative reporter."

"Wouldn't that be something?" Aubrey thrummed her fingers on the stack of questions and notes. "But to answer your question, Missy is never far from my mind. You saw firsthand how evil plays into this. But being in a house with Eli Serino, it's not the worst thing I've ever encountered. I know there's more."

He cut the engine, twisting in her direction. "How much more?" Levi grasped her hand and abruptly pushed up the sleeve of her pale blue sweater—a color that tended to be neither here nor there. "Tell me about the marks on your arm. Your chin. Is this more, Aubrey? Is that how this happened?" With her free hand, Aubrey traced the half-moon scar. From anyone else the question would have been intrusive, like someone asking, *"So how'd you get that fake leg?"* From Levi it felt more like concern, maybe serious fact-finding. "I need to know before we go in there. I have to understand the potential."

She didn't look at him. She couldn't. With her hand in his, Aubrey focused on the exterior of the Exit 43 Diner. Its dull silvery façade looked as though it had its own traveling secrets.

"When I was seventeen . . ." She stopped, breathing deep, squinting at the view. "When I was seventeen, the Heinz-Bodette Troupe was forced into an unexpected travel delay—hurricane weather headed up the Eastern Shore of Maryland. Charley suggested we check into a motel and ride it out. Her arthritis had progressed to a point where she welcomed a break. On top of that, she'd had some awful nightmares in the days leading up to that night. She said the dreams weren't vivid, just the vague face of a young African-American male. Even so, the dreams really seemed to upset her, which, in hindsight, maybe I should have noticed." In the midst of the bitter tale, Aubrey gave a small smile. "I thought the motel was a great idea. When we stayed in places like that, aside from a full tub, one of the best perks were separate rooms—adjoining but separate. When you've lived your life in a motor home, space and privacy is a splurge.

"We checked into the Delmarva Inn. It was nice for a mom and pop place. Everything seemed new, the bathrooms, the carpet. The mattress. It was thick, comfortable. The wind was howling, the rain pummeling, but the building was cement block. I felt incredibly . . . safe. And for a few hours, I was. We were pleasantly tucked away in rooms 112 and 114. Then, in the middle of the night, I woke up." Aubrey's hand rose, touching her neck. "There was a hand around my throat. You know how a motel room is, pitch black?" Levi nodded, his expression growing more wary. "I couldn't see anything, but I could smell it. It was rot, worse than the stench that came with Eli Serino, an anger that made his seem . . . well, now that I think about it, just spooky. I thought my heart was going to explode—or be ripped—from my chest. The sounds were inhuman, screeching . . . wailing that I knew no one but me could hear. I tried to get out of the bed. I couldn't move. It was holding me down, tearing at my nightgown. I couldn't scream; I couldn't breathe. Something raked across my stomach—I felt the dampness of blood. Then the groping sensation moved lower. I fought back and it dug into my arm, pinned it down . . . I realized it wasn't fingernails." Aubrey turned her palm upward, yielding the best view of the odd pitted marks. "It was teeth. It bit me, over and over. For every encounter I'd had with the dead, I'd never experienced anything so violent . . . so physical."

"That's . . ." A shaky sigh pulsed out of Levi, sinking into her. "Was its intention to . . ."

"Its intention was pure evil. Beyond that, I don't know. Thankfully, the damage was all . . . *external.*"

"You managed to get away."

"Somehow, I did," she said, lightly touching the scar on her chin.

"Did it . . . did it do that too?"

"No," she said, looking at him. "This was all me. As I broke free, I collided, chin first, with the nightstand. The whole incident couldn't have lasted more than thirty seconds—but when it's something that horrific, unknown, thirty seconds feels like a lifetime. It took just that long for Charley to make it through the connecting door. She flipped on a light. The energy was still there but not nearly as strong. I ran into Charley's room. It didn't follow. Very much like Eli Serino, it seemed stuck in that space. I was, um . . . I was a bloody mess, a flap of skin hanging from my chin. My stomach and thighs, they looked as if I'd tangled with a bed full of rabid cats. It, uh . . . it gave me new appreciation for the familiar confines of a motor home."

"I don't . . . It's almost inconceivable."

"That it could happen?"

"That you'd survive it. Surpass it. That you'd have to live the rest of your life knowing it's a possibility."

Aubrey watched his fingers move lithely over her pockmarked skin. Her brow crinkled. It was the same gentleness he'd applied to a splintered finger. Last time it was an anomaly, this time she felt something else. Aubrey retracted her arm, looking away from him and out the car window. "I've never spoken about it before. Not to anyone."

"Your . . . He's never asked?"

"Of course Owen's asked," she said, turning toward him. "But by then I'd put us in a position where the truth . . . Let's just say a scene straight out of *Rosemary's Baby* wasn't where I wanted to start the conversation."

Levi nodded, backpedaling. "So what happened after that, after you left the motel?"

"I begged Charley not to tell the other troupe members. I'd rather them think me clumsy and Charley eccentric. To this day, I'm sure Carmine, Yvette, the rest of them wonder why the Heinz-Bodette Troupe fled the Delmarva Inn like thieves in the night."

"And you have no idea who or what attacked you?"

Aubrey self-comforted, running her hand over the scars on her arm. "No, I definitely needed to understand what happened. Charley and I did some research." Aubrey took a deep breath, thinking back to a period of time she'd never forget. "The Delmarva Inn reopened the week before we stayed there. It'd been closed for two years. Most recently due to a complete renovation. More memorably because of an incident that occurred there. A convicted felon—a David Ray Tomlin—escaped an Eastern Shore prison. He robbed a convenience store, shot one clerk to death, and took the other hostage at the motel—a young African-American male. There he tortured and sodomized his victim."

"He was the boy Charley dreamed about."

"She does that, dreams of people connected to the dead—she even dreamed about you." She pursed her lips flat. "At the time, her dream about David Ray Tomlin's victim was too abstract. No one could have predicted how it might affect me so directly. According to old newspaper reports, it was a volatile hostage situation. It went on for two days . . . gunfire, threats . . . demands. Then it all abruptly ended when Tomlin took his own life in room 114, my room."

Aubrey could feel Levi's shuddering breath. She saw the angst on his face. Then she heard him take control. "Look at me." She did. "As awful as that was to hear, I'm glad you told me. The house on Acorn Circle is one thing, but what you just said . . . I don't want you to do this, Aubrey. I don't want you to meet with Delacort."

Thinking about the curious ring of leaves she'd drawn, Aubrey wanted to agree. Then she considered the *Surrey City Press* and what she'd promised Malcolm. "And that would leave you where? The paper would lose the biggest story connected to Missy Flannigan's murder."

"It's secondary. I'll talk to Delacort myself. You can write the story, take the byline. Your safety comes first. I thought I was tagging along because there's a possibility you'd be sitting down with a murderer. There's no way I'm taking the chance of you sitting down with his victim."

"Trust is everything with somebody like Delacort. You can't do that, Levi. Pull a last minute switch like that and he'll be the one bolting. You know that."

"That's a risk I'm willing to take. Your safety," he said, "isn't. Just let me go in there, talk to Delacort. I'll get around your absence."

"How? It's the one thing he stipulated."

"I'll tell him you have the flu." She cocked her head. "Okay, I'll say you were in a car accident. Not a bad one, but enough to keep you from coming. It doesn't matter. I'll think of something. Hell, I'll tell him that you decided to reinvent your life and move to Seattle—whatever it takes. Nothing," he said, breathing deep, "can happen to you."

And there it was, like a spotlight. They'd managed to circumvent circumstance, neatly avoiding a single word about last night. Aubrey looked into his brooding eyes: co-worker, friend, confidant . . . Whatever the label, Levi's solemn expression said how much he meant it. He'd help her pack if it kept her safe. Aubrey shook her head gently. She reached out, making feathery contact with Levi's clean-shaven cheek. "Talk about mysteries. You and I . . . I have absolutely no idea how we got to here." Beneath her touch, Aubrey felt an awakening. On the surface, there was the hard-to-see, but always there, considerate side of Levi—concern for things like personal safety and deep splinters. He would do it for anybody. It was a piece of Levi that you might not see at first glance—and truly a huge part of who he was. But this . . . this felt as if it exceeded those boundaries. His hand rose and covered hers. Aubrey watched a hard swallow melt through his frozen pose. "Levi, I'm grateful for your willingness to intervene. I really am. But I can't live my life like that. I can't stay locked in motor homes or cars. And I won't run away. Not from Frank Delacort. I want to do my job."

"It's an impossible situation that you shouldn't be anywhere near."

"Believe me; I'm not looking for the adrenaline rush, just the truth. I'm going into this eyes wide open." Aubrey's hand dropped from his cheek. She turned her attention toward the diner. "If this were your interview, would you let anything stop you?"

"Short of being hit by a train?"

"Okay, then," she said, looking back. "Why should I allow anything to stop me?"

He started to object, the dimple forced into a false smile. "On one condition."

"What's that?"

"If you feel the slightest bit threatened, whatever that means to you, and I'm not talking about Delacort, you leave. You don't take time to make excuses. You get up and walk out. I mean it."

Her breath was doing it again, the fluttery movement of air she'd felt last night. But inside the car was more intimate than a restaurant vestibule, a space busy with a bar and a longtime girlfriend a few feet away. "Levi . . ." No one leaned in; it was more like gravity, his mouth moving deftly over hers. Aubrey's arms rose, needing to hold on to him. Her mind took exception, feeling a sharp pang of betrayal. This was wrong. This shouldn't be happening. But like the woozy lure of champagne, Aubrey wanted more. She wanted Levi to kiss her again, to tell her he wanted the two of them to be someplace, anyplace where the focus was only . . . *kissing*. But before the moment clarified, the kissing stopped. Levi's forehead and heated thoughts bumped against hers. She still held tight to his arm. Aubrey blinked fast, her peripheral glance catching a man in a hooded sweatshirt, his gait hurried. "Damn, this is it."

Levi inched back. "Here?"

"What?" she said, looking between the diner and Levi. "No. Delacort. He just went inside."

"You're sure?"

"Yes." She let go. Aubrey only wanted to feel the crisp cotton of Levi's shirtsleeve—all businesslike and orderly. Instead it was the quixotic sensation of the taut muscle of his arm that lingered. "You . . . you'll follow right behind?" she said.

"Count on it."

Aubrey gathered her satchel and reached for the door handle. Her gaze flitted back. She smiled, wiping a smudge of lipstick from his mouth. "That might stand out."

"Thanks," he said, repeating the swipe himself.

"Thanks for the extra camouflage."

"Camouflage?"

"Color isn't the only deterrent at my disposal. The more divided my thoughts . . . emotions, the more difficult it becomes for any spirit to make itself known."

"So kissing is a tactic. Like you could have just as easily kissed Blake in photography?"

Aubrey stepped out of the car, then ducked back in. "No, it wouldn't work with Blake. Cute as he is, the wrath of his boyfriend would make it totally not worth it. And for that particular distraction to have any influence, I need to feel something in return."

CHAPTER
TWENTY-SEVEN

Aubrey moved through the diner, her focus not completely on Missy or Frank. The taste of Levi was redolent—powerful. She was halfway across a worn linoleum floor when the heady aromas of coffee and all-day breakfast finally grew stronger. Aubrey was grateful for unexpected and ordinary things. She saw vinyl-covered booths and a well-traveled atmosphere. People were scattered about, caught up in early-bird dinners and destinations. Seated in the rear of the diner was the man in the hooded jacket. He had salt and pepper hair, close-cropped to his head. Distance couldn't hide the awkwardness with which he sat, the come-and-go setting foreign and removed. "Mr. Delacort?" she said, approaching. He gripped a glass of water as if stunned by the simple sensation of ice. His head ticked left, reacting to her voice, a feminine voice, in the same dumbfounded manner.

"Yeah. I'm Frank."

"Aubrey Ellis." Extending her hand would have been the polite thing to do, but touch was more risk than she was willing to assume. He didn't seem miffed by the lack of etiquette, his chin cocking at the seat opposite him. It wasn't hostile, but it wasn't friendly. The immediate air, laden with greasy food smells, made her stomach churn. Aubrey tried not to glance in Levi's direction. He'd just taken a seat out of Frank's line of vision, a newspaper in front of him. Aubrey thought he might as well be holding it upside down.

"Thank you for agreeing to this," she said, sitting. Frank's gaze moved over her like a metal detector. "Let me, um . . . Let me start by saying that I'd like to hear things from your perspective. I'd like to help." Frank stared blankly, as though help was the last thing on his mind. "We can show the public, our readers, what this whole ordeal has been like for you. Everything from being accused of the murder of a girl you barely knew to your time in . . . well—"

"Prison?"

"Yes."

"Why?"

"Pardon?"

"Other than to sell newspapers, why would you be interested in any of it? No one from the *Surrey City Press* has come around on visiting day for the past twenty years." He held a pack of cigarettes in his hand. "'Course, guess I'd make a good . . . what do you call it? Human interest piece?" He turned the unopened pack over and over, tapping it on the tabletop. "Nobody's wanted to talk about the state of my humanity for ages. But a body falls out of a wall, and . . . *Bang!*" He let the pack of cigarettes fly, his fist splaying wide. Aubrey startled. "Suddenly everybody wants a meeting." He laughed. "Almost as bad as I want a damn cigarette." He glanced at posted *no smoking* signs. "You know how long it's been since I sat in a diner, Miss Ellis?" She cinched her shoulders. "I didn't have a clue you couldn't grab a smoke. That's how long."

"Fortunately, people better appreciate the hazards of smoking." Aubrey cleared her throat. "Your situation is news, Mr. Delacort. That's not my fault. It's just my job. I'm sorry if that offends you."

"I was right about you—you got guts, lady. I could tell that on the phone." He flashed a dazzling smile and Aubrey felt a tickle of déjà vu. "But here's the thing. The police screwed up plenty the first time around. Maybe they've got it all wrong again. So why should I believe that you're here to help me?"

Aubrey scrambled to organize her thoughts, amazed how swiftly she'd managed to botch the interview. She glanced at Levi, who offered an encouraging nod. Regrouping, she shuffled through her satchel for her phone. "Do you mind? I'd like to record our conversation." Aubrey tapped the screen. In reply, Frank reached across the table and grabbed the device. Aubrey's eyes went wide; Levi stood.

"It would be polite to wait until I answered." He handed it back. "Pass on the audio. Last time I sat with a running tape recorder, it was on a reel. It also didn't end in my favor."

"Fair enough," she said. She took the phone back, gingerly, and put it away. Levi lowered himself back into his booth, although it looked as if he were waiting for the sound of a starter pistol. "I'd like to begin with a few questions about you and Missy."

"I . . . I didn't mean to snap," Frank said, his mood revolving. "Bad impulse . . . A lifelong habit."

"Uh-huh," she murmured, wondering if he'd used the same excuse on Missy. "Is that all right? Could we talk about her?" Tentatively, Aubrey reached into her bag again. She took out a notepad and pen. She held them at eye-level for Frank's approval. He nodded.

"I been thinking this through since the second I heard about Missy's body being found—where it was found. And I decided that unless I was going to talk about Missy . . . I mean, really talk about her, there was no point. All or nothing."

"Why's that, Mr. Delacort?"

"Frank," he insisted. "I said you were gutsy. Let's not be a phony, okay, Miss Ellis?"

"Frank," she said, flipping the notepad open.

"Because what I have to say isn't going to make me look any less guilty." The waitress came by and asked what they wanted to order. It gave Aubrey a moment to process his remark. "Coffee," Frank said. Aubrey said she'd have the same.

Levi peeked up from his newspaper. He knew she wasn't a coffee-drinker, and that the order was a fine demonstration of her nerves. She skipped past it. "Then why say it? Why not just get on your bus and go? No more questions asked."

"Dustin Byrd is now physically linked to Missy and her murder. I got things to say about that—some of it is going to shock you." Aubrey remained poised, expressionless. "But first I need you to know one true thing: the last time I saw Missy she was alive. Banged up, but alive."

"Where was the last place you saw her?"

"In my room at the Plastic Fork."

"You stated she cut her leg running, that you offered first-aid. That was your explanation for how Missy's blood and hair ended up in your room."

"That's not exactly how it happened."

"Okay, Frank, I'm listening with an open mind. How did it happen?"

"To tell you that I have to explain what Missy was doing in my room . . . *really* doing in my room."

"Does it affect your story significantly?" she said, heeding Levi's advice to keep a back-and-forth dialogue going.

Frank picked up the pack of cigarettes, his focus on his thumb as it ran over the shiny label. "If I'd told the whole story twenty years ago, I would have looked big-time guilty, like electric-chair guilty." He shrugged, making serious eye contact. "So here goes. We were in bed."

"In bed?"

"Yeah. Doing . . . well, doing what you'd expect we'd be doing." Aubrey's sideways glance met with Levi's stare. "Missy wasn't an acquaintance, like the papers said, like the police said . . . like *I* said." Aubrey's pen jammed, forming a tiny pool of ink. "But saying that we'd been *together* all summer . . . for sure that wasn't gonna help my case."

"You're right," Aubrey said, absorbing the shock while smoothing out her cursive. "That is a very different story. The police theorized that you kidnapped her."

"The police and the DA would have told you my fingerprints were a match with the devil." He looked past Aubrey. "I'm a few light-years from perfect, Miss Ellis, but I'm not that kind of monster. Can you believe that much?" She was only convinced it could go either way. The waitress returned with the coffee and served them. Frank proceeded to dump four packets of sugar into his. "Habit," he said, "prison coffee sucks . . . you know?"

Aubrey dumped half as many packets into hers, nodding. "Newsroom coffee is almost as bad."

"So here's the second unexpected truth. The world saw Missy like she was as innocent as snow. I thought the same thing. It was easy to believe." He hesitated. "But it wasn't true. It also wasn't her fault."

"That's an interesting assertion. Can you elaborate?"

"I've watched nearly twenty freakin' winters come and go from one exercise yard. Plenty of time to study the color of snow. You know how it starts out, pretty and innocent—even in a prison yard. Fast-forward into February, maybe March. It drifts outside the lines of what you first saw, doesn't it?"

"It's kind of dirty, not so pretty anymore."

"Imagine what it looks like after twenty years. What I'm saying is the police saw Missy that way, and maybe even I saw her that way. But I've had lots of time to watch the snow change."

Aubrey navigated away from metaphors, aiming for facts. "If you and Missy were romantically involved, will you tell me about that?"

"We were planning on leaving Surrey together," he said. "She wanted out of that town for a lot of reasons."

"Name a few of them."

"For one, she'd been carrying on with Dustin Byrd since high school. He wanted to marry her, and she didn't want anything to do with that." His head tipped, eyes narrowing at Aubrey's blunt stare. "You don't seem surprised."

"It's one of our revolving newsroom theories. I think Dustin Byrd may have paid for her car. My partner on this story, Levi St John . . ."

"I seen his name with yours in the paper."

"It's Levi's contention that Missy paid for the car herself."

Frank frowned as he stirred his coffee. "You're still seeing white snow. Your partner's got a sharp instinct. I like sharp instinct. Missy paid for that car herself."

"Did she? But how . . ." Aubrey stopped. One thing at a time. She needed to steer. "Can you fill in some details about her relationship with Dustin Byrd? He was so much older—not really the image that jumps to mind. He was mid-life, she was just starting out. Dustin's life was stable but not very glamorous. He was—"

"He was one more thing. He fit the profile."

"What profile?"

"The kind of guy a teenage girl would latch on to after years of abuse."

"Abuse? What kind of abuse?"

Frank Delacort opened the pack of cigarettes and took one out. He tapped the unlit casing into the table. "The kind that nice folks in pleasant towns don't talk about. Tom Flannigan. It's another thing the police totally missed, what he did to his own daughter. But if you follow what I'm telling you, you'll see that it fits."

"Tom Flannigan sexually abused Missy? Do you have proof of that?"

"I told you, Miss Ellis, you'd be shocked by what I had to say. You also won't be inclined to believe me. Twenty years in prison—guilty or not—alters my credibility. But it's the truth, every goddamn word."

Aubrey tried to erase the stigma surrounding Frank, but she couldn't dismiss what she knew about his military past. She leaned back, clearing her head. Inadvertently, she cracked open a frame of mind she'd normally keep sealed shut. Like the turn of a page, aromatic coffee began to drift and the odor of greasy foods receded. Pastries. She smelled fresh pastries . . . cookies . . . sugary icing. On her palate was anise, almond extract, nutmeg . . . lemon squares. Nothing so refined was on the Exit 43 Diner menu. But Aubrey also didn't feel threatened by the sweet sensations. "Go on, Frank, I'm listening."

"When Missy was nine years old, Tom Flannigan started making frequent trips to her bedroom. Don't ask me to explain that part. I've spent decades wondering what could be so sick inside a man's soul that he'd do something . . . something that depraved. I don't have an answer. But I do know that when Missy turned sixteen she took control. Missy was . . ." Frank laughed; the sound was eerie and out of place. "Because of what she'd been through or maybe despite it, Missy didn't take much shit off anybody. I knew that from the day I met her. She told Tom Flannigan it was going to stop." Frank mashed the unlit cigarette into a saucer, crushing it until the casing split like a watermelon. "According to Missy, it did stop. Of course, by then, what's a girl like that supposed to do?"

"She could have reported him to the police, a friend . . . confided to her high school counselor, another adult." Frank's head shook more adamantly with each suggestion.

"Don't you think I said the same thing to her? To tell anyone meant telling her mother, and Missy couldn't bring herself to do that. You're aware of her mother's condition?"

"She has multiple sclerosis. She was diagnosed when Missy was about seven or eight."

"Her mother's illness, what she felt for her, it was the one thing . . . the *only* thing that kept her in that house. Still, Missy talked about a dream she used to have. She was at her mother's funeral. Standing by the grave, she'd see herself as happy. Happy because after they buried her mother, Missy went screaming to the police about what Tom Flannigan had done. Pretty twisted, huh?" He sipped his coffee. Frank put down the cup, his expression turning rigid—lifeless. "Imagine having to wish your own mother dead to find some peace? That's a big fucking burden for anybody."

Aubrey didn't say anything, trying to see between the rough edges of a tough life. It was raw but honest. There was also, in the distance, someone asking for Frank. The more he spoke, the closer it came. Aubrey turned it off hard, like a leaky faucet.

"You all right, Miss Ellis? You look kind of . . . distracted."

She sat up taller, a reassuring shift. A glance at Levi's face confirmed a repeat of Frank's concern. "I'm fine, just surprised . . . just like you said I'd be. Tell me why you think that kind of heinous experience resulted in an ongoing relationship with Dustin Byrd."

"I'm no shrink, but I get coping mechanisms—probably because I've tried most of them. Over the years, I've read about girls like Missy. Most of them end up on the streets or with a needle in their arm. Turning to Dustin Byrd wasn't a great choice, but it probably saved Missy from something worse—at least for a while. From what Missy said, Byrd thought the sun and moon rose over her, and . . . well, I guess that felt pretty good to her."

"But things changed when you showed up."

"By the time I showed up things had already changed. Dustin Byrd was obsessed with Missy. And the tighter he held on, the less she wanted it. He was a chump. Even a normal sixteen-year-old girl won't want the same thing at twenty-one. But he had that kind of arrogance about him, never questioning why Missy fell for him in the first place."

"He didn't know. Dustin Byrd can't corroborate the abuse."

"No. She never told him. She couldn't do that—ruin the image he worshiped. One of Missy's *hobbies* was hanging out in church. But she didn't tell them neither. She never could bring herself to confess something that wasn't her sin." Frank sighed. "So, lucky me, I'm the only person she ever confided in."

Convenient or tragic? It could be either. Frank waited as if Aubrey were his new jury. She felt like she had her opening. "Frank, I'd like to share something with you, something about Missy's murder." His eyebrows cinched together. "Eventually, the DA will release a manner of death. Missy died from a gunshot wound to the abdomen."

"A gunshot wound?"

"Point-blank range."

Frank was quiet, not reaching for the pack of cigarettes, not sipping his coffee, oddly not avoiding Aubrey's gaze. "Since I haven't heard a question, I'm guessing there's more."

"A ballistics expert matched the bullet lodged in Missy's skeleton to a rare military-issue weapon—a Ruger Super Redhawk."

He smiled again. Aubrey breathed deep, not at Frank's cool response, but at another pang of déjà vu. There was the crank of carnival music, a shooting game of chance. Then it was gone.

"My military record is sealed."

"We managed to unseal it."

"Aren't you gutsy and shrewd."

"We have a good team at the *Surrey City Press*."

"I get it. You're liking me for this murder all over again because my history tells you as much."

"I'm offering the information I have. But I would imagine you're awfully glad that military record didn't come to light during your trial, certainly not before they exonerated you."

"That's what this is about?" he said, his tone growing sharper. "I do twenty years for a murder I didn't commit, and now you want to crucify me all over again? You're going to tell the world I was no better than a mercenary? That Frank Delacort and the United States Army inadvertently killed women and children."

"Excuse me? I'm not sure what you're—" She traded a fast look with Levi, who seemed equally perplexed.

"Sometimes, Miss Ellis, things are classified for the sake of safety. Sometimes it's because the truth is so ugly nobody wants you to hear it."

Aubrey shook her head. "That's what you'd be concerned about? That's what you'd worry about me reporting?"

"My unit carried out orders. Anybody who thinks you can do that without collateral damage is a fool. Good as we were, missions like ours, innocent people died. Someday, I expect to be held accountable—but it won't be on this earth, by a jury of your peers."

Fast as she could, Aubrey recalculated Frank Delacort's sins—which by his admission were mounting. It was a startling confession, but it wasn't the one for which she'd come. "Frank. My reason . . . the reason I wanted this interview was to talk about Missy Flannigan. I wasn't aware . . . I don't have those kinds of details about your military history. Just your familiarity with the gun that killed Missy."

"Just . . ."

"Just the gun, Frank. That's all I wanted to discuss."

His line of vision crept from his ice water to Aubrey. He nodded, understanding that she wasn't going to demand an accounting of military injustices. "To answer the question you came to ask, the no-brainer one—yes, I was well trained with that particular Ruger. But I didn't shoot Missy. You said point-blank range?"

"Yes. That's what the coroner concluded."

"Had I wanted Missy dead, it wouldn't have been with anything as sloppy as a handgun—not unless I wanted to rip a hole in her the size of Oklahoma. That particular Ruger is a vicious firearm. If shot by one, the victim would have just enough time to glance at the mess in their lap before it was lights-out. My hit, it would have been from three hundred meters out with a high-end optical sight, assuming there was no breeze. She would have never seen me coming. Trust me. That's how you kill someone, Miss Ellis."

Aubrey didn't let the calculated conclusion rattle her. "Even so, you have to admit it's a compelling piece of information."

"I can't change facts. What you learned might be true. But I wanted to protect Missy . . . I loved her. I didn't want her dead. So who did?

Maybe the guy she dumped hard for me? That wannabe commando. Byrd shouldn't have been licensed to own a water pistol. But he was that type, the kind who thought a stockpile of weapons made him somebody . . ." Frank's weathered face looked more contemplative. "And here I sit, a free man. Why is that?"

She was quiet, forgetting Levi's advice not to give Frank an opening. He was quick to pounce.

"Byrd owns a Ruger. That exact Ruger, the Super Redhawk. Doesn't he?" Frank leaned back. "That's why the DA and judge cut me loose— not even a retrial. They think it's a done deal. A body in Byrd's wall and a weapon in his hand. And now a motive, which I just gave you."

"Despite your military history, Dustin Byrd does appear the more likely perpetrator."

"Particularly when you factor in the location of the body. I mean, good luck placing me at the scene."

"It's a valid point. You have no connection to the Byrd house."

"Which brings me back around to why I agreed to this. I've had plenty of time to consider my own ideas about . . ."

"Wait," she said, holding up her hand. "Back up a step. None of this explains how Missy's blood ended up in your room. Do you want to circle back around to that?" Aubrey flipped through her notes. "You said Missy was 'banged up but alive,' the last time you saw her. Your words. Did Dustin assault her? Did she come to you afterward?"

"Confirming that would seal that fucker's fate, wouldn't it? A jury might buy it, even if it came out of my mouth."

"But that wouldn't be the truth."

"I said up front, if I'm telling this story, I'm telling the whole story. Maybe Byrd committed a crime of passion, maybe it was a hair-trigger accident—who knows. But Dustin Byrd wasn't responsible for Missy being . . . banged up." The crow's-feet around Frank's eyes narrowed. "I was."

"You?" Aubrey said. The empathy she'd built up fell like a house of cards.

"Me," he said, as if he'd been waiting twenty years to admit as much.

"I'm sorry, Frank, but that does change my opinion about what you've said so far. How can it not?"

"Yeah, on my way here, I realized the truth might. Twenty years ago, honesty wouldn't have done me much good. It won't help me now. I'd just hoped . . . I thought, maybe, despite my shortcomings, you might be interested in the bottom line."

"You're asking for an awful lot of faith, Frank. Based on what you've admitted, based on what we've learned. Surely you can see how it doesn't ease my skepticism."

He picked up the pack of cigarettes and pulled a couple of crumpled bills from his pocket. "Yeah, I get it. People wanted this story to be black and white—*you* want this story to be that way. One good guy, one bad guy. It isn't. And now you know why I never used the truth as my defense. Tell you what. Go back to your paper and print that. Print it all if you want. My life's been nothing but a fucking mistake—from Laurel, to the army, to sweet Missy Flannigan—today's just one more. Coffee's on me." He stood and headed for the exit.

CHAPTER TWENTY-EIGHT

Frank Delacort moved and so did Levi, rapidly blocking his path. "Wait. I want to hear the rest of what you came to say. I *need* to hear it. I'm sure Miss Ellis does too."

Frank spun toward Aubrey. "A cop? You brought a cop with you?"

"No, she didn't. I'm Levi St John." He extended his hand to Frank. "You said you've seen my name on the byline with Aubrey's. And yes, I've been sitting here the entire time."

"Like I said, this was a fucking bad idea." Frank glanced at Levi's hand and brushed past it.

The reporter in Levi couldn't relent, so he spoke to the back of Frank's head with one-on-one zeal. "Most of what you said, Frank, it did sound like you wanted to protect Missy." Frank stopped, a few diners tuning into the exchange. "I was only doing the same thing for Aubrey. I apologize for the cloak-and-dagger setup, but I couldn't let her come here alone."

Frank did an about-face, but he didn't move forward. Aubrey sensed someone buzzing, panicking at the back of her brain. He . . . *she* . . . didn't want Frank to leave. "Miss Ellis seems like a capable person. Like she'd tell me to fuck off if need be."

"You're right. Aubrey can handle herself—in situations more precarious than the one you represent. Still . . ."

Frank nodded vaguely. "I get that, wanting to make sure Miss Ellis was okay."

Aubrey leaned into the table, the restaurant and people feeling detached from where she stood.

"Aubrey?" Levi said, having turned toward her.

"I'm all right." But she sat as she said it, sliding into Levi's booth.

Moments later, Frank agreed to sit too. Levi sat beside her. Staying engaged was increasingly difficult. An entity churned around her and Aubrey didn't object as Levi took the reins. "You're right about the truth, Frank. People will react emotionally to what you admitted. But my role isn't to judge. It's to gather facts. It doesn't make the rest of your story false or irrelevant." Levi picked up the pad and pen, which Aubrey had abandoned. "Start with why you assaulted Missy. Was it an argument?"

"It was a fight, a nasty one. Money was our only issue in leaving Surrey. Missy drained her bank account buying that car. I didn't have a bank account."

"You were fighting over money."

"Not exactly. We were fighting over the eighty grand she'd showed up with that day."

"Come again?" Levi said, now diligently taking notes.

"Byrd had saved pretty much every penny he ever made. He was going to build a house for him and the *new missus*. Missy decided, all on her own, that his nest egg was going to be ours."

"She stole it?" Levi said.

"She figured I'd take it as a prayer answered. She thought I'd be relieved . . . grateful. Missy was right about one thing, I was blown away. From nowhere, she unzips her backpack and dumps eighty grand—*cash*—onto the bed, like it was poker chips."

"But you didn't see it that way."

"Fuck no. The last thing I wanted was to start a new life with Missy by stealing her ex-lover's money. We both disappear and that puffed-up commando's safe gets sucked dry. Who do you think's gonna get blamed for masterminding that? Of course, joke was on me. Instead of doing time for grand larceny, I end up doing time for murder."

"That started the argument," Levi said.

"Started it, yes. But it's not what set me off. Not really. Some time had passed since Missy ended things with Byrd. Thinking about that made me wonder how she managed to get her hands on his cash. According to Missy, Byrd kept the money in a safe in his bedroom. To get it, she would have had to go there. One sentence led to another, and . . . well, she didn't deny it. In fact, I think she was proud of her coup. For a couple of sweet fucking hours, I'm sure Dustin Byrd thought Missy wanted him back. He got into her panties and Missy got into his safe. Apparently, a wet dick was all it took to blindside him." Frank's glance veered to Aubrey. "I, uh . . . I didn't mean to be so graphic."

She held her hand up, dragging her attention along with it. "That's how she got to the money, by sleeping with Dustin. That's what angered you."

"Nothing was going to stop Missy from getting that money. Remember what I said about snow?" Levi and Aubrey nodded. "A lot of things came clear that day. Until then, I saw myself as the more damaged one of us. But it was the *way* Missy took the money, her tough-luck attitude toward Byrd—and you know I'm no fan of his. But it was all okay with her, the way she thought things through—or didn't. Using sex as a means to her end. It made me realize just how messed up she was."

"And that pushed all your buttons."

"Wrong as it was . . . yes, it did. I lost it. I couldn't make her understand what was so bad about sleeping with Byrd. Not if it got her that money. Missy said to call it payment for services rendered. Had she charged Byrd for sex all those years . . . well, according to Missy, that eighty grand was interest." Frank's jaw tightened. "Like I told you, this story's not black and white. Neither is anybody in it. Missy had very solid ideas about the kind of money men would pay for sex, right down to à la carte services. It tore me up good to think of her like that, what Missy was willing to trade for cash." He sucked in rank diner air and swallowed hard, like maybe he was going to be sick.

While Frank and Levi heard silence, Aubrey combatted a soft but determined voice. It throbbed in her head. Levi's in-charge tone kept her clinging to the moment. "It wasn't the first time Missy did something like that . . . sold herself for money," Levi said.

"Once you get your hands on all the puzzle pieces, you can see it's a very different picture. Through no fault of her own, Missy Flannigan had no moral compass."

"How . . . how badly did you beat her?" Levi's question sounded matter-of-fact. Body language said otherwise, his leg stiffening against Aubrey's.

"Does it matter? If I hit her once, is it less excusable?"

"As a reporter, my opinion isn't the point. If you're asking me personally . . . no, it isn't. Still, I'd like to know Missy's condition when she left your room at the Plastic Fork."

"A busted lip, a bruise on her cheek." Frank stiffened, focusing on his folded hands. "Things escalated fast. I couldn't get my mind around it—Missy sleeping with Byrd so she could take his money. My wife, Laurel, she'd cheated on me while I was in Kuwait. She was killed by a drunk driver on the way home from her lover's apartment. That's how I found out. The cheating part, it seemed like history was repeating, even if Missy wasn't Laurel, you know?"

"I didn't know about your wife," Aubrey said.

"That she'd cheated on me or that she was dead?"

"Both. I'm sorry she died." Beneath the table, she gripped Levi's thigh. He glanced curiously at her.

Frank moved on, not elaborating or accepting the condolences. "I struck Missy once. But it, um . . . it was more than a slap. She bled on the sheet, on the bathroom towel. And there," he said, "is your blood evidence. I can't defend it. But I don't think I deserved twenty years in prison for it. After Missy got herself together, I packed up the money and told her to find a way to put it back. That she'd better put it back if she still wanted . . . *us*. Missy left the Plastic Fork and I never saw her again. It seems clear enough. Byrd caught her in the act, they had it out, and she lost."

Levi tapped the pen against the edge of the notebook. "The fifty-dollar bill. The one you used at the Plastic Fork. The one with 'Happy 21st Birthday, Missy' written on the edge."

"An innocent act that sealed my fate. Missy used to cash my paychecks for me—no bank account, remember? Aside from bringing me the eighty grand she stole that day, Missy also just happened to include the birthday fifty in my cashed paycheck from Holliston's Hardware & Feed."

"It was your money," Aubrey said.

"The fifty was mine. But I had no way of explaining it. I couldn't deny an envelope with a postmark from the twenty-eighth of September. I broke the fifty at the Plastic Fork the next afternoon. Reports of Missy's disappearance surfaced that evening. After finding her blood and hair in my room, how hard was it to believe that not only did I kill Missy, I robbed her too?"

Levi set the pen aside. "It's all very gripping, Frank. But here's the problem."

"I can't prove it, not a word. You won't do a story based on what I've said."

Levi shook his head, closing the notebook. "Your story won't make tomorrow's headline, that's for sure. But that's not to say we won't pursue leads based on your version of things. In fact, I'd encourage you to tell the police everything you told us."

Laughter sputtered from Frank. "You've never done time; have you, Mr. St John? There's no way I'm sitting down with any cops. As much as I want to see Missy get justice, I'm not the guy to do it."

"What you've told us is huge. The implications are vast," Levi said, picking up the pen again. "It's strong evidence against Dustin Byrd. But without hard proof, anything we'd print—especially your claims about Missy's father—it would read like slander. Give us time to work on it."

Frank sighed; it was all disappointment and resignation. "I admit, I was expecting a lot from the truth. It's the only thing I never tried." Aubrey focused on his face, her mind trying to erase the years covering it. Something subliminal seeped through, something in his smile, but she couldn't place it. "I guess my luck's only destined to change so much."

"Maybe more than you think," she said.

"I doubt that. But I hope Dustin Byrd pays for what he did. Missy's life went from bad to worse to over before she had a chance to live it. I thought if I could bury him—worse than the way he buried Missy, it would be worth telling. I'd also sleep better knowing Tom Flannigan's part in this was exposed. A sealed-up basement tomb is better than that bastard deserves." Frank rose from the booth. As he did, the earthbound conversation Aubrey heard became secondary.

"What will you do now?" Levi asked.

"My sister, Marie, she wanted me to come stay with her all those years ago. For now, that's where I'm headed, to New Jersey."

Aubrey fidgeted and raked her hand through her hair. She cleared her throat hard and Levi pushed his water glass in front of her.

"We should go . . . *now*," he said, half rising from his seat.

She sipped the water, trying to clear her palate. "It's okay, really." Levi sat again and even Frank hesitated at the table's edge. Her watery gaze volleyed between the men. "Sugar rush." Aubrey smiled. "Sorry. I sensed an incredible scent of fresh pastries, overwhelming really. It was like I could taste them."

"I know that smell," Frank said, looking queerly at her. "So much fucking flour and sugar it about knocks you over. Laurel was a pastry chef." He shrugged. "But the only thing I smell is coffee, maybe the special. Whatever that's supposed to be." With nothing else to offer, Frank nodded at the two of them. "For whatever it's worth, I'm glad I'm not the only person walking around who knows the truth."

"Frank, wait." Aubrey attempted to exit the booth, Levi pinned her in. "Will you let me out, please?"

"No. I don't think you should."

She patted him on the leg. "It'll be fine. I promise. I've got this." Reluctantly, he stood and Aubrey slid from the booth. As she did, Levi held on to her arm. "Frank, you asked us to take a leap of faith with everything you said. Would you do the same for me?"

"I don't follow—"

"I don't believe our meeting was for nothing. I also don't think it was just about Missy. Laurel, she wants you to know how sorry she is."

"Laurel what?"

"Unbelievable as this is going to sound, she's been here all this time. Think about it. You could have returned the phone call of a dozen different media sources. They all want to talk to you. But there's a reason you decided to call us. There's a reason you ended up speaking to me. Laurel's that reason."

Frank shuffled closer. "She . . . I dreamed about Laurel last night. I haven't dreamed about her in years. Not like that. It was vivid . . . intense."

"Dreams are one way of communicating. She very much wants the chance to talk to you."

"Talk to me? What do you mean?" His gaze moved around the diner, perhaps looking for an apparition, or an exit.

"Look at me, Frank." He did. "Laurel's right here. Incredible as this is going to sound, I can communicate with people like Laurel, people who have passed."

"You can . . ."

Aubrey drew a crumpled piece of paper from her pocket. She showed the drawing to Frank.

"A laurel wreath," he said.

"I drew it while we spoke on the phone the other day. At the time, I had no idea what it meant." A shaky breath filled Frank's chest. Levi's grip tightened around Aubrey's arm. It was curious. Usually, in this moment, she was so completely alone. Now, with Levi there, Aubrey felt a solid connection to both sides. "What Laurel did, it left you with the impression she didn't love you. It's what started you on the dark path to this place. She regrets that more than anything. She was so young . . . lonely. It's too late for her, but there's still time for you to make better choices. She wants you to know that." Aubrey broke eye contact, focused on the battered linoleum beneath her feet. She looked back up. "Laurel . . . she wants . . ." Aubrey held up her hand to empty air. "Slow down . . . I don't understand." She stared at Frank, her tone a recitation. " *The Christmas story, not the manger one . . . the hand-written version . . . the one with petit fours and sunglasses'* . . . I'm sorry," Aubrey said, feeling frustrated. "It doesn't make sense, but that's what I'm hearing."

Frank looked equally bewildered. Slowly his face relaxed. "The first Christmas I was overseas, Laurel wrote me a ten-page letter. We'd been married a year. We barely had a dime between us. The letter was her Christmas present to me. She wrote out our entire life, exactly how things were going to be. Where'd we live, the kids we'd have . . . everything a person could want. In the care package were new sunglasses. I'd lost mine. The letter was inside a box with petit fours. They were my favorite."

"That's incredible," Levi said.

"You're fucking telling me." Frank's eyes were damp, the back of his hand running across his nose. "The letter, it's at my sister's. I never could bring myself to throw it out, even after her affair, even after she died."

"Good. That's good, Frank. I think going to your sister's is the place to start."

"Yeah . . . maybe. Hey, could, um . . . could you tell Laurel something for me?"

"Absolutely, Frank. Just say it."

"It's just that . . . even after everything, I still loved her."

"She knows, Frank. I promise, she knows."

CHAPTER
TWENTY-NINE

"It's a good story, honey. Very well written." Yvette closed the A2 section of the *Surrey City Press*, where the continuation of Aubrey's and Levi's front-page story was printed. The former carnival seamstress smiled at Aubrey, the same way she had after reading her essay assignments for Carmine twenty years ago.

"Thanks, Yvette," Aubrey said, seated at one end of her dining room table, her long legs tucked tight to her chest. In her hand was a half-eaten pancake. "But it's not the one we wanted to tell."

"Doesn't your Dustin Byrd, bullets, and ballistics scoop trump the other media outlets?" Charley said, pouring cream in her coffee. "I didn't hear Nancy Grace say anything about adding a murder weapon to the evidence they have against him."

Yvette chimed in. "Nancy Grace would never admit that. Why, she's practically BFFs with Byrd's mother," she said as if they were characters in a TV crime drama. "Nancy will be arguing the other side by airtime tonight."

"Yvette has a point." Aubrey bit down on the dry pancake. It was the only way she ever ate them. "There's nothing wrong with the story," she said, poking at the paper. "It's good. Levi and I put enough effort into it. Malcolm held the press until two this morning. But still . . ."

"Perhaps you're being impatient, dear. Didn't you say Frank Delacort's story will take some digging?"

"It will. He gave us plenty to consider, but not much we can corroborate. It may take months until we get there, if we can get there at all."

"Speaking of getting there," Yvette said, rising. "I've got to get in the shower. Your grandmother and I are doing a little fabric shopping this morning."

"Yvette's insisted on whipping me up something new. Carmine and a few others are in the area on Monday. Didn't I tell you?" Charley said, crooked fingers brushing against a gray temple. "We're having an impromptu reunion down in Newport, spending the night. We'd love for you to join us. Maybe it would be a distraction from all this Missy Flannigan business."

"Sounds like fun," Aubrey said, smiling. "I can't. Not right now. There's too much going on. But I am glad Yvette's here to go with you."

"It should be a good time, sweetie," Yvette said. "Two of my four ex-husbands have threatened to show." Passing by, she gave Aubrey's shoulder a squeeze. In the air was a faint hint of lemon verbena. The scent followed Yvette everywhere and it took Aubrey back in time. She closed her eyes and tilted her head back, hearing carnival music, sensing breezy summer days. Aubrey leaned forward. The vision of a single September day was so clear, like a still photograph, one capturing an orb. Aubrey and Yvette were working the duck-shooting game. There was a man. His hands were dirty. His smile was dazzling . . . Then it was gone. Aubrey glanced toward the credenza where her box of ghost gifts sat. "I thought I put that away."

"You did. Yvette wanted to reminisce. But she didn't want to peruse the box without asking."

Aubrey shook off the déjà vu and the orb. Like the ghost gifts in the box, déjà vu and random orbs were impossible to place. She relaxed her balled position, stretching her legs onto an adjacent chair. "Look all you like. But seeing everyone from the troupe will be way more interesting."

Charley's mouth curved upward. "More interesting than you? Doubtful. As it is, Yvette's been clamoring to reminisce over your ghost gifts since she arrived." Her grandmother leaned back, arms resting across a rotund middle. "So, my darling girl, we've talked about everything from newspapers to new frocks. Seems you've exhausted ways to avoid personal information. Tell me, what is it you plan to do with your Saturday . . . maybe your life?"

Having finished the pancake, Aubrey picked up her tea and cheered the cup toward Charley. "I was waiting for that."

"I know it's hard to find time to share. Especially when you've been so busy, rolling in at two in the morning and all."

"I told you, it was a super late press. And to answer your Saturday question, I'm going to see Owen."

"How nice. A tidbit. If nothing else, it would be wonderful to know if I should look into other living arrangements."

"Nonsense. You'll have the option of staying here—either way."

"Meaning what, exactly?"

"Meaning I have no intention of selling this house."

"That's all well and good. But I sincerely feel three would be a crowd. Owen would agree."

"There is no crowd." Out of stall tactics, Aubrey slowly sipped her tea. "Charley," she said, putting the cup down. "Owen had some wonderful news the other night. At least I hope you'll think it's wonderful. Sky Secure Technologies has offered him a permanent job . . . in Seattle."

"Seattle? How very grand. Convey my congratulations." Years of dealing with hired hands made for practiced calm and Charley's expression gave nothing away. But her hands, clasped around her girth, rose at least six inches with the breath she pulled in. "So this is a plan."

"It's a discussion."

"Please, bring me up to speed. Is putting this marriage back together what you want?"

The question was too direct. She didn't answer.

"Aubrey?"

"It's what I've said since Owen and I fell in love—one life, one marriage, one address. I want roots and a routine. I realize that life doesn't appeal to you. But maybe you can appreciate how important it is for me not to have failed at this marriage."

"True enough. That sort of life was never for me, but it doesn't mean I can't appreciate the attraction." She sipped her coffee and Aubrey waited for Charley's point, which surely wasn't complacency. "But for whatever it's worth, it seems something is missing from that eloquently stated need not to have failed at marriage."

"And that would be?"

"Your husband."

She blinked at her grandmother. "Owen is understood."

"Is he? My mistake. Based on the past year, I wasn't sure Owen was a given." A stone-cold silence crept into an otherwise chatty relationship. "Look at me, please." Aubrey's gaze had shifted, stuck on her and Levi's bylines, printed above the *Surrey City Press* fold. "If I can offer unsolicited advice?" Aubrey shrugged; it was coming despite any objection. "Along with your need not to fail, carefully consider your feelings. Just because something surprised you, jumped in front of you, doesn't mean it's the right answer. Sudden circumstance doesn't give that man lasting substance. Employ some common sense and logic here, Aubrey. Consider where you were emotionally, only a short time ago and the way he's affected you. When I think about that, a change of heart seems rather unexpected."

"You think it's unexpected? Try it from my point of view." Aubrey rose from the table, busying herself with a flurry of activity. "My life was fine—close to ordinary, thank you very much. You talk about common sense and logic? Forgive me, but where's that logic here, because I'm feeling absurdly confused." Aubrey pursed her lips, fighting an unexpected rush of emotion. If she was a teenager, she might have run from the room.

As it was, she straightened items on the lazy Susan, shoved salt and pepper shakers into their designated spot. "Anybody who knows either of us can see that we're completely ill-suited, an absolute train wreck." Aubrey shuffled napkins into an orderly stack, imagining her life with daily doses of organization and preciseness—a singular counterweight to her ethereal gift. Finishing with the napkins, she grabbed up scattered newspaper pages. "And don't even get me started on that ridiculous kiss. Had it been a crappy kiss, fine. It would still be weird, but at least we'd be done. There'd just be some awkward moment to avoid. But it wasn't crappy. In fact, it was disgustingly perfect. Common sense and logic," she huffed, wondering if any two words could be further from describing what she felt.

Aubrey stared at the neatly arranged newspaper sections. *Great. Just the way he'd like them . . .* She smacked the pages, sending her story and his skittering in every direction. She eyed her grandmother, who showed little outward reaction to her fit. "From the moment he dropped in on my life, nothing has been what I expected."

"From the moment *who* dropped in?" Charley said, looking curiously at her.

"Levi, of course. Isn't that what we were talking about?"

"My dear, I didn't say a word about Levi."

◆ ◆ ◆

Aubrey took a deep breath and rapped her knuckles on the door. "Hi."

"Hey . . . it's, um, early for you, especially after such a late night." He looked sleepy, rumpled.

"I know. I just needed to see you . . . talk to you." The door opened wider and Aubrey glided through.

"Okay, sure. Sorry, the place is kind of a mess." Owen grabbed a sweatshirt from the sofa back, a pizza box off the floor, then shoved them both aside. "I wasn't expecting you. Not before nine anyway," he said, glancing at his watch.

"I don't think this can wait."

"Hang on. I'll make some coffee . . . tea. I'll make tea."

He headed for the kitchen. "Owen, wait." He spun back around. Standing bare-chested in the middle of their Boston loft, he was a vision from the past—his sinewy body in pajama pants, a tattoo, binary code in the shape of a heart, taking up a large portion of his right side.

"Are you okay, Bre?" he said, coming across the small space. "I got your text. I know you said you *worked* that story until early this morning."

"It was a late night. I had breakfast with Charley and Yvette. In between, I've been thinking. Maybe not so much thinking," she said, picking up the pizza box and sweatshirt. "More like ironing out the wrinkles in my head."

"The other night, you said you wanted time to think about going to Seattle. I admit; I didn't like it. But I'm open to giving you space. Should I assume your doorstep arrival means you've made a decision?"

"Yes."

"Awesome," he said, grinning. "That's great news." Owen looked as if he wanted to rush the distance, but the cardboard and sweatshirt impeded forward motion. She held on tighter. "Hey, it's early for champagne, but how about mimosas? I think I have orange juice that isn't expired."

Aubrey turned the words she'd come to say over in her head once more. "Owen. I'm not going to Seattle."

"You're not—"

"Could we sit down, talk?"

"No."

"No?"

"I don't understand. It's everything . . . every last thing we ever talked about, everything you wanted."

"I still want those things—someday. It's us I've changed my mind about. I've had a whole year to think . . . to grow, to be on my own. It was hard, but it was hardly awful. It reminded me that I did a pretty damn good job before I even met you. Before I got caught up in the whirlwind that was us."

His hand rose. "*Was* us? Aubrey, stop. Back up. Moving home, it's what you wanted."

"Right. To our home. I don't want to uproot my life, move to a place where I don't know anyone. I feel settled in Surrey, like I belong there. In so many ways, I've waited my whole life for that feeling." She took a couple of steps toward him. "But it's even more than that now."

"More. Like what kind of more?"

Aubrey needed to slow it down. She needed to explain her feelings, not come rushing at him with them. "Owen." She shoved the sweatshirt and pizza box onto the desk, which housed a large computer monitor. It jostled the mouse enough to wake the computer out of sleep mode, and the monitor went from Technicolor bursts to a big-screen selfie of Owen and Nicole—kissing.

For a moment, Aubrey's breathing and rational thought ground to a stop. She couldn't process what she was seeing—if it was a Photoshop feat, like erasing orbs, or maybe a carnie sleight of hand. Just as she eliminated either possibility, Owen dove for the mouse. Aubrey got to it first. "I think I'd like to have a look." She started flipping past image after image, her brain catching up with the simple but telling photos. There was no sound other than the click of a mouse. Nicole was in the loft, looking comfortable on the couch Aubrey had chosen, wearing Owen's shirt, which she'd also chosen. Aubrey's throat tightened, her grip around the mouse doing the same. Nicole showed off a thong and a butt cheek to whoever was holding the camera. In the background, Aubrey also saw a window air-conditioner. Her mind raced. Maintenance installed the units on June 15, and they removed them promptly the Tuesday after Labor Day. The photos were surely taken last summer.

"Bre, before you say anything, let me explain. I was deleting the pictures when you came in. It's over. It's been over for months."

"She still works for you."

Owen opened his mouth, then closed it again. "Her tech knowledge is almost impossible to duplicate."

"I'll bet," she said, laughing as her eyes welled.

"Aubrey, don't do this. I get that you're upset, angry. But we were separated. What happened last summer isn't the point. And I'll fire her today if it helps. But she doesn't matter—I swear. You and I, we'd be three thousand miles away . . . from her, from the past. What we need to focus on is our future. I wasted so much time understanding just how much you mean to me. If you just give us . . ."

Owen's hands closed around her shoulders; Aubrey pulled away. "You're not serious."

"All right. Clearly this is something we're going to have to deal with, but don't overreact. Don't throw everything away because of some stupid, six-week . . ."

"Affair."

His jaw clenched. "Not technically. I don't think so, Bre. We'd been apart since the winter."

"And you were sitting here deleting photos so I'd never find out. Who are you kidding, Owen?" Aubrey closed her eyes. The guilt she'd felt over one emotionally charged kiss between herself and Levi had sent her into a tailspin. But this, these photos, they had all the markings of nothing more than a down-and-dirty affair.

"Just listen to me. You need to understand how meaningless it was."

"Precisely what I was thinking."

"Okay. So it was a fling. I was passing time. We were working remotely from here, a lot of late hours. I was stressed. I felt shitty and I just wanted to feel better. One thing led to another and . . . Come on, Bre, this is nuts. I'm ready to upend my life to make this work. Don't do this because of her. Fuck Nicole." Aubrey looked from the amorous photos to her husband. "Okay, that was an extremely poor choice of words. But the point is—"

"The point is it's over. It was over before I got here." Aubrey brushed at a tear, considering what else was on his computer—their honeymoon photos, house photos, the rooms they'd painted where their life was supposed to have happened; all of it downloaded alongside meaningless images of Owen's answer to stress and boredom. "That's what I came to tell you." She took a step toward the door. "I still have my set of papers, which I'll sign. If you'd do the same . . ." Aubrey turned back, seeing him shirtless, hopeless, in the middle of the living room. "I'm sorry I don't love you anymore. I'm sorry if that makes you feel shitty. Maybe someone," she said, pointing to the computer, "will lend a shoulder to cry on until you feel better."

CHAPTER THIRTY

The following Monday Gwen and Aubrey stood in Malcolm's office, chatting. Gwen said she'd spent her weekend planning a Thanksgiving menu. Aubrey listened politely, thinking she'd spent hers planning an alternative life—one that didn't include Owen. She never got that far, brooding in her bedroom, not ready for Charley's "You're better off, dear . . ." speech. Aubrey was resigned to ending the marriage; she had no second thoughts. Still, she'd needed time to process Owen's betrayal. She'd witnessed his brilliant brain; she'd admired his commitment to the life they'd both wanted. She thought two people falling in love would insulate her from the reality of things like affairs. Most surprising, Aubrey thought, was how not being in love could result in a similar heart-whacking sting.

Aubrey refocused on Gwen, who was in the middle of a sentence about a congealed cranberry salad when Malcolm and Levi came through the door. Gwen abruptly shifted gears. "So what's all the fuss?" she asked. "Why the on-demand meeting?"

"Hang on a second." Malcolm held up his hand. "Go with it, Levi. It's the best we're going to do for now. Let Gwen and Kim handle the digging as far as Delacort's claims are concerned. You and Aubrey see if Byrd's attorney will address the latest statements in some fashion."

"For whatever either thing is worth," Levi said. "Proving Delacort's claim or trying to get corroboration from Byrd via his attorney—they're both needles in a haystack."

"But they're our needles. If we find one, we'll have something. Gwen," Malcolm said, turning to her. "I need you and Kim to take a ride over to Holliston's Hardware & Feed. See if they're open to talking, letting you look around. The store recently changed hands and according to Levi it looks like they're stripping the place bare."

"I drove by over the weekend. I saw a dumpster being delivered. It made me think about what they might be discarding," Levi said. "Producing anything to substantiate Frank's story will be tough, but it's worth a shot. His time in Surrey is ambiguous at best. Holliston's is the one anchor we have."

"It's a ghost of a hope, if you ask me," Malcolm said. "But it's all we've got at the moment." Aubrey listened, her editor's remark on earthbound options resonating. "Being as the Hardware & Feed is cleaning house, I agree. It's worth the trip."

"I knew the grandson sold the business," Gwen said. "Emmett Holliston's been out of the picture for years, dead the last ten—Alzheimer's. He wasn't terribly helpful during the original investigation. I believe his memory was failing then. After he passed, the grandson all but drove the place into the ground. But I did hear the new owners are from Surrey."

"They are, and that's good," Levi said. "It will give them a sense of community. They may be willing to let you and Kim poke around."

"I'm all for pursuing a lead, Levi, but it would be nice if Kim and I had some idea what we're looking for."

"I wish I knew," he said, his hands rising in a vague gesture. "Like

I said, a needle in a haystack—anything that might help validate Frank's claims."

"It's a fox-hunt long shot, no doubt," Malcolm said, looking up from a tablet where he was making notes. "But it's up to us to keep this investigation going. We've informed the authorities about Delacort's claims. They listened, but I wasn't feeling a whole lot of traction—particularly when it came to accusing Tom Flannigan of sexual abuse. The police, the DA, are satisfied that they have their guy and all the evidence they need. They're not about to drag the victim's father through the mud, not on Frank Delacort's word. As for the rest, Byrd's sitting in a cage at the county jail and he's not about to sing. Not if it cuts his own throat."

"Agreed," Gwen said.

"Sticking with the status quo is where following this murder investigation went terribly wrong last time," Malcolm said, "this paper's complicity included. Twenty years ago and today, the one thing this story has lacked is Missy Flannigan's voice."

Dragging in a long low breath, Aubrey clasped her right hand around her left arm. She felt the old indentations. Two marks, just to the right of her wrist bone, a little deeper than the rest. She stared at Malcolm's desk, unmoved and unmotivated by an endless maze of information. "You're right, Malcolm. The one thing missing from this story is Missy Flannigan's voice."

◆ ◆ ◆

After leaving Malcolm's office, Aubrey went straight to her cubicle. She needed to keep the distractions small. She gathered reporter essentials: notepads, several pens, a badge identifying her as a member of the *Surrey City Press*. She remembered her camera was in photography. Aubrey opened a bottom desk drawer, pulling out a sunny yellow sweater. She tugged it on.

"Where the hell do you think you're going wearing that?"

Levi stood at the cubicle entrance, inadvertently—or not—blocking her path. She shrugged. "To cover a house story."

"What kind of house story?"

"Excuse me?"

"You've done a damn good job of avoiding me, Aubrey. But I saw the look on your face in Malcolm's office. I heard what you said. Tell me, was the word 'ghost' some kind of cue? Where are you going and why?"

"Levi, I don't have time for this. I need to stay focused. Suffice it to say, if all goes well, you'll have some answers about Missy Flannigan soon."

"I don't give a damn about Missy Flannigan answers."

"Liar."

"I'll rephrase. I don't give a damn if the stakes are too high. Fair enough?"

"It's not your call." She continued to go about her business, stuffing a few sheets of paper in her satchel, leaving others on her desk.

"Maybe not. But at the very least, you're not going anywhere until we discuss it. That and a few other things we need to settle. I called you yesterday and the day before . . ."

"I saw," she said, trying to avoid other emotions. "Is that what you wanted, to tell me about the dumpster outside Holliston's? You could have left a message."

"You could have answered."

"I was busy." *Wringing my hands over Owen . . . Thinking how I'd like to wring his neck . . .*

"Busy . . . I see. Just so you know, I wasn't calling about any dumpster. But right now, if you're going where I think—"

"Blake," Aubrey said, looking past Levi. The chief photographer of the *Surrey City Press* came toward them. He held her camera in his hand.

"Excuse me." Blake made his way into the cubicle, squeezing Levi out of the frame. "I can't find a thing wrong with your camera, Aubrey. Every shot I take, not a single bright light floating around. I have no idea why that keeps happening to you. I adjusted your exposure setting. Maybe that will help."

"Right, the exposure setting." She took the camera from him. "Thanks for taking a look. I really thought I had it mastered."

"Sure thing. Keep at it. Photos are tricky, even if the subject is a house full of furniture."

Blake went on his way. Levi watched until he was out of earshot. "It's not the exposure setting, is it?"

Aubrey shook her head. "He's been trying to improve my photography skills since I came to the *Surrey City Press*. About a year ago, I started photoshopping out the orbs. I haven't had time lately. Look, Levi, added emotion is the last thing I need right now. If you'd just let me by . . ."

His arms stretched across to either side of the cubicle, impeding her exit. "Not if your intention is to go to the Byrd house."

"The Byrd house," she said quizzically. "What makes you think . . ." She stopped. "Fine. Yes. Are you satisfied?"

"Aubrey, if you think I can be a stubborn pigheaded bastard, you're about to find out just how much. You're not going to the Byrd house. It's not going to happen."

"Yes, Levi. It is. It's time. We're out of alternatives and realistic leads. Do you really think a scavenger hunt at Holliston's or ambushing Byrd's attorney is going to turn up anything?"

"Probably not. But I'm fairly certain that going those routes will leave you in one piece at the end of the day, physically and emotionally, and that's what concerns me most."

"I appreciate that," she said, which she did. "But you can't stop me."

"Okay, how about the police stopping you?" he said calmly. "I have no objection to you sitting one cellblock over from Dustin Byrd. His property is still under the domain of the Surrey police. How do you plan on getting in the house without breaking and entering?"

She smiled, returning the placid tone. "The Byrd house just came on the market."

"It's for sale?"

"I spoke with Marian Sloane earlier. You might remember that Happy Home Realty tends to get the listings nobody wants. Marian was anxious to share her news. She's just contracted what is sure to be a hard-sell Cape on Wickersham Lane, small commercial art studio in the rear. Marian absolutely gushed when I said I'd do a home portrait piece, paint the place in a family friendly light."

"Why are they selling?"

"According to Marian, Violet Byrd needs the money. Apparently, she's rather distressed over the idea of living there after such a grisly discovery. Can you blame her? And you're right, the police still have domain. But our realtor managed to bully her way past protocol and through the Byrds' front door—just to measure square footage, note the amenities. She also mentioned having installed a lockbox."

"And you think you're going to . . ." Levi stood firmly in front of her, his presence now a human roadblock. "No way, Aubrey. You're not," he said, his voice raising just enough to turn nearby heads.

"Interesting that the universe would deliver such a timely window of opportunity. In fact, I'd say that house is almost begging. I'm taking it. I'm going to give Missy Flannigan the best possible setting to connect with me—no matter the outcome."

"No matter the outcome? That's just swell." Levi stared hard. "Over my dead body."

"Whatever works," she said, flicking her gaze up and down all six feet and two inches of him. "If you like, we can finish the argument when you're on the other side." Every ounce of that pigheadedness pumped through his body. If she wanted out of there, she needed to appeal to his logical side, maybe tempt the reporter in him. "Levi, if Dustin Byrd killed Missy, he needs to pay for his crime. But I have another reason. No, make that an *unyielding need* for doing this. Let me ask you something. Do you believe it was more than happenstance or my press credentials that encouraged Frank Delacort's decision to talk to me?"

"I'd say that's a fair assessment," he said, one arm dropping to his side. "But I don't see what that has to do with—"

"I need to know the driving force behind it."

"The driving force?"

"What brought Frank to me—or me to him? We assumed it was something *good* at work. As human beings, that's our natural conclusion. You saw it yourself, how it was all touching and beautiful when Laurel came through. And if it was in the spirit of closure, fine. But what if it wasn't?" Aubrey gripped tighter to the leather satchel. "Consider that. As witnessed, evil can produce some amazing things—I doubt posing as a good intention is a difficult trick. Do you think it's unfathomable that evil put Frank Delacort in my path? Because from what we do know, I'd say the jury is still out as to which side he comes down on."

"No. I hadn't considered the possibility."

"I've come a long way, but understanding this gift has no rational end. At least none I can see. If evil can so easily mislead me, I want to know. Did it deliver me to Frank Delacort? Is evil sometimes the voice I hear; can it make me draw something without my own intent? Does evil wield enough power over this gift to summon me to a house with a horrific history? Is it the reason I'll end up talking to Missy Flannigan?" she said, all but hugging the satchel. "There are people who would swear my gift is nothing but evil. And if you don't think that hasn't kept me up a few nights . . ."

"You don't believe that. I certainly don't."

"But maybe my father did. Maybe he had good reason. Whatever tortured him . . . I'll be damned if it's going to do the same thing to me. I will own this gift," she said, slinging the satchel over her shoulder and smoothing the sweater. "You see my reason for visiting the Byrd house as dangerous investigative reporting. I see it as the chance to answer a burning question. If, in doing so, an encounter with Missy sheds light on who killed her, it would be a nice bonus, maybe a grand headline."

Levi still held on to the edge of the cubicle. He stared, his face confident. "Evil wasn't responsible for Frank Delacort's decision to talk to you. It didn't mastermind that kind of meeting."

"Really?" she said. "And what proof do you have? What possible St John logic could you file in that folder?"

"Neither proof nor logic. Instinct."

"Reporter's instinct?"

"Human instinct. Aubrey, I have no idea how or why you can do what you do. But I can't imagine someone so inherently evil would get the privilege of experiencing a gift like yours. I heard Frank Delacort confess to killing people in a war zone. I saw the burden that haunts him. We know what it's done to his life. Damaged as he is, what I did not see was a man who willfully murdered the girl he said he loved. I'm siding with faith here. I refuse to believe that the universe, and whoever's running it, would allow you and your gift to be used that way."

"That's a long way from a man who doesn't believe life is subject to any more influence than random chance. What was it you said . . . 'win the lottery . . . get hit by a bus'?"

"Your influence on how I view the world is a different conversation for another time. But that's where I am."

"That's some change of heart. I wish I had your faith. But this time around, I'm the one who's going to need solid evidence."

They were quiet, a moment idling between them. "Aubrey, there are so many reasons not to do this." Levi stepped closer, paying no attention to a room full of reporters. He reached toward the crescent-moon scar. He brushed his thumb over it. "I'm asking, please don't do this."

His hand fell away and Aubrey clasped it. "Thank you for being . . ." Aubrey squeezed it. "So extraordinarily pigheaded." A glimpse of a smile passed between them. "But after thinking about Frank and listening to the straws we're all grasping at . . . I know my role, Levi. I'm supposed to go to that house." She let go of his hand. There was a sliver of an opening and her thin frame slipped past his.

"Wait." She stopped and turned. "Do you still agree that this is our story—no matter what avenue we're pursuing?"

"It is."

"Then assuming there's no way of talking you out of this . . ."

"There's not."

"The way I see it, I have a right and an obligation to come with you." She wanted to say no. She couldn't.

"For whatever it's worth," he said. "Let me go with you to the Byrd house."

"It's worth a lot, Levi. But only if you're sure. You understand what we may be walking into . . ."

"Whatever's at the Byrd house, we'll walk into it together."

CHAPTER
THIRTY-ONE

Initially, Aubrey approached the Byrd house like she did hundreds of other properties—making a quick street-side assessment of its curb appeal. The Wickersham Lane house sat on a hilly plot—uncommon for Surrey. If Aubrey were to write a home portrait, it might be the first thing she'd embellish— *"charmingly private hilltop setting . . ."*

Together, she and Levi trudged up a steep driveway, shuffling through leaves no one had raked. The architecture showed off a quaint Cape. It was picturesque in terms of New England buyer appeal, less the giant X of yellow caution tape that marked the front door. "Kind of kills the homey atmosphere," Levi said as if reading her mind. They avoided the tape, walking around to the rear of the home where they discovered an ill-fitting addition. It wasn't visible from the front, built right into the slope of the land. A peek inside a window revealed Violet Byrd's ceramic studio. Aubrey tried the studio door, which was locked. It didn't matter as they quickly located Marian Sloane's lockbox hanging from the house's back door. Aubrey recalled the realtor's remark about being a Christmas Day baby, including the year. She punched in the code and the box popped open. But as Aubrey reached for the lock, Levi intervened by grasping her wrist.

"Give me the key," he said, holding out his free hand.

Maybe this was his plan. Without a key, she'd truly be subject to breaking and entering. But Levi had stopped to retrieve a flashlight from the trunk of his car. It indicated that he was on board. For a moment, the burden was all Aubrey's. *A flashlight . . .* It was his singular act of preparedness. What if they did encounter Missy Flannigan, a girl who'd died a death more violent than Eli Serino's? Aubrey could barely fathom the outcome. Could he? She held tight to the key, nearly changing her mind. Surprisingly, the faith she had in Levi dominated, and Aubrey placed the key in his palm. "Go ahead."

The modest Cape interior was filled with clutter, although impersonal in nature. Inside were the generic remnants of people who'd lived there for decades—stacks of *Field & Stream* magazines, an electric organ, a cabinet of mismatched mugs, and a brown refrigerator, the front covered by magnets from every state. Levi was momentarily sidetracked, insisting that South Dakota was missing. Aubrey pointed to the plain square magnet, which blended into the refrigerator's color. "Come on, let's keep going." She took long calming breaths as they toured the first floor, which included Dustin's bedroom. Her nose filled with the musty smells of a sealed house, maybe a permanent trace of coffee. Just to make certain her perceptions were obvious, Aubrey asked Levi what he smelled.

"Nothing but your perfume." He turned away, then abruptly turned back. "That is *your* perfume?"

It didn't register at first. Then Aubrey recalled Missy's Midnight Fire. "Blue Linen—it's new. And yes, it's mine." There was dated furniture and a plethora of bric-a-brac. Among the items was a half-naked nymph whose wand was the spout for a watering can. "An eclectic array, isn't it?"

"Looks like a flea market waiting to happen." In the dining room, near the buffet, Levi stopped, examining a group of ceramic hula dancers, the largest one providing the base for a lamp. He held it up. "Seriously?"

"Don't judge," she said. "Not everybody likes an Ikea look."

He put it back. "I'm sorry. But that's just plain ugly."

They continued on, noting other items, including a corduroy-covered recliner. It came with an imprint of Dustin Byrd's body. At least that was Aubrey's assumption. "Interesting," she said. "It's just a chair, but it seems like the most personal thing we've seen."

"I agree. The police stripped this place bare, everything from DNA samples to personal property," he said, pointing.

Wires hung haphazardly from a modular desk. The only items left were a coffee-stained mouse pad and a container of paper clips. In the den, painted in a dated shade of forest green, was Dustin's empty gun cabinet. Aubrey counted space for more than a dozen firearms. Except for one photograph, the den walls were empty too, nothing but naked nails left behind. "I'm surprised they left this picture," Levi said. It was a framed photo of Dustin at a ribbon-cutting ceremony for the new baseball fields the town had opened last spring. The fifty-seven-year-old director of parks and recreation stood beside the two-term town council president, Randy Combs, controller Ed Maginty, and Mick O'Brien, the project's resident volunteer.

"Curious photo," Aubrey said.

"How so? It looks like any one of a dozen ribbon-cutting ceremonies."

"The men. There's something about them." She touched the glass, which was room temperature. "Something in common. And I don't mean their dedication to civic duty." She arched her shoulders. "It makes my brain *rapid fire*—and not in a good way."

"Could you please not talk in cryptic phrases? I'd rather not have to overcome a learning curve right now."

"Sorry. It's nothing specific."

"Come on. Let's keep going," he said, repeating Aubrey's words. As they continued, Levi took hold of her hand, and Aubrey could not say she minded. They stopped at the bottom of the stairs, near the front door. "Up or down?"

Aubrey glanced toward the second story. "What I need to see isn't up there."

"Okay," he said, breathing deep, "the basement it is."

Levi went first, using the flashlight but quickly locating a light switch. He still didn't let go of her hand as they descended the creaky steps. Spotty egress daylight filtered in, barely enhanced by low-wattage bulbs. "You'd think they could have at least sprung for a few sixty-watters."

There were basement smells, mildewy and dank. Aubrey tasted nothing on her palate but that morning's tea and a blueberry muffin. Her gut instinct was even emptier, idling between disappointment and lingering terror. The Byrd basement was large and partially finished. The front portion held a messy workbench, laundry area, and a forgotten coffee cup. Wedged in a vise was a sprinkler head. "I guess Dustin was going about his business until Missy's remains turned up."

"Seems like it," Levi said, perusing the items. "The behavior of a cool killer or somebody oblivious to reality?"

She didn't answer, looking over an area filled with weights. "Seems like Dustin Byrd's man cave, in the most virile sense of the word." The basement smells were stale but real, making Aubrey's nose wriggle. "Over there," she said, pointing to a line of discoloration on the basement wall. "You can see how high the water came when it flooded. No wonder it's so dank down here."

"I don't think that's flood water you smell. It's a lifelong buildup of testosterone."

"Gross," she said, not realizing Levi was turning right while she veered left. Their hands parted. "It splits." On her side was a dark hallway. Directly in front of Levi was a closed door.

"The door first," he said. "Let me check it out. Just stay there." Levi tried the knob. "It's locked."

"Look above the door." He did, coming up with a key.

"Good guess."

"Homeowners and about a hundred locked doors. People can be weird when they put their house up for sale." She cocked her chin at him. "Do it."

He hesitated. "Anything?" She shook her head. Levi cracked open the door and found a light switch. He stepped inside and Aubrey waited, her gaze drifting around a space that was all cement and brick. He returned a few moments later. "It connects to the studio, just an interior hallway. Definitely not where they found Missy."

But Aubrey had turned away, distracted by a handyman's project. "This is interesting. The brick around this window doesn't match the rest of the basement." Levi shut the door and joined her. The flashlight highlighted unpainted window trim and brick. It stood out from the rest of the basement, about a dozen rusty orange bricks contrasting the vintage red.

"You're right. And this window's different from the others. Newer." Levi tipped the flashlight, the light shining on Aubrey, who brushed her hand over the orange brick. "What are you thinking?"

She zoned in on the cement seam, dragging her fingers through the groove. "I . . . I don't know. This brick, the window, they're just building materials, but they seem different from everything else down here."

"Different how?"

Aubrey's gaze moved across raw ceiling beams and dropped to the cold cement floor. Heavy damp air filled her lungs. It evened everything out and she shook her head. "Whatever it was, it's gone now."

"I guess that leaves the hall." Admittedly, she didn't mind letting Levi take the lead. Any natural light faded, eclipsing as they entered the dark vestibule. Levi came to a jerky halt only a few steps from the door at the end of the hall, Aubrey all but crashing into him. "Damn it!"

"What's wrong?"

Levi turned the flashlight toward the floor. "There's a bunch of junk here. I walked into . . . something." He squatted, coming up with a large object. "It's a cat." The flashlight shined on a giant, brightly painted ceramic cat. "Jesus . . ."

"What?"

"It's uglier than the hula dancers."

"Levi, could we finish the art critique later?"

He put the cat down and reached for the doorknob. "Damn," he said again.

"Now what?"

"It's not locked. I was kind of hoping . . ."

"Yeah, I get it." She shuffled back a few inches. "Just open it." The creak of the heavy door completed the horror-movie vibe. The window-less room gave new meaning to the term *pitch black* and Aubrey sniffed at the air like a bloodhound. She stopped, realizing her anxiousness. Scents connected to the dead came from the inside out, not the other way around. The only prevalent smell was the thick odor of heating oil, maybe a dirty cat box. "There must be a light."

"I'm looking." The flashlight lit parts of a room, shining on free-standing metal shelving, clearly meant for storage. "What the hell was that?"

"What was what?" Aubrey grasped for his hand. He tilted the flash-light up. They both sighed at an overhead light, its delicate metal chain dancing along Levi's neck. "God, don't do that." Aubrey's free hand flew over her pounding heart. Levi passed the flashlight to her and yanked on the metal chain. But relief was short-lived as the room brightened for only a split second, the bulb crackling as it popped. Darkness washed over them. Aubrey pressed flat against the wall, dropping Levi's hand and the flashlight.

"To hell with whatever's here," he said. "You're not doing this." The floor seemed to pitch downward as the flashlight rolled away. It left the two of them in eerie blackness. He managed to find Aubrey, pulling her tight to him. "Let ordinary people figure out who killed Missy. We're going." She didn't argue. But to retrieve the flashlight Levi had to let go of Aubrey.

"Don't!" The need for human comfort—*his* comfort—was strong and Aubrey reached for Levi to keep him where he was. Logic insisted he follow the rolling path of light, which dead-ended in a distant corner. As Levi came up with the flashlight, his head met with a sloped ceiling. In a cramped corner of the room, the flashlight illuminated an igloo-size hole. The broken brick outlined the opening to Missy Flannigan's tomb. Beyond the busted wall, markers remained where the police had noted crime scene elements. Toward the back of the cove was the repaired water pipe. Had the clay pipe never cracked, it could have flowed on for another twenty years or more. Nobody would have ever found Missy—not in that dark miserable hollow. "How horrifically awful . . ." Aubrey whispered.

"You wouldn't bury a pet in there," Levi said, focusing the light on the space, filled with pipes and mounds of soft, sandy earth. Aubrey inched forward, but his arm kept her from coming too close. "Aubrey?" His voice was steady, calmer than moments ago. The flashlight crept up, lighting their faces. She stared at the makeshift grave, feeling all the things any person would: fear, heartache, clenched nerves, and sorrow for the way a bright but battered young woman had died. Through the light and dark, she looked back and forth from Levi to the empty tomb. "There's nobody here but you and me."

CHAPTER
THIRTY-TWO

By the time Aubrey and Levi emerged from the Byrd house the November sun had given up on them. It made it feel later than it was. Without much discussion, they drove away. The car traveled from the highway to side streets, though Aubrey paid no attention to the route. "How's that for irony?" she finally said. "The first time I go looking for a spiritual connection and I come up empty."

"If you're waiting for me to say I'm disappointed, it's not going to happen. Particularly after what the average eye could see back there."

Aubrey concentrated on the sleeve of her yellow sweater, which looked blue in the dashboard lights. She ran her hand over the fabric, feeling the divots beneath. "Thank you for coming with me."

"Going alone wasn't an option—no matter how politely I might have phrased it. I hope you realize that."

Aubrey remained focused on her sweater sleeve. "Who would have imagined diplomacy being such an integral part of Levi St John?"

"Not me, that's for damn sure," he said. "I'll add it to my list of memorable moments from Surrey."

"Right. Like a keepsake after you've left." Aubrey thought about that, imagining Levi gone from the place she called home. "I'm glad you found more than a headline while you were here."

Aubrey saw Levi glance between the road, Brody's watch, and her. "What about you? When I arrived in Surrey, the only thing you wanted was to get as far from this story as possible. And now . . . If what you did today, facing Missy Flannigan like that, isn't owning your ability, I don't know what is. Seems like you have this story to thank for bringing you and your gift full circle."

"Levi, if I have anyone to thank for that . . . well, it's not Missy Flannigan."

His breath and nod were equally deep. "So what do you make of it, the fact that Missy was a no-show?"

"I've been thinking about it." The car turned, but Aubrey didn't look for a landmark, busy plucking at the sweater sleeve. "Seems like it's one of two things. Wherever Missy is, it's better than the life she lived here. Maybe she's at peace. Maybe it's only us who are so disturbed and driven by what happened to her."

"Something like your parents?"

"Something like that."

"And option B?"

Option B left Aubrey a bit more confounded. "In the basement, near the brick and window, it was the only place in that house where Missy felt like something more than a story we were chasing. Even then, it was vague. More like a long-ago memory than anything ethereal."

"Whose memory?"

Aubrey's head ticked toward Levi. "Mine," she said, not realizing it until Levi suggested as much. "The brick and mortar. It had the oddest sense of déjà vu attached to it. Like I'd seen it before, like I've overlooked something." Aubrey shook her head. "Maybe I'm just making excuses."

"I doubt that." Levi stopped the car and put it in park. "Tell me something else, less a meeting with Missy, where does this leave you with Frank?"

She gave up on the sweater and focused on Levi. "You really believe it? That Frank confessed all his transgressions at the Exit 43 Diner."

"The ones that matter to us. Delacort is flawed and troubled, but I don't believe he's Missy's killer. And yes, I realize that's a lot of gut instinct from a man who's never relied on it before."

Aubrey was about to say how much faith she had in Levi's gut instinct, but their location stopped her. "Oh, we're home." She sighed, unsettled, the non-connection with Missy leaving Aubrey feeling out of sorts. "Guess we were both distracted. My car's at the newspaper. You didn't have to drive me home."

"I know," he said. "I wanted to make sure you got here. We'll get it tomorrow." Levi picked up his phone. He scrolled through his messages, playing one from Gwen out loud. She didn't offer details, only saying that Holliston's new owners were open to her and Kim exploring the old building and its contents. "She left that message two hours ago, none since."

"Gwen's efficient. She'll get back to you if they find something." Aubrey looked at the dark house and back at him. Each stepped on the other's thought, saying their names simultaneously.

"Sorry . . . go ahead," he said.

"I was going to say, I don't feel like being alone—and I'm starving. Do you want to come in, have something to eat? It's barely dinner time, but . . ."

"You cook?"

She shook her head. "Not so much. Why? Can you?" There was a weighty pause. "Never mind," she said, waving him off.

"Right, it's probably not a great idea. I don't think Owen was keen on finding me in your living room last time."

"No, I just meant the cooking part." Aubrey continued to stare at the house. "Owen's not coming back."

"Tonight?"

"Ever." She turned to Levi. "I told him I didn't want to go with him to Seattle. I don't want to reconcile." Levi's always serious face looked even more solemn. "If I'd answered your calls this weekend, that's what I would have told you. I'm sorry I didn't," she said. "I, uh . . . I couldn't muster the courage."

"Why would you need courage? Personally, I think it was a damn smart choice."

Aubrey started to explain. Then she closed her mouth. Perhaps it was better just to leave it at that. "I really don't want to talk about Owen."

"Whatever makes you comfortable."

"Scrambled eggs."

"Scrambled eggs make you comfortable?"

"Uh, no. But they might be edible. I make decent scrambled eggs. If you want . . ." The car idled and he didn't reach for the ignition. Aubrey brushed her fingertips across her forehead. "Of course. You probably need to get back to the condo. I wasn't thinking. Bethany must still be—"

"Bethany took the train back to New York—the same night we were at La Petite Maison."

"Oh. I see. I hear publishing is a crazy, high-demand business. I'm sure she needed to get back. Did, uh . . . did the two of you talk any more about you moving to New York?"

"Not so much. After you left, the conversation got sidetracked."

"Sidetracked," she said, the interior of the car feeling extraordinarily tight.

"Yes . . . severely. She and I talked about how she's tired of being labeled 'the longtime girlfriend.' Beth said she was thinking about getting a tattoo to that effect."

"Monogrammed towels work too."

"What?"

"Uh, nothing. A tattoo. That's permanent."

"That's what I said. It was hardly our first foray into the subject of permanence. Beth had a point. In fact, I think we were kind of reading each other's minds."

"She did mention that about herself, a sixth sense and all."

"Beth admitted that part of her decision to go to Europe was to leave me with a wake-up call. Make me think."

"You are a careful thinker. It's a commendable quality."

"That may be, but Beth's position was difficult to argue. Besides, I believe we surpassed the 'careful thinker' stage a couple of Christmases ago."

"That long?"

"So before she left, I manned up. I did the sensible thing. Something I should have done a year ago—before she ever left."

"Did you?" Aubrey said, hearing a sharp pitch in her voice.

"I did. And I'm glad I did. It wasn't a pleasant conversation. But in the end, we agreed. If I was ever going to be more than the longtime boyfriend, it would have happened by now."

"Wow. I think that's won—" Aubrey blinked fast, hoping the dim light masked a wallop of emotion. "'Never going to' . . . as in she didn't buy a return ticket?"

"As in it was over and we both knew it. Somebody just had to pull the trigger."

"Can I ask why? Like you said, you've been together a long time."

Aubrey expected the logical parts of Levi to field the question: *After careful study, we realized we're incompatible . . . The timing was inopportune, not advantageous to our careers . . . I couldn't see myself living with all those fashion magazines . . ."*

"Because I'm not in love with her."

"You're not . . ." His logical nature would always trump hers.

Levi's hand hovered over Aubrey's and with a gentle landing it folded around hers. "That said, do you think we've finally gotten around to what we've been avoiding since the parking lot at the Exit 43 Diner?"

"Maybe. But pragmatically speaking, it would be wise to go about this carefully . . . thoughtfully . . ."

"In theory, I absolutely agree." The words came out of his mouth, but clearly it wasn't what he wanted. Instead, Levi kissed her, and Aubrey felt as if two people were melding into one. Moments later, the scene mirrored hot and heavy teenagers parked in a driveway. Things slowed a bit, just long enough for Levi to say, "Logically, pragmaticism is the way to do this. But I'd rather see where faith takes us."

◆ ◆ ◆

It took them into a quiet living room, where one small lamp cast a teasing glow over shadows that barely parted. Together they began down a heated path, a subtle discarding of clothing and caution. They lingered between the sofa and the stairs, Levi's hands caressing her skin, Aubrey encouraging his touch. Every part of her fluttered with anticipation, but she stayed steady and on task, the unbuttoning of Levi St John proving to be an intriguing mission. At the bottom step, he hesitated, his forehead having to dip slightly to meet hers. "Wait."

"Why?" she said, breathlessly.

"Because while I'm all in here, leap of faith and everything, I'm not that much of an exhibitionist. What about Charley?"

"She's with Yvette."

"And Yvette is . . . ?" he said, kissing her again.

"Our carnival seamstress."

"Of course she is." He sighed and kissed her almost simultaneously. "And they'd be . . ."

"Gone," Aubrey said, kissing him back.

"Okay, but later . . ."

"Gone for the night."

"You're kidding?"

"Not right now," she said, her hands running over the crisp cotton of his shirt, the hardness beneath it. "Troupe reunion in Newport. Yvette whipped Charley up a new dress. They were very excited."

"Damn," he said, his hands skimming beneath her blouse. "I hope they have an incredible time."

"Nice of you to care."

"I told you, I can be social in the right situation." Levi's mouth moved deftly over hers, then kissed the long line of her throat.

"Keep it up, and you'll convince me of *charming* by morning." It all felt so right, so honest, Aubrey found herself indifferent to the living room setting, happy to indulge in the moment right on her sofa. But the gentleman in Levi was having none of that—or so she thought as he insisted she show him the way to her bedroom.

Once inside, Aubrey slipped from his hold long enough to light candles. She watched as Levi looked around her space, his gaze pausing on the wrought-iron bed. "It's new to me," she said. "But is it too antique for you?"

"Does it, um . . . speak to you?"

She laughed, standing in the flickering candlelight. "It's never said a word. That's why I wanted it. It has no story. It's just beautiful to look at."

"I think we may have different opinions about what deserves to be called *beautiful to look at*," he said from the other side of the room. Not so long ago, logically speaking, Aubrey would have thought he meant sleek modern lines, clean edges. Now, his meaning was clear. Aubrey absorbed him from this new perspective, wondering what else she didn't know about Levi. He was quick to offer something. "The bed, all of this, it's what I imagined *here* would look like."

"You've thought about *here?*" He didn't answer, closing the distance instead, finding the zipper to her skirt with a smooth expertise she might not have imagined. The dark skirt obediently slipped to the floor. Aubrey stepped out of it and at the same time she pushed Levi's dress shirt off him. His undershirt followed, Aubrey admiring Levi's underlying physique. It complemented the room's ambient aura, making shirts of any kind seem like a sin. What remained was fast to follow, shoes, socks, trousers, until nothing was left but Aubrey's fingers, wrapped around the edge of his boxers, his hand cupped around the backside of her satiny, champagne-colored panties. She hid a smile, grateful to have bypassed plain white cotton panties that morning. It was serendipity really. Sex in her bedroom that evening hadn't seemed like a remote possibility when she'd dressed for the day. He held her close and Aubrey savored the feel of her body against his. She kissed his collarbone as her hands joined the effort, running hard over the broad muscles of his shoulders. He inched back. Her head tipped slightly as she studied the new point of view, watching as Levi removed his glasses and placed them on the nightstand.

"What?" he said, the faintest hint of inhibition in his voice.

"I've never stopped to think about that when we got to here."

"So you've thought about *here* too?"

Aubrey didn't answer, too absorbed in Levi's touch, which moved fluidly across her stomach and in between her legs. Light kisses traveled over the stubble on Levi's jaw, a private, sensual discovery. His dark gaze flirted with the flicker of candles before clinging willfully to her body. The boxers were the last thing to go as the two of them fell onto the bed, hands touching skin in a way that was destined to become a pattern.

He kissed her again and his thoughts tumbled forward. "You . . . like *this*, it's more incredible than I imagined."

"And did you imagine all this after the kiss at the diner?" she said, a little breathless as Levi's hands made logical yet intuitive progress.

"Not exactly."

"Really . . . Then when?" she said, making half an effort to keep up with conversation.

"Sometime after the splinter . . . before the night at the restaurant. Maybe the day you wore that clingy dress to the office."

"Ah, the one you referred to as *'different.'*"

"It was the only adjective I could come up with that wouldn't get me fired." In between kisses, she smiled. "Anyway . . . I had this completely inappropriate dream. I think I was fifteen the last time I woke up in that, uh . . . state."

"And what happened in the dream?" she said, not opposed to being cast in Levi's reverie.

"We were . . . Let's just say the word *salacious* is involved. I was actually damn sorry I woke up before it was over."

"That's disappointing. I couldn't keep your attention."

"Hardly . . ."

"How so?"

"My conscious thoughts tend to be more dominant than my imagination. The whole damn thing ended up in some crazy, *hot* . . . Jesus," he shuddered as her hand wrapped around the aching length of him. "A, um . . ."

"Fantasy?" Aubrey said, kissing him hard.

A moment later she was beneath him. "Yeah. A fantasy." He smiled; the dimple full on.

"Show me how it goes. . . ."

"Show you . . ."

"How it goes."

"It, um . . . Not a good idea. It doesn't include anything that would be construed as *charming*."

"So this was an intense fantasy."

"There weren't any handcuffs or a blindfold—just us. But I'd say *intense* is a fair description."

"Then I want to know."

"Are you sure?"

Aubrey bit down on her lip, the prospect of an unguarded Levi irresistible. "Completely sure." He didn't ask again, nor did he hesitate. Her eyes went wide as they turned onto a different sensual path. Levi grasped both her wrists, pinning them up over her head. Apparently, handcuffs were unnecessary. The binding knot of hands sank her wrists deep into a feathery pillow, the dominant act not subject to interpretation. Aubrey was sure—almost sure—that saying *stop* would take things down a notch. But she surprised herself, more inclined to demand that he keep going. The sense of touch belonged solely to him, which fit—Levi in control. It was all naughtily sublime. His mouth caressed her body as gently as his hands had when they first touched hers, taking out the splinter. He moved past her breasts and Aubrey was teased by the desire for his mouth to linger. It nudged her toward heightened passion and she embraced the commanding hold Levi had over her free will.

As he reached a physical point, a position where she felt sure he'd have to let go, let her touch him, Aubrey nearly relaxed. But the muscles in her body didn't take the cue from her brain. Her breath quickened as his lips flirted with a spot just below her breastbone, just above her belly button. It was titillating and wicked, even more so as he loomed back over her. His voice was edgy, his mood cradling enticement. "Do . . . do you want the rest of this, Aubrey? The rest of what I so clearly saw." Yet he released her wrists, his hands anxiously mapping what his mouth had explored. "It's your call." He paused, but then continued. "We can do this in a pragmatic . . . logical way—which, I swear, will be thoroughly satisfying, or . . ."

Her wrists stung a little, but it was nothing compared to the way her heart was pounding. Every part of Aubrey hummed, her toes curled tight into the sheet as her body clamored for total participation. "I want the 'or.' Don't you dare bring logic into this bed."

Levi kissed her hard. Aubrey was amazed by the sense of relief, the sudden permission to touch him, to run her hands over the thick ropey muscles of his arms, through his hair. The rhythm was disrupted, but only momentarily, as he leaned over the side of the bed. She admired the broad side of his back, a body that she wanted to wrap around hers. Levi came up holding a condom and a conversation about safe sex was implied. Yet, the fact that he carried one in his wallet was a surprising tidbit. Credit card, library card, insurance card, AAA card, she expected. If asked to make a list of must-haves for Levi, a condom did not pop to mind—not before now.

He laid a foiled wrapper next to them and returned to making Aubrey the center of his attention. Mouths and tongues mingled as his fingers moved between her legs, touching Aubrey until she reached an absolute precipice—a lusty, breath-holding edge that she wanted to tumble headfirst into. The moment hung in the balance, her one free hand gripped around the feathery pillow, the other around him. Then Levi stopped, whispering hotly in her ear, "This is a damn nice mattress. Sink your knees into it for me . . . *please.*"

For a second she couldn't breathe, wanting to force his fingers into finishing what they'd started. She was amazed how intrigue and torture could fit into the same sensation. With her body writhing against his, she locked a leg around him. The action offered a shapely lure, demanding that he respond.

But Levi was too tactical. "Do it. Please," he said again, the request husky and determined. Levi's hand closed around her chin, her own scent on his fingers. But Aubrey sensed that this was as much about her as it was him. Her fingertips raced over the candlelit lines of his angular jaw and his studious features. Her nose nuzzled deep into the hollow of his neck. She loved the smell of him—a trace of hard-worked aftershave, the lingering starch from the collar that had rode his neck, the scent of skin that was just Levi.

The invitation wasn't wildly outrageous, but it was wildly unexpected from a man whose public personality was inarguably *buttoned-up*. Aubrey turned her back to him, seeing the foiled wrapper vanish from her peripheral glance. What she felt, moments later, was Levi. First his hands, gliding strong over her back, his mouth painting light kisses more tenderly between her shoulder blades and down the small of her back. The act moved from pleasant to powerful, a dominating pulse of sensations as he thrust into her. His arm wrapped around Aubrey, his fingers finding their way, continuing on his earlier mission. The precipice widened, her body complementing his steady rhythm. She trusted Levi with every part of her life, and this reward fell beyond ordinary pleasure. It was delectable and uncharted. "This," he said, moving with a bit more force, "is what I thought about . . . in a bed that I dreamed about, pretty damn close to this one." Dream-like scenes spilled into reality. Aubrey's hands caught around the wrought-iron rails of the headboard as an unlikely curse word slipped from her mouth. It captioned the moment. Both of them shuddered, melding into one another and onto the mattress. Breathlessly, Levi replied, "Exactly . . ."

The after moments drifted toward sedate. Sexual adventure settled into a comfortable pocket that felt more like two old souls finding one another again. It just didn't translate into two people who'd never shared the same bed. The man Aubrey knew best returned to her. She was content knowing there'd be more to learn another day. His hands moved gently, protectively, over her body, the ambiance of Levi weaving permanently into her life. It was where Aubrey was meant to be, the exact result if you were the focus of Levi St John's undivided attention.

CHAPTER
THIRTY-THREE

It was just after eight, but it felt more like a decadent midnight meal. Aubrey and Levi were comfortable on her couch, indulging in a delivery order from the Plastic Fork.

Aubrey stretched her long legs across Levi's lap, glad she had managed to grab the silkier bathrobe from the back of the closet, avoiding the terrycloth one with a strawberry jam stain on the lapel. She'd dared Levi to venture downstairs in his boxers, but quickly relented. That side of him belonged behind closed doors. He'd shuffled on his trousers, though he'd opted for bare feet, and tugged on his undershirt. He seemed relaxed and Aubrey liked how that looked in her living room. As she'd arranged the food on a tray, he'd built a fire and lit more candles. One bottle of wine later, Levi said, "I'm a straightforward man. Wouldn't you say?"

Aubrey tilted her head, studying him from her end of the sofa. "If you mean straightforward in a fluid Latin sort of way . . . Sure. But keep in mind; I'm a dead languages kind of girl."

"No argument there." His tone was steady, though his gaze roamed the clingy line of the robe. It sent a fine shiver through Aubrey, thinking the sofa might get to play a part after all.

"Why do you ask? Afraid your bedroom comportment has sullied your image? That I might be tempted to kiss and tell in the ladies' room?"

"I don't have any doubt this will stay between us—at least until I vacate Surrey. I just . . . Maybe I'd better back up a step. Tell me if I'm wrong, but this didn't feel like a one-time thing—not to me."

Aubrey sipped her wine and smiled. "I don't think you're wrong."

"Good. So my question is: Do you know what you're getting into? A lot of what you see is what you get. I'm not as unyielding as advertised, but I'm also . . ."

"Not about to run away and join the circus."

"Not even a good carnival."

"I'm not asking you to be anyone other than who you are. I get that."

"Do you? I mean, everybody has idiosyncrasies, but mine . . ."

"Yours?" she said, inching back. "Levi, have you met me?" Aubrey traded the wine for chocolate sorbet, popping a spoonful into her mouth.

"Yes, but at times I can be . . . somewhat trying," he said, lifting his wine glass. "Surely there are plenty of examples, but most glaring would be my work. I get too involved. Absorbed to the point where I need someone to physically stop me."

Aubrey leaned over and placed the sorbet on the table. "I'd volunteer." She curled her long legs and adjusted her position on the sofa. They were eye to eye. "Do you think I'd stand any chance of curtailing your work habits?"

Levi tucked her hair behind her ear, his fingertips fluttering over the traffic jam of earrings. "Better than anyone I can think of."

"Although, just so I have some talking points, what sort of alternative activities stand the best chance of distracting you?"

His hand slid from her hair to her neck, drawing Aubrey into a lusty kiss. "You can always start there."

Poised on the verge of an encore to the bedroom scene, Aubrey said softly, "I'll start a file—alphabetical, of course . . ." She kissed him then stopped. "But, Levi, what about . . ." In the small space between their bodies, Aubrey tangled her fingers with his. "While I appreciate warnings about work habits, what about me—my *not so little* extras?"

"Listen to me. I was talking about my behaviors, stubborn, inbred personality traits. When it comes to you, it's not the same thing. It's indelible, like the color of your eyes. Yes, it's extraordinary—no one can argue that." He paused, his hand cupping her cheek. "But so are a lot of other Aubrey Ellis qualities."

Levi's attempt to convince her didn't stop there. In one swift movement, Aubrey slipped from beside to under him, Levi reaching for the tie on the robe. The moment was so enticing it took her breath away. Aubrey swore she heard chimes, maybe background music. Then it became an unwanted intrusion. She turned toward the drilling sound of the doorbell and they both sat up. "What overzealous Girl Scout is selling cookies at this time of night?" Aubrey rose from the sofa and Levi grabbed her hand.

"What are you doing?"

"Answering the door," she said as the chime sounded again. "Whoever it is, I don't think they're going away."

He stood. "Wearing that? I'll answer the damn door."

"Wait," she said, tugging on his arm. "I doubt it, but it could be Owen. I don't want . . . a scene."

His self-assured nature never faltered. "Then Owen will get a diplomatic final notice that this is definitely not his living room anymore."

Before she could object, Levi opened the door. It wasn't Owen. But Aubrey guessed her ex-husband would have been a more welcome sight. Three gaping mouths hung open, Levi just as shocked as Gwen and Kim, whose stares bore down on his severely underdressed state.

Aubrey didn't move; Gwen finally broke the silence. "I, um . . . I called several times—both your cells. No one answered."

"I guess they were busy," Kim said.

Levi ruffled his hand through his hair. His grip around the door-frame tightened, begrudgingly inching it farther open. The women shuffled inside as Aubrey tucked in the lapels of the robe. "When we couldn't locate either of you, Kim and I decided to drive over. We saw Levi's car and we assumed you were here . . . working. We, uh . . . we didn't expect you'd be . . ." Her co-worker's gaze moved from the wine glasses to the candles, from the crackling fire to Aubrey's flustered expression.

"To be picnicking in my living room?" Aubrey said, tugging hard on the silky tie.

Gwen cleared her throat. "Right. Yes. Exactly. Picnicking . . . with Levi. Just what I was going to say." She smiled crookedly and glanced at Kim. "Close your mouth, dear. Surely you've seen fireplaces and picnics."

Kim closed her mouth only to have it pop back open. "Yes, but whoever expected . . ."

"Precisely, Kim, whoever expected we'd stumble on such a coup!" Gwen said, steering with discretion. In her hand was a large ledger, which she waved like a flag. "It took us all day, but Levi's idea about Holliston's Hardware & Feed turned into . . . well, just wait until you see."

"What did you find?" Levi asked. He'd recovered quickly, though Aubrey fought the urge to run upstairs and retrieve his dress shirt. "Was there something to corroborate Delacort's claims—a letter from Missy, maybe one he'd written to her?"

Gwen pointed to the darkened dining room alcove. "Could we talk in there?"

"Good idea," Aubrey said, darting toward the dining room's less romantic setting and flipping on the lights.

"In our meeting this morning, it was mentioned that the new owners of Holliston's were from Surrey."

"I remember," Aubrey said.

"It turned out to be a lovely husband and wife team. Seems they met in rehab—eating disorders, apparently. Anyway, the wife, Heather, she went to high school with Missy. She remembered her quite fondly."

"Seems to be the way a lot of people remember Missy."

"I think that memory facilitated our present day efforts. Heather was sympathetic to Missy's death, the mystery surrounding it. Not only did she allow us to look through every nook and cranny in the place, she helped."

"The office area looked like a hurricane blew through," Kim said, picking up the story. "According to Heather, Emmett Holliston's grandson made a mess of the place inside and out, which made it hard to even know where to look."

"Eventually, we discovered older ledgers in a crawl space. They were fascinating—a nuts-and-bolts history of Surrey, and sadly the deterioration of Emmett Holliston's mind. Starting in the mid-nineties you could see the level of detail decline; even his handwriting changed. By 2000 it was vague, indiscernible babble. Prior to those years, I'd say . . . what, 1996-ish?"

"Yes, the mid-nineties," Kim offered.

"Before that, Emmett Holliston was a meticulous bookkeeper. He recorded everything—from the price of a flat of brick pavers to filling out detailed job tickets for the services people employed."

"That's interesting," said Levi, "but I'm not sure I see your point. How does this ledger document Frank Delacort's claims?"

"It doesn't. Not at all." Gwen, who had her hand firm on the blue-gray cover, opened the creaky book. The pages were musty, the handwriting so steady it looked like a vintage penmanship primer. But as Gwen turned the pages there was a noticeable shift in handwriting. "Here. Look at the entries for September 27, 1996. Plain as day . . ."

Gwen and Kim backed away, allowing Aubrey and Levi to get a closer look. It took a moment. The pages overflowed with scrupulous detail. Then Aubrey gasped, Levi's index finger bulls-eyeing a few lines of information. It was an order placed by Dustin Byrd for an egress window, replacement bricks, fifteen bags of quick-dry cement, and a half-dozen bags of lime.

"Hold on. That's not even the kicker." Gwen turned the page. Stapled throughout the ledger were pieces of yellow paper, the handwriting mirroring the other entries. "These are the work orders that match the materials purchased. Remember, Holliston's was well known for its handyman services. This particular work order corresponds to the items Dustin Byrd purchased."

Levi pointed to the recorded details. "The work order was issued on September 29, the day Missy disappeared. The day Frank admitted to fighting with her. Holliston even noted, 'work to be completed: replace window and surrounding brick. Deliver lime to back entrance—214 Wickersham Lane.'" His finger pressed harder to the page, as if he couldn't believe what he was reading.

"Oh my God," Aubrey said. "The ledger, it puts the man exonerated for Missy's murder at the scene of the crime. The work order is marked 'complete,' and it's signed by Frank Delacort."

CHAPTER
THIRTY-FOUR

For a moment Levi seemed frantic and confused. He stood in Aubrey's dining room, his unbuttoned appearance dwarfed by his chagrined expression. He'd been wrong. In front of them was solid proof, evidence that Frank Delacort had, indeed, been to the Byrd house the day Missy died. "Motive . . . and opportunity," he said.

"We've talked it through, and Kim and I presume that burying Missy inside the Byrd house was twisted irony—maybe the best payback Frank could come up with," Gwen said. "The fact that Delacort was there that day, it could have very well slipped Emmett Holliston's mind. As you can see," she said, flipping to November of that same year, "the entries become more sporadic, deteriorate significantly."

Aubrey mentally reworked the sharpshooter's version of events—a man documented as having anger issues. During his diner interview, Frank had even alluded to a motive. Learning that Missy had slept with her old lover, a man Frank admittedly hated, he'd boiled over, killing her. Aubrey recalled his gruesome description of the havoc a Super

Redhawk would cause: *"Not unless I wanted to rip a hole in her the size of Oklahoma . . ."* Maybe that had been exactly Frank's intention.

"This is unbelievable," Levi said, his eyes fixated on the facts. "I was sure . . . I mean, I had no tangible proof, but my gut said Frank didn't kill Missy. At the very least, I believed he was innocent of this crime."

"Levi," Aubrey said, trying to console him. "You made an honest assumption based on instinct. Don't beat yourself up for that."

"I shouldn't have let instinct or anything else that happened at that diner influence me. For all we know, Delacort could have taken that eighty grand from Missy, and it's been earning twenty percent in a Caymans account since. Goddamn it!" His fist made hard contact with the dining room table. Gwen and Kim skirted back, Aubrey moved closer. "He played us both. Frank's probably laughing like hell, cashing in his retirement fund. At least a new charge for grand larceny would have been something. Good luck even finding him now." He slammed the ledger closed. "Think about it. Taking a life was not an unimaginable thought for Frank Delacort—it was his job—and I never should have lost sight of that."

"You trusted your instincts. That's not a crime."

"Maybe not, but it makes me a weak reporter. And that's not something I ever thought I'd say about myself." He scrubbed his hand hard over his face. "But I can tell you one thing, we're bringing Detective Espinosa—the DA, anybody who'll listen, up to speed on this right away."

"To what point?" Aubrey said. "You've got something just short of a signed confession here, but it doesn't matter. Frank's not going back to prison for Missy's murder. It's double jeopardy—he can't be convicted of the same crime twice."

"Another thing, Levi," Gwen said. "Factor in Dustin Byrd. He may not have killed Missy. But he did take advantage of a desperate, troubled young woman. I say let him swing for a while. Stolen money or not, he's not the victim here either."

"No, he's not," Levi said. "But I'm reporting this regardless."

"In the morning," Aubrey insisted.

"No, tonight," he said, taking possession of the ledger. "Whatever the outcome, I won't be one more person who stands in the way of justice for Missy Flannigan."

◆ ◆ ◆

Levi was gone the second he had retrieved his dress shirt. It left Gwen and Kim in Aubrey's living room, tiptoeing around circumstance. "Aubrey, whatever else we . . . *stumbled on* tonight, I promise it will stay under wraps," Gwen said, shooing her young co-worker toward the door. "On our way home, Kim and I will have a long talk on the merits of keeping personal matters private." Aubrey thanked them as they left, though what they'd stumbled on wasn't Aubrey's most looming concern.

Hours later, sleep seemed to be the last thing she would do in her bed that night. Aubrey tossed and turned, absorbing the blame for Levi's miscues. Inviting him to trust something other than his factual nature had thoroughly backfired. Staring into the dark room and through an even darker window, Aubrey hugged a pillow that smelled of Levi. Eventually, she turned on the feather-filled thing and punched it squarely. The last time Aubrey looked at the clock it was just past three. She checked her cell once more and then shut it off. There was no text, no missed call from Levi. She should have gone with him to see Detective Espinosa. He'd been adamant about going it alone, the headstrong uncompromising side of Levi coming on in full force. Aubrey's last drifting thoughts were of Levi's misgivings. Perhaps about her, but more so for wholly buying into a gift that appeared to have steered him terribly wrong.

Light peeked through the blinds early the next morning. It felt like September sun on her face, not waning November rays. With a childhood spent in open air, the difference in early and late fall stood out, and that was what Aubrey sensed. No alarm was set, though she heard music. Her brain quickly corrected, recognizing the whimsical whirl of carnival sounds. It was familiar like a reflection. The grinding tune that captioned her childhood, it was the way songs on the radio caused other people to reminisce. Nowadays, Aubrey only heard the music in her dreams or by way of a memory. But it was there that morning, as if she were standing on some random fair ground or town common, surely a scheduled stop. From the place between awake and asleep, images flooded in.

Aubrey spied the carnival's Ferris wheel and heard the grave accusation in George Everett's voice. It haunted her still. Half awake, she forced her body to roll away, wanting out from under the memory. The music played on while she read *Watership Down*. Aubrey saw the book's brown and gold cover, the rabbit in the foreground. It hopped into the distance, maybe to the next town over. Then, like a ride on the Heinz-Bodette Whip, Aubrey swung around. In her mind's eye she was wearing a tie-dyed apron and manning the duck-shooting booth with Yvette. A feeling of nausea and worry clouded a late September sun. A man stood before her. Tall . . . young . . . an excellent shot. He showed her cement-covered hands and a dazzling smile. Her mind rode the Whip again, depositing her in a diner off Exit 43. Aubrey sat across from an older man. He wore salt-and-pepper hair and a weary life. But the smile, it was the same. It belonged to the man standing at the duck-shooting booth. Her heart pounded, the way it would if your stomach was about to unleash a violent spasm—fast, like a thundering race. In a blink, Aubrey was back at the booth. The man was gone and so was his smile. In his place was a beautiful blond girl. Aubrey said, "Can I help you?" The girl didn't speak. She only nodded in reply.

Aubrey jerked upright in bed, the wrought-iron frame banging harder against the wall than it had last night. Her heart and ears thrummed, but the ill feeling had vanished. She pressed her hand to a beating chest. Closing her eyes, Aubrey pieced it together. Her Exit 43 meeting with Frank Delacort was not their first. They'd met twenty years before, the same day she'd encountered an already dead Missy

Flannigan, right here, in the town that was now home. The newly dead, she thought, they never could convey anything, what they wanted, or their state of being.

"What . . . what do I do with it?" Aubrey wiped a bead of sweat from her lip, nearly panicking over what felt like suppressed evidence. She grabbed her phone and dialed Levi. There was no answer. She saw a message, left just moments ago. It was from Marian Sloane. "Hi, Aubrey. I wanted to let you know the police have cleared the way to the Byrd house. If you want to come by, take the tour, that would be fabulous! The homeowner will be there this morning, so I think it's best if we went later. Give me a buzz."

Aubrey tossed the phone aside. "Thanks, but I've already had the grand tour." With a head full of memories that looked like proof, Aubrey threw the covers back and headed downstairs.

She was halfway through the living room when Charley and Yvette came in the front door. Aubrey paid no attention to their point of view, which included abandoned wine glasses, fresh ashes in the fireplace, a necktie hanging over Charley's chair. The three women halted, a round of stares revolving. Charley spoke first. "I don't believe Owen owns a necktie."

"No," Aubrey said, zoning in on the bold Brooks Brothers print. "I don't think he does."

"Brava, my girl, and how absolutely delicious!" While she leaned hard on her walker, Charley's expression could not have been lighter. "Yvette, I believe our absence has facilitated a romantic encounter with Cary Grant."

"Gregory Peck seems like a closer fit, but never mind that now."

"Is he still here? Yvette and I can make ourselves scarce, perhaps have breakfast . . . maybe brunch out, if you'd like."

"No, he's gone."

"Gone? Already?" Charley said, satisfaction fading. "Aubrey, I realize you view man-hunting as archaic, but absorbing a few of my wheedling ways might have benefited."

"Charley, let me cut to the chase. The sex was incredible," she said, pointing to the romantic leftovers. "Why he's currently not here . . . That's more complicated. It has to do with . . ." Turning in a tight circle, she stopped and looked at the two women. "Where's my box?"

"It's in the dining room," Yvette offered, helping Charley toward her chair.

"Right, of course," Aubrey said, darting after it. She padded back into the living room, then settled onto the sofa and placed the box on the coffee table. Yvette sat beside her.

"Aubrey, what's going on?" Charley asked.

"I'm looking for something." She opened the lid and in a few sentences conveyed to the women how her co-workers turned up, the information they'd brought, and how Aubrey realized that she'd met Frank Delacort prior to their Exit 43 Diner interview. As for Levi's whereabouts, she told Yvette and Charley that he'd insisted on sharing the ledger discovery with the authorities last night. "As for us . . . I'm not sure. I can only navigate so many things at a time. I don't know exactly where he was on that when he left. But after what we learned last night, I doubt he sees me or my gift in the same bright shiny light."

"Oh my . . . and here I never thought you'd top our evening," said Yvette.

"Do you think the memories you experienced this morning, your first encounter with Frank Delacort, is the reason you've been unable to connect with Missy?" Charley asked.

"It makes sense. Like many spirits, Levi's brother included, once they felt their message was offered, their business concluded, they moved on. There must be something I'm missing, something that indicates Frank," Aubrey said, combing through the box. "Yvette, do you remember anything? You were there that day, at the duck-shooting game."

"Was I?" she said, looking clueless. "I'm sorry, baby. You and I worked lots of booths over the years. And, my memories, they wouldn't exactly be like yours."

"No, I guess not," she said, depositing keepsake after keepsake onto the coffee table. "Hell, memories can be pretty mixed up in my mind. Sixty-eight towns times what? Thirteen seasons, countless people—alive and dead? That's a lot of geography."

"Physically and spiritually," Yvette said.

"Put it in context, Aubrey," Charley suggested. "If you can place Frank in a specific span of time, what is it you recall? Did he make a remark about Missy?"

She shook her head, touching each keepsake with renewed fervor. "No, nothing. I just remember his fingernails being covered in cement . . . and I remember his smile."

Among the accumulated ghost gifts were a dented teething ring and foreign coins, matchbooks and the package of Skittles. Aubrey scooped up the marbles that had rolled around her apron pocket and the bag of sand she'd felt compelled to collect. Of course, she knew now how it connected to Levi's brother. It gave her hope. If a ghost gift that abstract could have meaning years later, there had to be something connected to Frank Delacort. Aubrey fished through the remaining contents, including a vintage postcard from Bayport, New York. The card bore no written message, but its aura remained intense, heated to Aubrey's touch. Completing the collection was a modern black and white photo. Two giant hearts intertwined, drawn in a dusting of snow. Aubrey had the most powerful sensation of love and loss when she held it. "Miscellaneous, disjointed . . . stuff. That's what it looks like," she said, tossing the last item on top.

"What's in there?" Yvette asked.

"The envelope? Just some dried flowers. But I saw Frank in Surrey. The flowers are from eighty miles away, in Holyoke."

Yvette picked up the envelope, dumping the contents into the palm of her hand. "No, they're not."

"Sure they are," Aubrey said, chewing on the thumbnail. "I remember. We were in Holyoke."

"You're confused, honey. But I get that. It was a rough patch . . . George Everett was in Holyoke—all that nasty business. It upset you so—you'd practically barricaded yourself inside the Winnie. I might not remember everyday events, but I do know where these flowers came from." Yvette tipped the brittle blossoms into the palm of her hand, their fine white tails still tied with the grosgrain ribbon. "These flowers, they grow like crazy around here. In my mind, they're like Plymouth Rock or California redwoods, a landmark—when I saw them, I always knew we were in Surrey."

Aubrey gasped. "Oh dear God, the flowers, they are from Surrey!" Her eyes went wide, her hand folding around the dead stems. "You're right."

"The flowers, Frank left them behind?" Yvette said.

Aubrey pressed her free hand to her forehead, as if willing the memory to surface. "No. Not Frank. Missy—they were her ghost gift. It was Frank's bond with Missy that enabled her energy to come through at all. I'd be willing to bet she wasn't dead more than a few hours. Tenacious in life and death, apparently. Her connection to the man she loved, it allowed Missy a window to tell me who killed her—and it wasn't Frank. Yvette," she said, testing her own recollections. "What color . . . what kind of flowers were they?"

"They were violets, baby. Pretty purple violets."

CHAPTER
THIRTY-FIVE

The victim had answered the decades-old question: Who killed Missy Flannigan? But it was Marian Sloane's listing that provided a serendipitous opportunity. Aubrey's heart thundered as the revelation sank solidly into her. She drove Yvette's rental car to the house on Wickersham Lane. Once there, Aubrey sat out front and focused on real reporter expertise. While her gift had played a role, it was only newsroom skill that now mattered. A gray Honda Civic sat in the driveway. It was the kind of car a woman of seventy-five might drive.

When Aubrey left her house, Charley and Yvette believed she was going to find Levi. And she might have, if he'd answered his damn phone. Staring pensively at the Byrd house, she tried calling him once more. Voicemail. She felt alone without him, even though she was well-versed in navigating big moments solo. But Aubrey also felt an urgent need to get the truth out of Violet Byrd—Missy, a man who'd served twenty years in prison, and all of Surrey had waited long enough.

As Aubrey stared, she worked to wrap her mind around the idea: the elderly widow Byrd, a cold-blooded killer. Of course, twenty years ago, she wasn't the fragile old woman the police, Gwen, and even Nancy Grace had interviewed. On the drive over, Aubrey had speculated at length—perhaps Missy's murder had been payback, Violet purposely killing the girl who'd broken her son's heart. Or maybe it had more to do with the eighty thousand dollars that Missy had taken from Dustin's safe. Whatever the scenario, Aubrey knew her first order of business would be to gain Violet's trust.

Going to the police had crossed Aubrey's mind, but after a quasi-conversation, she passed on the idea. *"Detective Espinosa, would you believe I've known for twenty years who murdered Missy Flannigan! Seriously, it was just a matter of some orderly recollection . . . honing those real reporter skills . . . How do I know? Um . . ."* Aubrey imagined the bemused look on the detective's face. No, what she needed was proof. The kind Levi relied on, direct and hardcore. With that in mind, Aubrey hit record on her phone and headed for the front door of the Byrd house. She rang the bell like she'd done at hundreds of houses before. It would not be out of place for the *Surrey City Press* home portrait reporter to turn up on the doorstep of a for-sale property.

Violet Byrd seemed surprised, but she was also quick to accept the marketing boost Aubrey's presence offered. The unassuming woman welcomed her inside. Violet appeared grandmotherly, with a head of tight curly gray hair. It seemed that osteoporosis had set in, and her body looked frail, unthreatening. "It's all so surreal." Violet clasped her pruned hands together as she conveyed her wear and worries. "I knew we'd sell one day. But who could have predicted such sordid circumstance. It's all so dreadful."

"I can imagine, Mrs. Byrd."

"Call me Violet . . . please."

"Violet."

"Marian said you'd be by—but later. I thought I'd be gone by then."

"Oh, so you're not staying?"

In the small entrance between the kitchen and living room, Violet turned. "Surely you understand?" she said, touching Aubrey's arm. "At my age, with all that's happened, I'm simply not comfortable in my own home."

"Since you mention it, I'm so very sorry about everything. It must be difficult."

"To say the least. One never expects to find a body buried in their basement, do they?"

"I was referring to your son's situation."

"Of course, my son. I've spent most of my life hoping Dustin's life wouldn't turn out like this."

"Like this?"

"His father never made much of himself before passing away. It hasn't been easy for me. I had higher hopes for Dustin." She shrugged. "Of course, I only pray he gets himself out of this mess. I'm hopeful that the sale of the house will help with his legal aid."

"That's generous of you, selling your home to pay for Dustin's legal expenses."

"What mother wouldn't do as much for her son?"

"Then let me get started. Is it all right just to walk through?" Aubrey said, taking out her notepad.

"It's a fairly basic floor plan. You know how Capes are—two bedrooms up, one down."

"I've seen my share."

"I'll be packing up my art. Marian suggested I pare down the personal items. I've collected so many." Light laughter pulsed from her wrinkly throat as a cat circled her legs. "Rodin is glad to be home. His brother, Bernini, is around somewhere . . ."

"Unusual cat names."

"Sculptors, dear. They're named after renowned sculptors. You know, ceramics wasn't my passion. Just the thing that paid the bills." Violet stroked the mother of a duckling family that dotted the stairs. "Even so, one gets attached to the work. See here, the brushstroke I used combined with the glaze technique gave their feathers real dimension. Of course, I may have to leave a few items behind. My nymph-fashioned watering can, she'll pack up easy. She was one of my bestsellers back in the day." She burrowed her fingers into her hair. "There are just so many!"

"I see that," Aubrey said, glancing at the living room bric-a-brac. "You may need an entire box just to get the hula dancer clan and lamp inside."

Violet paused. She picked up the cat and smiled. "You're right. I might want them as well."

"The ceramics studio, it's in the rear?" Aubrey said, pointing.

"It is. I'm not sure what the next owner will do with it. Sadly, ceramics is somewhat passé. In its heyday," she said, a reminiscent look brightening her face, "my place was the hottest ticket in Surrey. Moms loved it, an excuse to get out, have a few glasses of wine. Express themselves without any annoying rug rats hanging on. I didn't even need a liquor license, not in my own home. I have to hand it to Missy—it was brilliant, her Paint and Party idea."

Aubrey turned. "I didn't realize you knew Missy."

Violet's enthusiasm stumbled. "Lots of people knew Missy," she said. "She was active, volunteering with the town and whatnot."

"Sounds like you knew her well, well enough to have a conversation about your business."

"As I mentioned, ceramics was popular. Missy may have taken a class or two—almost everyone in town did. We chatted, like I did with most of the female population of Surrey back then."

Aubrey moved through the kitchen, pretending to take notes. "Do you think that's how they met, Dustin and Missy?"

"I'm not sure what you mean?"

"Your ceramics business. Do you think that's where Dustin and Missy met? I'm sure you're aware that the police are speculating about their relationship. You just said she took a class or two . . . so I'm just wondering."

The small woman filled with a deep breath. "Marian Sloane assured me that your purpose here was to take a tour, write a story—about the house."

It was Aubrey's turn to stumble. "My apologies, Mrs. Byrd. I didn't mean to get off track. Of course I'm here to see your property, write a wonderful piece that, hopefully, will help it sell."

"Hopefully. Dustin will need the cash. Look around all you like. You won't find anything but a house on a hill, an attached art studio. If you don't mind, I'll go about my packing."

"No, I don't mind. The appliances," Aubrey said pointing to the refrigerator. "Do you plan on leaving them?"

"Absolutely. I don't need a thirty-year-old refrigerator."

"So your new place, it comes with appliances?"

"Actually, I'm undecided about my plans. But I don't want the fridge. Aside from my art, the cats, I don't want anything from here. Washer and dryer are in the basement, much newer models than the fridge. You might want to take a look."

"I'll do that," Aubrey said. Violet left the kitchen, just missing Aubrey's shuddering exhale. In comparison, getting the dead to talk was a cakewalk. She'd inched forward with information, but it wasn't enough. Aubrey's best move would be to regroup and reapproach.

She went about her business. The bedrooms, up and down, showed what Violet had promised—nothing to note but two unmade beds. It made sense. No one had slept in the house since the night before Violet and Dustin had gone to Foxwoods and the pipe burst in their basement. Standing near the front door, Aubrey called to Violet, who was in the dining room. She asked if she'd mind making the beds before she took photos.

"Not a problem, dear. I'll take care of Dustin's then go up and do mine."

"Thank you," Aubrey said. "In the meantime, I'll check out the washer and dryer, take a look at the art studio while I'm down there."

"The art studio. Yes, that's a good idea. Help yourself."

On her way to the basement, Aubrey checked her phone again. Nothing from Levi. She texted a quick message: *Lots you need to know. I'm at the Byrd house. Call me . . .* Following the creaky steps down, Aubrey stood in the dank dark space. At least this visit came with zero trepidation about running into Missy Flannigan. She saw the washer and dryer, a matched pair located away from the workbench, closer to the newer brick. It was also diagonally across from the door that led to Violet's ceramics studio. Aubrey approached, looking lackadaisically at the front-loading, newer LG models. She jotted down the brands, mumbling, "Might be the only amenities worth mentioning . . ."

"I see you found them."

Aubrey didn't turn, but her head jerked up. "Uh, yes . . . just taking a few notes."

"Of course you don't want to miss my art studio. That's why I came down here. The basement entrance is unexpected—topography of the lot. You'd never know it was accessible from down here. But then it occurred to me, you knew that. You've been in my basement before, haven't you, Miss Ellis?"

Aubrey squeezed her eyes shut, guessing she'd been caught red-handed. She turned, finding Violet Byrd standing halfway between Aubrey and the door to her art studio. In her hand was a revolver. "What . . . what are you doing?"

"I think the question is, what are *you* doing?"

"I don't know what you mean," Aubrey said, stalling, scrambling for the best way out of the situation. "Marian Sloane asked if I'd come take a tour of your house, do a piece for the paper."

"Come on, honey. I've handled cleverer kittens than you. Exactly what do you know?"

"I don't know anything. The art studio entrance was an assumption. I didn't see a door that connected from the upstairs."

"I'm not buying that. Not when you add in your mysterious knowledge of my hula dancers. Be careful, Miss Ellis, with what information you offer, especially if you want to play that game with me."

"Your hula dancers? You were the one who went on about your ceramic collections. Look, could you just put the gun down? This is ridiculous."

"Is it? You mentioned the hula dancers first. Eye-catching, aren't they? But not something you can see from my front entry. They're more like something you'd remember. Explain how and why you were here. Unless, of course, you prefer I just go ahead and protect my property."

"Mrs. Byrd," Aubrey said, pressing her hands to the air, "I don't think pointing a gun on someone is the way to go."

"Why not?" she asked. "I believe in my Second-Amendment rights, Miss Ellis. Who do you think took Dustin to his first shooting range? I'm capable with a firearm. Right now, I'm defending my property after finding what I thought was an intruder in my basement. After everything that went on in this house . . . I think the delicate, jittery state of an old woman would be explainable . . . excused. Five in-depth interviews with the police so far. I can survive one more. My credibility with authority is stellar, ask Nancy Grace. I'm the helpless, demure Widow Byrd with a tragic life, everything from a dead husband to a disappointing son."

"To the girl who left him."

"Ah, some truth." The gun aimed higher. "Dustin couldn't manage to hang on to the one thing that might have made him something. If it comes out, his failure will only enhance my sympathetic appeal. Keep talking, Miss Ellis. It's currently keeping you alive." She aimed the gun slightly left and fired into the brick. The noise was deafening. Aubrey twitched involuntarily, turning her head in the direction of the bullet, but otherwise she didn't move. "Who else have you told?"

A fear of death ran like blood through most people. Aubrey braced for a rush of adrenaline, the feel of weak knees, an urge to beg for her life. None of it came to fruition. Surely Violet assumed otherwise, perceiving Aubrey's wobbly exhale as terror. It wasn't that. It was the realization that her gift, despite all else, had left her fearless. Imminent death did not frighten Aubrey. It didn't yield the state of mind Violet Byrd was counting on. Instead it empowered her. Aubrey stopped stalling and embraced the truth. "I know you killed Missy Flannigan. It wasn't Frank Delacort. It wasn't your own son. It was you."

"How could you possibly know any such thing?"

"I know because Missy told me."

"She . . . ?"

"Yes, years ago. She turned up dead by the duck-shooting booth at the Heinz-Bodette carnival. Maybe you remember it? We came to town every September—my grandmother owned the carnival. Odd as it may sound"—*mesmerizing as this conversation suddenly is*—". . . I have an incredible gift, the ability to communicate with the dead. Missy's spirit conveyed to me that you're the person responsible for her death. It was you, Mrs. Byrd, who murdered her."

"What a stunning claim!" Violet nodded deeply and waved the gun at its target. "Any chance you're going to get her to testify to that?"

"Any chance I'm wrong?"

"That beautiful girl would have been something on my Dustin's arm. I was actually fond of her. The way we viewed life—Missy and I had things in common. I have no earthly idea what drew her to Dustin, but Missy would have elevated him a step or two in this town. If only he could have gotten her to go through with it, followed my plan. It was a good plan," she said, taking steadier aim. "But in the end, not only did Missy break his heart, the little bitch stole his money."

"And you caught her."

"In the middle of Dustin's bedroom with his money—half in her backpack and half still in the safe." Violet shook her head. "As Missy pleaded for her life, she tried to insist she was returning the money. Missy had played Dustin for a fool. She wasn't about to do the same with me. My son never even noticed the area rug was gone. She bled all over it. Really, it was quick. Missy was dead almost before she knew what hit her. Then, with a bit of effort, I put sweet Missy Flannigan in a wheelbarrow. I rolled her out back and into my studio. From there we came right through that handy basement entrance." Violet smiled, nudging a shoulder at the door behind her. "The back storage room was perfect—no one ever went in there but me. The foundation, thanks to the slope and art studio addition, created the perfect tomb. The dirt in there is like play sand—easy enough to dig a hole. I covered Missy with lime—promotes the decaying process—and bundled her up in plastic. Some handyman had been here earlier that day. Naturally, Dustin over-ordered supplies." She shrugged. "Opportune, really. There was plenty of brick and mortar to work with—sealed her right in, no problem. Those materials weren't foreign to me. As for Dustin . . . Twenty years ago, I had high hopes for my son. I believed in possibility. Had Missy Flannigan played nice, not left him, not gotten greedy, things would have been different."

Violet turned the gun a bit, as if focusing her aim. Aubrey's phone rang. "That's my partner," she said, hoping it was. "There're too many people who know where I went, Violet. You can't pull it off again, get rid of me as tidily as you did Missy." The phone droned on. "He's a hell of a reporter, and an even better man. I made tactical errors today. I promise you, he won't do the same. He'll haunt you. He'll figure it out."

"Answer it," she said, pointing the gun at Aubrey's pocket. "Put it on speaker. Tell him you're fine."

Aubrey dropped her notepad on the floor and reached for her phone. "Levi . . . hi," Aubrey said breathlessly.

"I saw Charley," he said. "She explained . . . everything. I got your text. Are you okay?"

"Uh, fine. I'm fine. Where are you?"

"Not far . . ."

"What does that mean?"

With Levi's voice on speaker an echo was muffled. It surprised both Aubrey and Violet when the studio door creaked open and he appeared in the entryway. Violet turned in the direction of the new intruder. Aubrey lunged left, toward the room that had been Missy Flannigan's tomb. She grabbed the first thing she found—a giant ceramic cat. When she turned back, she saw Violet aiming the weapon at Levi, who stood frozen in the face of a gun being pointed at him. Aubrey propelled forward, swinging for the armed elderly woman. She made hard contact with the side of Violet's head, but it was a second too late. Not quick enough to keep her from firing the gun. The bullet struck its target.

Levi fell hard to the floor and so did Violet. The pieces of the ceramic cat lay scattered between two prone bodies. Aubrey dropped to her knees beside Levi. She heard herself cry "No!" but it sounded small and useless in the aftermath of gunfire. None of it seemed real, not until Levi spoke, a trickle of blood seeping from his mouth.

"Ellis . . ."

"I'm right here." Aubrey scrambled for her cell with one hand, trying to apply pressure with the other. But she fumbled, frantic and scared, unable to pinpoint the wound. His injury became evident as a sticky dampness met with the palm of her hand and Levi's dress shirt transformed, turning from white to red.

"I deplore weakness . . ." Blood continued to dribble over his lip, following the raspy whisper of his words. "But I gotta tell you, it hurts like a son of a bitch. "

"Levi, stop . . . You're going to be okay." But Aubrey's confidence began to wane. She started to panic as his breathing shallowed. She did gather the wherewithal to glance behind her and see an unconscious

Violet lying on the basement floor. "Listen to me, Levi . . . Don't . . . don't you dare die on me! You're staying right here," Aubrey insisted. "I don't want to finish any arguments from the other side!"

She hit the speaker button on her phone and connected to 911. Aubrey demanded what she needed. She and Levi traded unsure looks. His color had turned white, ghostly white—and Aubrey realized how it was that everyday people drew the conclusion. "Levi, please," she said, her voice more pleading than in the moments before. She looked up, considering places that she didn't really think about in terms of earthly needs. *Please . . . please don't take him from me . . .* She looked at Levi, whose eyes rolled back, eyelids fluttering.

"See that . . . you didn't think . . ."

"Didn't think what?" she said, pinching back tears.

He smiled, but it was weak, too weak to force the dimple. "That I'd see Brody again so soon . . ."

CHAPTER THIRTY-SIX

Three Months Later

"For the record, state your names, addresses, and occupations. And so you are aware, we are recording this investigatory inquiry in addition to the court reporter. Also present is Jennifer Hayes for the town of Surrey, assistant district attorney." Detective Espinosa inched the recording device toward the two women who sat opposite him.

"Aubrey Ellis, 54 Homestead Road, Surrey, Massachusetts. I'm a reporter with the *Surrey City Press*."

The petite Asian woman cleared her throat. Aubrey could hear her breath, light and steady. "Ginger Imai, apartment 8C, Highgrove Terrace, Surrey, Massachusetts. I recently retired as the assistant manager of Benjamin Franklin Savings Bank."

In the sterile conference room of the DA's office, where they'd been summoned, Aubrey glanced at Ginger. She seemed calm, even composed. Ginger had come alone. An older man who smelled of breath mints over cigarettes, an attorney from MediaMatters, sat to Aubrey's left. On the table, in between the two sides, was a safety deposit box. "The purpose of this interview," the assistant DA said, "is to determine if any criminal act was committed regarding a safety deposit box that belonged to Missy Flannigan. The box was delivered from Miss Imai to Aubrey Ellis and the *Surrey City Press*. This occurred after Violet Byrd's recorded confession, obtained by Miss Ellis, was turned over to authorities. Mrs. Byrd was immediately taken into custody and charged with the crime of murder, which she did not deny during further questioning. Miss Imai, would you please tell us how you came into possession of the box?"

"Missy Flannigan was a customer at my bank. Back then . . ."

"Could you please be specific about the dates in question?" the detective asked.

"When she was alive, approximately twenty years ago. Missy often came into the bank. She made a lot of deposits. Two years before her disappearance, she took out this safety deposit box. You see the original documentation for the rental of the box, Missy's signature."

"Yes, the evidence was entered into the record prior to this interview," Detective Espinosa said.

"Miss Imai, were you aware of the box's contents?" asked the district attorney.

"Perhaps you are unfamiliar with the privacy inherent to a safety deposit box, Miss Hayes. The contents were not my business. But Missy did tell me that the box contained pearls that belonged to her grandmother. I cannot confirm or deny this. I've never opened the box."

Aubrey listened to the exchange, recalling her surprise when she and Malcolm did open the box, the stunning secrets that had tumbled out. If Ginger Imai hadn't come forward much of Missy's story would have remained, not a mystery, but simply untold. Aubrey sighed, thinking it still wasn't enough.

"You're right about that . . ."

Aubrey sat up taller as the assistant DA continued on, vetting the elderly woman without apology. "Did you have a relationship with Miss Flannigan, beyond bank teller and client?" she asked.

"No, not really." Ginger Imai hesitated and her hands clasped in front of her. "Although I did believe Missy Flannigan was a troubled girl."

"Did you have conversations alluding to that?"

"Not a single one. In that regard, I cannot help you. What I can tell you is that I too escaped a difficult life in Japan. Perhaps conversation is not necessary to recognize this kind of confusion and pain in another person."

"And after Missy disappeared," Detective Espinosa said, "you deliberately chose to keep the box private?"

"I did. Naturally, it occurred to me that I should turn the box over to her family. I struggled with this greatly." A swallow rolled through Ginger's crepe-paper throat. She pointed to the box. "But," she said, her head tilting slightly, "I watched Missy's father come and go from that bank for as long as I worked there. There was something in his demeanor that I found . . . disturbing. I have good instincts about people and I trust them. From what we now know about Mr. Flannigan, I believe I was correct." The elderly woman frowned, looking at the box, looking as if it were all that was left of Missy Flannigan.

Aubrey swore a whisper wove through the room.

"It's not enough . . ."

"Back then," Ginger Imai said, "what I sensed about Mr. Flannigan prevented me from turning the box over to him. If I am held responsible for this, I accept it. But I would not have done anything differently."

Detective Espinosa leaned forward, his gaze steady on the former bank employee. "And it didn't, at any point, occur to you that turning the box over to the authorities would be the prudent and rightful decision?"

"When the authorities so swiftly caught Missy's killer and brought him to justice twenty years ago, I did nothing. I thought it respectful to keep the contents of the box private. I thought it was what Missy would have wanted. She secured the box for a reason. It was my perception that whatever was inside should perhaps die with her."

"I thought so once too . . . but not anymore . . ."

Aubrey cleared her throat and shook her head. She glanced around the room, seeing nothing but celery-green walls and office-grade furniture.

Detective Espinosa never missed a beat, pouring a glass of water and placing it in front of Aubrey while asking Ginger, "And when Missy's remains fell out of the Byrds' basement wall, you didn't feel any different?"

"Detective Espinosa, a man spent two decades in prison for a crime he did not commit. When a plumber discovered Missy Flannigan's remains, it did not enhance my confidence in the authorities. Since that time, another man was falsely accused of her murder. Missy's true killer was finally apprehended when Miss Ellis obtained a confession. I hope, finally, she'll pay for her crime."

"Count on that, Miss Imai," said the assistant DA. "Whatever life Violet Byrd has left will be spent behind bars."

"Good," she said, nodding.

But Aubrey heard two voices say "good" simultaneously.

"As for why I chose to give the box to Miss Ellis—she earned my confidence. With my retirement at hand and Missy's murder solved beyond question, the time had come. I felt the box would be *safest* in Miss Ellis's care." Her tiny shoulders shifted. "If the box contained nothing more than a strand of pearls, so be it. If not, I believed Miss Ellis was the person most capable of deciding what to do with its contents."

"Me too . . ."

Aubrey heard a curt "Miss Ellis, are you listening?" and looked at the detective. He must have said her name more than once. "What do you have to say for your part in this?"

Aubrey blinked at him. "To say it's been a tumultuous few months would be an understatement."

"Miss Ellis, if you could speak up just a bit," he said, pushing the recorder closer.

Aubrey tucked a piece of hair behind her ear, curious if she appeared as weary and vague as she felt. "I was stunned when I opened the box."

"And when you saw what was inside," the assistant DA said, interrupting, "you didn't feel a duty to turn all its contents over to the authorities?"

The attorney who accompanied Aubrey held up his hand. "My client was not under any legal obligation to surrender the contents of the box. We all know that while damning and inflammatory, the contents had no bearing on who murdered Missy Flannigan. However, as it was, Miss Ellis did turn over Missy's diaries. The state has made full use of this information in regards to the very disturbing crimes committed by Tom Flannigan. Perhaps instead of questioning Miss Ellis, you should be thanking her."

"Mr. Siegel, the state is aware of Miss Ellis's contribution in the matter of Tom Flannigan. The diaries proved most useful in obtaining a long-overdue confession. The state and a judge will see that Tom Flannigan is prosecuted to the full extent of the law," Miss Hayes said. "However, there's still the matter of the other items in the box. The items that Miss Ellis and the *Surrey City Press* used to produce a rather stunning exposé."

The MediaMatters attorney began to object again. This time Aubrey interrupted. "Miss Hayes, after carefully examining the contents of the box my editor, Malcolm Reed, and I determined what we wanted to present to our readers, and what we felt was best left in the hands of the authorities. We did nothing without serious deliberation, fact checking, and advice from our own legal counsel."

"I assume you're referring to the various men who solicited Miss Flannigan for sex rather than her diaries and their contents," Detective Espinosa said.

"Isn't that what *you're* referring to? The diaries supported Frank Delacort's claims about her father. I know you've spoken with Frank," Aubrey said, having told him about the diaries herself. Confirmation of Missy's suffering wouldn't change what twenty years in prison had done to his life. But Frank seemed to find peace in knowing that the story had been corroborated. "The diaries provided excruciating details about the abuse perpetrated by Missy's father. But everything else we found—the motel receipts, signed thank-you notes from Missy's clients, even some fairly shocking photos—that was fair game. And as for those men—"

"Those men? Please be specific," said Miss Hayes.

"People like Randy Combs, Mick O'Brien, Ed Maginty, a few other adults who took advantage of Missy. We knew that the statute of limitations regarding solicitation had long run out. It seemed to us that an above-the-fold headline exposing their part in Missy Flannigan's story was the only sentence they'd be served."

"You could do more . . ."

Aubrey slapped her hand against the table. Everyone looked in her direction. In turn, her gaze jerked around the room. She sat back in the chair, absorbing what was now no more than a distant whisper.

"You felt it was the right of the *Surrey City Press* to serve up justice," Detective Espinosa said.

"If you think a local two-part series exposing how adult men—trusted members of a community—took advantage of an already traumatized young girl, not to mention Dustin Byrd's part in this, is in any way justice—"

Jennifer Hayes interrupted. "As unfortunate and unsatisfying as it is, the police and my office are bound by the confines of the law. I can't speak for Detective Espinosa, but I understand what you tried to do, Miss Ellis. However, it's also our job to assess if a current crime has been committed."

"If you consider it necessary to press charges for my decision, have at it," Aubrey said, teary eyed, overwrought by the endless aftereffects of a girl gone twenty years. "And you're right. The law doesn't serve justice in Missy's case. Sadly, neither do the stories I wrote for the *Surrey City Press.*"

"You can do more . . ."

Twenty-four hours later, Aubrey was in the ladies' room of the *Surrey City Press* when the call came. She was relieved to hear that the DA and Surrey police had decided not to press charges. But she was having a hard time conveying much joy. As it was, she'd just exited a stall and was pressing a damp paper towel to her face. Aubrey was perplexed by a wave of nausea, curious that it didn't connect to an inbound entity—at least not the kind with which she was most familiar.

Later that day, still reeling from the cause and effect of Missy Flannigan, Aubrey drove out to the cemetery. She didn't relish the idea of walking among the dead, but she needed to pay her respects. Passing by dozens of headstones, she was surprised by her level of comfort. She'd had a lifetime with her gift, but Aubrey felt sure she'd come the furthest, gained the most confidence, in the past few months. Standing in front of a newer burial plot, she spoke to the stone marker, shiny granite carved with angels. She swiped at a runaway tear and hugged herself tightly. "I see your mother's been here. I'm glad about that." Fresh daffodils sat against the headstone, a charm on a ribbon that said "daughter."

Placed next to the spring flowers was a more permanent plant in a pot—a plastic red geranium that looked wildly out of place. She picked it up and moved it to the side of the grave. Aubrey felt sure Dustin had brought it by. After his mother's confession, he'd been released from jail and unceremoniously fired from Surrey Parks and Recreation. Aubrey had read Ned's piece that morning about how Surrey revoked Dustin's pension. She shook her head at the plastic plant. "It's not enough. Money, that's all this will cost you, Dustin. You should be made to understand the part you played. As it is, you'll probably try to turn your infamy into heroism." Aubrey knelt, refocusing on the headstone. "Maybe we can get a graveside restraining order."

She pondered the receding edges of winter, the way wet snow bled into loose dirt. Aubrey reached past the grave, glad for her long arms, scraping a layer of snow across the slushy mess. It looked too much like the life Frank Delacort had so poignantly described. Then she stood, reflecting on the white snow that covered Missy Flannigan's new grave. Branches rustled in the wake of a spring breeze and on a cutting wind Aubrey heard a last adamant echo: *"You can do more . . ."*

EPILOGUE

Three years later

"Charley, I'm not arguing. You're putting on this sunscreen and that's the end of it!" Aubrey's watchful eye moved between a glistening Connecticut shoreline and her grandmother's back.

"Fine . . . Just do it," she said, allowing Aubrey to smear a handful of sunscreen between her shoulder blades. "In my day, sunshine was the best thing a person could hope for. Now the sun's the enemy. When did that happen?"

"No credit to modern medical science, huh?"

"No credit for taking the fun out of a day at the beach . . . or a carnival." Charley pointed toward the water where Yvette stood with a toddler jumping by her side. "I tell you, my dear, that son of yours is half fish. Look at him splash in those waves—no fear!"

"Mmm, a little too fearless," Aubrey said, standing. "Reminds me of somebody. I'll go reel him in, relieve Yvette at the very least."

"He's a handful. That's for certain."

Striding through the sand, Aubrey heard only the echo of beach-goers, late morning crowds that had descended in large numbers.

Saturdays were busy days at the beach. The dark-haired boy spied her. His hand broke from Yvette's grip and he charged toward his mother.

"Hey, Petey!" Aubrey scooped him up, swinging him full circle. "Thanks, Yvette, I'll take over. I know he can wear anybody out."

"Oh, I don't mind, baby. I'd rather wade in the water than attempt to get your grandmother to wear sunscreen."

Aubrey laughed. "Mission accomplished on that front. She's all set."

"In that case," Yvette said, her hand swiping her brow, "I think I will get some lemonade."

"It's in the cooler." Yvette retreated to their spot on the beach. In a shallow stretch of water, Aubrey admired her son, watching him squeal at little waves and the blanket of silt that washed past his toes, again and again. She smiled at his fascination, the fact that there were no batteries to wear out. He stamped his pudgy feet, trying to trap rocks and shells beneath his toes, and pointed to a tiny crawling crustacean that he could not name. "It's a crab," Aubrey said, "like in *The Little Mermaid*." Granted, Disney movies held more interest for Aubrey than they did her always-on-the-go two-year-old. After a minute her son quieted. She'd noticed this about him too. For such a busy boy, moments came where his attention was captured by something only he saw. Aubrey knew the power of this shoreline, Rocky Neck beach. She imagined what it might bring—an uncle, perhaps a father. Aubrey never gave up hope on the idea of connecting with her own loved ones. The boy's feet stopped moving, his view fixed on the horizon. He looked up at his mother. "What do you see, Pete?"

He jumped up and down and flapped his arm in a willy-nilly direction—the beach, the sea, the sky. "Pa," he said.

On the other hand, the boy's exactness amazed her. The surrounding crowds were enough to unsettle the point of view of any ordinary adult. But through the masses, past beach-goers and beach umbrellas, running children, and swooping seagulls, he'd managed to spot his father. "You're late," Aubrey said as Levi drifted into focus.

"Not that late." He swung the boy into his arms, his chubby arms gripping tight around Levi's neck. "Sorry," he said. "Sunday layout ran longer than I'd hoped."

A canvas tote hung from Levi's shoulder. Aubrey eyed the non-beach bag. "Don't tell me you brought work. Remember, that's why you hired an editorial coordinator."

"Nope, not me. I remain the well-balanced editor in chief of the *Surrey City Press*." A glance passed between them. "Most of the time," he said, settling the boy onto his shoulders. As he did, the tote slipped and Aubrey caught it. "The work is all yours. Well, not so much the work, but the result of your labor."

Trudging through the sand, Aubrey shuffled to a stop with Levi alongside her. "Oh, is this . . ."

"The box was on the porch when I stopped home to change. Take a look."

She hesitated, thinking about Levi's remark. It had been a difficult undertaking—though worth every moment. Worth discovering where her writing talent belonged. Naturally, the temptation was too much and Aubrey flipped up the flap. She plucked out a book, holding a first finished copy of *The Unremarkable Life of Missy Flannigan* by Aubrey Ellis.

An hour later the group had thoroughly perused the pages, admired the cover art, and remarked on the fascinating story it told. The book offered Missy far more justice than the law or a two-part *Surrey City Press* series ever could. Aubrey felt satisfied; she'd answered the request. She had done more. She'd done everything she could for a girl now gone nearly a quarter of a century. But the feeling began to ebb almost as quickly as it settled. She sat up on the blanket, a sleepy Pete crooked between herself and Levi.

He pushed up as far as his elbows. "What?"

"It's nothing." She lay back down.

A moment passed. Levi sat up taller. "To your left or right?" he said, looking in either direction.

Aubrey sat up again. "Straight ahead." She bumped his arm, and Levi looked toward an older couple parked under an umbrella. "Their daughter."

"And?" Levi said, which had become his pattern.

Aubrey couldn't say it was necessary, but there was terrific peace in knowing that someone always had her back. "It's good. It's all good."

He stood, and Aubrey breathed a thankful breath as he brushed the sand from his body, oddly grateful for the scars that he would forever bear. It could have ended so very differently. Levi held his hand out to hers, the dimple full-on. "Okay then. We'll go together."

ACKNOWLEDGMENTS

Susan Ginsburg has been the voice of reason and positive input since I emailed her in 2008 asking if she would offer literary agent advice for my manuscript *Beautiful Disaster*. Her kind, detailed reply is still my favorite publishing story to tell. Many thanks to Stacy Testa and Writers House as well.

Thank you to JoVon Sotak and Anh Schluep, Editorial Director at Montlake, and most especially editor Alison Dasho, who saw *Ghost Gifts* to the finish line. Endless appreciation to the entire Montlake team for all their hard work with this book. Also, thank you to Anh for assigning this book to Charlotte Herscher, Developmental Editor. It was my jackpot win and privilege to have her edit *Ghost Gifts*; her editorial ideas and guidance were invaluable. I'd also like to acknowledge Hannah Buehler, copyeditor extraordinaire, and proofreader, Montreux Rotholtz.

Much gratitude goes to the talented professionals who lent their expertise during the research phase of this book. This includes Jennifer Lehman, Senior Deputy District Attorney, Schuylkill County, Pennsylvania; Walt Sosnowski, retired sergeant, NYPD; and *New York Times* bestselling author Grant Blackwood. Thanks go to Ken Wiesner for lending me his real computer genius brain. Locally, many thanks to

Jim Ginley and the Wednesday night critique group. A huge thank you to Richard K. Lodge, Editor-in-Chief, GateHouse Media, West unit, and Editor of the MetroWest Daily News. I could not have created the *Surrey City Press* newsroom without his generosity and insight.

Sincere thanks to Karin Gillespie, my most important first reader. She is the pace car of good writing and a wonderful friend. Much appreciation to authors Barbara Claypole White, Saralee Rosenberg, and Judith Arnold, as each offered perfect thoughts in just the right moments. May I never write a book where Melisa Holmes is not part of this page—every time I hand her a draft, I've cleared a hurdle. Every time I trip over one, she hands me wine and an answer. Thank you to Steve Bennett, founder of AuthorBytes. He tolerates my writing hours and always has something brilliant and humorous to add. Lastly, to everyone at home, Matt, Megan, Jamie, and Grant, you make books worth writing.

ABOUT THE AUTHOR

Ghost Gifts is Laura Spinella's third romantic fiction novel. Her first two books, *Beautiful Disaster* and *Perfect Timing*, received multiple awards, including a RITA nomination. She also writes sensual romance under the pen name L. J. Wilson, which includes the Clairmont Series Novels. She currently lives with her family outside Boston where she is always writing another novel. Visit her website LauraSpinella.net for more information.